THE WOMB OF INANA

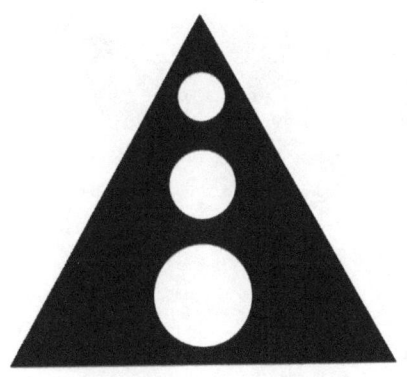

THE WOMB OF INANA

BOOK ONE

MATTHEW NORTH

The Womb Of Inana

This is a work of fiction. All of the characters, organizations and events portrayed in this novel are either products of the authors imagination or used fictitiously.

The Womb of Inana
Ages of Atalay - Book One

© Copyright 2023 by Tri-World Publishing
All Rights Reserved

ISBN 978-1-7386983-1-8 *(hardcover)*
ISBN 978-1-7386983-0-1 *(paperback)*
ISBN 978-1-7386983-0-1 *(e-book)*

mattnorth@live.com

First Edition (June 2023)
10 9 8 7 6 5 4 3 2 1

The Womb Of Inana

For Caroline

INANA
WESTERN HEMISPHERE

Duran
The Naga Valley
M'zhulu River
The Gonothi
The Quiniso Savanna
Mountains
Asa
The Blood Plains
Lake Zanele
Nolwazi
Sand Harbor
Oba
The Griner Valley
Vaccavane
Abelhalter   The N'erik River
Ardving
The Sindiswa Mountains
Centralia
Stoneshore
Lake Vala
The Stone Sea
Mt. Lapis
Meadowdell
M'lilo Forest
Red Savanna
Sizwe Plains
Redsnow

INANA
EASTERN HEMISPHERE

TABLE OF CONTENTS

The Womb Of Inana

Matthew North

The Womb Of Inana

CHAPTER ONE

N'damu I

"If our history lessons have taught us anything, it's that we should never sneak out of our history lessons."

—King N'aras Atalay, the Reuniter

The afternoon was too inviting to be bogged down by irrelevant curriculum and outdated quotes. "Blah, blah, blah … 30,330, Thraxian Cycles, Prince N'damu Atalay died of weaponized boredom." N'damu chuckled softly at his own joke as he slowed to a walk, confident enough that he'd outpaced his Prince's Guard. Unfortunately, escaping the city walls was no simple feat. Often, he'd been caught the moment his backside left his chair in the seminary.

The Womb Of Inana

I've finally lost them!

The sky was a bright yellow haze that rotation. The home star, Thraxis, cooked the air. Inana was a planet known for long and unforgiving summers, but he didn't mind one bit, having spent most his life indoors, under idyllic conditions.

Prince N'damu ran through the ebony canyons of the Glass Valley as fast as his spindly legs would carry him. A dust storm had passed the rotation prior, leaving the volcanic glass cliffs sleekly polished from the sandblasting—so much so that his reflection could be seen with impeccable clarity on their charcoal-black surfaces.

He had to get out of that infernal tower. He had to feel the warm wind on his face and the fields of tynn between his toes. The prince yearned for the sweet smell of skylar rose pollen and the music of the rasp dragon's circadian buzz.

Amongst hundreds of his likenesses, the maze of mirrors seemed the perfect place to go missing: no more training, no more lessons. N'damu just needed time alone before the pressures of being an Atalay swept him away.

He paused to observe his reflection on the hillside. His wiry body was undefined at best, and his creamy brown skin was smooth as a baby's backside. *Too smooth,* he thought, never having been worked very hard or suffered the elements.

N'damu held up his long, princely braid and twirled it, making silly faces in the glass. The deep black of his eyes disappeared in the rock, no matter how wide he opened them. His frizzy mohawk had a muted copper tinge he preferred to its regular bright orange.

In fact, his whole face seemed more handsome in the stone's midnight hue.

An Atalay was a deity to his people and needed to look the part. Mother had always made certain his royal adornments were impressive: ears studded with gems and loops of solid gold. His neck, wrist, waist, and ankles were encircled by rings of fine, jewel-laden ansyonite. His decoratively embroidered leathers shone every shade of yellow: shoulder bag, silky trousers, and a lustrous tunic that was split down the chest by buttons of polished obsidian.

"You must be *more* than a man to them, my son."

His mother's words often echoed through his head. When his family met with the natural-born commoners to give the needy food or to play with the sick children, he could see what Atalay meant to them. How happy they were when he touched their shoulders and "shared his light."

"You are the Shepherd of Men. You must dress to inspire," his Queen Mother, Anaqua Atalay, often said. "They give their hearts and souls for Atalay. For *you*, N'damu."

He clumsily spun his spear before striking an uncomfortable warrior's pose. An Atalay also carried the finest of weapons, though they'd always felt awkward in *his* hand. Today, it was a great spear of Sadah, a long blackwood shaft with a triple-bladed mount. He could barely swing it.

"When I am king, I will legalize blasters," he mumbled. The Doctrines of Atalay forbade such technologies on Inana, with few exceptions. Instead, he was expected to set an example by learning the spear, the holiest of weapons. Yet the prince knew no amount of training would help his feeble technique.

N'damu wished he saw so much more staring back from the reflective stone. His father, King N'joku Atalay, had muscles upon muscles, handsome to behold, the figure of a mighty Atalayan king. Growing up, the prince heard endless tales of his royal ancestors and their genetic perfection. His lineage was the pinnacle of the *Homo purist* class; people once called clones who'd risen to dominance in the spacefaring ages. Atalay was considered humanity's perfect version of a benevolent ruler, every molecule engineered to lead with selfless virtue. N'damu was destined to carry the burden of guiding humankind to prosperity next. It could be a lot of pressure at times.

"Sacred DNA—timeless and enduring." He shook his head, staring down at his sandals as he mocked his father's bottomless voice. *There was a defect in my embryonic vessel,* he thought. "Engineered perfection." The boy staring back from the hillside certainly wasn't. Not even close.

The prince focused his gaze down the valley, crinkling his nose at the bitter olyin yara spores wafting down from the hills. "I came to enjoy the afternoon—not to wallow in my shortcomings." Nesting ulanoids cawed from atop the amber-leafed vera trees, ovulating females calling for a mate.

N'damu continued to the riverside, a favorite landmark on his contemplative excursions through the valley. As usual, he went straight to skipping stones across the water. His father had always tried to teach him, but he'd never really picked it up, rarely getting more than two or three skims before his pebble disappeared into the murky abyss. Undaunted by each failure, he carefully walked the banks looking for more ideal stones amongst the thousands that shifted under his sandals.

"You must always be alert in the wilderness of Inana." His father's voice resonated in his head as though he were there. "Crongrins patrol these rivers, my son." Crongrins were deadly aquatic exophiles that hunted the riversides—he'd grown up learning all about them. With bony shells that mimicked jagged rocks, they could blend seamlessly with the shoreline, snaring unsuspecting victims with their bone-crushing jaws in an instantaneous and fatal strike.

"Aren't you afraid, Father?" N'damu remembered asking him, wide-eyed.

"My eyes are trained to spot them," he'd said. "You will learn too, in time." The king nodded with a broad smile. "N'damu, the Kingdom of N'gaia is your home, but you must be vigilant. Often the gravest threats lurk in plain sight. In your own home."

Kerplunk. Another hapless pebble sank to the riverbed.

"Crongrins are just one of many dangers out here, N'damu." He could remember the first time his father brought him into the valley, down from the Tower of Atalay. "The valley *itself* is a maze many have died trying to solve. Remember the G'higari words, Son. *Our* words. 'When you're lost, seek the home star.'" The mantra never strayed far. Thraxis rose in the south and set in the north. It would always orient him.

Fear of leaving N'gaia weighed heavy as he picked up a seamless-looking skipping rock. Prince N'damu was forty-two cycles now. He was coming of age, and his father had decided the time was upon him to take an imperative step into adulthood: the journey of N'jikota.

Instead of tossing the ideal stone across the water, he bobbed his head and dropped it at his feet, continuing down the riverbend. Atalay followed the G'higari faith, and this meant N'damu must make his quest to commune with Khanya, the Womb of Inana, to clarify his essence and calling. The ancients had called it N'jikota, but today it was more commonly known as a spirit-link.

"You will love it, N'damu," his father had promised. "Clan Novojoh are Masters of N'jikota. Every devout G'higari must travel to their home, Meadowdell. Atalay most of all. The spirit-link is most potent in *us*."

The visceral energy of Inana was potent indeed, and all Homo purist humans interacted with it differently. For some, the experience was powerful and accompanied an intensely intimate relationship with a wild creature; a bond that lasted for life. It was now his time to see what spirit-link the Womb of Inana might gift him.

N'damu climbed to the edge of a rocky overhang, which stretched out over a sizable pooling in the river. It was his favorite swimming spot. The prince hastily stripped down and, with a running start, dove from the rocks into the cool water.

As a small boy, he'd obsessed over the wild animals of Inana and dreamed of the day he would make the bond. What would it be? The mamidons of the great Sizwe Savannah? N'damu could imagine himself on the back of one of those mighty, towering beasts, shaking the ground as he charged into battle against some mountain warlord, bandit tribe, or rebellious scourge.

Or perhaps he would spirit-link with the dushnah, the bone-horses of the tynnland. Some of the greatest Atalayan heroes had ridden aback these noble animals; their power and speed was unmatched. He could feel the goosebumps on his arms tingling with excitement at the thought.

However, the one he dreamed of most was the atranoch. It was this beast that had captured his imagination all his life: the colossal bone-dragons. Who wouldn't want to fly on the back of such an godlike animal, high amongst the clouds, with its massive wingspan casting a shadow over the countryside?

The prince swam down as deep as his lungs would bear and clenched his eyes as tight as possible before letting his body go completely limp. Floating up slowly, he tried in vain to silence his mind.

There were, of course, less romantic possibilities. N'damu realized N'jikota could bond him with himpheah ants. Inglorious, though the enormous colonies of mites could serve as a dangerous ally when their masses rallied. Or maybe he would be a healer of the sick and wounded by bonding with the microbial throzeids. The tiny bacterial creatures could enter the bloodstream to regenerate tissues and even stimulate cell reproduction.

Or perhaps he would not bond with anything. What kind of Atalay would he be then?

Refreshed by the dip, he lay naked on a flat stone, resting his arms behind his head. The prince continued to daydream as the warm beams of the Eden Star dried his cocoa-brown skin. Stretching in the sunlight, he let out a melancholy sigh, inhaling the sour dander of the tynn grass. Despite his excitement, he'd be homesick without question. The journey could take many cycles, and to someone who'd never left N'gaia, it was terrifying.

N'damu dressed casually, then gathered his shoulder bag and staff, lamenting everything he would miss. *My father, my friends ... and her.*

His thoughts were interrupted by an odd sensation on the back of his neck. Then, an unnatural shadow darkened his peripheral vision.

A cloaked assailant sprang from the bush, thrusting a spear at him. N'damu repelled the blade with his own, but the buckling force of the colliding shafts knocked him onto his backside.

The attacker flipped toward him. Their dark-brown cloak spun through the air like a saw blade. Another spear slash darted in his direction, missing by inches as he frantically rolled out of the way. A red visor glowed under the stranger's hood. N'damu bowled backward, dodging another lunge. Seized by adrenaline, the ill-prepared prince reacted just quick enough.

He continued resisting the blows with his staff, barely able to get back to his feet. The prince knew he was outclassed and couldn't keep up his defenses for long. Finally conceding the high ground, N'damu found himself caught with his back to the cliffside, thrusting again and again like a cornered animal. One slice caused his phantom aggressor to pause, shredding the side of their cloak.

"Dammit!" the attacker cried out. The voice was distorted and mechanical, yet recognizably female. *A girl,* he thought.

Her spear technique was Sadah, though that was not enough to identify her. She vaulted forward, kicking him in the abdomen. The prince lost his wind with a grunt, stalled long enough for her to disarm him. Her next kick sent him to the ground with an undignified thud, then the blunt end of her spear rattled the side of his head.

N'damu faded out of consciousness for a moment … and dreamed another life.

When you're lost, seek the home star.

He saw a distant light and ran toward it. The throbbing pain pounded in his temple as the world spun back into focus.

"That's *one* life down. You only *get* three!" She peeled back her hood, revealing familiar N'gaian armor, silver and shining. Her visor glowed, staring down as he struggled to his feet. *N'gaian armor. Sadah spear. She is a warrior of the Royal Guard.*

Throwing down her weapon, she engaged him in hand-to-hand combat. Jab, cross, hook. His foe landed blow after blow, and it was clear he was outclassed again.

"What is this?" he cried out as he tucked his arms in to shield his face. "Do you know who I am?" Despite his rich ornamentation and extravagant finery, and his sacred name notwithstanding, Prince N'damu Atalay could be beaten—wounded. He could be killed.

The enemy in soldier's attire tossed a small chrome ball at his feet. Before he could realize his mistake in looking, a flash of dazzling light blinded him. Disoriented, the prince could see only pulsating ripples of white. Then, with a finishing uppercut, he was on his back again.

Unconscious once more, he dreamed. Inana raced around its home star, faster and faster. Seasons came and went as he lived and died and lived again. Out of the darkness, he could feel his heart beating, pounding like a drum, reminding him he was still alive. The world blinked in and out of existence as the figure standing over him came into focus.

"That's two lives down; luckily, you have *one* left," she said. "I think I'll let you keep it."

"This is no holo-game," he shouted. "Reveal yourself. I will decide the allotment of lives." She removed her helmet, and a fuzzy orange mop shook free from restraint, back to its fiery fullness. *Her*!

N'damu sat up with a jolt, suddenly concerned with his emasculating position. He staggered to his feet. "Nalia Chuku? Damn you, girl! You hide your face in N'gaian armor and attack your prince?"

"Yes, and you cut my cloak. So, what of it?" Nalia retorted, tearing away some tattered fabric. "I wasn't really going to hurt you!"

"Uh. What if *I* hurt you?" His reply made her chuckle. "I thought I was dead."

"Good," she snapped. "If you are going to go off to train with the Novojoh, you need to be able to defend yourself. Besides, it serves you right for sneaking out alone. Milushi bandits are known to come down to the valley."

He tried to broaden his shoulders as he stood up to her. "So, this thrashing was—what? Training?"

She scoffed and rolled her eyes. "What if I was a bounty hunter from the Jade Moon? What if I was an assassin from Anu?" She puffed out her chest—one of the few who did not fear him. "Would they go easy? You purists think you're all invincible." Nalia was a *natural*—born the old-fashioned way.

"Well, you do make *some* valid points," he said with an aching chuckle that ravaged his bruised ribcage. "But still ... I know *that* isn't it. Why don't you tell me the real reason you nearly killed me, Nalia?"

"Well ... maybe I'm angry..." she said with a shrug, her voice trailing off evasively. "I don't know. Never mind."

As she began to turn away from him, he grabbed her hand and pulled her back around. "Tell me, Nalia," N'damu demanded, staring her down as he rubbed his injuries. "What did I do? I know you don't care that I skipped my lessons."

"You're leaving ... you're leaving, and I worry, okay? I couldn't help it. Why does he have to make you go *now*? You're not ready!" Her eyes began to tear up as they stood with

11

entangled gazes. It was as if she radiated an aura of light that only he could see.

"Confident in your prince, I see."

"Look what I *just* did to you," she reminded him.

"Perhaps it is out there, Nalia." He pointed to the south at the distant mountains, so far off they seemed transparent.

"What?" she asked, exasperated.

"My strength, my calling … my power." He trembled as he struggled for words.

"Your power is that tower," she said, pointing north at the colossal spire on the horizon. "Your power is the loyalty of the clans. Your power is in your people. In your friends, and … and me."

He'd known Nalia Chuku since before he could form memories. One of the Two Spears of his Prince's Guard, she had trained from her youth to defend him. As he learned to be a monarch, she learned to be his guardian—her oath to live and die for N'damu.

"I don't remember spending a single rotation without you," he said as he reached for her hand, lost in her cavernous brown eyes. "I don't know anyone stronger than you—I mean, look what you just did to me. You don't need *me* half as much as *I* need you, Nalia."

Dust covered her soft brown skin, but still she seemed to glow. He thought she was the most gorgeous person he'd ever seen. But, standing this close to her, he reminded himself, as he always did to stifle his attraction: loving him would be her death.

"You underestimate yourself, N'damu Atalay," she said, laughing as she meekly looked at her feet to avoid eye contact. "Some battles can't be fought with a spear, you know. Some people's weapon is their heart." Nalia looked up, locking eyes with him once again. "Believe me; you've got me bested in that arena."

She was a natural-born, a line of Inanean Homo sapiens with uncultivated DNA reclaimed by time. He was Atalay—elite among the gene-obsessed Homo purist society. The blood of Atalay could never mix with a natural's; the Doctrines of Atalay forbade it. Khanya and the spirits of his ancestors forbade it. Someday he would marry a noble of the high clans who would be his queen and foster the next Atalay son—the next king. That, above all, must happen. It could never be Nalia Chuku, regardless of his feelings for her.

Doctrine IV: Natural reproduction is forbidden. The Homo purist genome must never be subjected to variability.

He would have to choose a queen nonetheless. *Princess Enahdra Vesta, perhaps?* Enah was a true beauty, and he knew he could do much worse. Or if not her, then some noble debutante of Rhyolite, Duran, or Centralia.

N'damu leaned closer to her, knowing he shouldn't. She smelled like ocha-nut berry armor polish. "I don't want to leave you, Nalia."

13

Instead of stepping away like he expected her to, she gazed unblinking, unflinching, staring through him, as though he had no opacity. "I'm sworn to defend you … yet when you face true danger, I'm forced to stay behind."

"It is the G'higari way," he said. "I'm afraid we are both slaves to the juggernaut of duty."

"Service to you is blessed penance." She smiled, and the last of his defenses melted away. Maybe it was the wound to his head or the sadness in his heart, but he put his hands on her waist and pulled her close until their faces were less than a finger's length apart.

"As you've sworn your spear to my life, I swear my heart to your service, Nalia." Each breath seemed impossibly long as he moved his lips toward hers. Each heartbeat came further apart from the last, as though dropping its rhythm. It felt like an eternity—or at least he wished it were, but unfortunately, some moments just don't have that much time.

Just as he grazed his bottom lip on hers, an abrasive yell rang from atop the canyon. Then, as reality regained tempo, their blissful moment crumbled to dust.

"N'damu! Get up here, you mamidon's ass." His First Spear, the young Lord Noba Sadah, looked down on them from the rocky cliff with a troop of guards at his back. They seemed unaware of what they'd interrupted. "What in the Barren Void is your problem, N'damu?" he called out before looking back over his shoulder. "Over here, Enah!" Moments later, Princess

14

Enahdra stepped to the edge beside Noba and looked down in relief.

"So … I found him!" Nalia called out before anyone could say more. "We were just going to head back, but we got caught up in some … *ahem*. Training exercises. My fault!" Even then, she tried to protect him.

Finally, N'damu's heart slowed to its normal pace. As they walked up the canyon, he could only lament the kiss that almost was.

CHAPTER TWO

Myriam I

Port City was less than fifty kilometers from the Axis Solaris, the border between day and night that cut the tidally locked planet Anu in half. It was on the edge of the dark side in the region known as the Tropic of Dusk. With the city in a perpetual state of twilight, the sky was always a blackened haze of violets and blues. Stars dotted the heavens, crystal-clear despite the light pollution radiating from the unsleeping urban center. The waning gibbous shape of the planet Ra formed an ominous bloodspot in the sky, a red eye over the rows of towering skyscrapers. The buildings seemed to merge, layered silhouettes, speckled with cascades of window lights, each with less detail the more distant on the horizon.

Called "Tokyo Vegas" by some, Port City was unquestionably the hardest and most dangerous metropolis in the Tri-Worlds. Limitless nightlife. Streets awash with drugs and sex for sale on every corner. It was a crime capital to which criminals gravitated from all over the system: tech smugglers, weapons dealers, gangsters, organized syndicates of bounty hunters, guilds of thieves, hackers, and assassins.

The chill tonight is unusual, she thought. *The height, perhaps.*

Myriam Yamada had grown up under the Eden Star, Thraxis, on the light side of Anu, accustomed to its comforting warmth. The cold gave her goose-pimples, swinging and flipping from rooftop to rooftop, dancing amongst the high-rise towers with the grace of a ballerina. Her lush pink hair whipped in the wind as she acrobatically traversed the skyline. Dressed in a tight black bodysuit, slick and suitably aerodynamic for her line of work, she wore dark gray knee-high boots and matching gloves. Spooled at her shoulder was a length of rope, and around her waist her katana hung in its scabbard.

My soul is empty. My mind is alight. My exile, my shame: sharpen me to the task at hand.

Once, she was a defender of life—a warrior of the Knights of Yosai. Devoted to Atalayan justice, she'd held the rank of Yon Astra, second in the order's command. Previously a beacon in the Light of Atalay, she was now relegated to darkness. The former Yosai could only exist in shadow after her dishonorable expulsion.

The Womb Of Inana

Like a ghost out of phase, Myriam seemed lighter than air. Her skin was tanned bronze, her eyes sparkling violet. Eternally focused on her mission, she wasted no motion in her effortless acrobatics, vaulting from flagpoles and sliding down balcony covers, grappling up the taller buildings and diving to those below.

I am only a sword, mid-swing. Tonight, I am nothing but a lethal lunge bound for my enemy's heart.

She scaled an Izlagosi industrial tower called the Factory, one of the tallest engineering hubs in Port City. From its roof, the streetlights sparkled like glitter amongst the bustling life below. Accepting her exile with dignity, Myriam committed to cleansing herself of the weakness that had undone her. Redemption required her to destroy the flaw in her heart that proved her bane: love.

My heart is empty, and my blood is cold. I am death, she thought. *I am the emotionless void.* But despite the chilling monikers, "Death" had to eat sometime. She had to use what she had left to survive on her path to ultimate detachment. Tonight, the former Yosai was a living weapon to be wielded by the highest bidder. Tonight, Myriam had a mark.

She unspooled her rope, attached its grappling hook to the roof's edge, and began to rappel silently down the edifice. The western face shone purple and maroon in the light of Ra as the Anutian assassin descended to the windowsill she sought.

Quietly, Myriam pulled out her sword, the relic she'd kept from the Yosai. *I deserved at least THAT.* She'd bled to earn the great katana: the Sword of Pegasus, forged from legendarily rare metal, taken from the Earth Ark itself. *It's a part of me now,* she thought. *I wasn't about to give it back.*

Launching herself out with a kick, she swung away from the window to gain momentum. Then she announced herself with a crash, shattering the glass as she bounded through.

She landed at the end of a long hallway lined with armed security sentries. *Izlagosi Guard. What are they doing in Port City? Meat to the cleaver, sadly.*

There was an elevator door at the far end. That was where she needed to go.

Alarmed by her entrance, the men of Izlagos drew their weapons. "Halt, intruder! Drop your sword," demanded the one nearest, "or we will drop you." The hum of plasma rifles charging followed, reverberating down the corridor as Myriam calmly stood up, shaking the glass from her hair.

"I'm looking for Thar'vak. *Oddis Thar'vak.* If any of you gentlemen would like to escort me to him, you needn't die today. Decide quickly. I'm rather anxious to kill." Scanning the eyes of the guards, she counted twenty. Probably well trained; from the way they were standing their ground, it was clear they were at least confident.

The one nearest to her began to raise his rifle, likely only intent on aiming, but that was all the excuse she needed. *All right, let's commence.*

In a blur of black and pink, she leapt to the middle of the hall and planted her sword in the floor tiles. Then, spinning upside-down, she helicopter-kicked two men, breaking their jaws on the first rotation and driving their skulls into the wall on the second, leaving wet, splattered bloodstains. *Two.*

Somersaulting forward, Myriam spin-kicked another guard at his legs, taking his feet out while at the same time driving her katana deep into the adjacent man's abdomen. The one she'd kicked fell to the floor, crushing his knees as he erratically discharged his rifle. Then, before his desperate spray of plasma bursts could find her, the exiled Yon Astra spun with her sword, ripping it from the dead man's stomach. A bloody trail followed her blade like a comet's tail as she drove it into the skull of the wild rifleman. *That makes four.*

The corridor was tight. They could only attack two at a time or risk killing each other. Throwing the bloody corpse of the man she had just gutted into the next guard, she drove her sword through his back, skewering them both like meat on a stick. *Five.* Myriam continued counting as she leveraged their corpses, grabbing the sixth guard in a leg scissor and snapping his neck. *That's six.*

The pink-haired assassin then dove behind the next Izlagosi, grabbing him by the shoulders to use as a human shield as three others opened fire. *Seven.*

She caught the electron rifle of the blast-riddled man-shield and answered fire. Myriam shot one in the forehead and another in the heart before the third could rush her. He tackled her to the floor, able to detain her for a moment under the bodies. She reversed his hold, however, and with a loud crack snapped his neck in a headlock. *Eight, nine, ten.*

Regaining her feet, Myriam wiped the iron flavor of blood from her lips, her face and hair now spattered in hot, wet death. She pointed her sword at the next two with the eyes of an emotionless executioner, signaling for them to come with her free hand. Looking at each other first, the two guards panicked and made a break for it. Desperate to escape, one tried to run past her. She lopped off his head with a graceful pirouette and a spray of red. The other dove from a window, preferring to take his chances with gravity rather than face her katana. *Should have stayed on the sunny side. Anyways ... eleven, twelve.*

Like a maestro conducting a symphony in blood, Myriam Yamada cut through six more men like they were nothing. The hallway turned white to red as she passed. Slicing off heads and punching through hearts, her blade painted abstracts in blood as she slaughtered them, until at last only two remained between her and the elevator door.

"Now, I only need *one* of you to open this door. Whoever does first, I'll reward with continued life. Choose." Myriam cocked her blade behind her head, ready to strike.

The guard on the right broke down, raised his arms, and dropped to his knees before her. "I surrender. I'll open it! Kill him, not…"

Spineless. Not bothering to let him finish the pointless plea, Myriam slashed her katana. With a single stroke, she cut through

21

the guard who'd answered too slow, his insides falling to the floor with a succession of squishy thuds.

She nodded at the last man. The Izlagosi turned to the access panel, timidly removed his glove, and placed his palm on the scanner. The light turned green. Then he stepped back and nervously tiptoed past her, negotiating the mounds of corpses littering the floor. "Hey, sunshine." He turned to Myriam in terror. "Kiss your kids goodnight tonight and give your mother your love."

The door opened, revealing two more operating guards. She walked into the clean white elevator, soaked in death, marking the stainless-steel floor in bloody boot prints with each step. Then, turning around to face the door as it closed, she calmly made her request. "Penthouse, please."

***

Aggressive electronic music pounded, filtering through the doors before they opened. The blood-spattered elevator dripped red from the ceiling as Myriam stepped out over the operators' dismembered remains.

The penthouse was a discotheque. Subs pulverized the room with bass beats as psychedelic melodies soared dreamily through the enormous ballroom. Mirror balls reflected a kaleidoscope of light beams in perfect sync with the music. Myriam walked in with a crooked grin, about to spoil the party.

22

Plants of all origins decorated the hall: garlands of Oshunese ipabites, Inanean aiku, and fresh janelle bouquets. Leviathan ivy sprawled out amongst headless statues of chrome, abstract hologram art, and avant-garde sculptures in cast ansyonite.

At the opposite end of the room was a fine couch stitched from tanned mamidon leather. On it, a naked blond man reclined over luxurious pillows, watching a hologram monitor with great fascination. He puffed smoke rings through the rainbows of light, nodding to the beat as two young girls lay on each side of him. Naked, with legs draped over his lap, they adoringly caressed his muscular bronze chest as he stared off in a trance.

Myriam walked up and put her sword through the hologram, its point half an inch from his eye. Then, peering indifferently, she mouthed words she knew he couldn't hear. The two women panicked, their breasts bouncing as they jumped back to their knees in retreat. The man, however, still pretended not to notice.

After a moment, he began laughing hysterically. Next, he gave a brief flick of his finger, and the music cut. His laughter awkwardly became the only sound in the room, and he pulled the girls back to his side. "I was watching you work just now … LOVED IT!"

Clearly a man of Izlagos, his hair was styled with meticulous care and carefully trimmed from head and chest to golden pubis. His face seemed familiar, but she couldn't place it. Some forgotten nightmare, perhaps.

He made air quotes with his fingers as his laughter continued. "Oddis Thar'vak." The yellow-haired noble of Izlagos clapped in apparent approval, then gently pushed her blade from his eye. "Do you think *these* whores got me hard like this?" he asked, gripping his erection and thrusting his pelvis. "Fuck, no." He continued his raucous laughter as he shoved the girls away again. Then, scooting on his knees, he drew closer to Myriam with his rigid cock flapping about wildly. "Seeing you kill those useless cretins; it was a fucking murderous masterpiece. I mean, stone-cold heartless. Absolutely callous!" He roared with amusement again. "I thought I would blow my load just watching."

The former Yosai nudged her blade closer, grazing his neck.

"I'm so glad I hired you to kill me," the Izlagosi said. "Well, to kill 'Oddis Thar'vak,' that is."

"Who are *you* then?"

He scoffed. "You don't recognize the son of the Steward of Anu?" *Is that why I recognize him? No.*

Confused, Myriam stepped back. "Wait … what?"

"Theodus, of Clan Darius, at your service. Well, actually, I suppose you are at *my* service, Myriam Yamada."

She knew his dossier. Theodus Darius, privileged son of Lord Cassius Darius—N'joku Atalay's acting steward on Anu. High Clan Darius was the premier Homo purist family on the planet, and Theodus had the clone-blood of ancient emperors. He was a mogul in the robotics industry and had credits to burn—indeed, his credits had credits to burn. Seventy-nine cycles and in his prime, he was ruggedly handsome, with a physique like chiseled stone.

"What sort of game are you playing with me?"

"Yes, yes, exactly. Only a game," the lordling said, clapping softly. "The Cypras Foundation?" He fell back on his cushions, continuing his condescending applause. Theodus grabbed one of the girls like an inanimate object, burying his face in her chest and gyrating. He emerged, hooting again in intoxicated pleasure. "I'm sorry. Ha! No, no—really, I'm sorry. For the deception, you know. But ... *Vel Lucilius Litorius*? The man who hired you. I am actually HIM as well. I have so many aliases; even I lose track. The Cypras Foundation is a subsidiary of Darius Corp., a little cover I use sometimes. You know how it is ... I mean, I know you're new to this assassin thing. But *I've* done my homework too. Been playing this game all my life—I was engineered for it. *I* know who you are. Believe me..."

"So, I guess the 200,000 credits...?" Myriam asked, staring him down, looking more and more ready to kill.

"Pintah nuts," he responded with an arrogant smirk. "Minerva berries. An artist of your talent shouldn't settle for such trifle compensations. Not under *any* circumstance. I just wanted to see what you could do for myself." She scowled at him, not happy to play the pawn. "You know, if you could really get to me. You see, I require a murderer, and, especially after *this* display, let's just say I'm a big fan of your murdering! Whoooo!" He screamed erratically until the other girl passed him a tray of powdered ether. Darius snorted a line and finally slouched back.

"You might not be a fan when all is said and done." Myriam held her sword aloft once more, ready to bring it down on him. She couldn't tell if he was toying with her or there was truth in his words. *I should kill this devil now. Though perhaps he is exactly the devil I need.*

"How about a *billion* creds?"

After a moment of consideration, Myriam stayed her katana, sheathing it calmly. She walked to the edge of the bed, sat down, and crossed her legs. Tilting her head slightly to the side, she separated a strip of her hair and began wringing out blood. A red pool splashed, slowly seeping into the fine Inanean leather. "And the mark?" she asked.

This may be the kill I need to cleanse my heart of love's infection.

"Oh, that would be the son of my former guru, *hahaha*." He fondled one of the girl's backsides as he guided the other into oral service. Laying back, Theodus lit another concoction, puffing a hazy cloud as the girls worshiped him in tandem. "Oh, yes ... this will be a *very* sensitive target. And there will be some travel involved. Have you been to Inana? It's a shithole of a planet, but we *are* talking a billion creds here."

The pink of her hair started to show through again as Myriam continued to work out the gore. "I don't really buy that you'd want to pay those kinds of credits just to settle a personal vendetta. What's the name?"

"Ha! Oh, *ummm* ... the prize of the Tri-World, innocent little *N'damu Atalay*." Theodus shifted and writhed in gratification as the second woman joined in the oral pleasuring. "Ever heard *that* one? I'm guessing you have."

"Wait, you want to assassinate the prince?"

"If it were anyone less than the future king, would I need a murderer of your caliber? A Yosai gone dark? *Whooooooo!*" His eyes rolled back in titillation.

"But why?"

"Because Atalay stole something from me—and I want it BACK! Then, I want the Tri-Worlds to feel the way I have felt— to suffer as I have suffered. You want billions? Well, I want trillions—and still, I'd be empty without my princess." Darius took another hit as the suckling sounds intensified. "I was N'joku's ward. Let's just say I didn't leave on good terms. I want him to watch while I take what is most precious to him. Like he took…" His attention trailed off for a moment, and then he began to shake in a frenzy. "Atalay, Vesta, Sadah—*they* spite us. Our planet is plagued now by Tri-World capitalists, waving the flag of Atalay in my business. MY BUSINESS!" His eyes bulged as he frothed at the mouth. "On this planet … MY PLANET! Time to upset the status quo and for me to reclaim my property." He screamed, thrusting into the girls' mouths as his emotions boiled to an explosion.

"The Tri-World Alliance is more than just the Seat," she said as she wiped her arms and chest with a silk throw from the couch.

"Is it?" he asked. "Tell that to my father. Tell that to my cunt of a sister, who would suck off anyone sitting on that throne. We bow to Atalay from afar when, in truth, Izlagos is the greater empire. They smuggle weapons tech to darksider rebels and drugs to sunnyside innocents. It's time to get rid of those orange-headed fuckers once and for all."

"The council of Izlagos will not necessarily collapse without an immediate successor," she explained. "Nor will Vesta … Sadah … Duran. Konga Dreau will stand with Atalay…"

"I don't care about Inana or that fucking jungle moon, Oshun!" Theodus stood and pulled up his pants. In an instant, the noble Izlagosi's demeanor flatlined. All signs of intoxication disappeared, and he was all business—sober and focused on the deal. "Listen, I can credit you 200,000 for tonight's entertainment," he said. "No sweat off a botsora's balls! I work for a powerful organization that has been in operation longer than your cute little Knights of Yosai, even. If you don't want to be rich beyond belief, you know the way out, I'm sure. Maybe you could tell someone about my plan. There may be a reward for that little tip. You can kill me where I stand now, as easily as I take my next breath. It could be you'd even survive those who would seek retribution. Yes—you could cross me, but we *both* know you're gonna take that sweet cred. You're gonna go to that shit planet, and you're going to kill that little fucker, N'damu. Am I wrong?"

"And how would you expect me to get to Inana? Your people ardently police the spaceports in Izlagos."

"I'm sure in your time as a Knight of Yosai, you heard of the Hangar," Darius said. "Perhaps served some 'justice' there?"

"Zharr?"

28

"Zharr—City in the Dome. Go to the Hangar … find Kat'har Rio." He bent down and leveled out his palm, knee-high. "About this tall, can't miss him. He has a pirate or two in his employ. He can get you to Inana." *Kat'har Rio? That smarmy dwarf.*

The visceral conflict was tangible. Myriam's mind could only do battle with itself. Perhaps this was the steel that could redefine her blade, the whetstone to sharpen her heart's edge to nothing. The Yosai had made her an instrument of death and cast her out. She'd tried moral obedience. She'd been Yon Astra, a servant of justice. Was her mistake tipping too far toward the light?

"Half. Up-front," she said, polishing the last of her boot heel clean. She returned to the elevator, turning back before the doors shut. "I believe you have my account information, Mr. Litorius." *As flowers grow and ulanoids fly, as manta swim the oceans and shadow panthers stalk their hapless prey, so too does a weapon kill.*

There was nothing left of Myriam Yamada but a weapon.

CHAPTER THREE

N'joku I

The throne room atop the Tower of Atalay looked as much like the command bridge of an ageless space vessel as a royal hall. It was a chamber befitting the most powerful men ever to have lived. As he walked the long scarlet carpet leading to the Seat, King N'joku Atalay let out a long, foreboding sigh. Colossal columns of granite towered from the floor, reddened from the light of the braziers like his personal hell. *Only a dull-minded twat would envy the excitement of being Atalay,* he thought.

He wished *he* could run off to the valley like his truant son. Instead, like a prisoner returning to his cell, the king looked around his elegant court, wondering how a room so grand could bore him so completely.

N'joku's two imposing ten-foot-long nagas slithered behind him as he waddled his husky frame up the steps, grumbling with discontent. He sat upon his radiant throne of white ansyonite—the Seat of Atalay—encrusted with gems that formed a great eye on its backrest. The Omnipresent Eye, they called it. Ornate as it was, the chair had always given the king a sore ass.

His rattling nagas curled up beside him, Usoca on his left and Urnas to his right. Long, worm-like exophiles, nagas had been top predators on Inana for millions of cycles. Their internal anatomy and spinal column were vaguely visible through the transparent flesh of their underbellies as they sat up begging for treats as usual. The animals' suction-cup mouths frothed violet foam, dribbling from between their razor-sharp fangs and pooling on the carpet.

N'joku patted Usoca on her belly, then winked at Urnas, smiling lovingly. They seemed to glimmer in his eyes. Since the king had spirit-linked to them as a young prince, he carried the moniker The Naga King. He and his companions had so much in common, it seemed. Apex predators—alphas of their kind. Too wild for captivity.

The vibrato of murmurs made the court feel animated, rhythmic like it was the heart of the Tri-Worlds. Two hundred Homo purist nobles loaded their ears with whispers and gossip so they might spread through the veins of the system, giving life to the realm of three worlds.

M'demke Vesta, his Lord Chancellor, always announced prominently in court. The king's old friend was more than happy to address the endless line of insignificant quibblers come to call. "And now for Article Twelve of today's proceedings. Atalay will hear the noble Elsa E'sizi, esteemed purist of Clan E'sizi,

Masters of Defense and Lords of Mountain Shore. Please, state your business with the Council of Atalay, My Lady."

For Inanean naturals and noble Homo purist alike, this business was their livelihood, but for N'joku Atalay, the Naga King, hero of the Charonese Wars, it was the same monotonous drivel he'd been listening to for a hundred cycles. His mighty mount of dreadlocks spilled over his face as he propped his chin on his knuckle. A mix of silver and orange, the king's mane was connected in front by an equally lush beard that crunched under his fist as he sulked. *Surely, my ancestors did more than sit on this chair and fatten to their old age.*

"Clan E'sizi thanks the council for hearing our grievance," Lady Elsa said. "For thousands of cycles, our people kept faith with the Tri-World Alliance. We have held back the raids of the savage Zolan mountain bandits for generations. Unfortunately, their tribes have recently ravaged our stocks, and dust storms from the Fuza have left our yields this quarter … tenuous. As Masters of Defense, we are a critical cog in the security of Inana and the stability of the Tri-Worlds. We feel our hardship will ripple through the kingdom if we do not receive aid."

The Lady of E'sizi continued, but the meaning to her words seemed to evaporate before reaching his ears. The king stared at the purist woman with a glazed gawk, making no effort to feign focus as he imagined the shape of her breasts under her ridiculous dress.

He rolled back his dark black eyes and stared up at the ceiling as the woman droned on. Along the upper rafters perched icons of his Atalayan forefathers cast in gold and ansyonite.

32

Eavesdroppers with hands to their ears, constantly staring down with watchful eyes on the floor, where nobles of the high clans would socialize and scandalize. "An Atalay is always watching," the old adage went.

"...thousand men required to fortify the basin..." She seemed to yammer on endlessly. "...swarms of zogolaths from the Tundari Savanah have also devastated our..." His eyes crossed, going in and out of focus as he imagined he was somewhere else: playing music, drinking, painting, dancing, smoking, fighting, fucking—anything but this. When he opened his eyes, Lady E'sizi was gone.

"The crown will now hear the..." M'demke stopped for a second, as if choking on his words. "Ahem ... *noble* Jahr'rod Wahlt, the Master of Waste, Lord of Abelhalter."

The old and rotund man spoke in a high-pitched wheeze. He had a noble name but carried himself like an animal from the jungles of Oshun. The gift of engineered DNA, squandered. "It is an honor to address the council once again. I come to ask a royal blessing for my sixth marriage, to the lovely young noble..."

The aloof king tossed a couple *grats* to his ravenous nagas who obnoxiously wrestled for the little, bony, snack-sized creatures. The gaudy upheaval caused a commotion in the court, but he didn't care. The noise thankfully drowned out Lord Wahlt's mewling. *Let M'demke handle this mamidon shit—he still has the will for it.*

M'demke was the lord of High Clan Vesta: Masters of Technology. The two comrades had come to rule side by side as their fathers and grandfathers had before them. As Lord Chancellor of his council, M'demke was N'joku's most distinguished ally and closest confidant.

"If the girl's clan consents—and she is of appropriate age, then Atalay will allow the union." He was happy to let M'demke speak for him as the king tapped his foot, imagining beats in his head. The Lord Chancellor wore a tall black cylindrical headpiece that towered over everyone, embroidered with the Tri-World pyramid in metallic blue, three circles inside a triangle.

The thin old man still stood with dignity, despite his aging backbone. Vesta was the richest clan on Inana, and it showed in his ceremonial blue armor. His family was trusted to regulate the Tri-World's most significant technologies. M'demke fingered through the holo-screen of his tech-infused wrist bands, casually making notes as he called the next noble.

"Article Thirty-Three, the Lady France Babbyanna, natural-born, married into Clan Babbyanna, Lords of Ardving..."

It seemed like the longest string of disgruntled whiners he'd ever endured. The obnoxious, loud-mouthed woman was unbecomingly plump and hid her lack of class behind tacky finery.

The king threw a couple more grats to Usoca and Urnas, then glanced over to see his wife taking her seat, the ever-elegant Queen Anaqua Atalay. *Now that's how you take care of yourself,* he thought. *She is the perfect woman for a king.*

Even at 135, she looked as lovely as the day of their match. N'joku could already see the glazed look of boredom on her face, despite her reputation for proper court etiquette. His father had called her to N'gaia as a lady in waiting, purist daughter of the High Clan Tattrila, Lords of Stoneshore. She was an angel of the water and immediately became the goddess of his heart. Most importantly, she had the nobility required to raise Atalayan children.

"I'm sorry, Lady Babbyanna," M'demke proclaimed as the discontented noblewoman huffed. "Unless you have physical evidence or an admission of guilt from your husband, Atalay cannot pass judgments regarding marital fidelity ... rumored adultery or no."

"Can you blame him for the adultery?" Anaqua smiled and even let a giggle slip, further exposing the crack in her royal demeanor. Hypnotically gorgeous as always, the queen wore a sapphire tiara that shined like a halo atop her silver weave and an elegant white crystal sequined gown that hung to her toes. Her skin was light brown, and though her age showed under her glowing olive eyes, her rosy cheeks and red lips still had their youth.

"Article Sixty-Five of today's agenda: the council recognizes Colt Dunkarr, the noble son of Clan Dunkarr, Lords of Vaccavane, City on the Mountain. Please state your business with the Council of Atalay." M'demke beckoned to the man with a tired flick of the wrist.

"Thank you for hearing me this hour. I come with dark whispers from high in the Sindiswa. I addressed my lord father

35

and now come before you at his behest." He bowed uncomfortably. Colt was a simple young man in brown leathers, no more than sixty-five, and unkempt beside the smooth-shaven courtiers. *The boy struggles to fake his formalities*, the king thought, *a lordling after my own heart.*

"Do continue, young Dunkarr," M'demke said.

"Well, you see, I live as a guide through the mountains. I go through Yi'fava or Ardving, Vharti Pass, Jhiph—even Meadowdell from time to time—leading people safely through the passes and on to Vaccavane." Colt's face was ruggedly handsome. Brown-eyed and black-haired, he had an evening shadow of stubble on his face and a scar that ran from the top of his left eye down his cheek, as if from a blade's slash.

"Anyway, I'm sorry to admit in front of you noble lords, but sometimes the travelers I accompany are not of the most honorable character. Naturals, mostly—some may stray from the Doctrines of Atalay from time to time. I've interacted with the mountain tribes often enough, even lodged in their village encampments. I am always hearing savages brag of their kills— of their spoils from raiding. Making a sport of rape—a competition of who'd eaten the most purist flesh."

N'joku was oddly intrigued, noticing the boy stop and look at his feet as if the memory brought on a recurrence of some trauma. He carried a whip at his side, a common weapon of the mountain people. *The boy must have seen a fight or two.*

"Anyway, I was at this … establishment. A place one might go to find some *company*, maybe a pint of japhid spiced ale. You know, we're two clicks up the mountain, so the options aren't great. This one night, there was a particularly shady individual having one too many." The more comfortable he became, the more Colt's phony decorum faded. "He's feeling good, and so he goes on and on with this woman. He's trying to impress her, telling her, 'I killed this guy and fought that guy.'" Chuckling, he paused and shook his head. "He acted as though he were the hardest man on Inana. But she's *not* having it at all, not at all, and she calls him out as a liar."

M'demke interjected just then, hoping to hurry the lad. "Please, if you could move on to the point."

"Yes, apology, My Lord," he replied. "So, the guy gets pissed off and goes on a rant about his next job. Apparently, there's a hit out on *all* three worlds—a prize on the head of none other than the Prince of Atalay." The entire court seemed to exhale at once, but N'joku just rolled his eyes. "Word is going around the tribes of the Sindiswa. This fellow was intent on cashing in, trust me. Possibly just a drunk or a liar, but my father thought it prudent to share what I heard with you."

Now on full alert, Anaqua interjected, "Who was this man?"

"What his true name is, I couldn't be sure. All I know is they say he came from Oshun, and around the mountains they call him 'The Volturis.'" He was clearly frustrated that he couldn't be more helpful. *Another threat from the mountain tribes,* N'joku thought. *Silly barbarians. When will they learn?*

"Volturis? *Hummmm*. From the Jade Moon, you say." Despite his skepticism, the king mimicked his queen's concern. "Troubling," he whispered to her. "Most troubling."

"What will we do, my love?" Anaqua's eyes began to tear.

Take the afternoon off? he thought. *It's the perfect excuse to end this drudgery.*

N'joku finally stood to address the court for the first time all day. "Atalay thanks you, young lordling Dunkarr, for your loyalty. Lord Vesta, bring up everything you can find about this Volturis. I need to contemplate this development with my councilors." He walked down and put his hand on Colt's shoulder. "I bless you, in the Light of Atalay. The Tri-Worlds are in your debt—the hospitality of N'gaia is yours." As he walked off, the king turned with melodramatic urgency, gazing wide-eyed at the Lord Chancellor. "I will hear no more appointments this rotation. Empty the court!"

M'demke didn't need to repeat the king's words. The assembly began to clear the hall the moment the order left his lips.

CHAPTER FOUR

N'damu II

"N'damu Atalay!" Princess Enahdra said, waving her finger.

"Enahdra Vesta!" the prince replied, mocking her stern expression.

"Thank Khanya you are safe," she said. "I was worried sick." Enah was the daughter of the Lord Chancellor. N'damu was surprised she'd forgone whatever social event was on her agenda to come after him herself. Certainly, Noba was capable enough of leading the guard. It was *not* the first time an Atalay had skipped class, after all. *This level of concern seems a bit ... unwarranted.*

"I was tailing him the whole time," Nalia said with a nervous chuckle. "He was perfectly safe." N'damu's grin went crooked. *I was,* he thought. *Until you found me, Nalia Chuku!*

Enahdra didn't seem to acknowledge Nalia's comments. "My father has called us to the throne room. Come, My Prince, the royal magnus awaits." She waved her hands, beckoning him to make his way up the cliffs where their hulking land tank was waiting to take him home. Enah's long indigo gown matched her glossy hair flawlessly—she was not one to sacrifice beauty for utility, even in the valley. "Your sisters are here too, and I'm afraid they aren't happy." The aroma of flowers trailed her, and glitter sparkled on her flawless umber skin. A lineage as ancient as Atalay, Vesta was one of few clans to name their children "prince" or "princess." It was a Homo purist custom of respect traditionally permitted only to the oldest blood.

Noba shuffled up, trying to beat him to the princess's side. Enah, however, boxed him out with her elbow. "Shouldn't you be guarding something, Noba? Silently, perhaps?"

"Don't worry, Princess," he said, winking with an alpha's confidence. "I am guarding your heart. Have no fear. It is safe with me." DNA engineered for warfare, Noba was the noble son of Clan Sadah: Masters of Arms, genetically designed to be a warrior. "As for silence, no. I can only scream of your beauty from atop a mountain." The handsome lordling shimmered in his dazzling chromium armor.

Enahdra rolled her eyes, reaching for N'damu's hand and pulling him next to her. "Come on," she said. "We should not keep the king waiting." Enah pouted, tilting her head slightly. He looked at Noba and shrugged while Nalia fell behind with the guards, disappearing in his periphery. They walked up the foothills like they'd done a thousand times growing up, but something felt different. The situation's gravity was abnormal, unbefitting *one* truant afternoon.

"What *were* you thinking?" Enah asked as they passed under a grove of vera trees. "I love a stroll in the valley, N'damu." She leaned to whisper in his ear. "But you *need* better guards."

"Please, Enah, I'm forty-two now!" N'damu pursed his lips, kicking a tuft of dirt. "I don't need *any* guards, in all honesty."

"Fun fact!" she said. "On Earth, you'd only be sixteen." Princess Vesta was a keen admirer of Earth lore.

"A man is a man," the prince replied, puffing his chest. "No matter the star they orbit." His bruised ribs throbbed from the gesture as he favored his side.

She flashed a lopsided grin. "Father says sexual maturity comes early in an Atalay." The princess glanced back at Nalia, squinting. "I mean, she's cute, I guess … for a natural. But still…"

"What are you *talking* about," N'damu said, grinding his teeth anxiously as the light flickered through the trees.

"Don't think I didn't notice," she said with a huff. The prince looked to ensure no one was in earshot. Enahdra lowered her voice, clearly delighted to gossip. "I get it. I get it. Trust me … I like to explore my wild side too." She looked off in wonderment. "There are a lot of gorgeous naturals on Anu."

"Enough of this, Ena—wait … what?" His face went crooked as she giggled mischievously. "You? You were interested in naturals?"

41

"What do I look like, some Earth ape?" She flashed a devilish grin and winked. "No … I would *never*."

Suddenly, Noba interrupted another intimate moment. The First Spear, the captain of the prince's sworn guard, swung his arms around their necks as they came out of the shade and into a clearing. "Did I really want to spend all afternoon with your stuck-up sisters, N'damu?" He shivered. "This was my rotation off!"

Enahdra shook free of his arm and scurried ahead to the magnus. Noba stared him down with a frustrated grimace, clearly unimpressed. N'damu's mind, however, was still on the opposite sex. *Princess Enahdra,* he thought, *and a natural? Did she actually?* "Are you even listening to me?" Noba complained. "This armor is *not* comfortable."

N'damu snapped back from the daydream, smirking a moment before laughing at the lordling in his unnecessarily bulky battlement.

"What's funny, my *holy* Prince of Atalay?"

"No, you're right. That looks most uncomfortable. Can I help you loosen your shoulder pads?" N'damu massaged Noba's shoulders mockingly. His friend was taller, and, of course, a much better fighter. The son of Sadah had a neatly combed coif, black with a tint of maroon, held back with his ruby visor slid up over his forehead. A few cycles older, Noba had been the prince's companion since parturition—his closest and most trusted friend. He was like a brother.

As they approached the magnus, the hatch of the colossal land rover opened, and a long row of stairs lowered. Noba put his hand on N'damu's shoulder and looked at him with a seriousness that was rare for his friend. "I'm not always going to be here when you want to play games, My Prince," he said. "When you're in Meadowdell or out on the Sizwe with the Novojoh, this reckless foolishness will get you killed."

"Such faith you have in me, my friend. I'm truly moved. You forget the very *first* Doctrine of Atalay."

Noba straightened up like a boy at seminary recital. "Atalay was created with the burden to serve as captain through the void. He is the Shepherd of Humanity."

"Very good," N'damu said. "Wouldn't you think such an individual should be capable of going for a walk on his own?"

"Look, Clan Sadah are Masters of Arms." His friend scoffed and threw his arms up. "I can defeat anyone on Inana physically, but I'm not going to engage you in a battle of Doctrine passages."

While he loved Noba and respected him wholly, winning his esteem felt nearly impossible. Noba worshiped Atalay like all others; still, he possessed an ego designed to be alpha. They stepped up the giant black magnus's docking ramp, entering the immense vessel. A rumbling castle on tracks, the vehicle's engine whirred as the door closed quietly behind them. The company entered the elevator, ascending to the command bridge as the magnus embarked for home.

N'damu's ego felt bruised. *Someday, you will see. I'll be on my own, and I will thrive, Noba Sadah.*

43

Princess Enahdra scooted beside him again as they stepped onto the conveyer belt to cross over the cargo hull and passenger quadrant. She kissed him lightly on the cheek and whispered, "I have faith in you, my Prince of Atalay. I ran away too once—if you remember. A little girl, just looking to feel."

He smiled and leaned his head against her shoulder for a moment. Princess Enahdra had her own experience with truancy—and it didn't end well. Entering the amenity sector, the Vestian beauty took his hand before raising her voice for the others. "Well, I really *must* freshen up. Afterward, I hope you will join me for appetizers, N'damu. I'm serving *azu* and *chi sisi*." She squeezed his hand lovingly before skipping off to her quarters.

The prince walked into the bridge flanked by Noba and Nalia and was met quickly by his sisters. He braced for the wrath of Atalay. Cawing ulanoids circled both his sisters, pink and blue feathered, wings flapping in a rage. The bone-hawks reflected the twins' anger through their spirit-link.

"This behavior is unbecoming of one who will be king," Ala scolded. "People will look to you for an example, N'damu! Should everyone—all *your* people—sneak out of their lessons to frolic the riverside with their girlfriends?"

N'damu and Nalia both interrupted at the same time.

"She's not my…"

"I'm not his…"

"Are you trying to embarrass Father?" Aku, his other sister, asked. "You're over forty cycles now. Will you ever grow up?" The rumbling of the motors seemed fittingly furious as the magnus tanked along.

"*You're* really one to talk of this, Aku!" N'damu indignantly stepped up to her. "Maybe some people are fooled by that arrangement of pillows under your blanket. Certainly, *I* am not. Perhaps we should discuss *your* nightly escapades outside the tower."

Princess Ala stood between her two siblings, pushing N'damu to his seat and leaning over him. With her hands on the arms of his chair, she scowled down. "Seriously, brother, do you think you will remain prince forever?" she asked. An ulan landed on her shoulder and squawked aggressively, glaring with its six ebony eyes. "You know your place in my heart is infinite, but you are to be the king of our generation. Your name is Atalay. The Shepherd of Humanity. That *really* means something to me." She stared as if she were examining his soul's integrity, and he was suddenly overwhelmed by guilt. "What does it mean to you?"

Beams of light hit his eyes as they cut through the mountains and into the window. "Dammit, Ala, okay! Fine ... you're right. I don't *want* to disappoint anyone. I just needed some time alone. The journey of N'jikota is stressful…" Ala was the older twin by minutes, though her maturity made the gulf between his sister's ages seem more significant. She had always been the more stoic of the two. Princess Ala was nurturing yet firm in her resolve, like Mother.

His sisters were beautiful, like all Atalayan women, with soft brown skin and fiery orange hair like his own. Both wore gold-plated armor ornamented with royal jewelry: obsidian beads, ulan feathers, chains of ansyonite, and hoops of mamidon ivory. The Tri-Worlds crest was chiseled on their breastplates and painted red. The great pyramid and its three circles within, representing the three worlds of the realm, Inana, Anu, and Oshun.

Aku ordered the guards to leave them alone with their brother. The younger twin grinned at him as the ulanoids all settled quietly and the room cleared out. "So, what exactly *were* you doing down there?" she asked, holding back some strange excitement. "You know … with *her*?"

"She was beating me half to death, to be honest," N'damu replied.

Princess Aku was the free spirit in their family. She and N'damu always had a playfully competitive relationship of one-upmanship. Aku taught him about practical jokes, tricks on the servants, schmig slinging, dushnah tipping, and other such nonsense. Sneaking out of history lessons was, in no small part, Aku's influence. As was gossip. "I don't know. I hear from Enah it might have been a little more than some training exercises." She snickered. "Ala, I think little brother might be developing a love life, among other things."

"I would hope he knows better than that," Ala said. "No sense toying with the natural girl's heart, especially when her task is to protect his life." N'damu's sisters were a perfect contrast, designed to inspire the people and protect them. Princesses of the high clans were traditionally made in pairs.

"Exactly," N'damu agreed, patting Aku on the shoulder. "And I *do* know better."

The great Tower of Atalay loomed large through the windshields as they came into the city. N'gaia was built on a volcanic valley around steaming thermal vents. A perpetual haze coalesced at the base of the city gates and outer walls. "Father wishes to speak with you immediately, N'damu," Ala announced. The prince nodded in acknowledgment as he stared at the passing city. "He did not let on his intention, but I'm sure today's excursion will be no small part of the subject matter."

The magnus rumbled down the central highway that ran through the city and up to the tower. N'gaia was comprised of cylindrical buildings of white steel—towers cast a tannish yellow color as Thraxis sank into the horizon. The city's architecture was styled to complement its grand central tower, overflowing with iridescent gold spires and citadels of polished white ansyonite.

Love for his people swelled as he watched from the window. The prince smiled as the magnus passed the grand bazaar, where diverse citizens from all three worlds came to N'gaia freely, in the Light of Atalay. To trade their goods and services, bathe and sing, drink and gossip, laugh and eat—to share their thoughts and dreams. He so yearned to be one of them, especially now.

"Father says he used to give his guards the slip all the time," N'damu said as he gazed out longingly. "He would masquerade as a poet or a painter—or a musician performing street side."

N'gaia was a cultural hub unmatched. Every corner had some theater showcase. Comedy routines, sporting events, religious ceremonies—the capital had whatever the human heart might desire.

"Yes," Ala said. "But not at forty-two cycles." She pointed. "Do you think the casino strips are safe for a young prince?"

He shrugged and let out a long, slow sigh. "Enah says they're nowhere near as sordid as those in Centralia." The home of Clan Vesta was also known for its delights: fine vintages, intoxicating chemicals, and, of course, the companionship of the most beautiful men and women creds could buy.

"Well, this is not Centralia, little brother. But that does not mean there are no dangers." They both stared up at the Tower of Atalay as they came to the outer gates. The first man-made wonder of the Thraxian system, it was constructed on the site of humanity's initial settlement on Inana. Built with the remains of the ship that brought them across the galaxy, it marked where the seed of humankind landed after migrating from Earth. On an overcast day, the spire's peak scraped the clouds, a standing symbol of the might of Atalay.

The white tower was lined with circular windows, lit according to activity within. It had veins of red and yellow running from top to bottom, pipelines that fed water and energy throughout the structure. Large balconies of chiseled quartz adorned the building, placed extravagant botanical gardens, reflective fountain pools, and luxurious stages where purist nobles would hold balls and celebrations. At its peak sat the throne room, the Seat of Atalay, where N'damu's father, the Naga King, was waiting for him.

Exiting the magnus, N'damu turned to his sisters. "Well, at least I'm leaving for Meadowdell soon," he said. "The punishment will be short! *Hahaha*." His laugh was scratchy and nervous and met with a woeful silence.

CHAPTER FIVE

N'joku II

The throne room was empty except for N'joku's appointed council. The queen and M'demke sat at the throne's annexes while his other trusted allies approached the Seat. The king was at ease, relieved to be alone with the people he trusted and free of his griping subjects. Colt Dunkarr's regicidal tale was nonsensical to him, and he was confident his council would confirm as much.

"My King, what do you command?" Lord Vesta asked with concern on his dark brown wrinkled brow.

N'joku gave a sideways smirk. "You don't believe the lordling, do you?"

"Dunkarr is an honorable clan," M'demke replied, pinching his pointy goatee of azure. "The boy may be unrefined, but his father would not have sent him if not—"

"What do you say, Jambi?" he asked, looking to his Chancellor of Peace. The husky man's shining silver armor jingled as he stepped up from the line of councilors.

"This is not something we can treat idly," Lord Jambi Sadah said. "We must organize a detailed investigation. We do not tolerate threats against Atalay in any manner."

"Please," the king replied. "We tolerate them all the time. You are the general of my armies. Would you have me deploy men for every anti-Atalayan whisper?" His nagas began to circle, increasingly agitated. "Who would dare plot against my progeny? Ridiculous." N'joku rolled his eyes. "Comets are a threat, my friends. Volcanoes—solar storms—these are threats."

"The people adore you, my love, it's true, and our children are beacons to a hopeful future," the queen said. "But envy is a part of human nature. Many would want that adoration for themselves." She spoke solemnly, clearly alarmed by the sudden specter over their son.

"What would the mountain tribes stand to gain? Certainly, *they* would not rule in N'damu's stead. Natural-born fools." *They must be high on Mountain Mist.* The thought reminded him of his own supply—he could use a puff, if only he could get out of this court.

"I'm afraid I must second the queen, King N'joku." The G'higari Head Priestess, Elle Li'asaga, stood tall in her long pastoral shawl, the color of sage. She was Chancellor of Faith. "Any affront to the sanctity of Atalay is a threat most paramount. Therefore, we must postpone the boy's N'jikota quest."

"Unquestionably," Queen Anaqua added.

N'joku made no reply. *Impossible,* he thought. *The Womb calls to N'damu, and it WILL be heard.*

"I agree," Jambi said.

"Have patience, My King," Elle Li'asaga added. "Khanya is not going anywhere. N'damu can find his spirit-link when—"

"Nonsense!" He stood abruptly from his throne. "Threat is a part of being Atalay. Like a great many things, this is something the boy must learn. Something none of *you* comprehend as *I* do. Do you not think the darksiders wanted me dead when I stormed the nation of Charon with my nagas and liberated Anu?"

"My King," Jambi replied. "We only ask you to delay the prince's journey to Meadowdell, just until—"

"And you, Starr?" N'joku locked eyes on Serivicious Starr. "What says my Chancellor of Science?"

The brown-haired man from the moon Oshun bowed low in his fuchsia robe. "The more data we compile, the easier it will be to formulate a strategy." Clan Starr were cosmologists, a line of Homo purists engineered for immeasurable intelligence. "With minimalized variability and a favorable likelihood of desired outcome." Serivicious always gave him sound, calculated advice—not that the king gave it any more credence.

"What about N'damu? You would risk his life?" The queen grew angrier. "He is to journey to Meadowdell in *three* rotations. I don't feel comfortable with him away from N'gaia right now, not in light of this, my love."

N'joku scowled in derision. He looked to his final counselor. "Does the Chancellor of Finance have *anything* to add?"

"The queen is right," Lord Naris Commodus said. The pale blond man from Anu shook in his stately gray vest and slacks. "The stability of the Tri-Worlds is rooted in the Seat of Atalay. Safety is paramount, I am afraid. The prince must remain in the capital until we get to the bottom of this."

"Do you have any expertise in matters of security?" N'joku asked, staring him down with a scowl of disapproval. He knew he could intimidate the son of Anu into siding with him.

"I am an expert in preserving my assets," Naris replied. "What greater asset than the future King of Atalay?"

The king threw up his arms and scoffed. Usoca and Urnas began to flail wildly, lashing their long purple tongues as they slithered around the courtroom.

"Umm..." Lord Commodus trembled as the nagas wormed past him. "Unless your majesty feels otherwise. I trust in your wisdom, of course, *ahem* ... my liege." The king exacerbated his grimace, then looked to the queen again.

"Anaqua, my love." He held his hand out to his councilors. "My Lords, how can I allow fear to dictate my actions and expect our great realm to feel safe under my rule?"

"I've had enough of this discussion," the queen said, turning red with rage. "My son is staying."

"I concur with King N'joku," M'demke said, causing the council to gasp collectively. "It would be a tragedy for the boy, I know, and for you, My King. I understand what N'jikota means to Atalay. The pilgrimage is vital; I am well aware." M'demke was like a second father to N'damu. "The spirit-linking quest is a formative journey for every man of Inana. But for an Atalay, it is essential."

"Then you agree, it cannot be compromised," N'joku insisted.

"I do. But it would be prudent to proceed with caution as we gather the appropriate information. My King, allow my Vesta Enforcement Officers to investigate the claims of the Dunkarr lordling. They will have informants in the Sindiswa region and beyond. The VEOs will uncover this threat's legitimacy."

"Yes, good," he said. "Lord Vesta, invoke your spies, but they are to observe only. To listen, not to whisper—not to put *themselves* in danger. Forget not; these are mountain savages. If this 'Volturis' character is real, I will cast him to the Barren Void." The king closed his eyes and massaged his temples. "Concession to one threat only begets two more. We will investigate the matter. The quest will commence as planned."

"You fool," the queen replied curtly. "You let your ego determine your actions here when it is a matter of our son's safety? Remember, we do not all have the bravery of a king."

"Yes, well, N'damu must. The boy needs to become a man— a man and much more."

"N'joku!" Anaqua snapped as though he were only king at her allowance. "N'jikota will be postponed—indefinitely!"

"Postponed?" The voice of his son called out from the entranceway. The prince charged across the crimson carpet without announcement or formality. "Father, you *must not* postpone my N'jikota quest!" N'damu Atalay cried out, his squeaky voice ringing through the court as he shook his fist.

"Child, wait outside," Anaqua shouted, pointing to the exit. Still, the prince defiantly continued forward, despite his mother's attempts to intimidate.

M'demke stepped forward, majestically waving his cowl. "My Prince, we are only having a discussion. No decisions have been made." But even Vesta couldn't calm him. N'damu continued charging forward regardless until they were face to face. *Like a true Atalay, the boy will not be denied,* N'joku thought.

"Don't do this, please. It is my time, Father. You said so. I can feel it too. Something is calling to me. Now. Not in ten rotations, or fifty."

The king and his son had a connection born of deep love and respect. Their rapport allowed the prince to influence him, as he could influence his nagas. He loathed letting the boy down. N'damu reminded him of his relationship with his own father. As a baby, his charm was like mind control—he couldn't say no to playing games, telling stories, and even sleeping in the royal bed, cuddled between him and his wife.

"If I miss my opportunity..." his son said with a sympathetic head tilt. N'damu clearly hated the notion of stalling his destiny as much as N'joku did.

A proud determination washed over him. "How can I let some mysterious threat deny my son of his birthright?" The king rubbed his over-stressed eyelids. "Do the mighty Atalay live in fear of those who conspire in shadows?"

"I'm sorry, N'joku, I just don't like this. It seems foolish to leave ourselves vulnerable. I am shocked you would send him in this situation." The king could tell his wife was cautious not to reveal the nature of the threat to their son. However, Anaqua's eyes implored as much as her words.

"What situation, Mother?" N'damu demanded, frustrated by the lack of clarity.

"My King, perhaps if my private guard were to accompany the prince on his journey to Meadowdell," M'demke suggested. "My daughter, Princess Enahdra even; someone N'damu is close to—to see to his protection."

A babysitter, N'joku thought with a chuckle he couldn't hold back.

"A babysitter?" the prince cried out. The whole court seemed to snicker and giggle. "For what possible reason would that be necessary?" N'damu continued pulling at the heartstrings. "Father, how am I to be a man if I am minded like a child? What will the Novojoh think of me? It's not the way of the G'higari."

"N'damu, please." N'joku looked to his wife. Her glare of disdain was like a spear to the heart, and he knew he had to do something to make her happy. If not, she would be likely to leave his pleasure to his palm indefinitely. "My son, we have received some…" He paused a moment to consider his words carefully.

56

"Security concerns," Anaqua finished for him.

"Yes. It could be nothing; however, it may be sensible to have some protection. You will leave for your pilgrimage as scheduled, but I agree with M'demke. The VEOs will accompany you."

N'joku could see his son's irritation, but the boy knew when his father's command was final.

Vesta assured the king that he would make the arrangement for three rotations. "Worry not, My Prince," M'demke said. "My Vesta Enforcement Officers are highly trained. They are specially equipped to ensure your safety from afar." Clan Vesta was responsible for policing dangerous weapons and technology on Inana. Therefore, they controlled who was sanctioned to carry such armaments.

"But remember, M'demke, the VEOs must not interfere in *any way* with N'damu's training. They need to be shadows and wind. Make certain they understand that."

"Unquestionably, My King, it shall be done," he replied, confidently flipping his long blue cape.

Anaqua interjected again, clearly annoyed to be overruled. "I want his Two Spears with him as well," she ordered.

"Mother!" N'damu objected in horror. N'joku couldn't imagine the embarrassment. *If I'd had to march into Meadowdell with protectors—Sal'aah would have laughed me back to my tower.*

He could tell his queen had reached her line and was putting her foot down. After over eighty cycles of marriage, sensing her limits was second nature. Without words or even eye contact, he could feel his lover's energies as they shifted in the room.

"Quiet, N'damu! The Spears will accompany him—Noba and Nalia love N'damu—they will not be flies on the wall. They will stay near and stay vigilant."

"Mother, please," N'damu cried.

"And don't worry…" Anaqua paused a moment, then started walking out of the hall before turning back one last time. "My King. Lord Chancellor, noble council members: I will give the command myself." None dared deny her the final word as she exited the throne room with authority.

She is truly glorious.

N'damu continued to whine after she'd gone. "Father, she is being unreasonable."

"My King, I do believe my guard will be sufficiently capable of the task," M'demke reasoned.

"Though she wasn't born to it, she carries the name of Atalay well," N'joku said with a hearty chuckle. "I'm sorry, gentlemen, I believe my queen has spoken."

CHAPTER SIX

Nalia I

The clang of steel on steel resounded throughout the training yard as the soldiers of N'gaia vigorously engaged in their morning sparring. The Tower of Atalay loomed, an enormous silhouette against the auburn sunrise, as Nalia Chuku trained with maximum determination. Thrust, parry, swipe, jab. Each effort was accompanied by exacerbated grunts between the whir of twirling spears slicing the air. She exerted everything she had with each swing, but her opponent seemed to best her at every turn, as though she'd telegraphed all her moves three steps in advance. Nalia's every attack that morning was answered with the perfect counter.

"You're slow today," Shyla Sadah said. The high commander of the Royal Guard, Lady Sadah was a ruthless mentor.

Grimacing, Nalia lunged again, hoping to pick up the pace. Her sandals slid across the gravel, kicking up a cloud of dust as her guru effortlessly sidestepped the advance. Spinning her staff like a turbine, she turned hastily, only to meet the blunt end of Shyla's spear with her bottom jaw. With a painful crack, her feet were in the air, and she was on her back.

"Slow … *and* stupid." Shyla stood over her, scraping dirt from her fingernails. "Aren't you the Second Spear of the Prince's Guard?"

She's right, Nalia thought. *Get him out of your head, Nalia. You're better than this.*

She rolled back on her shoulders and sprang to her feet with a bound, then let out an enraged shriek as she charged again. This time plunging her pike into the dirt, Nalia vaulted, attempting a dropkick. Her mentor dropped in a split and uppercut her ribcage as she flew by. She hit the ground again with a hard thud, and her spear was flung from her hand.

Dead. That's it. I'm dead, Nalia thought. *Atalay's ass!*

The student looked up at her master, her bottom lip curled in as she fought back the tears. Her insides ached from more than the rib shot. *How could you even think about kissing him?*

"Back on your feet, Nalia!" Shyla yelled, brandishing her spear. She rose again, the broadcloth of her sparring robes tattered and her orange hair browned with dirt. Nalia reached for her spear as her master swung at her face, grazing her lip. "Now refocus. You're better than this!" *You're natural, and he's purist,* she thought.

This time Shyla Sadah, of the Six Swords of Atalay, rushed at her, whirling her spear so fast, it looked like some dark vortex.

Like her fighting style, her attire was simple and pure, apt for a lady of Clan Sadah, who were Masters of Arms. She wore a traditional brown kando'rah robe, still unblemished after a morning's dueling. Her head and face were hooded in a white headdress, exposing only her dark umber eyes when she fought. *It's wholly absurd, Nalia. You can't kiss him.*

Their blades clashed again and again as they traded swings and repels. Clan Sadah were Lords of Ulundia, N'gaia's sister city to the west, though more a military outpost than a metropolis. Shyla's honored grandfather, Lord Simit Sadah, had trained spearmen in the ancient style of Sadah'anah for two hundred cycles. It was he who had taught her to be the greatest fighter Inana had ever known.

"You must learn to silence the voice inside your mind that tells you what moves to make, that voice that gets angry when you miss. It only distracts you. It only drowns out the now. Let your instinct take over. Your body has already learned what it needs to know. Quiet your thoughts, Daughter." *But still, he seemed like he was going to...*

She swung her spear with all her might. As their weapons collided, both women were disarmed this time by the buckling impact. Having spent all her life in the Royal Guard of N'joku Atalay, it was not particularly unusual to lose when sparring with Shyla Sadah. In fact, it was the norm.

In a fury of fists, Nalia relentlessly went on the offensive. The playing field was far more even when it came to fists as they matched blows. She struck a hard hook, then flipped backward, with a jackknife kick to Shyla's chin. Nalia landed in a handstand over her fallen spear. Coming back up with the high ground, she held her blade's tip to her adversary's heart.

"Better. Much better," Shyla said, extending a congratulatory hand. "You will be a great fighter." She regained her feet and wiped the blood from her lip. "Though you don't carry our name, I will always consider you Sadah. I'm proud of the capable woman you are becoming." She beamed with pride. "Nalia, I have something to tell you. Something big. The time has come when you may truly need to use your spear."

If only I could believe that, Nalia thought, observing her torn robes in a huff. "Can I not get through a simple training session without shredding my clothing?"

"Nalia, are you listening to me, girl?"

"Of course I'm listening. Only I've heard this tale, again and again, growing up. I never actually see any action. Just glorified babysitting. All … day … long. At some point, I just want to swing this at something for an actual purpose."

"Well, I have received orders from Queen Anaqua. She has commanded the Prince's Guard to accompany him on his spirit-link quest to Meadowdell. There is reason for some level of concern for his safety away from the capital."

Nalia tried to conceal her excitement, but it took over her face. "You mean I get to go with N'damu?"

"You don't *get* to—you're *ordered* to. This is duty, Nalia. The queen wants eyes on him at all times. Both you and my nephew must be vigilant."

"Noba is more prepared than anyone in the guard. You can count on us, Mother." Nalia bowed to the woman that took her in as an orphaned natural and gave her a home among nobility. "We will not let the queen down."

Shyla walked up and embraced her warmly, careful not to aggravate her bruises, as always. "I know you won't. You could *never* let me down." For a purist woman, motherhood had nothing to do with DNA, and Nalia was every bit a daughter to her. She was lucky to have her guidance, yet still, as a natural, she couldn't help feeling this wasn't her real family. *She is a remarkable woman, able to be a hardened authoritarian one moment and a nurturing mother the next.*

"I never dreamed I would see an atranoch." Nalia scratched her head, staring off as the rising home star broke through the brilliant bronze clouds. "Imagine it, Mother, like riding on the back of a living airship. What a dream!"

"You'd fall to your death, girl," Shyla said with a dry chuckle. "The Prince's Guard is your dream. Go now. You're dismissed." Her mother flippantly waved her toward the gates. "You leave tomorrow with the prince—prepare your things."

Nalia bowed low, then ran off to her chambers, beaming.

Her heart raced as she scampered down the lower halls of the Tower of Atalay, making her way to the southwest wing and the O'taji Fortress. It was the place Nalia had called home since she was very young, and as much as she loved it, she couldn't wait to leave. She'd always yearned for adventure, even if it wasn't hers.

The Womb Of Inana

The tower had various sectors purposed toward providing everything a human could desire; in fact, one could easily never leave and still want for nothing. Nalia skipped through the halls, whistling and beaming at the bustling residents going about their daily business. Chefs of all specialties prepared foods night and day, fine Rhyolitan cuisine, Nolwazi-style feasts with the freshest produce imported from the Griner Valley, and spices from Tilo and Redsnow. She couldn't help but try the jupiter fruit pie samples in passing.

The Second Spear greeted each of the cleaners by name as she passed. "Good morning, Nhiles. Ju'hana—Mari—Hipothah." They scoured the tower, polishing the stonework and washing the rows of tall, long windows that lined the halls. She pulled a purple flower from a vase and handed it to Ms. Riah, a sweet older woman from Asa with whom she often chatted in passing.

Nalia crossed the weapons guild next, where soldiers could come to buy and repair their armaments. Then the infirmary sector—hospitals, medicine dispensaries, and resynthesis chambers.

Finally, she reached O'taji, a vast gray castle accounting for half the tower's base, built by the ancient Lord O'taji Sadah, who first galvanized their military traditions. The Soldiers of Sadah were the finest standing army ever known—eternally loyal to Atalay. Hastily, she ran past rows and rows of security sentries at target practice and then a company of legionaries rehearsing their synchronized marching.

Nalia saw the noble lordlings of Clan Rhyona tending dushnah in the stables. Twin brothers Ryus and Ryun were visiting N'gaia to deliver a herd of newly trained animals to serve the guard, all the way from their home in Eastsage, where the Lords of Dushnah resided. Their younger sister, Rachana Rhyona, had received them that morning. She was spirit-linked to the dushnah and served as one of the Six Swords of Atalay. Nalia had always been impressed by her bone-horse, trotting across the Utondan plains at her mental command. Upon its mighty back, Rachana seemed quite unstoppable. All three siblings had olive skin with black hair and wore magnificent golden armor with a rearing dushnah painted on their cuirasses, their clan's symbol. Nalia stopped to bow respectfully and offer pleasantries before moving on.

Flowers perfumed the stone complex as her footfalls echoed through the hall. Rounding the corner to her room, she met another member of the Six Swords. The desert ranger Haldir Nolan lingered at her door. "Chuku, I've been waiting to talk to you."

Nalia ground her teeth. Every encounter with Nolan was awkward, to say the least. *Damn me to the Barren Void, not again!*

Haldir was a purist ranger from the vast deserts to the east— a noble warrior of the Fuza. Twice her age, he'd always been aggressive with his attraction. He was a handsome man indeed, with dark brown skin and wavy black hair—six and a half feet tall with a muscular chest openly exposed by his fine, crystal-studded robe. Rings of gold and silver covered his arms, and on his head he wore a jeweled wrap. "Haldir, you would have been waiting here a *long* time were it any other rotation."

"I know, but I heard the news in court. I knew you would be running to pack your things this morning." His smile was uneasy, as if forced. "I wasn't sure if I'd get a chance to see you again before you leave." He placed his hand against the wall, arching his arm over her and leaning in. "I'll miss you, Chuku." He tried to force eye contact.

Oh, please, Haldir, have you ever heard of perfume?

She squeezed her nostrils tight and spun under his arm, slipping through the door to her quarters. "You'll hardly notice I'm gone before you find I've returned," Nalia said, forcing a courteous grin. "Let's not be overdramatic, Lord Haldir." He was her superior officer, so it was sometimes difficult to navigate his affections. "And that's not to say I won't miss you too, my friend."

"You name me as *friend,* but I have told you what you mean to me. Every moment we spend apart is agony." He followed her into her apartment, grabbed her hand, and pulled her back around. "Please don't deny me. I suffer without you."

The Second Spear looked up at him, her face betraying no emotion. "It is not fair to put that on me," she said. "Believe me, your feelings are moving. I appreciate and respect you. You are a warrior of genuine honor, and I could think of no better person to share my heart with." Nalia paused for a moment, staring at her feet and carefully considering her words.

He ran a finger across her brow, pushing a lock of orange behind her ear. "But?"

"I'm sorry, Haldir, you're a great man, truly you are. But my heart, it's just somewhere else," she said. "This is my first mission. I need to be there for N'damu."

She felt his frustration as his demeanor grew cold and robotic. "He's the Prince of Atalay," he said. "You're not even purist! What hope do *you* have when you give your heart to him? He would never marry an orphaned natural … but *I* would never care about something like that."

She knew that he was right, of course, but when Nalia thought about loving someone else, it stung like a betrayal of her soul. No matter how much sense it made for her to become Nalia Nolan or how good it might feel to be married into a noble clan, she just couldn't do it.

The worst thing was she couldn't allow herself to be with N'damu, even if he *did* love her. Even if he were willing to sacrifice everything for her, she would never be able to. Nalia couldn't let him put her over his people, even if her wildest fantasy did come true and he professed his love, no matter the rules.

"I'm sorry again. I know it's not what you want to hear. I am not interested romantically in the prince, of course," Nalia said. "Still, I would recommend looking elsewhere, Haldir. Your affection for me is imprudent."

His face sank, and he retreated from her quarters, slouching and dragging his feet. Nalia felt cruel—guilty, as though *she'd* done something wrong. *Why can't I be too low-born for HIM?*

Once the discomfort of the encounter subsided, the excitement of the adventure ahead returned. Carrying on with her business, she began packing everything she would need for her time in Meadowdell—her time alongside N'damu.

Nalia wanted him to think of her as beautiful, even though she knew duty should be her focus. *I can be elegant and dangerous at the same time, right?* She hummed an old melody as she packed her silver gauntlets securely in her satchel, "The Overture of N'gaia," a famous Atalayan anthem. Next went her linen undershirts and extra-long stockings. She would have to wear her armor all day and didn't want her thighs to chafe. Finally, she tossed in one last item, a beautiful dress of violet silk fabric, soft as a cloud. *You never know*, she thought.

After packing, she ate her lunch of boiled ghayn leaf, fried in yhonid seed oil; of course, doused in hot sauce. Nalia loved spicy food. She ate like a starved botsora and let out an uncourtly belch. *I wonder if he knows I'll be going with him yet*, she thought. *He will be red as Thraxis with rage, I'm sure. Such a shot to his pride.*

***

Later that rotation, the Second Spear reported for duty to the O'taji Fortress's war chamber, N'gaia's military operations base. She was immediately alerted by the sentry that the Chancellor of Peace, Jambi Sadah, was waiting to brief the guard. She ran there without hesitation, entering the chamber where the Lord of Sadah paced the stage impatiently. "Good, you're here. But where in Adam Atalay's asshole is Noba?"

Her mother's brother, Jambi was a hard man, general of Atalay's armies; he was a leader of men who had to be a living example to his soldiers. It came through in the way he treated his officers, including the members of the Royal Guard, and especially his son.

"I don't know, General Sadah. He was not in training this morning. I assumed he was in his quarters packing for the journey."

"Damn that boy. How can he be responsible for the prince's protection when he's not reliable enough to show up for a briefing?" Jambi barked at her as if she were Noba's proxy. In natural culture, he'd be her uncle, and Noba would be her cousin, but without the DNA, she'd never be one of them. The general was a husky man, standing just less than six heads in his shiny silver armor. Gray streaked through his maroon dreadlocks and especially his bushy sideburns. Dark-brown eyes detailed his wrinkly face, battle-weathered beyond its age.

"My apologies, Lord Sadah. Noba is late because of me."

Nalia turned around and saw N'damu and Noba enter frantically. Her heart seemed to lose rhythm for a moment.

"Don't come in here with excuses! Even *you*, N'damu, do you believe it is princely to keep your soldiers waiting? Is it kingly?" he asked. Both boys looked to the floor and shook their heads. "Will the Volturis and his collection of murderous, anti-Atalayan rebels accept your apologies, My Prince?" Before N'damu could answer, Jambi turned his scowl to his son. "Noba, I am extremely disappointed. You disrespect me. My father would have put me in the hole if I had done this to him. You will send me to the Eternal Womb."

"I'm sorry, Father … I … I…"

So that's how you shut him up, Nalia thought, letting a chuckle slip. *I'll need to take note.*

Jambi didn't want to hear his son out and quickly got to the briefing, killing the lights with a snap. The hologram projector whirred softly as a large city map sprawled out in front of them— light, given form.

"This is the layout of the city of Meadowdell. Noba knows it well enough from his time training there, I'm sure. The main estate in the center is the Hall of Novojoh, the chief monastery of the G'higari faith. This is where N'damu will spend the majority of his time. It's the home of Clan Novojoh and an institution for N'jikota training." Jambi carried on for some time, explaining the entrances, exits, and various palaces around and outside the castle walls where N'damu would train. "The situation presents something of a dilemma. Queen Anaqua insists that at least one of you always has eyes on the prince. The king, however, commands your utmost discretion insofar as you are not to interfere with his instruction. The Novojoh are masters of the wild, and the bonding brings natural danger. It is part of G'higari training. Leave this to the Novojoh. Your attention must be human threats. Guerillas of the Sindiswa, tribes of the M'lilo Forest, even bounty-hunting pirates of the Stone Sea. You must be vigilant of any threat."

"Believe me, we will joke of this overkill upon our return," N'damu said with a flippant wave. *He's the only one brazen enough to interrupt Jambi.*

"That may be true, young prince," General Sadah replied, "but you should be taking this seriously as well. And believe me, if Noba or Nalia need to save you from yourself, I have faith they will do their duty." He turned to his son next, placing a hand on his shoulder. "Someday, my son, N'damu will be king, and you will be general. This mission is an important opportunity for you. I pray that nothing happens. I became a man in a time of war, fighting a foreigner's cause on another world. Every rotation, I thank Adam Atalay that such is not the case for you."

Noba clanked his staff on the stone floor and bowed, crossing his forearm over his brow in salute. "You can count on me, Father. Any would-be assassin's fate will be death by my spear."

As the meeting adjourned, Noba and his father returned to their quarters in O'taji while Nalia took over guarding the prince. She was always happiest on duty. Maybe it gave her a sense of purpose and meaning, but more likely it was N'damu. She couldn't help but think how handsome he seemed. She knew he was as nervous as her, yet his confidence pacified her.

"Care for a sunset swim on the terrace level?" N'damu asked, extending his hand. Her mind returned to their afternoon in the Glass Valley, where they'd almost...

"Yes, My Prince," she said with an overly professional salute.

But DID we almost? Nalia wondered if she might have misinterpreted what had happened. Or perhaps she had only

71

imagined that he was going to kiss her. *Was it an instance conjured in a dream?*

The terrace level of the Tower of Atalay was the most picturesque place Nalia could imagine. Every memory here was joyous. You could get lost in the maze of thick olyin yara hedges and endless rows of polished white quartz pillars. A few large meridian falls formed violet umbrellas with their branches, shading granite tables and paved stone leisure areas. Beds of flowers and exotic plants filled the garden, enclosed by stone borders covered in ivy. The arched outer walls at the edge of the balcony were formed of black glazed terracotta—engulfed by the climbing vines of skylar rose that ran up from the tower walls below.

Being here with N'damu felt like home. As children, they had both loved to spend hours roaming the gardens, catching os muscas and feeding them to the rasp dragons. Basking in the summer sun rays or playing water games in the grotto, this was their most special place.

"Shall we train before we swim? If we learned anything lately, it's that your spear work needs improvement." Her affections for him were ethereal and defied all explanation—feelings born at first sight, so long ago. To ask her why she loved him was like asking the stars the purpose of their motion. The Light of Atalay was more real for her than anyone in the Tri-Worlds. She felt it so intensely, it burned. What girl would not give her heart to the Shepherd of Men?

"Enough training," he answered. "I would not spend this beautiful evening with 'Nalia Chuku' of the Prince's Guard …

not if I had the choice to be with Nalia Chuku: my best friend. This may be our last night home for some time." His smile affected her like a slaver's whip, and she forgot about training for the evening.

She grinned and nodded, then put down her spear and helm at the pool's ledge. Nalia kicked off her sandals and wiggled her toes in the water. "The temperature is delightful."

N'damu stripped down to his shorts and sat next to her. His thigh grazed hers in a way that seemed intentionally accidental. "So, the other day. Down in the valley, you know, before Noba found us—" He playfully kicked her foot.

"Yes. I remember," she said, urging the prince on while not wanting to be the one to say it, in case she'd misread the moment.

He turned and looked at her. "It felt like … like…" The words seemed to get stuck on his tongue like tinkercane syrup on a dry day. He trembled as if losing his nerve.

"It's okay," she reassured him. Nalia could see him struggling, and it was instinctual to protect him. Like General Sadah said, even from himself.

"I felt like I wanted to kiss you. I *want* to kiss you," N'damu said, falling into her eyes again, just as he had in the valley.

Her heart fluttered at the thought of their lips touching, but in the back of her consciousness loomed the specter of their love's impossibility. A reminder: their society would condemn any kind of union between them. She smiled at him and then scooted her butt off the granite edge, disappearing into the warm blue pool.

Nalia emerged under the waterfall after a minute and turned back to look for him. The shower came down on her face, flattening her afro and blurring her vision. *Did he trick me into the pool so he could sneak off again?*

"N'damu," she called out. "Where did you go?"

Suddenly she felt his hands at her hips as he spun her around by the waist and pulled her close. They sank neck-deep in the water, and he wrapped his arms around her neck, drawing her nose to nose. "Don't be afraid. I have loved you my entire life. I can resist no longer, Nalia Chuku."

She dropped her stare and put her forehead to his chin, fighting the impulses pulling her in every direction. "I would love you with all that I am ... but I'm sworn to protect you." Nalia pulled away. "You cannot love me in that way. I cannot allow you to do something that I know will only lead to harm. Being with me would send the realm into chaos and insult everything your ancestors stood for. You're an Atalay, a fact we are both reminded of every rotation." His stare cut her like a spear to the heart, achingly alluring. His mouth an inch from hers, her resolve washed away in the falls.

"I don't care about DNA—about Homo purist tradition or the throne. Next to you, I care for noth—"

"The time may come when you will. When you become king," she answered.

"I'd be the king of nothing without you," N'damu Atalay said, then he pulled her that final inch closer and kissed her deeply.

The electricity jolted through her body. His words were complete. A cinematic moment beyond reproach. *Perfect.*

They both went silent. Bobbing in the water, Nalia and N'damu finally embraced in the kiss they'd anticipated for so long. She could feel his hands moving down the small of her back as they slid behind the shade of the waterfall. Their kissing began to intensify. She knew she should stop but felt out of control. Nalia locked her legs around his waist as he clawed at her shirt, managing to pull it off over her head. She was in ecstasy as his lips moved down her neck and onto her breasts—grinding on her, getting harder, making her hotter.

Are we actually going to? What if I get...? No ... no, this is too much. Something in her snapped back into place, like a dislocated joint, as a typhoon of reality rushed over her.

"I can't do this," Nalia said as she pulled away and grabbed her floating shirt.

"It's okay, Nalia, you can," N'damu replied. "I will take care of you. I know you want this too. I will love you till the Eternal Womb."

"I am one of your sworn spears." She began crying inside but held it back as best she could. "It's an *honor* for me to be in the Royal Guard. I took an oath to protect you. I'm sorry I let this happen. I failed you, but I won't let it happen again."

"No ... *I'm* sorry," he said with heartbreak and pain in his expression. "I shouldn't have done this. I shouldn't have pushed you." He slid away from her and climbed out of the pool. "I got caught up in the excitement of my N'jikota quest. That's all."

"I hope you can forgive me," Nalia said. She could see his heart fall from his chest and shatter on the ground. It was a lousy rotation for such things.

"There is nothing to forgive. Thank you for this moment. It's one I will never forget." He was gracious, yet his words slashed her heart.

Nalia Chuku knew it was her duty to forget this, as a soldier of Sadah, a disciple of Sadah'anah and the Second Spear to the Prince of Atalay. *Wake up, Nalia. You have drawn enough fortune from Khanya. You're not a queen,* she thought.

After they dressed, she hugged him, leaning slightly to the side. "I'll always be your best friend, you know. I'll always be there for you. I love you, as my prince and someday as my king." *I love you as my one and only.*

He looked at her with a sad smile that kicked the pieces of their broken hearts to the wind. "We must do our duty." His yawn seemed disingenuous as he stood to excuse himself. He clearly had to get away. "I think I'm going to retire early. We have a big rotation ahead of us."

CHAPTER SEVEN

N'damu III

"This is the threshold, my friend." Prince N'damu looked back at N'gaia from the rear deck of his royal magnus. The Tower of Atalay's tip was thin as a pin on the horizon, reduced to an impression in the clouds. "This is officially the farthest I've ever been from home."

"It was bound to happen eventually," Noba Sadah replied. A slow settling brown haze of dust followed the tank as it headed southeast over the endless Utondan Savanna. "Can't hide behind Daddy's nagas for the rest of your life. Time for a spirit-link of your own."

"Remind me of *your* bond again," N'damu asked with a crooked smirk.

Noba chuckled. "A warrior of Sadah—"

"A warrior of Sadah needs no spirit-link," N'damu said with sarcastic accentuation of Noba's accent. "*Right.*" He mocked his friend's salute, tapping his spear on the steel decking. "You don't need to be embarrassed about it."

"Please…" Noba's armor jingled as he shook his head and stared at his feet. "Instead of your light, o holy Atalay, I ask only for the blessing of your silence!"

"Noba, Khanya forgive you for mocking Atalay." N'damu chuckled, shielding his eyes from the sun's rays as he gazed west. *It's gone,* he thought, no longer able to make out the spire. "So, three rotations until we arrive in Centralia?"

"Yeah," Noba replied with wide eyes as he flittered his fingers together like bug's legs. "I hope I get a chance to tour the strips. Centralian girls are a feat of Homo purist engineering."

"Well, we're meeting with the Vesta entourage there," N'damu said. "I'm sure someone else can babysit me for a while. There's also Nalia…"

"So, what's going on with Chuku, anyways?"

Noba's question was like a punch in the gut. "Ahem, Nalia? Going on? I–I…" N'damu tripped over his words as he slid his sandal across the floor.

"Yeah," Noba barked. "She's acted strange all morning. Didn't want to train with me—didn't laugh at any of my jokes. She even crossed me in the bunking deck this morning…" He turned and ran his hands down his chrome chest plate. "I was shirtless, and she didn't even look up."

"Wow, and you have such manly nipples." N'damu rolled his eyes. "I never miss a chance to gaze upon your impeccable physique."

"I know. Exactly." It appeared the prince's sarcasm escaped the lordling. "What has made her so … lethargic?" Noba scratched his frizzy maroon hair and tilted his head.

N'damu's thoughts trailed off, left behind with the rolling plains. He knew the answer and that he wasn't going to say it. Instead, the prince simply shrugged as he looked out to the passing Utondan. "Inana is beautiful this summer."

"The *second oct* brings summer's end, officially," Princess Enahdra said, popping out from the hatch. "Take it in while it lasts. It's technically storm season now." The moment he heard her voice, the air seemed to drop two degrees. Her silky blue hair flew about wildly, despite her attempts to keep it in place.

"I thought Clan *Bravah* were Masters of Climate," N'damu said, smirking back.

"It doesn't take advanced meteorology to know the seasons, N'damu." Enahdra began to count them off on her fingers. "Summer, storm season, flood season, spring. The magnetosphere is volatile at this time of the orbital cycle. The troposphere is unpredictable and uneven." She flitted her long black lashes and hopped with a half spin. "Weird fun fact: Earth had four seasons too, just like Inana. What are the odds?"

Noba dropped his head and mocked snoring, and Enah huffed with her hands planted at her hips.

Nodding, the prince rubbed his chin, feigning a smile. "So fun," he said.

Suddenly, Noba pretended to jerk awake. "Aren't you worried Thraxis will blanch that pretty dress, Princess?" he asked, hovering over her with arms outstretched, as if providing shade.

Enahdra laughed, crinkling her nose as she slowly pushed him away. "Oh no! Not my dress. How can I look pretty enough for *you* warmongers if I ruin my dress?" She rolled her eyes to their whites. "Aren't you worried about N'damu's fine, princely leathers? You're his First Spear, after all."

"Have you seen this boy's closet? I expect not." Noba chuckled. "It has its own devoted servants and an elevator system. He can afford to ruin a few shirts."

"Is this true, My Prince?" Enahdra looked N'damu up and down. "Why all the yellow then? You must have other colors … something darker perhaps?"

"Gold!" N'damu snapped back. "Not yellow. Gold." He adjusted his collar, then swept the Tri-World pyramid patch on his chest. *An Atalay must adorn himself in gold,* his mother would say.

"I've got to say," Noba interjected, "you do wear a *lot* of yellow." N'damu looked down at his outfit, brushing his fingers across the lustrous fabric. The magnus began to rumble through the outskirts of a village, and his mind wandered again.

"What town is this?" he asked. The prince was intrigued to meet his subjects, Inanean common folk who seemed all too alien.

Enah squinted, stepping up to the rails beside him. "We're in Ulundian country—Sadah territories originally. This is the town of Argoset." As they got closer, the habitats grew denser; expertly crafted wood, stone, and stucco houses lined the road. "Earth architecture was a *lot* like the natural villages out here. Nature is a beautiful thing, people using what the planet gives them to survive."

"Is that not what *we* do, Enah?" N'damu noticed Nalia step out of the deck just then, her boots tapping along the grated steel floor. "Don't *we* use…" His Second Spear's hair was wild and chaotic as wildfire, and its delightful fragrance wafted through the air, to the delight of his nostrils. "…use … what Khanya … *Ummmm* … gives us."

"Please, N'damu," Enahdra replied. "The purist race bends the universe to our will. We make our materials from the constituents of reality."

Unlike the princess, Nalia didn't care about her appearance. She didn't worry about being beautiful for the world, yet she was the most gorgeous thing in it, even in the thick silver armor of the Second Spear.

N'damu snapped out of his daze. "Are those constituents not a part of 'nature'?" He looked away from Nalia before she realized he'd been staring. "We eat and drink and love, like naturals. They are not animals, and we are not clones—we're both human in every sense—born to live lives filled with wonder-filled purpose. Our differences are only social constructs."

"You will see the difference when we get to Centralia. My city makes this lovely village look like a himpheah ant mound," Enah said. "These people are quaint … to be sure. But most of them don't even *believe* in Earth."

He couldn't stop thinking of the grotto, no matter where Enahdra's banter went. Nalia's presence outshined everything around him—like a black hole to which all his attention was funneled. She beamed as she stared out at the village, clearly trying to take in every detail of Argoset herself. "We should go down," she said. "Let us meet some of them."

"Fun fact: the G'higari religion evolved from a denomination of the old Milushi faith," Enahdra said, going on as though she hadn't heard Nalia. "They actually executed Earth believers for sacrilege at one point."

"Why not stay *here* for the night?" Nalia asked. "The captain said the magnus needs to recharge soon anyways."

"Meadowdell has a vast subterranean vault—a chamber where they tortured people who still believed in Earth—"

"I bet the Earth naturals were hot," Noba said.

Enah grumbled and crossed her arms. "Ewwwww." Her blue ansyonite bracelets jingled as she shuddered and stuck out her tongue. "You're disgusting, Noba. Imagine how unhygienic they were."

"Nalia is right," the prince proclaimed. "Let's visit the village. I need a break from the incessant droning of this magnus." *And the people on it.*

***

Golden sentries of N'gaia followed N'damu and his companions as they ventured into Argoset. Their armor shimmered in the beams of the Eden Star as it lowered to the south. The sky was unusually bright for the hour, but the prince didn't give it a second thought as he marveled at the town. The architecture's intricacy was more evident up close—vera wood buildings sanded and polished to a beautiful luster—carved with G'higari glyphs and ornate Ulundian art.

The locals gathered around as they entered the city square. People formed a parade behind the N'gaian guards as dushnah riders and hover-bikers began to circle. "Hail Atalay!" a man shouted, punching the air triumphantly. Cheers followed, and like a swelling wave, soon the entire village joined in the streets to sing ovations.

Noba and Nalia flanked N'damu and Enah, their Sadah spears at the ready, just in case the Atalay worshipers grew unruly. The prince decided to leave his weapon behind on the magnus. After Nalia thrashed him in the valley, he'd become disheartened with his Sadah'anah training.

Gravel shuffled under his sandals as they passed domed stucco apartments, wooden storehouses with red shingled roofs, and giant pyramid tents filled with local vendors. The citizens continued to call out to him. "The Womb blesses us," a woman shouted, holding her baby up in the air. "My Prince, please consecrate my child with your light! He is sick—"

"N'damu! N'damu!" A louder man spoke over her. "My mother has passed ... will you shepherd her to the Eternal Womb?"

"I beg you, Atalay, for your light!"

"My Prince, my brother is injured. Heal him in your light."

"My father has dementia! Show him the way..."

Bless the parents with health. Bless the children with happiness. N'damu lost his sense of self, realizing what he meant to these people. These strangers to whom he'd never devoted a single thought, yet all loved him with such ardor. It both delighted and frightened him. *I'm not a human to them.*

He knew the truth—he was only an idea in their minds. More a slave than a leader. A faceless figure they expected to solve their gravest troubles.

"Prince N'damu … my daughter died. Bless me with your light so she might find me in the Eternal Womb." Soon enough, all the voices bled together into one static noise.

The throbbing of his heartbeat slowly moved to his head. Even when N'damu shut his eyes, there was no darkness. Only a glow, pulsating to the rhythm of his heart. He began kneading his temples. *Please, one at a time,* he thought.

"So, where can I get some good tucsabura chops?" Noba asked a young Argoset girl. The crowd eased up enough for the prince to hear. "My stomach is rumbling."

"There is an excellent restaurant on the north side," she replied with a giggle. "Let me show you."

"Sounds good, tinkercane, I'm so hungry I'm seeing stars." Noba grinned back at N'damu, licking his lips. "Shall we indulge, My Prince?"

He looked across the crowd. They had seemed to figure out the futility of yelling all at once; still, the villagers stared at him as if awaiting attention. Finally, he looked down at a sweet little girl in schmig tails, her freckled nose twitching with nerves as tears rolled down her cheeks. "I'm sorry, my friend, I must spend time with these people."

"You guys can go eat," Nalia said. "I will stay with N'damu." The prince tried to make eye contact, but she lowered her visor and tapped her spear on the pavement, snapping into a guard stance.

Enahdra touched N'damu's shoulder, closing her eyes. "I'm starting to get flashes; I think I need to eat something as well."

N'damu nodded. "Go, Princess, these people are no danger to me. I will be here when you return." A few guards stayed with

Nalia, but most followed Princess Vesta and Noba as they walked off, opting for food over standing guard.

His face was calm, flat, and emotionless as he kneeled to the small girl's level. "Hello, little one, what is your name?" He wiped a tear from her cheek and smiled.

"Ceefah," she replied meekly. "Ceefah Chi'dova." The prince placed his hand on her shoulder, and her sadness seemed to evaporate like ice in a flame. "My momma died from radiation. Will she find me in the Eternal Womb?"

"I can see the good in you, Ceefah." N'damu took her hands in his. "She would want you to live your life happily. Let the Light of Atalay ease *your* pain and know that you *already* shine bright enough for her to find you when the time comes." As if a sign of his divinity, the sky seemed to get brighter, more intense despite the evening phase. Like spirituality had overcome the atmosphere, clouds seemed to flash with extraordinary auroras. The prince, of course, knew it was a silly notion, reminding himself of the second Doctrine of Atalay: *Though he watches over us all, Atalay is man, not spirit or divinity. No known gods exist.*

He placed his hand on the shoulder of the next in line.

"Thank you, My Prince." The elderly, brown-skinned man smiled through his jagged teeth, then stepped aside and rolled a woman forward in a wheelchair. "I'm askin' ya ta bless my wife, though." She looked decrepit, arms and legs twisted with eyes focused on nothing. "She was my life, but now she's lost in paralysis. Trapped in 'er own body."

N'damu gave her his blessing, touching her bony shoulder and staring into her vacant expression. "She is lucky she has you, my friend. What is your name?"

"I'm Photah. She is Vhodinya." He began to sob as he crouched down to hug his wife. "Please, bring 'er back ta me."

"Photah," N'damu took his hands and joined them with his wife's, "she is *still* here, my friend. She hears you—draws strength and comfort in your presence. I am confident that in the Eternal Womb, you will be reunited as you were." N'damu's head began to ache as sparkles of light seemed to flicker at his eyelids.

"Is something wrong, N'damu?" Nalia asked.

"No–no … I…" The strange effervescent barrage seemed to intensify as he shut his eyes tighter. "Do you see that? Feel the—" A bizarre electrical drone filled the air. Then, suddenly, all of the hovering vehicles crashed to the ground at once with a bang.

"I am Ewyela," a voice said as a wrinkly hand pawed his arm, trying not to let the circumstances deny her. "The Volturis killed my son—" A heaving behind him drowned her out. The prince looked back at Nalia, now clenching her eyes, covering her face with her palms. The sky was whiter than mid-rotation, and the clouds seemed to pulse with veins of lightning.

"N'damu!" Princess Vesta called out, running back across the square. She looked oddly perplexed. "My comms are down." She tapped at her earing communicator. "We're getting a solar storm."

"Back to the magnus!" Noba called out with a commanding voice, waving the golden sentries into action. "Immediately!"

N'damu looked to all the people in the streets. Everyone now seemed affected by the flashes, keeling over in anguish. "What is happening?"

"It's solar particles burning your retina," Enahdra said as he pulled his hand away and began to run. "These wooden houses won't withstand it. Noba is right. We need the shielding of the magnus."

"Then we need to get these *people* to the magnus as well," N'damu cried out. Then, the lights went out in every building. Electrical panels began to erupt with sparks as wiring burst into flame and melted.

Enah pulled him by the arm and whispered in his ear. "This could be a coronal mass ejection. Not so fun fact: though rare, Thraxian CMEs are extremely deadly during storm season. The electromagnetic wave can be devastating to the planet's tech, and the radiation is hazardous for human DNA."

He tried to focus, to block out the flashes. His father had taught him about the ancestral kings who ruled over civilizational collapses. *Thraxis is a violent star at times,* he'd said. *It can take life as well as give it.*

Nalia was already following his order, filing the people down the road. N'damu pulled his arm from Enahdra. "Go, get to safety."

"You can't wait for all these old, sick naturals," Enah yelled as he fell back. "You are more important." Pale-faced and trembling, he tried to orient himself in the luminance. *I can't leave them to die,* he thought. A high-pitched tone grew louder in his ears. Deafening.

Noba and the golden guards hurried the crowd along. Instilled with the morals of Atalay, they seemed of the same mind. The sky was blinding, and everything shimmered. Sweat began to bead as he ran back to help the slowest of villagers. Nalia aided Photah in pushing his wife's wheelchair as Noba took Ewyela in his arms and carried her. Enahdra came back as well, grunting as she hoisted little Ceefah onto her back.

The prince commanded his guard to carry the slowest elderly. His skin began to peel and blister—the entire atmosphere now washed in white—and it was impossible to look up. The air grew increasingly hot, and an alarming sickness permeated his gut. *Radiation poisoning,* he thought. *Run! We have to go faster.*

His will was the extra push they needed. The entire world grew whitewashed as they reached the magnus. The captain and crew waved the villagers through, staggering up the ramp to safety.

"Get inside, N'damu!" Noba shoved him up the ramp against his will.

"Not until … where is…? Nalia?" He looked around desperately, his eyelids swelling from the strain.

"Get him inside!" Nalia screamed as she helped Photah carry his wife in and set her down. N'damu reached out for her, but he was too late. His Second Spear ran back down into the dazzling radiance of the solar storm.

"Dammit, Nalia Chuku." The prince tried to get up, but Noba held him down.

"It's for your own good," he said, pinning N'damu with his knee. "Can't save anyone else if you're dead."

"We have to help her," N'damu said, eyes wide and breath wrought with panic. "Don't let her die!" *Go, save her. NOW, you coward.*

Inexplicably, Noba let up on his chest and sprinted for the door. However, before he could get out, Nalia burst back through the glow, holding Enah in her arms. "She's the last one." Princess Vesta was limp, unconscious; her hair was falling out in chunks as bloody scabs peppered her once smooth skin from head to toe.

"Enah. *Noooo!*" N'damu struggled to get to her. Noba closed the gate, and the magnus's cargo bay went dark. It felt like the most soothing darkness he'd ever experienced. Stumbling down next to Enahdra, he ordered medics to come for whatever use they would be now.

"She'll be okay, N'damu," Nalia said.

"Are *you*?" he asked.

"I had armor ... *she* had a silk dress."

"What in the Barren Void was that?" Noba said, his voice trembling.

"The princess believed it was a coronal mass ejection," Nalia said, kneeling and pouring water from her canteen on Enahdra's lips.

"They're only supposed to hit once in a hundred generations." The First Spear stepped out of his armor, assessing his damage carefully.

"I guess we were lucky one hundred." Nalia rubbed ointment on Enah's wounds as the medics hoisted her onto a stretcher and wrapped her burns.

"I don't understand what happened," Noba said with a flabbergasted expression. "N'damu could have died out there.

That is unacceptable. The entire guard disobeyed my command. *I* disobeyed my *own* command." The magnus smelled like death already. Melted hair and charred skin. Shit and vomit. Cries of suffering filled the chamber.

A horror that will haunt a lifetime, he thought.

Noba scoffed. "Half of these people are as good as dead."

"What would you have us do?" Nalia asked.

"We should have saved our prince," Noba insisted. "Not elderly ladies. Not cute little children, adorable as they are."

"I couldn't leave them," N'damu said, sobbing over Enahdra. Her breath grew fainter and fainter. Suddenly, a wet croak accompanied a crash as Vhodinya fell from her wheelchair. *She's dead.* Her husband collapsed over her, but there was nothing more to be done. *The Light of Atalay failed her. It failed all of them.*

"You couldn't leave them? Well, *I* could have. We are the 'Prince's Guard,' not the 'villagers' guard.'" Noba punched the wall as hard as he could. The bang reverberated through the cargo hold, and all the moaning went momentarily silent. "Something is wrong here. That storm must have messed with my mind!"

"What will we do now?" Nalia asked, handing a canteen to Noba.

"We go back," he said. "To N'gaia. The princess needs resynthesis, and there is no way this magnus will run after that storm. So, we rustle up some dushnah and ride home once the solar maximum passes."

"Centralia is closer," N'damu said. His retinas were still too burned to make out faces, but he assumed Noba's was angry.

"I am here to facilitate *your* protection." The First Spear sat down in a huff, guzzling back an entire canteen. "Why override me?"

I can't go back, N'damu thought. *We're going to make it to Meadowdell. I will not give up on N'jikota!*

Just then, a whisper came from Enahdra. N'damu put his ear to her lips, straining to make out her words. "Take me … home … before I…" With a long gasp, she slipped into blackout again. N'damu looked at Noba with sad, desperate eyes, trying to will him into agreement.

The lordling crossed his arms, a dry scowl on his sunburnt face. "Fine, Centralia then."

"We only have *two* rad suits," N'damu said. "It could be a quarter cycle before the radiation clears."

"Mamidon shit! How is that possible?" Noba pursed his lips tight as if implosion was imminent.

"No one was expecting this," the prince replied. "These roads are traveled regularly—for millennia without consequence."

"Maybe the universe is telling us something," Nalia said. *Punishment for our kiss in the grotto?*

"What?" Noba scoffed. "Time to walk two thousand kilometers over dangerous radioactive wildlands. That's what it's telling me!"

"That's one way of putting it," she said. "What is life without a challenge? Don't tell me Noba Sadah is afraid."

He pointed to the cargo lockers. "You heard him, little girl. Two rad suits. I'm purist. I can resynthesize, so I know *I'm* not getting one."

91

Nalia's bottom lip began to quiver. *She knows the truth,* he thought. *Healing chambers can't reverse radiation's effect on a natural's DNA.*

"They will go to Enah and Nalia." N'damu stumbled to his feet. "Noba and I will endure the exposure."

The lordling of Sadah shook his head but did not argue. "We leave in the morning."

CHAPTER EIGHT

Nalia II

The Utondan tynnland skewed red through her rad suit's visor. Nalia wished she could see the terrain in its usual vibrancy, but the solar storm's fallout was too much for her human frame to endure. With her spear clipped to her back, she carried Princess Enahdra's stretcher's foot-end while N'damu carried the head.

Noba had gone scouting east, ensuring the pass was safe enough as they trudged behind. "We should have brought more guards," Nalia said, trying not to push too fast for the ailing prince. "I think we should have listened to Noba—"

"Without rad suits? Those soldiers are parents—husbands and wives, Nalia." N'damu's cracked and peeling skin looked twice as dark as the rotation prior. "How can I ask *them* to do this?" Lesions bubbled on his neck. She could see himpheah ants piled at cuts in his arms and legs, feasting on pus.

"At least take my suit for a little while." *I can't watch him suffer like this anymore.*

He began to hack a violent cough that rang out across the savannah. "Absolutely not." She felt his determination like an invisible force. Sensing the futility in arguing, she carried on. *Is this my penance for the grotto—to watch him hurt?*

They walked for hours, sticking to the shade when possible. The prince dragged on, weak, moaning uncontrollably at every incline. Yet despite his apparent agony, he didn't falter in carrying Princess Vesta—not for a moment. Not once. "Where in the Barren Womb is Noba?" N'damu's hoarse whispers served as little reply. "We need to rest a moment," she said, finding a shady vera tree and carefully setting down her end of the stretcher. *He can't even speak—enough of this.*

N'damu groaned as he lay down beside Enahdra. Nalia unscrewed the nozzle of her air supply and pulled off the helmet. "Nalia!" He stared daggers with his bloodshot eyes. "Put it back..." She pulled her arms out of the thick brown suit and began to force his arms in. "I can heal ... resynthesize. Dammit, Nal—"

"This is my oath, My Prince." She crammed the helmet over his orange mohawk. He had no strength left to resist; even his will to argue was broken. "You can't resynth in Centralia if you die here."

He grabbed her hand. "If *you* die, then no chamber can ever heal me." Despite the lovely sentiment, she slid the pants over his kicking legs and screwed in the air supply.

"Take a nap," she said as she settled him down next to Enahdra. The air was dense, and poisonous radioactive fallout distorted her vision. Her skin had hardly healed from the solar storm's direct wrath—it would not last long in its ghostly aftermath. She had no armor this time either, only broadcloth scrubs to shield her.

"Hey, you." A strange man's voice called out. "You, girl!" Nalia grabbed her spear and whipped her neck around.

"Who are you?"

He emerged from the tree thicket with two other men in tow. They all had chains hanging from their shoulders that jingled with tools, cutlery, and other assorted articles. *Junkers?* Nalia thought. Naturals, like her, their skin was ravaged by exposure. "Name's Lusk." He gave a nod, and a pained-looking smile as the other two waved from behind. "Dese here my brothers, Kort and Varm." *Ulundian. All three.*

"I am Nalia Chuku, Second Spear to the Prince of Atalay." The men looked at each other with doubt in their eyes. Without her grand Sadah armor, she looked like a commoner.

"I'm da Emperor of Anu," Lusk replied, chuckling. "Ya don' need the spear, girl. We are just hiding in the shade 'ere. Diggin' a shelter out—or a hole to die in. Time will tell, eh?" He winked.

"My fellow guard, the son of Jambi Sadah, scouted ahead." Nalia noticed him looking over her shoulder at her two companions and stepped sideways to recatch his eye. "We're just resting."

"Dose are rad suits, eh?" His eyes lit up. "'Dose two look good as dead ta me, eh?"

"They're asleep. My friend and First Spear will be back any minute, and we will be moving on."

"Come dig wit' us. Ya look terrible, girl," one of the others said. They were all dressed in mamidon leather, tanned and stained forest green. *You don't look much better,* she thought. *Those scrubs don't look any thicker than mine.*

"Yer crazy, Varm. She looks a lil' overcooked but not dried out yet."

"'De other two 'er lookin' burnt crispy," Lusk said, squinting while he scratched a scab buried in his wiry black beard. He took two steps closer, and Nalia held her spear up, threatening him with its edge. "Come on, little girl, ya can't save 'em. Or yourself."

"They are purist," she said. "The radiation damage is reversible." *Better not tell them it's the Prince of Atalay ... or the Princess of Vesta, for that matter.*

"'Den dey don't need dem rad suits, eh?" he asked.

"The suits stay on." She drew back the shaft, ready to thrust.

"What de fuck ya doing out 'ere?" Kort said, his tone soaked in ire.

"Yeah, bad day ta leave de tower," Varm added with a callous frown.

"Get back, *now*!" Nalia swung her spear, a broad stroke that skimmed an inch from their eyes. "It will be hard to dig with your guts spilling out, vermin." Adept at nonlethal grandstanding, if not at killing, her heart raced.

"I get it, yer takin' care of yer masters." Lusk pulled two daggers from his dangling chains. "But dese are my lil brothers, eh? You understand." He sprung at her with a wailing screech. She ducked as he swiped off a tuft of her afro. Nalia came around with a spinning trip kick, sending her foe to the dirt. She sprang up, holding her spear to his heart with one heel pinning his neck. *Don't make me do this. I don't want to kill you.*

"Do it, girl." He spat at her. "I'm dead either way. I'd give dem suits to my brothers anyway." He sat up, pressing his chest against her blade until it pierced his skin. "You say yer de Spear of Atalay. If dat's true, it's a good giveaway who's in dem rad suits."

"Fuck Atalay, Lusk!" Kort said. A pus-covered wound spewed down his forehead as he scratched at it.

"My brothers, dey *one* of a kind, eh?" Lusk pushed up even harder. Nalia could feel her spear-tip piercing his flesh and stopping at his breastplate. "Can't just make another one … if *dey* die, eh?"

Suddenly, the two brothers charged her at once. Varm pulled a dagger and flung it at Nalia. She somersaulted, narrowly dodging the projectile before coming up with a jump kick. His chin exploded, a gush of blood and teeth. As Varm fell into the dirt, trying to hold his jaw together, she came around with the blunt end of her spear, driving it into Kort's stomach. She knew the nonlethal approach would not last if they didn't back down.

The Second Spear grunted as her calf flared with an unbearable sensation. Lusk embedded his dagger in her leg. She twirled her spear with a hard swing, taking off his hand with a sickening *shoop*.

"Brother!" Kort took up Lusk's fallen dagger and flung it at her. Using her whirling spear as a shield, she deflected the shot.

"Why are you doing this?" Nalia asked. She fell to one knee, favoring her bleeding calf. Her eyes watered torrents, straining to focus. Varm suddenly hit her like a truck from behind. Spear flying into the bush, she tried to roll away, but the desperate man landed on her, his face still a cascade of crimson. *Dammit, Nalia Chuku!*

He wrapped his fingers around her throat and squeezed. The dripping gore blinded her as she choked on the metallic-tasting fluid spilling into her mouth. She reached up, gripping his throat and punching his wounded jaw over and over.

"Get dem rad suits," Lusk yelled.

"On it!" Kort replied. Nalia knew then her mistake in holding back. It was "kill or be killed," and she'd been too slow to realize. With an enraged scream, she punched harder, gritting her teeth and delivering a knockout blow to his temple. With a huff, he landed on top of her. Before she could push him off, a stiff boot hammered her ribs. Lusk was hovering over, handless and bleeding from the chest. He began kicking her repeatedly. Relentlessly.

"Got 'em?" he cried out.

"It's really him, Lusk! De Prince of FUCKING Atalay."

Just then, she noticed it, a stinging stench in the air. Nalia's stomach began to cramp up. "Get de fucking suit, Kort. Or you boy's're done for."

"You smell dat?" Kort asked, a second before he heaved a gob of yellow spew.

"Barren Void!" Lusk fell to his knees, then dropped down beside her, spasming. "Fucking botsora spray." Nalia watched, pinned down, an arm's length away as he began to retch blood. Noba's blade seemed like mercy by that point as he drove it through Lusk's temple like a melon.

"Chuku?" She staggered over and began to vomit. The lordling of Sadah kicked Varm off and impaled him in the chest. Next, he cocked back his spear in a fluid motion, sending it flying like a javelin, skewering Kort as he loomed over N'damu. "What is wrong with you, Nalia?" After hacking up her breakfast, she looked up with bulging eyes. The First Spear huffed as he picked her up and carried her to a collection of dushnah he'd gathered. "Why are you not wearing the suit?" Noba asked as he hoisted her onto a bone-horse and strapped her to the saddle.

"He was in agony. Dying." She winced, palming her leg wound. "I couldn't…" Her stomach finally settled as the smell of botsora spray diffused with the wind.

"What in Khanya are you thinking?" The First Spear fixed Enahdra's stretcher to a dushnah as well. Domesticated for thousands of cycles, dushnah were the Inanean beasts with which humans had the most intimate symbiosis.

"I'm thinking of protecting N'damu."

"We had a plan. I need you alive to help get N'damu to Centralia." Noba scoffed. *Maybe he's right.* "Look at him. He has already wrecked himself to give *you* the rad suit. Now *you* are broken as well." He showed her his arm, scabbed and blistered, cracked, burned, and peeling. "Stupid."

"These thieves tried to take the suits," she said.

"And you almost let it happen because you couldn't kill them. Is *that* correct?" It was, and she knew it. Noba saddled N'damu and then climbed on his mount.

"I am ashamed," she said. "It will never happen again." She could see now why she would need to kill. "Forgive me, Noba."

"I shouldn't have left for so long."

"Noba, no." She looked down as the animals trotted across the fields of tynn. "This is my failure alone. I will lose my place in the guard, surely."

He flipped up his visor and looked over with his dark brown eyes. "I won't say anything … as long as you promise not to mention the botsora stench."

She squinted at him, tilting her head slightly. "Wait, what?"

"No talk of botsora."

Just then, it dawned on her. "So, your spirit-link is with botsora?" She belly-laughed, despite her discomfort. *The beast with superpowered farts,* she thought. *So appropriate for Noba Sadah.*

He shot her a stern grimace, putting his index finger over his lips. *Shhhhhhhh!*

CHAPTER NINE

Myriam II

Interplanetary space travel was extremely difficult under the rule of Atalay. The Homo purist authoritarians paid close attention to comings and goings on all three worlds they governed. Strict quarantine protocols and procedural background checks were mandatory—*and* accompanied a hefty price tag. If Myriam Yamada was going to get off Anu unidentified, she would need to crawl out of the light completely. To kill the prince, she'd have to set integrity aside, either way. The law was her enemy now.

With her pink hair hidden under a shawl, the former Yosai cruised across the sunny-side continent of Vrinas on her QF Quanta. She'd spent two rotations riding from Port City to the space-faring capital of Zharr. The bike's quark flux engine lightly hummed between her legs as she sliced through the traffic, which grew thicker the moment the city's enormous dome appeared on the horizon.

The Womb Of Inana

The adjustable opacity of the dome's tinted glass gave the entire urban center a perfect simulation of day and night. Myriam ditched her jet-bike on the outskirts and made her way into the city on foot. Night-phase provided enough shadow for her to keep out of sight as she made her way to the notorious Hangar. There were observant spies here carrying badges that entitled them to judgment. The Izlagosi Guard, Vrinasi Patrol, the City Watch—Knights of Yosai, all best avoided if you were an exile *or* an assassin.

Unlike Port City, Zharr kept its crime infestation hidden under a guise of TWA compliance—a perfect embodiment of Atalayan hypocrisy. It was beautifully landscaped, with glowing hedges surrounding interconnecting walkways of polished pave stones. Few cities on the sunny side slept, and here was no different. Hovercraft zipped across the multilevel skyways above her head, making crosshatched streaks with their forelights. Myriam wore black specs as she walked among the bustling citizens, invisible in plain sight.

Maintenance robots scoured the streets, humming up and down the obelisk-shaped buildings, keeping them sparkling. The Hangar was easy to spot among the hundreds of pristinely smooth structures—a dirty iron square in a city with few edges. Ugly, noisy, and scuffled by rust, the dilapidated industrial warehouse billowed smoke. As ancient as the Empire, the Hangar was a metropolis unto itself, a massive compound with its own set of rules. Guarded by armed battle synthetics, it had always been too wild and unruly for the forces of Atalay to police, so they rarely worried about what went on in here.

Theodus Darius told her to seek Kat'har Rio, a loathsome dwarf from the jungle moon, Oshun. She remembered him well from her time with the Knights of Yosai, arrogant and beyond justice. No surprise he kept company with scum like Darius. *Repulsive little wretch,* she thought.

Hovercraft lowered in single file, preparing to enter the Hangar's clearance outpost. Myriam crept down behind a wall and unbuckled her belt. Then, as a luxurious hover-limo passed, she latched herself to one of its chrome exhausts. Tucking herself into the undercarriage, she reclasped her belt.

The limo slowed into the checkpoint. The richer the guests, the lighter the security—some of the freighters would undergo complete inspections, but this limo was high-class. Footsteps began to circle as the vehicle's doors opened and the passengers stepped out, six pairs of glass high heels in succession.

"State your business." The Hangar guard sounded gruff, a masculine Vrinasi in every sense. Surely he'd be vulnerable in the pants to women in heels like those.

"We are the entertainment, tinkercane!" Their heels clicked and clacked as they shuffled around the guard. "We're here fer Mr. Rio, handsome." Myriam heard the smack of kisses on his cheek, and she couldn't help the quietest of chuckles. *Purist males—so predictable.*

The limo's weight shifted as the other guards moved in and out, conducting their search. All in black, she held utterly still as one guard flashed his light down and scanned the undercarriage.

He seemed to pause the light beam on her face for a moment. *Fuck.*

She fingered the edge of her katana's handle, ready to kill to keep her anonymity. Her grip tightened as the guard scooted lower to get a closer look. The Sword of Pegasus slid out, half an inch from its sheath, and the nerve hit her gut, the guilty anticipation of butchering innocents. However, she forced out the feeling, convincing herself they were all soul-less meat.

"All good," he said as the light clicked off.

"You're clear to enter, ladies." Myriam's grip relaxed as she slipped the sword back.

After another series of wet pecks, the girls piled back in. *Brilliant strategy,* she thought. *It might be easier to get to Kat'har Rio in a skimpy dress than all in black.*

The artificial light grew amber-toned as they entered the Hangar's dank corridors. The limo sped down a zigzagging tunnel that led to the casino strips. Sounds of industrial machinery mixed with bustling laborers, slaves to whichever tycoon's whip lashed at their back. Hustlers ran rackets on every street, markets for anything from illegal weapons tech to Oshunese teas, from drug houses to schmig sandwich shops.

After reaching the bowels of the parking garage, the limo floated to a stop. Myriam slipped out the back before it settled on the pads. She silently vaulted onto its roof before the driver got out, peeked in the back window, and tipped his hat. "Message when you need me. I'm hitting the alehouse."

The passengers marched out again, one by one, gorgeous Izlagosi women, flamboyantly adorned with bright makeup that spanned the color spectrum. They wore sprawling cloaks of stitched ulanoid feathers draped over tight, revealing dresses. The first in red tones. The second in blues. Then came oranges, greens, and yellows. *Perfect,* she thought as the final girl stepped out in vivacious violet. Myriam slipped down behind her and applied a sleep-inducing neck pinch. Then, hand over mouth, the former Yosai quietly pulled the girl back into the limo. Releasing her pink hair to its full body with a wild shake, she quickly slipped into the skin-tight purple dress—at least two sizes too small. It cut off at her upper thigh and stretched uncomfortably at the waist. *A net positive,* she supposed.

She hid her katana between her shoulder blades, nestled under the cloak's pastel feathered shawl. Myriam's skin was two shades too bronze to hide her southern, Minician heritage, but by the smell of ale and Vhimhilian vintage, she doubted they'd notice in the dim lighting.

She hopped out and scurried back in line with the rainbow-colored girls. *You'd think Yosai training would be more helpful for walking in heels.*

The lady in yellow turned back, flipping a lock of her golden hair from her brow as she reached her pinky finger into a small vile. *Ether.* "Want a bump, darlin'?" Myriam smiled and nodded with an aloof grin as the girl held the finger to her nose. Instead of snorting, she puffed from her nostril, blowing the ether away. "Amazing rush, isn't it?" The young ladies walked the maze of tunnels like they'd done it hundreds of times, leading Myriam to a dingy club. A blinking fluorescent sign hung over its cracked-stone threshold: *Mongrel's? This must be Rio's place,* she thought.

"Mongrels" were the apex predator on Kat'har Rio's homeworld of Oshun. Circling the gas giant Set, the small green moon was covered entirely in an alien jungle. Among Rio's mutate tribe, he would be considered a runt; nonetheless, in the Hangar, this diminutive man had risen to a mighty status. Of course, when you're *that* tiny, you develop a talent for hiding things, and he had a reputation for making anything disappear.

An Oshunese quartet played somber melodies on a dimly lit stage. As they passed through the smoky club, shirtless waiters served drinks and trays of narcotics to the crowd. The local Vrinasi were indulgent, unruly Anutians. On Myriam's left a fight broke out, and on her right was a full-blown orgy. The line of girls, however, continued unfazed. She followed them to the back through a cascade of silk and bead curtains and into a circular room filled with ganga fumes and japhid spiced incense. Laughter rang out among random natters in the guttural language of Charon, Anu's darkside nation. Lit by blood-red lamps, half the room was a crescent-shaped couch made of gray incerta leather.

The girls lined up, side by side, in front of the couch. Myriam instinctually stepped in at the end as if she'd done this before. Across and in the center sat the dwarf himself, Kat'har Rio. He had dark russet skin with curly black hair that continued down as an inch-long fur covering his entire body. The dwarven man lifted his reflective silver specs and grinned with gold teeth sparkling under his bushy beard. He hopped up for a closer look, his crongrin tooth necklace jingling as he looked the girls over. "Let's see what they sent us, eh?" He covered a cough with his palm. "Eh, friends?"

Three men and three women lounged in metallic kilts. *Chieftains from Charon*, she thought. *Warlords, from the look.* Gray-skinned darksiders were not particularly welcome in Atalayan realms like Vrinas, but the Hangar was a different story. With overall looks of disapproval, the Charons were giant warriors with even bigger proton canons. Adorned with silver and leviathan ivory jewelry, they no doubt came to sell slaves or buy weapons. Black mesh covered their arms and legs, and straps of glossy leather hung loose on their shoulders, filled with munitions charges.

One of the males stood and spat at the girls' feet. "Disgusting sunnysiders. Over-fried by Thraxis." He grabbed the woman in red by the throat and pulled her closer. "What is this? Purist?" He ripped off her crimson wig, showing her sandy-brown hair in its tight skin-net. Next, he wiped his hands across her face, smudging makeup across her cheeks and smearing her lipstick. "How can a warrior of Charon debase his cock with such an unnatural creature?"

"Gorda, my friend," Kat'har Rio interjected. "In the Hangar, we got everything ya might desire. Say the word, and 'ese skanks're gone! We got more—pretty girls, pretty boys, natural and purist. Pussy, dick, and everything in between. Ya want Charons? Oshunese? Inaneans? Something more … exotic? Mutates?"

"We are not *friends*, jungle midget." The Charon general was the only one Myriam recognized, Tonn Gorda, who turned to his fellow warlord, a female of equal stature. "What do you think, Sigrund?" She'd been staring the entire time, scanning the disguised assassin, assessing her carefully through moon-white eyes.

"I think the ignorant midget should shut his hole," she replied. Rio scoffed as she stepped past and walked straight up to Myriam, brushing a chalky finger across her cheek. "This one's different—" She twirled a lock of her hair. "Not from the north like these others, I see. This color—the pink is real. Not like *these* pretenders." The line of girls looked over, finally noticing that Myriam was not the associate they'd come with.

"Hey!" the one next to her jeered. "Who in Atalay's ass are *you*?"

Gorda tossed down the girl in red, smashing her knees with a hard thud. Ignoring the excruciating cries, he marched over and backhanded the girl in yellow. Sigrund ran her fingers down next, across Myriam's cleavage, inhaling long and slow through her nose. "Anutian women are all the same," she said. "Squeeze their genetically engineered tits into a dress two sizes too small. Notice me, Daddy. Notice me!" The Charon woman brandished the blaster on her hip-holster as she mocked the light-side culture. "Where I come from, only killing makes a woman wet between the legs—and only valor in battle brings a man's cock to attention." She tossed her head back, brushing her hair through her muted-blue mohawk. "What I like about you is that you've killed."

108

"I smell it on her." Gorda leaned over and sniffed Myriam's hair, muttering an unnerving tune to himself. "The copper is hard to wash out."

"Minician, eh?" Sigrund asked. "Yeah, you have seen a kill or two."

"Oh, *she's* a killer herself," Rio chimed in. "She's famous on the sunny side. She's killed lots o'—"

"Silence, grat-shit!" The gray man whipped out his cock and began to slowly stroke as he looked Myriam up and down. "Who'd you kill, Minician?"

Sigrund ran her hands down her dress, caressing the silky, purple lacing as she leaned in for a kiss. As beautiful as the Charon warrior was, however, Myriam sidestepped. *Perhaps another time.*

"How dare you!" Gorda shouted as Sigrund recoiled with a gasp.

Myriam looked over her shoulder at the dwarf. "Kat'har Rio. I need to speak with you."

"Yer the Yos—"

Sigrund hissed, then grabbed Myriam by the shoulders and pushed her down to her knees. "You're not here to speak, Minician. You're here to *suck*!" She pointed to Gorda's erection.

Myriam tipped her head to see around the Charon's absurdly oversized appendage, catching Rio's beady eyes. "Theodus Darius sent me."

"She's Yosai! Let 'er up, you dumb gray fuckers!" Rio shouted with a scornful tenor. The other Charons laughed and picked up their cannons. The dwarf turned around, waving his arms for them to stand down. "Stop, dammit." Instead, they charged their weapons in unison, taking Myriam in their sights. "Ya don't wanna fuck wit Clan Darius, trust me."

"Suck!" She shoved Myriam toward Gorda's hard manhood. The former Yon Astra looked up with a poisonous scowl, emotion raging in her inner cage. With a swift *shoop,* she spun her sword from behind her cloak. Blood rippled through the air like a circular saw blade, and the Charon's cock dropped like a floppy worm between his feet. His balls fell next, one by one with wet plops, and Tonn Gorda screamed in agony, gore gushing from his crotch.

The girls shrieked, bolting out through the curtains like panicked schmiglets. Sigrund hissed like a naga as she held her blaster to Myriam's head. "Fucking cunt!" Rio immediately fell back, cowering defenselessly on the floor. The newly cockless Charon went berserk, flailing around the room as the rest of the warlords waited for their signal to fire.

"Ya can't kill 'er," Rio said, his voice a high-pitched squeal. "You'll bring the Hounds down on us!"

"Good, more Izlagosi to kill," one Charon called out.

"Death to Izlagos!" The rest began to chant in ominous harmony. "Death to Izlagos!"

Enraged, Gorda grabbed her sword at the blade with a bloody squelch between each finger. Next, gripping a handful of

Myriam's hair, he forced her face into Sigrund's blaster. "SUCK!" His creamy white eyes flared with tiny red veins as froth dripped down his chin. "SUCK NOW, WHORE!" She clenched her mouth tight as Sigrund pressed the barrel against her lips.

"She refuses." Sigrund squeezed the trigger. Instantaneously, Myriam pulled her katana down, slicing off the Charon general's fingers to free her weapon. With another quick lash, she lopped off his other hand, forcing him to drop her. The errant blast missed her head by inches, exploding into his abdomen. Gorda's stomach sizzled as spurts of blood and intestines rained down. With a twirling butterfly kick, she disarmed Sigrund, sending the blue-haired woman's blaster flying in the air. "FIRE!" Like a serpent, the former Yosai wrapped around her, making them indistinguishable targets. "Kill HERRR!"

Myriam booted Gorda's collapsing body into the closest Charon as he discharged his cannon. In a flash, what remained of the vile warlord disintegrated in the white of proton spray. Then Myriam caught Sigrund's blaster and unloaded its charge between another Charon's eyes, making her head pop like a volcano of brains, teeth, and eyeballs. She gripped the darksider's long blue braid from behind and held the Sword of Pegasus to her throat.

"Fire and Sigrund dies," Myriam said with a deadpan expression. The Charons did not flinch, keeping their weapons drawn.

"She's Yosai!" Kat'har Rio squealed from under the couch. "Put down yer weapons, ya ignorant darksiders."

One of the Charons unloaded her charge at the dwarf in a frenzy. "Die, Oshunese filth!" Rio squirmed through an escape hatch under the couch as it burst into flame and ash.

Like a cyclone, Myriam spun Sigrund by her braids, slicing her neck. She flung the warlord's head into the barrel of the next cannon, causing it to discharge wildly, bathing the room in light. In the blinding flare, Myriam tumbled toward the last armed Charon. Slipping off a high-heel mid cartwheel, she flung it like a throwing star into his eye. He jolted back with a spray of tooth-filled blood. Next, she cut off both his arms with a jarring slice, sending the primed cannon flying. She caught it in the air and landed, holding it on the wounded and defenseless warlords that lingered.

"We surrend—"

Myriam disintegrated them in another blaze of white proton plasma. "I accept your surrender," she said as she tossed the weapon on the ashy pile of remains.

Laughter and applause broke out behind her as Rio reemerged from his hatch. "Fucking grays are savages, eh? Excellent work. Darius said they'd be no problem fer ya!"

"What the fuck are you talking about?" She pointed her katana down, grazing the abhorrent dwarf's beard.

"These dark side scums've been extortin' me for half a cycle," he replied. "Ol' Teddy Dee told me ya'd waste 'em fer me." He lifted his specs and let out a long, unsettling groan. "He didn't mention ya'd be in such a tight little number."

"How would *Darius* know—?"

"Powerful clan, them gold-headed fuckers can even track a rogue Yosai."

Myriam rolled her eyes and sheathed her blade. "I remember our last encounter," she said.

"Unforgettable, o' course." Rio chortled as he opened a panel in the wall, accessing a red holo-grid. "Not every rotation the Knights of Yosai come snooping 'round the Hangar, eh. Falsely suspected me o' smuggling. Me!" The dwarf placed his palm in the grid, hooting as it turned green. "Good thing ya found zero evidence. *Ha!* Ironic, ain't it?" The floor began to shift slowly, lowering to a winding staircase.

"Can you do it?" she asked. "Smuggle me off-planet?"

Kat'har began to hop down the steps, waving her to follow. "O' course, I *can*." Myriam took off the remaining high heel and tossed it aside. "But will I? You're an exiled Yon Astra—legendary defender o' the Light of Atalay." Kat'har laughed harder as he led her down. "Now, yer workin' fer Theodus Darius. Must be an interestin' story."

"I'm not here for storytime." The white quartz stone steps were cold on her bare feet.

"Right, right," he replied, flashing his gold teeth again. "Ya want ta enlist the very same service ya once tried ta arrest me for." He tilted his head with a pitiful expression. "How can I trust ya now?" Rio gave a smarmy wink. "How can we trust each other if we can't share stories?" They entered a sumptuous chamber,

113

ornately chiseled out of bedrock and brimming with luxurious self-indulgence. The dwarves of the jungle moon dug deep caverns to hide their treasures, it seemed. Rio clearly had vast wealth—more of a kingpin than she'd suspected when investigating him as Yon Astra.

"I don't need you to trust me," she said as she surveyed a line of demonic statues, life-like replicas of Oshun's mutates. "I need you to get me off this planet—quietly." She poked her finger against one of their bone-covered faces. *So sharp,* the former Yosai thought, looking into the eyes of the monstrous humanoid covered in spikes. *An exosapien, carved in real bone?*

"Theodus told me enough, tinkercane," he said as he took off his metallic-mesh vest and tossed it on the head of one statue like a coat hanger. "The daughter of an angler and a prostitute, from a manta-harvesting village on the Minician coast." He scratched his head and plopped down, kicking his feet up on an exosapien statue posed kneeling in front of his golden chair. "Which one was it? Jentrilius, right? One of Atalay's forgotten, sold young—traded to a Port City slaver for drug credits. Musta been rough. Eh?"

"My past is silence, dwarf." The seam of her dress shredded at the hip as she drew her sword again. Her brain shut out the torture she'd endured on the streets, the abuse that molded her into what she was now: a silent assassin. Now, her adolescence was only a gravitational presence, an inference, a clue in the darkness.

"Come on, Yamada! We 'ave a lot in common. Ya think I was born wit' all this?" He waved his arms around, pointing out his rich belongings. "We don' have ta talk about Madam Cha's." Her inner turmoil raged as her grip on emotionless began to slip. "I know what she has 'em 'kiko moda' girls doin'." She squinted, grinding her teeth. It took every ounce of focus not to take off the dwarf's head. "I'm more interested in how ya got out. Purchased 'n freed by Clan Shingen!" He bounded onto his statue ottoman, wide-eyed and with great interest.

She nodded indignantly. It was true; her years of horror ended when she was sold for the last time. Lord Azuma Shingen was head of the Knights of Yosai: the honorable Yon Justia. She'd assumed he wanted her for servitude or some secret sexual perversion—instead, he granted her freedom and made her his prodigy.

"Odd fer Azuma Shingen ta place a street urchin in the Disciples of Yosai," Rio pointed out. "What made a little pink-haired scamp worthy of such an honor?"

Myriam still refused to answer. *He just saw something in me*, she thought. *Felt something, I dare say.*

"And you climbed the ranks quickly, didn't you? Yon Astra is second in command, if I ain't mistaken?" The fur-covered dwarf stood on the kneeling statue's head to match her height. "The Sword of Pegasus?" He ran his greasy finger across her blade. "Shouldn't the *current* Yon Astra be in possession of that lil' artifact?" Myriam heard a soft wheezing in the ambience.

With a scowl, she put the katana back in its scabbard. "The rich and resourceful Clan Shingen had founded the Knights of Yosai during the time of Queen N'dida Atalay's genocidal Reign

115

of Madness. For eons, the ancestors of Clan Shingen trained Yosai warriors to uphold justice on the three worlds." No temporal power was above Yosai code, even Atalay.

Kat'har opened a bottle of ale on the exo statue's forehead and took a deep swig. "And let me guess: no one embodied the honorability of Yosai more 'an Azuma Shingen? The greatest hero on Anu, they say. Ladies love that sanctimonious clone!"

Myriam could not dam the dark memories as they cascaded over her defenses. "His abilities were undeniable, but I didn't love him." Her face betrayed the lie. To this day, Azuma was never far from her thoughts. The Yon Justia was her champion. Truthfully, no one moved like him. Silent and invisible, her master was liquid light—a tachyon in motion.

"No ... o' course not," Rio said with a snort. "Yosai don't love, eh? No affection, lust, envy, or greed. Bet that cooch is dry as de Fuza under that skirt."

She let out an exasperated groan. "Are you going to get me to Inana or not?"

He looked at his comp-band. "Next shipment don' go out fer half an oct. We got time ta kill, pinky! I gotta hear the rest." Rio reached into his cooler. "I think ya did love 'im." He cracked open another bottle with the statue's horns and gave it to her.

She shrugged and sipped frothy ale. "I was young. No one spoke like Azuma: a calming, low, resonant voice." Myriam cracked her lip, almost smiling. "His every passing quip was poetry to my ear." The Lord of Shingen so enchanted her, she could not help but fall in love.

Rio put his pinky finger in and out of his mouth, waggling his eyebrows. "Did you?" He made a suckling sound.

"No!" Her brow lines crinkled. "You are a disgusting creature."

The dwarf nodded in agreement. "Right … 'A Yosai does not suck cock.' That's one o' them mantras, right?"

"DO NOT MOCK ME, DWARF!" She kicked him from atop the statue, sending him toppling into a glass vase. Breaking his fall with a crash, it shattered into a million pieces under his ass. "I thought I'd heard it under the whisper of his breath. That I'd read between the lines, a secret revealed in his eyes … that he loved me too."

Rio stood back up with a grunt and began to pick glass out of his backside. "Umm, ouch," he said, looking up at her.

"I was wrong," she continued. "And for everything his mentorship offered, my love for him came to strip away." The cinematic scenes played out in her mind as she slammed back the bottle of ale. Myriam had made the mistake of letting her feelings be known to Azuma. She trusted he would reciprocate. "The great Yon Justia and his Leviathan Hammer do not feel love. His only emotion was judgment."

The dwarf handed her another bottle.

"As he told everyone at my trial: 'No Knight of Yosai can allow their heart to be dulled by such a raw emotion as love, let alone our Yon Astra." She had his diatribe memorized, repeating it over and over in her head every night like a lullaby. "Despite the Light of Atalay, the time will come when our enemies rise again, those who would commit genocide … or worse. Madness *will* return, as it always does. We cannot risk weakness when the time comes. When such an enemy discovers a vulnerability, they exploit it without hesitation. They will slit your throat with your own limitations, leaving such notions as love to bleed out on the floor.'" She devoured the next bottle and threw it against the wall with an abrasive smash.

"He wielded the fascination of the council as expertly as his war hammer. His perfect demeanor hypnotized the jury and all in attendance. 'A warrior of Yosai must be a vessel of justice with unflappable focus. A balanced scale of life and death, we cannot tip one way or the other. Only then can we impartially judge. A Yosai cannot be vulnerable at heart. Myriam Yamada, you have proven your ultimate unworthiness. I strip the rank of Yon Astra and cast you out." None disagreed when she was exiled from the Knights of Yosai, forever.

"You really do got that speech memorized! *Ha!* I would kill the motherfucker who did that to me!" The dwarf popped open another ale on the exo statue's face-bone extrusion. Myriam thought for a moment she heard something odd—an almost imperceptible gasp as she grabbed it. She looked around the room, but it seemed they were alone. *This is why I do not drink.*

"My love for Azuma Shingen and my desire to kill him sit like an angel and devil on each shoulder."

"Instead, yer runnin' away to Inana?" He laughed condescendingly. "Ya know what's purer than love? Revenge, sweetheart."

118

"You know nothing, dwarf." She turned away, slugging back another gulp. As she swallowed, she stared into one statue's eyes. It seemed so real, glossy and wet—they appeared to tremble in the stone.

"Back on Oshun, I grew up a slave too." Kat'har glared as he violently kicked over the statue footstool. "Fuckin' exosapien tribe raided our city, took me from my momma's tit. Do ya wanna know what happened next?"

Myriam couldn't help but wonder how he'd come into such power on Anu. "Do I?"

"They worshipped an arcane god called Otu. A god meant to unify the mutate tribes—except for dwarves, of course." Rio scoffed as he pushed over another statue. "Were just powerless—stunted naturals."

"Poor little man." She would be hard-pressed to sympathize with this sleaze.

"The Order of Otu had some self-proclaimed high mages. I was afraid the religious zealots would do what I heard they did with dwarfs." He ground his teeth and closed his eyes. "But what I endured was far worse."

"Abuse is not specific to the Jade Moon, Rio. I grew up in Port City!"

"I wish it were only that," he replied in a huff. "They used me for their esoteric experimentation—drugged me wit' concoctions that paralyzed my body but did nothing to cloud my senses. The

119

exos recited incantations that made my skin peel and my bones contract—made my blood burn inside my heart."

Myriam crossed her arms and sneered in disbelief. *I can't believe anything from this cretin's mouth.*

"The mages sodomized me. The bone-freaks beat me in masses—even the exo women and children joined in." The dwarf looked down between his legs with a melancholy expression. "They cut off pieces o' my body—important pieces—throwing them into the fire as an offering to the demon-god." He held out his hand, sprawling what remained of his fingers. Three were missing. He held out his leg, showing her the divots of flesh absent from his thigh.

The former Yon Astra focused her gaze on him, somberly finishing off her bottle. *No sadness,* she thought. *No sympathy. A Yosai feels ... nothing. A Yosai ... feels...*

"The worst part was the visions. Otu, taunting me from the flames; the malevolent voice mocked me as they cut and burned away my body." He picked up his exosapien statues one by one. Dusting them off, he meticulously set each back in place exactly as before. Again, she heard faint pleas in the ether. Whispering tones that were desperate for help. "Finally, the exos left me in the jungle, alone, to die."

This time Myriam reached for an ale and passed him one. "But you refused."

"I resolved to survive—only long enough ta get revenge on 'em bone-covered grats who did that ta me." He took his golden throne once more and sat back. "I made my way to Dusk. One unpleasant act after another, I rose from nothing—got my gang together—made my fortune."

"Did you get your revenge?"

He kicked at the kneeling bone-man statue again. "I dunno, exo scum? Did I?"

This time the low, resonant mumbling was unmistakable. She knelt close to listen. "Kill—me," the statue muttered. Myriam recoiled in shock, then scanned all the other figures. *They're all real exosapiens!*

"These statues—are they...?"

He broke down in demented laughter. "The '*high mages*' of the Order of Otu."

"You keep them alive?" she asked with one lip raised and eyebrows furled.

"Oh, they're alive," the dwarf replied. "In cryostasis wrap. My prized possessions. I feed 'em intravenously, in 'n out through their assholes." He beamed with childlike enthusiasm. "They're multifunctional. Make great decorations, footrests, bottle openers, and punching bags." He kicked one between the legs, then swigged back his drink and smashed the bottle on its face. "Most importantly, they remind me of my revenge—and that the past doesn't control me. I control *it*."

Is the past holding me back? Myriam couldn't help but feel inspired. The dwarf left his homeworld and found his empire here. Perhaps she could follow a similar path on her journey to emptiness—her murderous pilgrimage to emotional nothingness.

121

"You got a half-oct before Inana's orbit is aligned and my shipments go out," Rio said. "I have three cargo vessels, undercover, headed for the ports in Duran. So I suggest ya finish up yer business 'ere. Tie up yer loose ends—might be a long time 'fore ya get back round Anu."

CHAPTER TEN

Enahdra I

Twelve cycles ago

"Father, why is Ahdia such a botsora's ass?"

"Enahdra, please." Lord Chancellor M'demke Vesta always sat rigidly straight at the dining table with legs tightly crossed and his long blue cloak draped over the back of his chair. "Do not soil your mouth. A Princess of Vesta knows not to admonish a family member—under any circumstance."

"Let me go to the gala alone, Father!"

"Yes, Father," Enahdra's twin said. "Let her go alone; spare me the misery."

"I told you," he replied, pursing his lips as he patted them with a napkin. "Attending the N'gaian Spring Gala is a signal to the realm that you are available for courtship. It is customary for both princesses to undergo this rite of passage together."

"I am ready." Enah batted her lush indigo lashes at him. "Why wait when it comes to love?"

"Everyone's heard the moaning from your bedroom, Enah." Ahdia squirmed in her seat, mockingly rubbing her hands up her hips to her tiny breasts. "Her availability is already sufficiently signaled."

"You both have too much to learn," Lord Vesta said. "You are the most precious commodity in the Tri-Worlds. Men would fight to the death for either of *my* daughters. But you must understand only the purest of blood and the noblest of hearts can win your hands. One of you could even be Queen of Atalay when the time comes."

"Ahdia could never be queen!" Enahdra flicked her spoon at her sister. She covered her face, bracing for a mess before realizing the scoop was empty. "She hasn't the fortitude I have."

"We're thirty-three, Father." Her sister smacked on maraphite tartar, then stuck out her gunk-covered tongue. "Why does she pretend she is grown?"

"Why do you insist on acting like a child!" Enahdra threw down her silver spoon and pouted.

"I *am* a child," Ahdia replied.

"Well, I am not."

"We're twins, you twit. Do the math." The two girls began as embryos in the same chamber—perfect copies, princesses of Vesta, two sides of light, as per the old way.

"On Earth, we would be thirteen," Enahdra declared as she spooned a bit of pudding with ladylike etiquette. "Adolescent women … but *women* nonetheless. At a time of metamorphosis."

"My friend Ja'sara says the Spring Gala is a meat auction for noble-blooded pedophiles," her sister said.

"What would a natural know of it?" Enah sipped at her cup and then slammed it down.

"Girls." Lord Vesta lifted his napkin from his lap and slid his chair out with an abrasive creek. "With your brother gone now, the leadership of Clan Vesta falls to you two alone. You must find equilibrium." Curling his goatee around his spindly finger, he flashed a crooked grin. "I will let you two decide. Enahdra, you can attend the gala..." Father gazed at her, pausing as if for dramatic effect before pointing at Ahdia. "...if you convince your sister to accompany you."

Her identical twin burst out in laughter as Enah groaned in agony. "But Father!"

Now?

Her stomach churned, though, from nausea or hunger; she couldn't be sure. Everything was dark—the color a pool of oil would be if you added a single drop of blood. Enahdra's sense of self skewed as the world move up and down in slow, steady paces. Skin covered her body still—but it would be made of pain, if pain had substance. Her mouth was inaccessible—sealed like cement, though air seemed to flow through her nostrils. *I'm alive.*

Enahdra seemed to levitate in the darkness. Somehow, she was both inside and outside her body at once, lapping in the waves of an invisible ocean. Like a baby on her father's belly, rising and falling to his breath, the princess could only wait out the sands of time.

"How much farther?" a voice said. A warm, wonderful voice made not of sound but somehow of light. "How much farther to Centralia?" The words made waves in the very matter love was formed from, like ordinary words carried on the air. How she wished she knew the answer or could hear some reply.

Suddenly, someone tugged at the hip of her dress. "Enah, Enah." She looked down, gasping when she saw the bright blue eyes looking back.

"M'davah?" She could hear her voice yet still had no sense of her mouth. *This is a dream,* she thought. *One from which I would never awaken!* "Little brother? Is that you?"

"Where are we, Enah?" He held out his arms, and she scooped him up, peppering him with kisses as sensation returned to her lips.

"You're alive!" She cradled the small toddler and as her feet regained feeling began to dance.

"I'm alive," M'davah said. It had been so long since she'd seen him. Not a rotation passed that she didn't picture his face. But looking at him again now, she realized she'd been remembering it all wrong. He was the most adorable child ever made. "Or are you dead?" Suddenly his sky-blue eyes blinked to red—bloodshot as his pupils disappeared. His young face began to decay right in front of her eyes. Her little brother's skin started to blister and crack as veins pulsated violently in his forehead. Enahdra screeched in horror as she dropped the boy and stepped back. Writhing on the ground, the young M'davah Vesta seized as his arms and legs began to flail like they had no elbows or knees to join them. Flopping around like a maraphite out of water, he hissed as his eyes collapsed.

126

"Why did you leave, Enahdra?" It looked up at her in the throes of death, gagging as it choked on its words.

"I'm sorry, my little M'davah. I wasn't there."

A loud clicking commenced as its head began to spin around on its neck. "Did you leave, Enahdra?" Soon, his skin melted away, and he was a skeleton—still, the chattering teeth kept repeating the question. "…you leave, Enahdra?" With dry bone fingers it pawed at her dress again. "…leave, Enahdra? … Enahdra?" Her silent scream filled the void as her demonic brother crumpled into smoke and ash.

Twelve cycles ago

"Please, Ahdia, what can I do to convince you to go to the gala?"

Her sister tilted her head and sighed. "This again?"

Enah hadn't left her twin's room all morning, begging—offering concessions over and over—deals that might convince her to attend the N'gaian Gala. She pleaded at the edge of the plush ulanoid feather bed as Ahdia lay on her belly, smiling with her bare feet joyously flitting in the air.

"I'll give you my leviathan pearl broach," Enah said. "You know? The one with the little ansyonite dragon on it?"

"No."

"My Earth collection…" *That's it!* The princess's eyes were wider than Thraxis as she looked up, hoping for a 'yes.'

"Nope."

Enah smacked her own forehead. "Anything you want, take your pick, and it's yours—jewels, dresses, tech. I'll do anything.

Humiliate me! I'll wash your boots with my tongue. I'll walk the streets naked."

"Nah."

"I'll go with you to Duranaut camp next spring! We can even go to the space station." Enahdra wrapped her fingers together and dropped to her knees.

"No, Enah! Father says I can do that without you," Ahdia said.

"Please. Purists from all the olden clans are coming—from Oshun to Anu. The Tri-Worlds' best and brightest."

"Yeah? I thought *we* were the best and brightest clan?" she replied. "Who might *they* be?"

Enahdra began to count on her fingers. "Well, there's Noba Sadah."

"Ewwww. Try again."

"There's Haden Winters," Enah said with wide eyes. "Lordling, son of the Steward of Oshun."

"He's okay, I guess." Ahdia giggled. "But would you ever want to live on a jungle moon?"

Enahdra shook her head as she scrunched up her nose. "Aku and Ala are going."

"But not N'damu, right?" Enah huffed as she turned away, dejected. "Exactly. When a princess marries a princess—what do you get, exactly?"

"You could do worse than a Princess of Atalay, Ahdia!"

"But only a *prince* is getting under *your* skirt," her sister said. Enah looked down at her sequined gown, running her fingers lightly over the opulent violet embroidery.

"Just because N'damu isn't ready doesn't mean we can't be— that we should wait here in Centralia all our lives."

"Only the Prince of Atalay is fit for us, according to Father." Ahdia rolled her eyes, flipping her long glossy-blue hair. "We are *Vesta*, after all," she said in a sarcastic tone.

Enahdra scoffed. "One of us is." She glared at her sister. It was like looking in a mirror—an exact reflection, inverted. They were two sides of a coin. *The light side,* she thought, chewing her bottom lip and twitching one eye. *And the dark side.*

"Exactly," Ahdia agreed. "I'm not a princess, and I'm not going to that ridiculous gala. I'm going to be a Duranaut. I won't need a husband or a wife in space."

"Just because M'davah wanted to be—"

"Don't talk about him, Enahdra!" Her sister shrieked like a banshee. "I want to be a Duranaut. For ME! Not for … for…" She broke down in tears.

"I'm so sorry, love." Enah sat and embraced her twin. "I just meant … he always wanted to go to space." She began to weep as well. The two princesses huddled their heads together, frizzing both of their hair as they caressed each other's backs. "Please don't cry."

Ahdia rubbed her nose as she sniffled. "I miss him." The indigo of her eyes sparkled as tears streamed down her soft brown cheeks. "I miss him so much, Enah."

"Me too." Enahdra used her dress to dry her sister's tears. "I think of him every day."

"You'll ruin the fabric," Ahdia said, pulling away a moment.

"I don't care, love. I would do *anything* for you." Enahdra patted her sister's hair as she sobbed on her shoulder.

They gazed at each other before hugging again. "I'll go to the gala," she said.

"Really?" Enah asked, tilting her head with a crooked smirk—unsure if it was a trick.

Ahdia shrugged. "Sure. Besides, I hear the king's new ward is pretty cute. The lordling from Izlagos?"

Enahdra nodded and smiled as she stared off dreamily. "Theodus Darius. He *is* gorgeous," she said.

Now

With a miserable groan, she peeked out from under her eyelids. The world looked burned—tinted red. *I'm dead,* she thought. *This is the Barren Void.* In a disoriented panic, she rolled and kicked, trying to get free from straps that held her down.

"Help," she cried out. "Atalay, help me!"

"Enah? Enah, are you all right?" She looked over, and he was there, like an answer to her prayer. He was in a rad suit, riding next to her on a charcoal black dushnah.

"N'damu?"

"I'm so glad to hear your voice," the prince said. "Guys, she is awake."

"I told you Thraxis would ruin your dress," Noba said, smiling down at her as he trotted over. She felt delighted to see her friends.

"We are a rotation out from Centralia, Enah," N'damu said. Noba loosened her straps, and the prince helped her sit up on the stretcher. Noba had tied it to the shoulder blades of her bone-horse, a steel-gray dushnah. *That explains the motion sickness.*

"My comms?"

"Out," Noba said, wincing as he massaged between his eyebrows. "All of Inana, it seems, has been crippled by this solar storm." The words were harder to hear than his wheezy, labored voice. Enahdra looked back at the natural girl, riding behind, scarcely conscious, it seemed. *Poor thing looks half-dead.*

"The chambers in Centralia run on geothermal," N'damu said. "They should still be up and running." *More than that will be up and running in Centralia,* she thought. *Vesta has tech that will be immune to the electromagnetic effects of the solar storm.*

"Won't do Chuku much good," the First Spear said. Her skin was baked by radiation as she keeled over on her saddle. "She won't survive this."

"She saved my life." Enah could see the pain in the prince's eyes—Noba's as well. "I remember her picking me up when I couldn't walk anymore. She carried me to the magnus."

"We all owe Nalia our lives," the prince said, slumped in his saddle, his voice toneless. Even through both of their ruby-red visors, she could see the anguish written on his face as he stared at the natural girl. *Wow, I'm starting to think he really does have a thing for her.*

She'd never cared for Nalia. The girl had abhorrent hygiene and never dressed like anything but a soldier. Not only that, since becoming the prince's Second Spear, she never left his side. Like a rasp dragon on a botsora's ass—the girl's relationship with N'damu seemed parasitic. Like a naga embedded in a mamidon's leg, sucking its blood.

"We can save her. Heal her." Somehow, she felt the prince's need and couldn't deny him.

"No, Enah," N'damu said. "She can't resynth. You know that." His heartache was palpable—as much a force in the air as the nuclear fallout.

"Vesta Tech can," Enahdra admitted. "Just get me home before we all die out here."

"Tech I am suspiciously unaware of," Noba said.

"We will also have transportation and coms—at least short-range."

"How is that possible?" the prince asked.

"We have some experimental batteries that run on ultranium eleven."

Noba scoffed. "That compound has been banned for ten thousand—"

"I'm sorry. Clan Vesta are Masters of Technology. We must use discretion when it comes to prototype technologies. What risks to take when cracking open the cosmos. There are long-ancient, time-tested safety protocols."

N'damu squinted his bloodshot eyes suspiciously as he trotted alongside. "What else is Vesta hiding?"

Twelve cycles ago

Enahdra held up two dresses for the hologram reflector, one in each arm—presenting each out in front of her in succession. "What do you say, Rigel? Cobalt blue or aquamarine?"

"Them sparkles would get you clipped in the Konga, little princess." Rigel Kong, the captain of her guard, never broke from character. "Mongrels would see you a kilometer away." Like his shaded visor, he always kept the persona on—a dangerous transient mercenary from the Jade Moon. Her father had imported Rigel from Oshun himself, claiming he was the most dangerous man alive—the only man capable of guarding his daughters. Especially after what happened to M'davah.

"I'm glad I have you here then," Enahdra said. "I hear the Tower of Atalay is far more treacherous than your little jungle moon."

Rigel nodded, grumbling muffled profanities. Captain of the Vesta Enforcement Officers, his stubble made a scruffy brushing sound as he rubbed his face.

"You *do* realize all the blasters have to stay home when we enter N'gaia," she explained. "I know Father lured you to Inana with the promise you could carry them at all times, but I'm afraid King N'joku would make more fuss than it's worth. No powered weapons in the capital."

"You people are pedestrian," he said as he tossed down his plasma rifle and unbuckled his hip holster full of hand blasters. "I can handle the lot of you with my fists alone." Rigel slid his hands down into the front of his pants and pulled out another pistol. Last, he opened his long leather trench coat and emptied his thermal darts, neutron grenades, and quark-flux decimators. *This guy is insane. But that long black dushnah tail is pretty hot.*

Enah laughed as she skipped over to the changing room and slipped into the aquamarine dress, shimmering with crystalline jeweling from neck to ankle. *Perfect,* she thought, looking down at the fit.

"Are you almost ready?" Ahdia called out. "The airship is cleared. Father is letting us borrow the M'dasa XR." Enah rolled her eyes and sighed. *She cares more about the flight than the gala. Whatever, at least she is going.*

"Right out, beloved twin sister," she said. Enah put her face in the makeup printer field and pulled away with her ideal blend of cool pastel blues.

"You look beautiful, Princess," said Ahdia's guard, Ivy Freya. "As always, Khanya blesses Vesta." The curly-haired brunette woman was always suited in polished lavender armor. Rigel Kong was the captain of the Vesta Enforcers, and Ivy Freya was the first lieutenant. Clan Freya was a Vestian offshoot that had served Enah's ancestors loyally for eons. "I'm envious! They will love you girls in N'gaia."

"And then all my dreams will come true." Ahdia waved her azure hair, worked completely straight; Enah had opted to weave hers in a bun. Her sister was ever as beautiful as Enahdra could hope to be, wearing a long, flowing black dress. *Tonight, Ahdia, you are a Princess of Vesta. Whether you like it or not.*

The princess tittered as they stepped toe to toe. They'd both chosen ipabite-scented perfume, though not surprising because it was their father's favorite. Enah pulled a black box from her handbag and opened it, holding up the contents for Ahdia.

"What are those?"

"And old Earth relic Father gave me for my collection," she replied, placing a shiny white beaded necklace around her sister's neck and guiding her hair out from behind. "They're called 'pearls.' They come from a strange sea creature that looked like a stone on the ocean floor."

She grinned and bobbed her head. "Thanks, En."

"You look gorgeous, sister," Enah said as she locked arms with her.

Ahdia looked her up and down. "*You* look … dangerous."

Now

"Who goes there?" A guard's voice called down from atop the silvery chrome wall that surrounded Centralia like a membrane.

"I am Princess Enahdra Vesta." She took off her helmet to show her face, no longer afraid of the radiation. Her skin had burned, her face unrecognizably blistered and scarred, but they would know the blue hair of a Vesta when they saw what remained of it.

N'damu took off his helmet as well as the radiation shields of the city made it safe. "I am N'damu Ata—" With a drone, the gate slid open. Enahdra's word was enough for her people. *Who needs Atalay,* she thought, chuckling as she shrugged at the prince and rode through on her dushnah.

Her city glimmered, so clean—pristine, just as she remembered it. Every building—every palace, and tower's polychrome coating glowed gold under the yellow skies of Inana. Hover-pods, chariots, and jet bikes would normally pulse through the streets, but today the people were on foot. Centralia was still alive yet ghostly quiet.

"It's been a long time, Princess Vesta." A woman in sparkling purple armor approached from down a white marble road, smiling ear to ear.

"Lady Freya …" She limped over and hugged Ivy, nearly collapsing in her arms. "It's been too long—and it was almost never."

"We feared the worst," Ivy said. "With you out there when the CME hit."

"Take this girl to the recombinant neo-genic lab." Enahdra pointed to Nalia, commanding a squad of VEOs who stood behind Freya. "She's a natural. I want every measure taken in her full restoration. Is that understood?"

"Yes, Princess Vesta," one VEO said as they carried her off. "We will take care of her."

Enah said nothing, looking to see if N'damu was pleased.

"You need resynthesis," Freya said as VEOs came to lead them to the chambers.

"Yes," Enah agreed. "And tell Captain Ariwyn to prep the Ghost Ship. I want the megamagnus fleet ready when we awaken; we leave for Meadowdell as soon as possible. And tell Rigel I want his unit on point."

"Yes, Princess Vesta," the Purple Knight said with a salute. "I will make all the arrangements."

"Thank you, Enah!" N'damu said, looking inches from death.

"I need a nap." Noba was panting, resting his palms on his knees.

"Come. This way," Ivy said. "I'll show you to the lazarus chamber, where we keep the resynthesis modules."

Enahdra, N'damu, and Noba followed Lieutenant Freya and her men into an ivory tower at the city's center. There, a steamy stone corridor led down a series of escalators. Passing two decontamination grids and two more quarantine stations, they finally came to a vast chamber. It was white, spherical, and filled with resynthesis capsules. Enah smiled. *Like the inside of one of the pearls I gave Ahdia the night of the gala. The night I met...*

Ivy and the VEOs helped Noba and N'damu as they stumbled into the blue crystal cylinders. "You will be good as new when you wake," Freya said. The boys laid back and closed their eyes as the cover slid down. The tube sealed with a crunch, and a pink gelatinous liquid quickly flooded in. Steam poured from the vents as the resynthesis tube reclined back into a cavity and the doors closed.

Ivy then turned to her and held out her hand. "Your turn, Princess Vesta."

Twelve cycles ago

The N'gaian Gala was everything she'd dreamed. King N'joku announced the princesses in court as they walked down the crimson carpet in the presence of Atalay for the first time. The king seemed like more than a man—a god, with his fiery mane of orange dreads. The great congregation of purists applauded the Vestian beauties as they passed, waving and offering their blessings.

Ahdia seemed dazzled by the star maps that decorated the walls, demarking the grand voyage their ancestors undertook to find the Eden Star.

For Enah, it was the people. They were so strange and exciting. So much more diverse than those in Centralia. The Konga Dreaun Symphonia came all the way from Oshun to play at the gala. Centralian music was far more synthetic; it was terrific to hear such ethereal compositions.

Ahdia quickly fell off, chatting with Princess Ala. She was still gazing up and pointing at the golden murals as the Atalayan princess explained each one. Enah sipped her drink as she walked around the floor, taking it all in. There were so many people—so many energies orbiting her at once. She hovered around the buffet, picking at the decadent snacks. *Isn't anyone going to talk to me?*

Rocking to the melodic overture, she pranced across the floor, stopping at the various art displays to appreciate the Tri-World masterpieces. She looked again at Ahdia, who now had both Ala and Aku's full attention—as well as a slew of other nobles. *What can she possibly be saying to them?*

Enahdra noticed Noba Sadah making his way over to her. She pulled at her dress, adjusting the hip. Then, smacking her lips, she turned around, smiling, only to see him dodge her as he jaunted over to join Ahdia's growing crowd. *This is so humiliating. What is so much more interesting about HER?*

The evening rolled on as she paced the crowd, pretending she wasn't alone. Ahdia danced with every noble in the room. Ala and Aku—Haden Winters. Her sister danced with socialites from Konga Dreau: Cyril Starr and his sister Persephone—with Haldir Nolan, Revis E'sizi, and Tiana Tattrila. She danced with Colt Dunkarr and his sister, Cassie. Even Noba got a whirl.

Enah found a small glass table and hunched down, trying not to cry. *What is wrong with me?* she thought. *Ahdia didn't even want to come.* She looked down at her reflection on the tabletop, which became increasingly obscured with each teardrop. *Oh great, cry now. You're pathetic! This pathetic night is complete.*

Suddenly, a handsome blonde man sat down across from her and reached out for her hand. She knew right away by the smirk on his face that he was trouble.

"I'm Theodus." He sniffled as if he had an allergy to the air. "I'm the king's ward."

"Theodus Darius … you're the Steward of Anu's son."

"I suppose you could put it that way." He laughed as he drank half a glass of vintage in one swig. "I prefer to say the Steward of Anu is my father."

"Wow," Enah said, blushing and giggling. "And now Ward of Atalay."

"Yes!" He jerked to his feet and took a theatrical bow. "I am so fortunate to bask in the Light of Atalay. No doubt about it." She thought she noticed the hint of an eye roll.

"He does seem amazing."

Theodus scoffed. "Well, it is your first time at court. *Anything* would impress you."

"I don't think I'll ever come back," she said, sulking in her chair as she dried her eyes on a napkin.

"You're too intimidating for this herd of schmigs! They're all afraid of you. Of the illustrious *Clan Vesta*." He made air quotes with his fingers as he said her name. "Trust me, on my planet I encounter this all the time."

"Why would they be afraid—"

"I am of Clan Darius," he said. "Masters of Robotics. My ancestors were Emperors of Anu. Whomever I marry would not only inherit a fortune but also a global conglomerate *and* the adoration of the Tri-Worlds."

Enah shrugged. "Yeah, but they are all talking to my sister."

Theodus scoffed, then finished his vintage. "She's a kid. They don't take her seriously." She couldn't help but get the giggles as he winked at her.

"We're the same age, thirty-three," Enahdra said.

"Yes, but *you* are a woman. It's clear. A woman only a rare man could handle."

He was so much older than her. "Why aren't you afraid of me? My father would never let me marry a man twice my age."

"Who said anything about marriage?"

She gave him a curious look. "Not me," she replied. "I just came to have fun, but this party sucks."

He extended his hand. "Would you care to take a stroll?"

She nodded. "Without question."

CHAPTER ELEVEN

N'joku III

The mid rotation clouds had a yellowish-gray brindle with the softest accents of white. N'joku stood on his royal bedroom's terrace atop the Tower of Atalay, staring to the west—out to the Utondan Savannah. He'd done little else since N'damu left for his journey of N'jikota. "What on Inana have I done?" He tugged on his dreads as his golden robe flapped in the breeze.

"Just come inside, you oaf." The queen came out of the archway, unfolding the curtains and scooting the king's nagas aside with her foot. Usoca and Urnas hissed, then slithered aside, grumbling as they recoiled for napping. She wafted the air from in front of her nose. "It still smells like burned tar." The solar storm's odor lingered.

"Now that he is out of reach, it is so clear, my grievous error," N'joku said as he reached for his beloved's hand. "I was only doing what I thought was right, Anaqua. Trying to be strong like an Atalay should be."

"You couldn't have anticipated the wrath of Thraxis, my love," she said. "Rebel warlords—treacherous criminals like this Volturis are not equivalent threats. Even Clan Starr failed to forecast the coronal outburst."

"It is as though Khanya were teaching me a lesson," he said, shaking his head and looking at his fat brown feet. "Reminding me of its power over us—how insignificant Atalay is in comparison." He clenched his fists and took a long, deep breath.

"We can't lament the past, N'joku," Anaqua said. "There is no sense. We must be forward-thinking if we are to help our son." He knew she was right, and yet regret seemed to overwhelm him.

"I can't help it, Anaqua," he said. "How could I have been so reckless with N'damu's safety? It is like I was under a spell."

"You were. It's called ego—or testosterone."

He sneered. "Be serious, woman." Usoca and Urnas began to circle N'joku anxiously as he paced the promenade. "I am afraid I may be losing my mind."

"Ridiculous," she replied. "We both know your DNA is in perfect order. If you would only lay off the sweets!" Anaqua patted him on the belly, making it jiggle. He let out an empty chuckle as he waved her away.

"You're not going to want to hear this, but I want to go after him myself."

"No," she snapped. "Absolutely not."

"Excuse me?" N'joku asked, massaging his brow. "Are *you* the king of the Tri-Worlds?"

"Even better, I'm the queen of the Tri-Worlds." Anaqua pressed her body against him from behind and reached around his waist. She slid her hand down into his golden toga, cupping his flaccid manhood. "I know who *this* is loyal to."

He exhaled long and slow as she fondled him. "You are an evil woman—to the core."

"I do what I must," she said. "M'demke has already sent scouts after N'damu. He has everything under control. He's with Noba and Nalia. And Enah—don't forget."

"I should be the one—out there…" N'joku's eyes rolled back as his words trailed off. Anaqua came around in front of him and gripped his shaft, now stiff in her hand. She gazed at him lustfully, smelling of sweet tinkercane suckle. "I am—the—Naga … Kin—"

"If you would have listened to me in court, N'damu would be here, safe." His wife began to tug him, pulling him back inside by the cock as if it were a leash. His nagas looked up at him with six eyes each, panting with a strange arousal of their own. Anaqua, however, only scoffed as she guided N'joku through the curtains and shut the door behind her. The nagas whistled and whined, protesting their defeat until the king willed them silent.

Anaqua dropped her dress to the floor. "We both need a distraction. Can you think of anything?" *Perhaps I can,* he thought as he looked her magnificent naked body up and down. *Though I fear I have been distracted for my entire reign— preoccupied with my ego for too long.*

"What's wrong?" she asked with a crooked grin and a raised eyebrow. N'joku blushed when he realized he'd gone soft again. Anaqua, on the other hand, grew red with ire. "Am I not attractive anymore?" In a huff, she marched to her closet and grabbed a robe. Watching her backside bouncing with each stride, he realized attraction wasn't the problem.

"My love, you are a singularity. Your beauty eclipses the natural world—it is the reason I have eyes. My lips exist to kiss you. My hands exist to caress you. My cock exists to—"

"All right, enough," she barked. "You're a botsora's ass."

"I am *your* botsora's ass, my love," N'joku replied. He crossed the room and swung open a large wooden dresser with the Tri-World triangle painted in red on the doors. His face beamed when he saw it—his great Atalayan war armor. Gold-plated krotrium—the most rigid metal ever synthesized—polished to a shine. There it was, waiting for him to put it back on and return to action.

Anaqua popped up behind him. "It would never fit now." The king looked down and patted his gut before sucking it in.

Behind the dresser hung his astonishing array of weapons. Sadah spears of all sizes, forged of gold, silver, and ansyonite. Broadswords, six heads long with ruby-studded hilts. Katanas and nunchakus—he had a two-balled chigiriki with emerald spikes and, of course, his favorite: a diskarmor of pure krotrium. He pulled it down and latched the chain to his wrist, then expertly whipped the spinning shield around the room

"Feels good to swing this," he said, tapping it into his chest with pride.

Anaqua crossed her arms with a glazed visage. "I was hoping for the spear, personally."

The next rotation

N'joku had shifted his big butt back and forth on his throne all morning. His unease was apparent to the entire court, no doubt. He still couldn't shake the feeling—the strange sensation that something coerced him to send his son away. Like he'd smoked too much ganja or had too much japhid-spiced ale the rotation prior, he felt hungover. "Report," he shouted as he tied back a mound of orange dreads. "Any word of my son?"

"Nothing yet," Lord Vesta replied. "Though it's too soon to expect news."

"Ala, Aku!" The king looked over at his daughters. "The ulanoids—can you sense him out there?"

"We have tried, Father," Ala said, shaking her head.

Aku crossed her arms with a frustrated grin. "It is not something either of us spent any time training to do."

"The ancient Milushi communed from across the planet through their winged companions. Keep trying, sweet daughters."

"Have faith, My King," General Jambi Sadah said with a tap of his spear. "He will be safe with Noba and Nalia. The Two Spears are highly capable."

"And Princess Enahdra, of course," the Lord Chancellor added. "I'm afraid communications are devastated across Inana, my liege." M'demke tipped his colossal headdress as he fumbled through a paper notepad. *Missing his tech, it seems.* "Satellites have been knocked out on a planetary scale. I've sent emissaries to get word from Duran. But it could be an entire oct before they return."

"The Duranauts will be grounded," said the Chancellor of Science, Serivicious Starr. "A CME of this magnitude can unsettle the entire Inanean magnetosphere."

"Indeed," Vesta agreed. Concern marred his old, weathered face.

"The fleet will be crippled, unquestionably." Starr rolled up his fuchsia sleeve and held up his charts. "As long as the electrical network is in flux, half of the essential systems will be inoperable."

"A double-edged sword, I'm afraid." Vesta twisted his finger through his wiry blue goatee. "Without access to space, we could be without communications indefinitely."

"How long, Serivicious?" the king asked.

"A cycle?" Lord Starr replied, scratching his lush brown hair. "Maybe two. I would have to speak with the Lords of Duran to assess the damage to the atom-breakers. After that, the entire mainframe must reboot from square one."

"So we will be cut off from Anu and Oshun." N'joku stepped down to the floor with his nagas slithering behind. "The economy will be devastated. Displaced citizens trapped. Critical trade routes for medicine and food are now severed."

"My envoys will return with news of Duran and of the prince as soon as they can," Lord Vesta said. "But aback dushnah, they must make the treacherous ride through the irradiated zone. We need to focus on reestablishing global transportation, firstly."

"Perhaps we can find some alternative energy source?" N'joku shifted again. "Lord Vesta, certainly your clan has some contingency for this."

146

"There are ultranium engines." Serivicious Starr looked to Lord Vesta. "Don't the megamagnus in Centralia have backup engines that run on ultranium eleven?"

M'demke flitted his hand like his wrist had no bones. "The compound is too volatile. Stockpiling ultranium eleven violates several weapons laws."

"The Doctrines of Atalay forbid all weapons of mass destruction," the Chancellor of Faith added. "Doctrine eight: Perversion of science to enact violence is forbidden. Death begets death under Atalay."

M'demke grinned, pinching his blue goatee. "Precisely, thank you, Lady Li'asaga."

"My King," Elle Li'asaga said. "The great tomes of G'higari also tell of such solar storms and the dark ages that follow. Might I suggest we turn to Khanya now? There is great power in N'jikota if we choose to harness it. Send word for all spirit-linkers to come. Sal'aah Novojoh and his daughter, Sho'nee—they command the atranoch. Princess Ala and Aku can send word on the wind with their ulanoid bond once their training is complete. We are not helpless without tech."

N'joku thought of the golden armor of his ancestors—of his diskarmor and his savage nagas. Tech did not mean power to him. Usoca and Urnas wrestled in a frenzy as the king tossed them some grats. "Khanya bless us, let N'damu return from Meadowdell on the back of an atranoch then. Thus, solving all our problems."

The Chancellor of Faith bowed in her white gown, her silver hair spilling to the floor. "The Light of Atalay will guide him, My King."

When you're lost, seek the home star, he thought.

CHAPTER TWELVE

N'damu IV

Light beams of honey and sepia pierced the clouds over Meadowdell as the prince's entourage of Vestian magnuses crossed the open moors leading up to the holdfast. The shadows of the Sindiswa Mountains were slowly creeping up the southern end of the castle's outer walls as the afternoon waned. The great Hall of Novojoh shone white, a magnificent manor of polished marble floating in the Eden Star's light above the mountain's rising shades. Its roof was a pyramid of oak and topped the chateau like a dark-brown wizard's hat pointed to the sky.

As the sun sank imperceptibly behind the vistas, the light flickered like wheel spokes off and on in N'damu's peripheral vision as he marveled at the beautiful castle. Stone walls surrounded the keep, making a perfect circle around the city, protecting the inhabitants within. He could see guards on the parapets above the gates signaling below. The drawbridge lowered, and the iron-plated portcullis began to rise, Enahdra's megamagnus, the Ghost Ship, only barely clearing the entryway.

This is truly humiliating. What will the Novojoh think of this production?

N'damu leaned his head out of the window and inhaled deeply through his nose. Meadowdell smelled of pleasant aromas, a mix of sawdust and spices. "Enah … can we slow our approach?" he asked. "There is no rush … I would prefer the sights over the embarrassment ahead of me."

Princess Vesta nodded to the captain at the helm. "We've made excellent time," she said as the colossal tank slowed to a leisurely crawl. The interior of Meadowdell was a quaint wooden village with interlinked apartment houses, stores, and gazebos connected by elevated deck walkways of stained vera wood.

"Only a few *minor* delays," N'damu said. "One or two solar storms! I'm just happy you agreed to take me on to Meadowdell. With the comms down—"

"Our fathers commanded it," she said. "I do not take *failure* lightly. Besides, nothing has changed. My orders were not to report back to N'gaia; they were to get you here and to keep you safe."

N'damu snickered, gently scratching his arm. "Thank you, Enahdra." His freshly resynthesized skin was still sore but looked brand new.

"It's a bit itchy, isn't it?" she asked. Enah also looked like her old self, her smooth, dark complexion flawless as ever.

"A little," he said, "but it feels all right." *You'd never know any of us were ravaged by a radioactive storm.*

"My sister, Ahdia, resynthesized an entire arm once," she said. "The itch kept her up at night for a quarter cycle."

"I'm just thankful to be alive," N'damu said. "All of us."

"Yes, even your little natural has recovered well."

"Thank you for saving Nalia."

"I told you Vesta's med-tech could restore her. Hopefully, she will learn to follow orders after this ordeal."

"She did what she thought was right," N'damu said.

Enahdra giggled softly as she joined him in admiring the passing city. The prince was most captivated by the people. *So beautiful.* He'd never seen so many natural-born southerners. They looked wild, dressed so differently from the subjects he'd met in Argoset: leathers vibrantly decorated with bright paints, hanging beads of maroon and amber. Ulanoid feathers adorned their hair, which they all seemed to wear long past their backsides.

He saw a portrait painter toiling over the likeness of a sweet old couple, happily posing in each other's embraces. Children ran through the alleys, clacking sticks together as they played at Knights of Yosai. A street musician's beautiful song was cut awkwardly short by the galling screech of a broken string. A little older lady sold cookies, yhonid seed cakes, marvets of cinnamon, or japhid spice at a small bake stand.

"I've always found Meadowdell so charming," Enah said.

"Well, it's no Centralia," he said with sarcastic intonation.

"I love my home," she replied. "But I still appreciate the beauty of Inana's more rustic cultures. It is a window back in time—to Earth." Surrounded by VEOs, Princess Vesta now was his highest-ranking babysitter, overseeing the glorified security protocols his father commanded.

N'damu stared, wide-eyed, out the window. "Will *you* ever seek N'jikota?"

"Ewwww, no!" The scorn in her voice was surprising. "I never liked pets, and Father says Vesta DNA is not conducive to soul-bonding." Enahdra was only a few cycles older, but she'd always raced to grow up, it seemed. She already knew the complex workings of interworld politics and diplomacy—she hardly lacked power without N'jikota. "Do you think I need an animal's help to get what I want, N'damu?" she asked with a sinister wink.

"You're much more than a princess. I know that," he replied. *Genius-level businesswoman and next in line to the Vesta helm.* "M'demke has taught you everything he knows."

"My sister begged Father to let her come study here, but he'd never risk his favorite daughter in the wilderness."

"She settled for the spaceports of Duran, I guess?" N'damu asked.

Enah laughed and shook her head. "Yes, as though space travel were safer than spirit-linking."

"Adventure is in Ahdia's nature. I always admired that about her," he said. "I hear she's become a worthy Duranaut."

"Well, Father could build a castle of ansyonite with the credits he's made selling Vesta tech to Duran anyway. Atom-breaker engines are *not* cheap."

Having been snacking on extravagant appetizers the whole trip, she offered him giheci on white keka buns. Accepting one, N'damu wondered how she maintained her impressive figure eating the way she did. Perfection seemed effortless for Princess Enahdra Vesta, and he was happy to have her on his side. "Just remember, My Prince, this is *your* journey. You worry about N'jikota—about the Novojoh. Leave the guard to me."

"I appreciate it, believe me, I do."

"I know it's not how you envisioned it." She reached out and patted his shoulder. "I can assure you, the Vesta Enforcers will be invisible as ghosts. My men will keep you safe yet remain like himpheah ants on the walls." Enahdra drew N'damu close and kissed him gently on the cheek. "I'll be the unseen angel watching over you."

She hugged him and kissed his cheek again before walking over to speak with the captain about fleet security protocols.

Soon the Ghost Ship came to a stop in front of the great hall in Meadowdell's center. N'damu prepared his courtly persona as he stepped into the docking bay, adjusting his collar nervously.

The front yard of the Hall of Novojoh was an enormous field of uniformly cut tynn, surrounded by picturesque gardens filled with flowers of every variety. The house was fifteen stories, fashioned of white marble so smooth, it looked carved from a single massive block. Two large balconies constructed of the same stone jetted out from the top level, looking over the Sizwe Plains. Twin pavilions of solid vera wood mirrored each other on the house's west and east wings. These were the schoolhouses where Inanean pilgrims, the devout G'higari, came to find their spirit-link, to live and study under the noble Clan Novojoh.

The hovering tank's thrusters quieted, and slowly the docking bay ramp lowered, revealing steps lavished in red carpeting. The Novojoh family was waiting in front of their colossal home, lined traditionally from oldest to youngest, ready to greet their monarch. The prince could hardly bear his embarrassment.

N'damu watched from behind, following Enahdra's protocols, as the Two Spears emerged ahead of him. Noba and Nalia walked up to the family and bowed graciously before taking guard on the left and right sides. Next went the princess, followed closely by three of her top VEOs, who promptly turned and took security positions. Finally, after Enahdra announced him, the prince stepped down.

N'damu Atalay walked across the field, fully aware this was not a conventional sight for these people. He felt debased by the grandstanding but swallowed his shame with each step as he approached the line of Novojoh.

On the left end of the line was the oldest, Mother Shi'nah Novojoh, who was the first to break the silence. "Steaming pile of atranoch dung's what *this* looks like." At 265 cycles of age, she had a long-cemented reputation as a sassy, opinionated

154

breaker of silences. Indeed, her bluntness seemed to come as no surprise to the rest of the Novojoh. "All this security, these ridiculous ships. Boy, what the Barren Void do ya think this is?"

"Apologies, Lady Novojoh—" N'damu began.

"My Prince, I have not been a *lady* for a hundred cycles. Don't try to flatter me. It doesn't suit you. This is a school and a place of great spirituality; it is certainly no vacation getaway." The wrinkled old woman had electric white hair splayed in all directions as she rolled her wooden chair. She wore a dress covered in ulanoid feathers dyed bright yellow and smelled of bitter pickled wompa root.

"Again, I do apolo—"

"And another thing," she interrupted again. "I was going to make some nice roasted rhybites tonight, but ain't feeding all these!" She pointed to the Vesta entourage.

"Mother Novojoh, perhaps we should let the prince *speak*." The current lady of Meadowdell, Marique Novojoh, stepped up to N'damu, taking his hand. "You are most welcome here, N'damu. Your father is an old friend. My brothers and my husband served him in the war." She wore a white fleece dress that hung loosely over her short, bubbly frame. Her mocha skin was smooth in his hand and two shades lighter than the rest of the Novojoh, giving her an even more foreign aura. "N'joku and I played as children when Atalay visited my home in Duran."

"It's an honor to meet you, Lady Novojoh. Thank you so much for welcoming me into your home. I apologize for the untraditional accompaniments. I mean no offense, but my liege father has ordered it," N'damu tried to explain through his humility.

She bowed low to him. "An Atalay is always watching."

"It's okay, Son," Lord Sal'aah Novojoh said as he hopped forward, sweeping the prince off his feet and embracing him—not unlike his father might. He laughed uproariously as he shook N'damu by the shoulders. "The son of the Naga King. Ohhhhhhh, I was with him that rotation, N'damu. Out on the Sizwe!" He put his arm around N'damu's neck, raising his hand to the heavens as if to project the image of his story onto the sky. "N'joku was good with a spear back then, sure, but a spear can only do so much when wild nagas get your scent."

Sal'aah had dark, leathery skin, reddened from his many cycles in the Thraxian heat, and his smile shone brightly from amidst his puffy gray beard. His hair was matted in locks that hung to the middle of his back. He draped a black poncho decorated in brown Milushi symbols over his broad shoulders, leathers worn and weathered like his face. "We were on our mamidons, N'damu. I almost thought he had soul linked, N'damu, but mamidons are deceptively cooperative beasts anyways, so you can never be sure with them. N'jikota works in mysterious ways, N'damu." His southern accent was thick, and his mind clearly tended to wander, but all the same, Sal'aah immediately felt like an old friend. "That rotation, he got bucked from the beast. So, the prince—I mean, well, you're the prince now, but *he* was prince *then*." He pointed his fingers in every direction, drawing knots in the air. "I'll just call him the king for the sake of this story!" He paused to think for a second, calculating in the air. "Actually, probably should have just gone with N'joku."

"There will be time for stories, my love," Marique interrupted as she retook N'damu's hand and led him away from her husband to meet her children. The first was a lovely woman of no more than sixty cycles draped in a violet throw. Her eyes were bottomless brown, her skin bronzed, with long amber locks of hair that waved in the breeze. "This is Sho'nee, my oldest daughter. She is the Kota of Atranochs, sage of the flying beasts."

Sho'nee bowed to him. "My Prince, it is a great honor to meet you. I look forward to flying together." She had a warm smile that reminded him of his sister Ala, exuding an undeniable regality. Her beauty filled him with awe.

"That would be a dream realized. I used to draw atranochs on my nursery walls—with myself on their backs, of course." He returned her bow with a chuckle, and Lady Novojoh led him to the next girl.

"And this is Sar'ah. She is a Kota of Throzeids."

She curtsied politely in her little yellow dress, lifting the white-laced fringe to her knees. "I'm sure you never dreamed *my* little critters. Everyone has thousands of throzeids in their bloodstream—but still, no love." She had the same soft tan skin as her sister, but her hair, dyed iridescent red, was split down the middle and tied in schmig-tails on each side. Tattoos covered her arms, mysterious tribal patterns that were unbelievably intricate and attractive.

157

Spirit-link achieved, he thought. "I look forward to your lesson, Sar'ah." The girl's intoxicating effect gradually faded as Marique led him on.

Next came S'ike Novojoh, the oldest son, who shyly extended his hand to greet him. "I'm S'ike, happy to make your acquaintance. I am a querghil sage, ahem. Yes." He was fat, a bit younger than N'damu—about thirty-five cycles, at a guess. Dressed in an orange tanned leather tunic, S'ike wore a braid in his reddish-brown hair that rolled over his shoulder down his belly. Querghil were massive, lumbering beasts—slug-like exophiles covered in plate shielding and equipped with a spiky, pronged tail. He seemed the perfect Kota of Querghil.

Next came Shar'nah Novojoh, a wiry girl, tall and awkward. She dressed in a brown leather jumpsuit with tasseled sleeves and a black fedora. Shar'nah had a masculinity about her that was almost intimidating to N'damu, despite her being ten cycles younger. As Kota of Dushnah in Meadowdell, perhaps she needed to be edgy. She simply nodded to him and tipped her hat.

Finally, Lady Novojoh introduced her youngest children, juvenile twins. The boy was Sab'ano and the girl was Sab'ina. They struggled to sit still and were continually poking and jabbing and whispering into each other's ears. Sab'ano had a puffy maroon perm and was shirtless with short brown pants. Sab'ina wore a rose leather dress with a tasseled collar. She had slanted eyes and long red hair that hung to her waist. Lady Novojoh told N'damu they would show him his quarters and give him a tour of the grounds.

"You're kinda skinny to be an Atalay," Sab'ano blurted out.

"Shut up, Sab'ano! You idiot," Sab'ina yelled. "The king is just fat."

N'damu kneeled to the children's level. "Can I see your muscles, Sab'ano?" he asked. The boy raised both his arms and flexed his little biceps. "Wow," he said as he squeezed the boy's arm. "I *would* seem small to *you*, with muscles like that."

The boy smiled and grabbed at his wrist. "Come on. I'll show you your room." Sab'ano pulled at N'damu, who looked to Lady Novojoh for confirmation that he should follow.

"Go now, settle in. We will discuss everything at dinner." The Novojoh all bowed respectfully as Marique gave leave. N'damu's entourage followed suit, save one.

"Just a moment," Enah interjected, as politely as she could. "Apologies again for the inconvenience, but Queen Anaqua ordered a complete sweep of the grounds before the prince is permitted to enter." She nodded to VEO Commander Rigel Kong, preparing him to initiate the procedure.

Aghast, Shi'nah barked out again. "Steaming pile of atranoch dung's what this is!"

"Mother, please, let them do their duty. What have we to hide? Besides, I am hungry. Let us hurry this along." Sal'aah Novojoh rubbed his pot belly as though he were famished.

N'damu shook his head with his eyes on his feet, too ashamed to look anyone in the face. "Again, my apologies, noble lords."

Lady Novojoh gave her leave, and Rigel Kong led his men into the house. Princess Enahdra curtsied to N'damu before making her exit. "I wish you good fortune in your N'jikota. You will fly before long, I am certain, My Prince. Rest assured the VEOs will stay out of the way after this." With one last hug, she returned to her megamagnus.

The Two Spears stood through the ceremonials like sentinels of stone. Noba exchanged a few grimaces of pity with the prince, but Nalia wouldn't look him in the eye since her recovery in Centralia.

N'damu tapped his feet awkwardly in the grassy tynn as the security inspection ensued. *Why won't she look at me? Do you think this makes things easier, Nalia Chuku? Look at me!* Oddly, as if hearing his thoughts, she locked eyes with him at last.

"All clear," Kong cried out. The twins each took one of the prince's hands and led him up the steps and through the oak gates. Sab'ano and Sab'ina instructed N'damu and his friends to remove their shoes—one could only walk barefoot in the Hall of Novojoh. The prince slipped off his sandals and began to explore while Noba and Nalia clumsily fumbled around armor plates, trying to access their boot laces. The house's interior was like a gallery, with ancient artifacts from vanished cultures and fossils of creatures long extinct presented within glass display cases.

"Is that a tondazar?" N'damu asked, staring up at a titanic skeleton.

"Yes," Sab'ina told him. "It's 800 million cycles old."

"Most impressive," N'damu replied. "Before *our* time. Imagine what the world was like back then."

"Father says humans are even older than—"

"Shut up, Sab'ano," the girl interrupted her brother sharply. "He gets confused at storytime, N'damu. Come this way."

Crystal chandeliers hung from the ceiling, casting a golden light on the walls decorated with ornate artworks: portraits of ancestors, ageless tribal motifs sacred to the G'higari faithful. The furniture, which smelled of saturn oil, was hand-carved from solid meridian, polished smooth, and upholstered with suede and ulanoid feather.

N'damu followed the twins up the stairs and down a long hall until they finally came to his room. The children could hardly contain their excitement. "It's the same room your father stayed in—do you like it?" asked Sab'ina as she swung the door open to present N'damu with his princely quarters.

Noba and Nalia took guard at the doorway as he peeked inside. "Yes, I like it very much, thank you," he replied. It was a simple room designed for introspection and meditation. No holo-projectors, no games, or musical instruments. No weapons or tools. Not even an ink pen. *How did Father of all people not go insane?* There was only a bed and a chair in front of a stone chimney, alongside a shelf lined with books: G'higari tomes, guidelines for N'jikota, humanity, and Khanya, the Womb of Inana. There were also some naturalist texts, including the most relevant information for all known Inanean wildlife.

"It's perfect, Sab'ina," he said, bowing to the sweet little girl. "Thank you, Sab'ano." He scuffed the boy's mop playfully and gracefully herded them to the doorway.

"I hope you like it here with us, N'damu." Sab'ina gave a slight head tilt, batting her lashes before bolting out of the room.

"I'll show you my rasp dragon collection after dinner," Sab'ano promised as he followed his twin, not to be outraced.

"Okay, see you at dinner."

Sab'ano slammed the door behind him, and for a moment N'damu was alone. He changed from his royal leathers into casual broadcloths, a brown hooded robe and trousers. *Wow, this is what they train in? Enah wouldn't make it past this test.* Next, he fingered through a few of the books on his shelf before back-flopping onto his bed to test its comfort level. *Surprisingly soft.* Despite all the stimulation, again, his mind drifted to Nalia. She was right outside the door yet a million light-years away. *She has been so cold since the terrace. How can I thaw this deep freeze, Nalia Chuku?*

He flashed back to the grotto, under the waterfall—embracing her—touching her body. N'damu wished she could be lying here next to him and not stationed outside, following orders. He thought about her lips and noticed himself getting hard below. *Everything that has happened today, this monumental rotation in my life ... and all I think about is her.*

An abrupt knock sounded at the entryway. "Can I come in?" Noba asked, his voice muffled by the thick door. *He even interrupts my fantasies.*

The prince took a moment to compose himself before bidding his friend enter.

"What do you think so far? Those Novojoh girls are astounding, aren't they? Well worth trekking across a radioactive wasteland and a couple rotations in a resynth tube. Tits of Inana! They were flat as skipping stones when *I* came for N'jikota."

"Well, it would appear they've grown up, if your erection were any indication." N'damu mocked his guard's stance while thrusting out his pelvis. "Couldn't we at least get through introductions in a noble manner, Noba?"

"Sar'ah is so sizzling. I think I was getting heatstroke." Noba wiped his brow and pretended to flick sweat at N'damu.

"Yes, she is a beauty … but where is Nalia?"

"I gave her first rest. She's settling in her room—she'll be at dinner, buddy. Don't worry. You won't decompose without her. You won't explode or melt or disintegrate if you spend two moments without Nalia Chuku." The prince rolled his eyes with a perplexed expression. "Come on, brother! Would it hurt you to smell the skylar roses? There are some very cute blossoms here. Noble, Homo purist ones too."

"And S'ike would be a splendid match for *you*, my friend." N'damu let out a wheezy chuckle.

"Well, now that's weird," Noba replied. "Though his breasts *are* bigger now as well."

"I'm hungry … do I smell maraphite soup?" N'damu asked.

The dining hall was a long cafeteria of tables in rows where everyone sat as equals. Atalay, Vesta, Novojoh, Sadah … Chuku. All fed from the Womb of Inana, together as one flock on a shoreline. Brothers and sisters within Khanya, come together to break bread with differences buried in times of war and peace alike. This was the way of the Novojoh.

He followed Noba as they took plates and bowls and chose from the buffet of foods. N'damu had indeed smelled maraphite soup, his favorite. He loved seafood.

"Wow ... do you see the size of those roasted chaladha nuts?" Noba seemed to marvel at every dish as he began to pile his plate. His muscular frame required high-calorie sustenance, to be sure.

Nalia sat beside Sho'nee Novojoh, having a polite conversation, the content of which was beyond his hearing. The seat across from her was still available, and N'damu quickly filled the vacancy, asking politely before setting his plate down. Next to Sho'nee sat S'ike, who leaned over his sister, asking Nalia what it was like being trained by the famous Lady Shyla Sadah.

"She is an artist with a spear. Truly, it is an honor to be her ward. I couldn't be luckier." He noticed her tighten up as he sat down, trying hard to pay him no mind.

"Well, I've heard a lot about you as well. Sadah'anah is such a challenging style to master," Sho'nee said. "One of the Two Spears, at your age—it's quite a remarkable achievement." She made her regal pronouncement with genuine awe, complementing Nalia to the entire table. "Prince N'damu, do you train with Lady Sadah as well?"

"I do—I mean, I try. More so with Nalia. My spear skills are still a work in progress." He conceded another weakness, humbly giving up on his last shred of dignity. He didn't care as he put his foot on top of Nalia's warm toes under the table. She smiled finally and petted the top of his foot with her other sole. It was so soothing, so invigorating. He felt invincible to indignity.

Sab'ano laughed. "So, the greatest spear fighter that ever lived hasn't been able to teach you yet?"

Lord Sal'aah finally slowed his feasting enough to speak. "Ask N'damu's father if he ever needed to use a spear after he left Meadowdell," he said, putting his unruly son in his place. He drank deeply from his mug of vintage and continued. "Ask the *Naga King* if he ever needed to bother his hands with silly sticks. In the Wars of Charon, do you believe N'joku Atalay triumphed because of his spear? No, no, no. The Charonese legionaries were the deadliest standing army of all time, but they had no answer for nagas. It was not sword or sharpened stick, but Usoca and Urnas who were the heroes that paved the field in carcasses!"

"Sal'aah," Marique interjected. "Let us not be so graphic in the retelling, my love. Not while we eat. Please."

"Apologies, apologies. Lady Novojoh is right, of course." He wiped the froth from his beard and honed his stare in on the prince. "The point is, N'damu has yet to discover his true power within. As I was telling you earlier, N'damu, the rotation your father fell from his mamidon, he was beset by a pack of wild nagas. He brandished his futile spear, to no avail. They snapped and snarled as they closed in his direction. Now, don't tell *him* I told you this, but he tripped and fell on his backside. Surely, he was about to die when suddenly one naga started to attack another, and the pack began to frenzy around him. *Around* him, like a wall—it was a protective circle, you see."

"He never tells the part about falling on his backside," N'damu said with a giggle. "Of course, his recap has him grabbing the naga by the mandibles and heroically mounting them to submission."

Sal'aah burst out in glee, soon joined by everyone at the table.

"Seriously, N'damu, it was the heightened emotion, N'damu. N'jikota! This is why people come to Meadowdell. You need to get out in the wild. You need to fall and get back up. Get your hands cracked and filthy black. Even an Atalay—"

"Especially an Atalay," he interrupted, to Sal'aah's obvious delight.

"I will show you the way," he promised.

"I'm ready, My Lord. I've been waiting all my life for this!" N'damu, finishing his last spoonful of soup, set his bowl aside enthusiastically. "When do we begin?"

Sal'aah laughed his jolly chuckle, a grin stretching ear to ear under his bushy beard. "Sleep well, young prince. We rise with Thraxis, when the mamidons are most active."

CHAPTER THIRTEEN

Sal'aah I

A haze of mist blanketed the savannah floor, seeping through the tall grasses, a ghostly remnant of the cool night passed. Scattered groves of vera broke the morning light into beams, warm gradients of auburn and yellow as Inana's mother star slowly ascended from behind the distant Zola Mountains to the south.

Ulanoid choirs sang their beautiful calls as the wild Sizwe Plains awoke to the new rotation. Herds of dushnah amassed at the riversides, bumping and bustling for their morning drink while trying to avoid being quilled by the spikey tucsabura, which crawled around their feet, also looking to quench their thirst. Botsora lay basking on the flat rocks, exposing their soft bellies to the warmth of Thraxis, as grats picked himpheah ants from their spindly back shells.

"The mamidons will start to come down from the foothills soon. They spend their nights up there, then come down here to graze and forage and drink before it gets too hot." Sal'aah Novojoh was Kota of Mamidons, teaching thousands of faithful G'higari to ride out here. This morning he crept through the tall grass with his new student, the Prince of Atalay. He couldn't help but bellow with laughter as N'damu continually fumbled through the roughage, tripping and stumbling behind him as he struggled to keep up. Sal'aah knew every tree and rock, every field and river bend in these, his ancestral lands. Blindfolded, he could still walk the moors of the Sizwe. Indeed, each foot met the ground like an old friend, with a muscle memory that had become second nature to him.

Sal'aah wore a russet half-cape over his right shoulder, embroidered with Milushi symbols in gold stitching. Though the religion had fallen out of favor now, Sal'aah loved to dress as his ancient ancestors had done when they first spirit-linked. Underneath that, he bore a tan tunic, half laced in front by black strings, his silver chest hair blossoming in a V. Like all Novojoh, he wore no shoes on his hairy feet, which were muddied beneath the tattered ankles of his black pants.

"Why do you not keep a mamidon with you?" asked N'damu as he huffed and puffed. "If they are your spirit-link, why not ride one at all times?"

Lord Novojoh tied back his massive gray dreads and smiled behind his puffy bristles. "I have a love for these animals, N'damu. As your father has for his people," Sal'aah explained. "N'jikota is not only a symbiosis, but it must be an equilibrium as well … the spirit-link is not a relationship of a slave and a master. Nor one of a virus and host." He scaled a boulder that jetted from the field and squinted, gazing east to the foothills of the Sindiswa Mountains, looking for mamidons. "Mamidons are meant to roam the savannah. They feed on the vera trees. They drink from the river. They draw life from Khanya. Who would I be to dress them in trousers and force table manners on them?"

"I never thought about it that way," N'damu said.

"Besides, the plumbers of Meadowdell would revolt. I doubt our toilets could handle a hefty mamidon shit," Sal'aah joked. "Better they drop those out here."

They both laughed. "I think I've stepped in a couple of them," N'damu replied finally and was met with another roar of amusement. Sal'aah extended his hand and helped the prince up onto the rock.

The young Atalay wore his training robes well. Their fabrics had sullied fast from his multitude of tumbles, a good thing in the guru's eyes. His braid was secured in a tight black skullcap, dampened as sweat poured from his brow. The boy had no aversion to working or a lack of enthusiasm.

"Look, N'damu, I see one now," Sal'aah said as he pointed out the silhouette of a long-necked, boney-headed mamidon bobbing across the treetops of a grove to the west. "Oh, it's Rosalie." He put his index and middle fingers to his lip and let out a powerful whistle that sent unnerved ulans flocking from their nests in the tall tynn. "Over here, girl," he called out with his voice and mind in unison.

After the animal rounded the tree line, it headed in their direction. Sal'aah smiled as he saw his new pupil's eyes widen in astonishment. "Wow—she's so beautiful."

"Now remember, N'damu, she will sense you through my bond with her. She will accept most riders with me, but don't mistake that for N'jikota. Spirit-linking, when it comes to mamidons, is gradual. You must ride alone eventually, but for that, they must accept you first. They must trust you."

As the towering beast lumbered their way, Sal'aah could see N'damu's visage betray his fear.

The huge mamidon finally came up to their rock. Rosalie's back stood as high as their perch, at least twelve feet from the ground.

"Forget everything your scientists told you back in N'gaia, N'damu." They liked to classify them as "exophiles," the sort of mega-arthropods that had taken a dominant course in Inana's distant evolutionary history. "Theories come and go. Let them believe what they want. I know our souls were created together. Birthed to Khanya."

The beast was mostly gray but covered in microfibrous fur that made patchy brown, beige, and gold spots about its hulking body. Atop her long bristly neck, at least eight more heads long sat Rosalie's cranium. It looked like an elongated skull, plates of interconnected bone with a mohawk of horns. Three sockets on each side housed her fleshy yellow eyes, which seemed to emanate a warm glow as they reflected the sunlight. She had four long quadric-jointed legs, each ending in a hard enamel hoof that created deep thuds as she walked. The animal had a long, thorny tail that extended behind for stability and a weapon against nagas, crongrins, and other predators.

Sal'aah handed her a jupiter fruit from his bag and stroked lovingly at the bridge of her nose. Then, with a huff, the Lord of Meadowdell launched his weighty frame up onto her back. Rosalie seemed almost to purr, a content breath that vibrated the bone plates around her mouth. He dropped a leg on each side and scooted up her neck. "Okay, N'damu, it's safe. Just hop on her back here behind me," he explained as he patted a soft patch between Rosalie's shoulder blades.

The boy leaped meekly from the rock and landed with a soft pat on the mamidon's back, quickly straddling where he'd pointed.

The prince's nerves were evident as the animal's purr slowly quieted to silence. Sal'aah could feel the incline angle increasing as the mamidon began to rear up on her hind legs. Out of instinct, he took hold of one of her spikes and held on. Thirty degrees, forty-five degrees: N'damu began to slip behind him, Rosalie's torso too wide for his arms to clasp. Sixty degrees, seventy-five. Sal'aah looked back and reached out, but the prince had skidded out of range. The mamidon stopped at ninety degrees and stretched out its neck to the sky. Somehow, N'damu still managed to hug tight enough to its backside until an abrupt shudder rippled through Rosalie's body, a shiver that jostled the boy's hold, sending him careening into the mud below.

Immediately she went back down on all fours, and Sal'aah laughed like he was a child again. "Rosalie," he called out, jokingly scolding her. "How dare you buck your royal prince?" Sal'aah chuckled until his belly ached.

"Yes … well, it's my pleasure to entertain, My Lord. But what should I do? Did I do something wrong?" the prince asked, brushing the mud clumps from his shoulders.

"She senses your fear, N'damu. She doesn't like it. Try again but try to be less, *ahem*, nervous." Sal'aah shrugged.

N'damu climbed back up the rock, but before mounting again, he pulled a fruit from his satchel and offered it to Rosalie. The mamidon stretched its long purple tongue and wrapped the fruit, accepting it happily before resuming its purring. Once again, his pupil jumped on the beast and sat behind him. The animal then began her slow stride, clumsily shuffling away.

"Graceful, isn't she?"

"She's a gorgeous beast," N'damu said in a shaky voice as he patted Rosalie on her side. However, out of nowhere, the animal leaned over a nearby meridian tree and drove N'damu into an out-hanging branch with clear intent. Whacking him like a bungee ball, the impact suddenly and unceremoniously unseated the prince for a second time, and with a hard, undignified smack, he again hit the grass.

That was when it first occurred to Sal'aah. *She can feel THEM watching.*

After three more false starts, it was clear Rosalie was not suffering N'damu as a passenger. *His father was such a natural at this. But he didn't have the Royal Guard hiding in the grass.*

We can ignore them, but we don't have a mamidon's sense of smell.

Sal'aah pointed at the moors to the west. "We need to go to the foothills. Your training commences at the mamidon's social grounds. If you start walking now, you should make it in about two hours." Sal'aah tossed the prince a canteen. "After Rosalie has a drink, we will head that way."

"Okay." N'damu sighed, looking discouraged.

"Don't worry, N'damu. When you're lost, seek the home star. Remember the G'higari words."

"My father says that to me all the time," he said. "Since I was a baby, actually."

"Do you know the rest?"

"No … no, I don't remember exactly."

"It's '*Find Atalay atop the highest of totems*,'" Sal'aah said. "You are the next Atalay. You have the spirit of kings inside you. But for some, even some of the best, it takes time. I believe in you, N'damu."

His student nodded as he headed toward the pass.

I believe in you, N'damu?

***

Sal'aah squinted as the Eden Star rose in his left peripheral. He chewed the end of a long strand of sugary tinkercane, bobbing up and down aback Rosalie as they arrived at the beautiful green hill dappled with herds of mamidon. This was their hallowed mating ground. Mamidons were generally solitary animals, but after their extensive wanderings, they always had a place like this, where they came to socialize as a herd and find a mate. Each of the animals raised its head as they rode past, hailing the Meadowdell lord with a trumpet, recognizing their link to him. Sal'aah felt as happy here as they did. He led his mamidon-mount near a hanging tree branch, grabbed on, and shimmied down the trunk. She let out a whooping trumpet of her own as she thundered away to join the herd.

The guru plopped his backside on a soft tuft and took a deep swig of cool water from his canteen, then sighed with satisfaction. He unwrapped a dry-roasted maraphite sandwich and took a huge bite. Crumbs peppered his chest hair as he devoured his lunch. Afterward, he laid back, crossing one leg over the other, and slipped into a midmorning nap.

His eyes began to flicker under their lids as his soul seemed to exit his body. Clouds split like parting seas, leaving rippled waves of smoke in his wake as Sal'aah soared the heavens. White-tipped peaks of the tallest mountains looked like tiny mounds from this height. He could see out of both sides of his head a 360-degree panorama of all horizons. The human brain wasn't equipped to perceive such detailed information—yet somehow he did.

Where he would have had arms, long wings spanned sixty heads long, bone frameworks connecting thinly stretched sheets of skin that caught the draft like a kite. With spiky horns at the joints and jagged talons at the wingtips, he was a mighty atranoch—master of the sky.

Dreamily soaring through the mountains, he saw another atranoch's silhouette below him. Sal'aah shifted in the air, instinctually triggering his descent. He could feel his three-ton body drop as his massive wings captured the updraft and steadied to gliding position.

As he drew closer to the other bone-dragon, he could see a shadowy rider on its back. The figure seemed to jitter in and out of reality, flickering like dark flames as it looked at him with ominous red eyes. The clouds blackened as the atranoch began to transform beneath its rider. It phased from gray to red as fur transmuted to flame. The beast tripled in size, dwarfing Sal'aah in comparison as he began to beat the air with his wings again. Lightning cracked around him, winds pounded, and thunder drummed the pitch-black clouds. Torrents of rain showered from above as the fiery rider pursued him, shooting black flames at his underside. The heat charred Sal'aah's tail as he weaved and dodged, trying to escape.

As if conjured from thin air, there were suddenly riders on his back. Behind his head was his eldest daughter Sho'nee, with her arms outstretched, holding each of Sal'aah's two massive shoulder spikes. He instantly felt a connection to her, a light that soothed a fire within him, the glow triggering an explosive release of chemical gratification. *Is this what an animal feels when it spirit-links?*

Another burst of black flames engulfed his armored atranoch belly. Behind Sho'nee rode Sar'ah, holding tightly to her sister's waist. Sal'aah knew his second daughter hated to fly. Behind her was S'ike, followed by Shar'nah, Sab'ina, and Sab'ano. All his children were on his back. The future of Clan Novojoh hung in the balance, threatened by this spectral creature of reality-warping flame.

The black plasma cooked his bone plates red as Sal'aah screeched in pain. He flew erratically, trying to shield his children with his body while evading a web of lightning bolts. Struggling to remain stable, he saw another figure falling from the clouds ahead. Without thought, he dove.

It was N'damu, skydiving, his training robes flapping in free-fall. Sal'aah looked back at the black rider on his crimson atranoch of flames and noticed him taking form. With an orange braid whipping in the storm, the dark figure now wore golden robes of Atalay. *N'damu as well. Two of them?* Red plasma continued to pour from dark N'damu's eyes as Sal'aah tried to save the falling double. *The children!* But they were gone as well, replaced by six more N'damus. One by one, each slipped off his tail, falling, disappearing into the lightning-illuminated clouds below. As they each fell into oblivion, he could hear each prince cry out. "Sal'aah … Sal'aah … Sal'aah."

"Sal'aah … Sal'aah. Wake up! Lord Novojoh—I'm here," the prince said as he shook his arm, rousing him from his nap.

176

He jolted up, unsettled by the dream. "Oh … N'damu. Apologies, I must have dozed off," he said, shaking off the nightmare. His heartbeat returned to a reasonable pace as he stood up and drank some water. "Wow, four hours? Did you stop for a nap as well?" Sal'aah joked, shielding his brow, assessing the time by Thraxis. His eyes throbbed, not yet readjusted from sleep.

"Sorry, I'm not the fastest hiker," N'damu said.

The traumatic vision faded, and Sal'aah patted the prince on his back. "Worry not, future king. A true warrior doesn't walk. A true warrior rides." He bid N'damu follow and strode down the grassy hill to a broad, sprawling valley. In its center stood a wooden perch erected atop a tall totem pole, carved with the long unworshiped Milushi gods' likenesses. He stopped and scratched his beard, gazing at the small pedestal on top. "Can you climb it, N'damu?"

"I grew up climbing trees in the Icici," N'damu said. "I think I can make it up." The prince spat on his hands, slapped them together, and hugged the pole. With some effort, he shimmied up, grasping at the outcropped noses, tongues, beaks, and horns of wooden deities. Slowly but steadily, he made his way to the top.

"Excellent, N'damu. It took your father twice as long to mount the mamidon totem! Now, you must get to your feet." The boy tried to stand, whipping and waving his arms for balance. Sal'aah clenched his teeth, bracing for the prince's fall, but he seemed to find stability. "You leave yourself vulnerable to the mamidons atop the perch." He let out another loud whistle. *Which of you will bear the prince?*

A huge mamidon named Mirabeth approached from the hill with her two young calves in tow. She was even larger than Rosalie and had a rusty hue to her spots. "That's Mirabeth," Sal'aah said. "Up there, you're at their level, N'damu. They will come to know you as an equal. You must stand eye to eye without fear. You must earn their respect." Sal'aah took about a hundred paces back and plopped down in the tall grass to observe his student. He could sense his apprehension through Mirabeth as she approached, no matter how brave a front he offered. Indeed, Sal'aah could not avoid the nagging feeling of disappointment creeping in.

The boy is not the second coming…

The Lord of Meadowdell buried the feeling deep, knowing his faith in Atalay would always compel loyalty. N'damu could surprise him still. It was unfair to hold him up to N'joku—wasn't it?

The mamidon marched up to the perch and came face to face with N'damu. Their eyes locked as she sized the boy up. *It's okay, girl.* The prince put out his hand, reaching to pat Mirabeth on the brow. *You can trust him. You can have faith in Atalay—always.* The mamidon reared back, however, its chest expanding as it took a deep breath. With the bang of a proton cannon, Mirabeth let out a wild sneeze. Her purple tongue flapped from her mouth as translucent goo sprayed from it with a burst. Along with a deluge of hot malodorous mamidon breath, N'damu fell from the perch, coated in slime.

Landing with a jarring thud, the prince clearly strained not to cry—not to show his weakness. Sal'aah saw it nevertheless. "It's okay, Son. Don't give up."

Struggling to his feet, N'damu rubbed the back of his head, working the kinks out of his shoulder. "Perhaps my spirit-link is not to the mamidon," he said. "They would rather see me bonded to the soil, it would appear."

"Nonsense," Sal'aah replied. "This is the first step of ten thousand. If you do not have faith in yourself, neither will the beasts. You must *believe*. They feel your doubt—I feel it *through* them. You have the blood of a hero. The DNA of Atalay comes with a mighty calling. Even if you do not find N'jikota with the mamidon, it must still respect you. Reach out to Khanya, N'damu. All are one, connected by the Womb of Inana. You must stand atop the perch, not only to prove to them but to yourself as well." *Will one of you please just let the boy ride? I'm getting hungry.*

N'damu made his way up the pole once again and stood atop the perch. This time a bull mamidon approached. It was Jasper, a husky blonde-striped giant. This time the boy stood his ground with more confidence as he faced the boney beast. *That's it. That's it.* Jasper, however, took no interest in the prince, only walking by him with an arrogant snort. *Jasper, why do you do this to me?*

N'damu gave a meek little whistle. "Hey, you. Mamidon! You will show me respect!"

Jasper showed his respect, or lack thereof, as he gave a final flick of his tail in passing, whacking the pole, and sending a wild tremor through the wooden gods. N'damu's arms whirled like rotors spinning for balance, to no avail. Again, he went careening down to the hard, unforgiving turf with a groan.

Sal'aah stood and walked up to him, still chuckling. *N'joku would be shepherding the herd by now.* Inside, however, frustration began to mount, since he'd never had a student struggle like this. *Do they sense my doubt? Or do they feel something else? Spears in the tynn grass? Scopes, targeting them.* He clapped the dust from his hands. "Well, I leave you to it. Takes rotations for some." A lie. "Others, not so much. If all goes well, you'll be riding a mamidon back to Meadowdell in time for rhybite stew." The frustration was too much.

"You're leaving?" N'damu said, surprised. "I'm to do this *all* night?"

"As many nights as needed, yes," Sal'aah told him sternly. Though he was an easygoing man, he knew how to be a master when necessary. He let out his whistle, and Jasper turned back. The beast lowered his neck and lifted Sal'aah into a rider's position. "I'll come back in the morning if you haven't returned. Try not to fall asleep up there." Sal'aah laughed heartily as Jasper began to plod across the valley.

Thraxis was getting lower in the horizon to the north, blanketing the sky in mustard yellows as he rode away to the sound of N'damu crying out as he impacted the ground once again. He turned one last time to see him climbing back to the top of the perch and standing. *Can't keep the boy down for a second, though. I like that.*

As Sal'aah crossed the hill just out of the prince's line of sight, he led Jasper to a small cropping of olyin yara. "You know, just because N'damu didn't notice you today doesn't mean the mamidons were *as* unaware."

Nalia Chuku popped out of the bushes in her clanking armor, followed by Noba. "Do you think we spooked them or something?"

Noba continued to keep a vigil on N'damu through a pair of enhancement specs. "Nah, we kept the necessary distance." His indignance was clear. "I've studied enough about mamidons to know how close we can get."

"It's hard to say. I respect the command of my king, but you can only harm the spirit-linking for N'damu. Like a quantum wave turns particle under observation, the watcher taints this ritual." Sal'aah felt like he was explaining rain to the ocean.

"If they *taint* this ritual, *I* must bend it over and sodomize it!" At first, he couldn't place the deep, scratchy voice until he heard a stir in the brush. Sal'aah and the Two Spears all looked to a parting of the tall tynn as a blond-haired Oshunese dwarf showed himself. "You knew these two rookies were here, huh, old man? But ya had no clue 'bout me," he said. Sal'aah recognized the little man from the prince's circus act arrival in the Meadowdell courtyard; he was one of Rigel Kong's lieutenants. A Vesta Enforcement Officer, he was bearded and ruggedly muscular, wearing a tight white and orange suit of body armor.

"I'm Sal'aah. I didn't get your name."

"Name's Frigg," the dwarf said as he pulled his specs and eyed N'damu in the distance. "Calitro Frigg. I'm the one who's *actually* keeping our princey-poo safe here."

"What are you even doing out here, Calitro?" Nalia asked. "The spears had this watch."

"I'm doing the work of the king. The will of Atalay, basically." Calitro Frigg chuckled dismissively. Though he said the words, the sarcasm in his tone implied he didn't take it very seriously, if at all. "Princess Enahdra deployed me herself. Don't like it, take it up with her."

The sky began to darken as the Eden Star waned. Next came a drop. Then another. Drop—drop: one by one, rain began to pelt Sal'aah's head. Again, laughter beset him. He stretched his arms to the heavens in uproarious mirth as a storm shower dumped on the Sizwe. "I love the storm season!" He struggled to regain his composure, holding his belly as he cried out over the rain patter. "Khanya has spoken. Have a pleasant night keeping the prince safe. I'm glad I can sleep easy." He looked down at the dwarf and patted him on the shoulder. "Keep dry, little one. I'll have some hot cinnamon swirl marvets in your honor."

The three rain-drenched guards all grumbled and complained.

"Mamidons sleep standing up, even in the rain. It doesn't bother them at all—but I'm sure you knew that, young Sadah." Sal'aah resumed his chuckling as he marched back to Meadowdell on Jasper, singing the songs of his ancestors loudly to the beat of his mamidon's footfalls. He always loved to sing in the shower.

CHAPTER FOURTEEN

Nalia III

The Vestian megamagnus fleet was encamped twenty kilometers northeast of Meadowdell, on the fringes of the M'lilo Forest. Comprised of sixteen Evanthide Tens, the age-old war tanks were stationed in a row across a sprawling grass meadow. Each magnus had a massive titanium-armored hull with a large reflective domed windshield over the command bridge. Due to the solar storm, they were newly equipped with ultranium eleven engines that required no electricity. Vaulted cupolas lined the flanks, each with its own proton cannon beneath black-tinted viewports. Huge chrome pipes jetted from their rears to pump out exhaust fumes when its tracks barreled over the land. *Princess Vesta will use any excuse to play with her toys, I guess.*

Temporary inhabitations peppered the field to the west, a small village erected overnight by Vesta Enforcement. The prince's protection force seemed bizarrely large to Nalia Chuku.

All this for N'damu's security, she thought as she strolled the encampment.

Her spear looked like a joke compared to the armored VEOs around her. They were at least a hundred strong now, and more seemed to arrive every hour. *For a phantom threat based on a rumor? It's just too absurd. There must be more to the Volturis they aren't telling us.*

She'd just returned from three rotations out on the Sizwe, watching N'damu struggle on that perch to the point of exhaustion. Three miserable rotations, hiding in the bushes, standing shadow guard in the freezing rain—or the sweltering heat.

Finally, this morning Lord Novojoh came to relieve him. It was heartbreaking to see N'damu come down from that pole in bitter failure. So pained, so spent he couldn't even walk. It took everything in her not to run and help him as Sal'aah made him crawl back to Meadowdell.

"I hope Noba didn't notice my tears," she whispered to herself as she looked for a cafeteria hab. The Second Spear had a few short hours off duty, and she needed two things desperately: a bath and a bowl of rhybite stew. Even though she smelled of swamp and mamidon turds, her belly took top priority.

The cafeteria was a large metallic geodesic of black and blue, the azure of Clan Vesta. Officers patrolled the columns, and Nalia greeted a group with a courtly bow as they passed. They acted as if they didn't notice her, although she knew they had. She shrugged it off and hung her coat of arms in the entryway.

Placing her spear casually on the weapons rack made only for blasters, she lifted her filthy helmet and put it on a hook beside. Her hair was matted flat from the weather, its usually vibrant orange dulled ruby red. Next, she kicked off her mud-caked boots, gasping from the burst of her own foot odor. Her scrubs were ripe and soaked brown from three rotations of body sweat and rain, trapped under her hefty armor.

The famished young woman grabbed a tray and approached the counter. Androids kept the buffet stocked with fresh rations, with a wide variety of options, yet no rhybite stew. *Just my luck.*

She settled on yhonid seed loaf, ghayn leaf salad, and four cinnamon swirl marvets for dessert.

Three VEOs fled the table quickly after Nalia took a seat near them, due to her stench or her social charms, she wasn't sure. She shrugged it off again, too exhausted to care. After ferociously devouring her meal, she chugged half a glass of dushnah milk and let out a thunderous belch. Sometimes her plebian origins shone through, despite her place in the Royal Guard.

"That sounded wholesome." A familiar, irritating voice came from behind. *Atalay's ass, wasn't three rotations enough? Calitro fucking Frigg.* "Is this seat taken? Where's Nimba? Numbo? Um, Nabu?"

"Inana is a large planet. There are many other places you could eat, Calitro." She waved an arm, gesturing to the rest of the tables. "And it's 'Noba,' as I'm sure you know." Her rudeness notwithstanding, the dwarf plopped himself down in the seat across from her with a huff. His buttery yellow beard and curly mop were puffed and frizzy and still damp from the showers. She could no longer blame the stench on him, as she'd done in the bush. He smelled of skylar rose cologne in his fresh white cape and taupe trousers, much to Nalia's chagrin.

"I just can't get enough of your company, sweetheart. Even though maybe ya *coulda* freshened up a bit," he said as he waved his hand beneath his nose to fan the odor. Several of his fellow VEO grunts began to fill out the table, including Frigg's commanding officer, Lieutenant Ivy Freya, who took the seat next to her. The dwarf creepily licked his lips and gave Nalia an unctuous grin. "Is it just me, or did we spirit-link out there in the sticks?"

"My foot is about to spirit-link with your balls," she snapped.

"I'm told the prince did not fare well," Freya said. "It must have been equally trying spending three cycles with Frigg. I commend your fortitude, Lady Chuku." Freya had overseen Nalia's recovery in Centralia. Her skin was fair, and she had large, round, umber eyes, with curled hair that arched at the bangs like a toppling wave in a sea of auburn.

"I knew the Sizwe would be no vacation, and the himpheah ants biting my backside *were* difficult to endure, but suffering Calitro's foul mouth was far more trying." Nalia enjoyed the comforting presence of another woman, and Ivy had an honorable manner, making her easy to trust. "And as I've said, it's just Nalia, if you please."

"See, I knew you felt it too, baby," Frigg said after he tossed back a pint of Nolwazi ale. "And let me add one thing, Lieutenant

Freya: 'the prince did not fare well' is a *colossal* understatement. I think watching her faith in Atalay pulverizing into the sod time and time again was worse than them bites on 'er sweet little ass."

Nalia scowled. "My faith in N'damu is unfazed, you shit."

Frigg roared in laughter and was joined by several of his fellow officers. "Mine was. That little wiener is going to rule the Tri-Worlds?" He snorted obnoxiously, spitting ale on his whiskers. "I thought their DNA was supposed to be *legendary*." He flitted his stubby fingers mockingly. "Genetic perfection, my ass!"

Freya giggled passively, but she only seemed to be humoring her fellow VEO. "Watch your tongue, Frigg," she ordered. "Please forgive the soldier talk, Nalia. It can grow coarse. This buffoon knows the Second Spear is loyal to her prince." Ivy wore a glossy violet suit of armor with long white gloves. Her shoulder armor displayed the Tri-Worlds emblem embroidered in red over a black field.

"Relax, tinkercane tits," Frigg said after a hefty belch. "Don't get yer little panties in a twist." *Even that idiot Frigg has power-weapon clearance. A true warrior doesn't need such a crutch!*

"You know, Calitro, if you're going to speak with the adults, might I suggest some manners," Nalia quipped. "And also perhaps a booster seat." *That neutron rifle would not help you against my spear.*

The little blond man reddened in anger, but he returned to his drink to cool off after seeing Freya's glare. The other men continued to laugh and snicker, which seemed to stoke his ego further. "I guess you know about booster seats," Frigg said. "Being nothing but a glorified babysitter. Do you burp that little grat too? Wipe his little backside and change his whiteys?"

Nalia kicked out her chair, sending it toppling behind her with a loud bang. "You will show Atalay your respect!"

He looked up at her from his seat with a satisfied grin and patted his rifle suggestively. "Yer a long way from yer fat king, sweetheart. You might wanna sit back down," Frigg said. "Besides, I can see it in your eyes: you're better at *taking* a shaft than swinging one."

That was the last straw. Nalia vaulted onto the table in a handstand. She grabbed a prong from her place setting and drove her heel into Calitro's face. The dwarf crashed onto his back with a thump. She landed on top of him and held the prong to his throat. "I need no spear to teach *you* respect, whelp," she said, completely losing her cool. "I'd cut your neck with my cutlery as easily as my loaf."

Before she could speak again, she heard several plasma rifles cocking simultaneously. The mechanical hum of their nuclear cores emanated as they charged. Red targeting dots speckled her face. Before Nalia could react, she felt the tip of a blaster poking into her hair.

"Desist immediately," Ivy Freya said as she pushed the barrel against her skull. A Seti-8, class five energy blaster, illegal to average Inaneans. Of course, Vestian weapons were unaffected by the coronal storm—and only VEOs were authorized to carry them. "Nalia, I worked hard to restore you after the fallout. If you want to keep that pretty little head, let reason prevail."

"The prince will hear of this," Nalia said as she tossed the prong aside. Then she stood up with her hands behind her head in surrender.

"Oh? You're going to disturb the prince's training because *you* lost your temper at dinner?" Ivy asked. Blood poured through the dwarf's fingers as he palmed his face. "You're better than that, Chuku—and you know interference is against orders. Princess Enahdra is in charge here. She will decide the best course. Until then, I must detain you. I'm sorry." At her order, four VEOs sprang to grab Nalia, quickly slapping restraints on her wrists.

She raged as they carried her off, kicking and screaming. The VEO men dragged her down the column of magnuses until they reached the deep blue hulk at the far end. The Ghost Ship was dark navy and at least half a size bigger—with twice as many proton cannons. The command "megamag" of Vesta Enforcement was Princess Enahdra's mobile palace. Nalia was brought up the loading ramp into a long cargo tunnel leading to the craft's bowels, a small prison hold where they put her in a tiny cell.

She gritted her teeth, clenching her fists tight. The situation seemed to match her own stink, which overwhelmed her senses again as she plopped to the floor. *There goes my bath, and I have guard duty in an hour.*

Soon enough, the princess emerged. Despite their mutual closeness to N'damu, she'd never been anything to Enahdra. It was a mutual disinterest—from rotation one, they had been content to ignore one another. Why would a princess want to be friends with an orphan natural? Worrying about it wasn't going to change anything. *I don't think she's ever even said my name.*

Surprisingly, Enahdra seemed as irritated by Nalia's imprisonment as she was, giving the order for her immediate release. The gate slid open as the blue-haired Vestian beauty walked up to her. A few paces from Nalia, however, she came to an abrupt halt.

"Sorry, I was supposed to be taking a bath right now."

"Quite all right. Still, I'll stand over here if it's acceptable." Enahdra held her hand to her mouth as though bracing for vomit.

"Of course."

"I've spoken to Lieutenant Freya, but I need to hear you now."

"I was just trying to eat quickly after three cycles on, but Frigg was spouting treason at the table," Nalia said. "I'm sorry, I lost my patience. It was not worthy of my post."

Enahdra gave her a troubled look. "Treason, you say?"

"Well, he was insulting N'damu. He was questioning his fitness to rule."

"Yes, well, Calitro Frigg is from another world," Vesta said with her graceful benevolence. "The culture of Oshun is not like ours. They are accustomed to a variety of behaviors considered unruly here on Inana. He struggles with our courtesies, but the

191

onus is on *us* as the higher society to set an example." She turned her back and began to pace away. "Being natural-born and adopted into a noble clan, surely you can appreciate variations in class?"

"I can," Nalia said. "As I said, I lost my temper. I was in the wrong."

"Frigg is my loyal man," Enahdra said. "And he is the most accurate marksman in the system—a master sniper. Spears are wonderful, and no one respects Sadah'anah more than I, but the true asset in this mission is keeping our distance. For N'damu's sake, wouldn't you agree?"

Nalia nodded.

"Also, perhaps we should not trouble N'damu with this drama."

Nalia nodded once again. She panicked when she noticed the time, however, and requested Princess Vesta's leave. She had to be in the Hall of Novojoh *right now*. N'damu was to begin his subsequent trial, and Noba had been on duty since the Sizwe. She sprinted from the Ghost Ship and made a break for her dushnah.

On the way out of camp, she passed Calitro Frigg exiting the medical tent with his nose wrapped in gauze. Even though she was in a hurry, Nalia still paused to offer her apology—he didn't seem to notice the obscene gesture on her way out.

She hopped on her mount and galloped across the plains with her frizzy orange curls flickering behind her like flames. The bitter odor of pollinating vharnum swallows assaulted her nostrils as their dust made waves of yellow smoke in her wake. Rancorous as the scent was, it was a welcome break from her own.

Thraxis was starting to sink in the sky, and she knew Noba would already be furious with her. "Heya, heya!" The ink-black dushnah ran hard to her calls. The white walls of Meadowdell quickly came up on the horizon. Nalia recklessly blew through the gates, dodging pedestrians as she trotted to the city center. There she jumped from her bone-horse, tossing it a jupiter fruit before sprinting to the Hall of Novojoh.

She took the stairs four steps at a time, putting on armor piece by piece as she ascended the complex's west wing. Nalia entered a sector with glass windows, white walls, and a large yellow door. There were instructions posted: *Do Not Enter without Adhering to Quarantine Protocols.* She pretended she hadn't seen it as she pulled on her helm and slipped through the doors.

The inside was much the same, walls of white with all-glass furnishing. It was a training facility for micro-organic bonding, with rows of glass benches facing a head table. All the seats were empty but the one front and center where N'damu sat, his lecture already underway. Today's instructor was Lady Sar'ah Novojoh, Kota of Throzeids. She was spirit-linked to Inana's most abundant species, making her one of the more formidable people on the planet. Throzeids communicated with pheromones, directing them in legions toward a chosen task within the body. Be it healing or harmful, this influence over people's internal systems could be a powerful tool or a dangerous weapon.

Nalia quietly scooted toward Noba, who kept guard, slouched, and fighting off sleep by the side of the entranceway. She hastily took up position next to him.

He sneered at her. "Where the hell have you been?" the lordling whispered.

She simply shrugged and put her finger over her lips, reminding him that he could not disturb the lesson. Flabbergasted, his face boiled brown to red as he marched out the door in silent fury.

I'm sure he will have plenty to say later. I'll probably never hear the end.

"...can control various functions of the body through pheromone manipulation. You see, N'damu," Sar'ah Novojoh explained, "throzeids amass in droves within all humans on Inana but themselves alone have little effect on us, living happily in our bloodstream biomes. We born on this planet think nothing of them, but visitors from Anu or Oshun often get throzeid illness. They regularly confuse this with rotation sickness—it's their bodies adjusting to the throzeid influx."

"So it's only the pheromones the throzeids *use* that can have effects on people?" N'damu asked.

"Yes, exactly. And only when manipulated in unnatural ways, through N'jikota. Alone about their daily business, the creatures would never influence noticeable amounts of any pheromone." Sar'ah displayed a pliable silicon sculpture of the human microbial landscape, conveying the creatures in action. "When I give them a little nudge, they can pollute you with enough toxin to have you vomiting in minutes."

"I've heard of G'higari healers. I've never heard of making someone sick," the prince said with a tinge of disbelief.

Sar'ah must have noticed his skeptical tone, shooting him a mischievous grin. "Is something the matter, N'damu?" she asked as she scooted up onto her glass desk and crossed her legs.

"No, why?" he asked with a crooked, confused grin.

"How does your stomach feel?"

A pale green washed over his suddenly sweaty face. "It's fine. I feel, fine … I feel … it's…" N'damu obviously tried to keep his composure, but it was clear he was *not* fine. He clutched at his belly as his face went ghostly white.

"Over there," Sar'ah said, pointing to a glass waste bucket. He made a desperate break for it, sliding down to his knees and barely getting his chin over the rim before spewing like a geyser. The greenish-brown fluid filled half the bucket as he convulsed again and again with loud eruptions. Nalia could see the little bits of undigested ghayn leaf and hunks of poorly chewed stew. *Hey, how'd HE get rhybite stew?*

"Apologies," Sar'ah said as she offered him a hand towel. He wiped his face, trying to stay collected and smacking his lips in disgust at the vomit's flavor. "Let me help with that."

"I think you've been helpful enough."

"Notice that feeling in your mouth?" she asked him. "It's a cleansing antitoxin. Better than any toothbrush. Your teeth will have never shined so white."

"Wow, I've never had fresher breath." He glanced back at Nalia and smiled, noticing for the first time she'd replaced Noba.

"And your stomach?"

He put his hand over his abdomen and grinned. "I feel fine now. Amazing, actually!"

"Indeed. Throzeids can do a lot more than that," Sar'ah said. The Novojoh girl was stunning. Nalia couldn't help a hint of envy. She adorned her long thick red hair with ulanoid feathers and colorful beads threaded on leather tassels. Her face was flawless, with amber eyes and lips that were creamy lavender. Sar'ah wore a traditional brown G'higari robe, tied up like a miniskirt—an untraditional fashion in the south.

The Kota of Throzeids gazed at her thoughtfully for a moment, as though sensing Nalia's attention. Then Lady Novojoh's grin turned mischievous. "Can I ask you something personal? Perhaps you can excuse your guard a moment if you aren't comforta—"

"No," N'damu interrupted. "Nalia knows me like no other." He looked back at her again, tuning into her gaze. Time and space went away for a moment, and they were the universe's sole inhabitants. "Ask me."

"Have you ever been … *with* someone, N'damu? A lover? Even a kiss?" she asked. Nalia's eyes strained to keep his stare,

196

but it flitted about the room like an uncontrollable hose before stopping bashfully at his feet. *Would he admit their encounter to her? Would he actually...*

"No ... never." The lie hurt, despite her relief.

Sar'ah hopped off her desk, flipped her hair, and approached N'damu. She leaned toward him until her nose was a fingernail's width from his. Her toes brushed the tips of his sandals. "Have you ever wanted to? A girl? A boy? Do Atalays have ... urges?"

"Of course, yes. But..." The prince tripped on his nervous words. "I'm an Atalay. I must be heedful."

"Really? Not even a kiss?" she asked. "Would *that* be so wrong?"

"No. Quite the opposite, I'm sure."

She started to step away, but out of nowhere, N'damu grabbed his instructor by the waist, pulling her close and kissing her with energetic enthusiasm. Nalia couldn't tell if Sar'ah was kissing him back, but it didn't matter. All she saw was N'damu's hands clawing at her backside. Struggling to maintain her composure, she grimaced in sickened derision. Luckily, it was not long before Sar'ah released her bewitching influence, and the man Nalia loved stepped off, shaking his head in a baffled haze. Regaining his faculties, the prince apologized as if *he* had chosen his actions.

Sar'ah gave a cute little giggle that made Nalia want to slap her. "No ... no. In time you'll come to realize it's *me* who owes the apology. But can you blame a girl for stealing a kiss from a handsome prince?"

Still in an intoxicated stupor, the kiss obviously on his mind, N'damu only grinned like a slobbering idiot. Undoubtedly, the rest of her lecture went in one ear and out the other before she dismissed him for supper.

"Don't forget the bucket," Sar'ah reminded him as she collected her things.

N'damu took the pail of puke and marched out as Nalia followed close behind. The moment they stepped out the door, he turned to her. "Why, when I'm holding a bucket of my retch, do I gag when I walk by you?"

Nalia blushed brighter than Ra as blood rushed to her cheeks from embarrassment. "Yeah." She dropped her head, having hit rock bottom. "Yeah … I'm disgusting. It's been a long rotation. Dump your vomit. I need a bath—obviously."

N'damu took off down the hall looking for a hygiene vestibule while Nalia waited. Suddenly, as if out of nowhere, her nasal passages felt the fantastic relief of cool, clean scentless air she'd not experienced for days.

"Thought maybe I could help you out with that," Sar'ah Novojoh said, passing on her way out. "It's a deodorizing pheromone. You're still dirty, however, so don't let the fresh smell fool you. You can still rash."

"Thank you," Nalia said with a polite bow. *What a bitch.*

198

"No worries," she replied. "Sorry I had to kiss your man in front of you. But you *did* contaminate my chamber, so I guess we're even?"

Is it the throzeids—or do I love her? The two ladies shook hands, sharing a sweet smile. "The prince is certainly not *my* man. Though I do apologize for my infraction all the same."

"Well, either the boy really wanted to kiss me, or today's lesson was an abject failure. He showed no resistance to throzeid pheromones," Sar'ah explained. "Your boyfriend will need to try again, it seems."

Annoyed now, Nalia reiterated the point more forcefully. "Again, he isn't my boyfriend. I am the prince's Second Spear."

"That *is* odd. You two have a pheromonal synchronicity characteristic of mating couples."

"Yeah, well, we're not a couple."

"Really? I'm seldom wrong abo—"

"You're wrong," Nalia insisted. Continuing their duel of courtesies, Sar'ah curtsied graciously and bobbed her head.

"See you at dinner." As she pranced away, she brushed her skirt down over her butt, back into place after N'damu's groping. As the Kota of Throzeids turned the corner, Nalia's love for her faded to indifference, though admittedly, she'd never smelled as fresh.

CHAPTER FIFTEEN

Enahdra II

Now

Enahdra Vesta unzipped her sky-blue dress and slipped it down, revealing her scandalous black two-piece. "Eyes on the prince," she said as she lay down in the sand to bask in the sun. Her VEOs all heeded her command, Rigel Kong, Ivy Freya, and Calitro Frigg all about-faced, keeping watch from the riverside. Noba, however, stared her down with a hanging jaw. She rolled over onto her belly, kicking her feet up over her backside and wiggling her toes. "Um, Noba! N'damu is out on the river, not under my bathing suit."

The Prince of Atalay was out wading in the water with S'ike Novojoh, Kota of Querghil. For the third rotation in a row, they'd come out to the wetlands at the eastern edge of the M'lilo Forest. These rivers were apparently the perfect place to commune with the amphibious slugs.

"Yes, Princess," Noba Sadah replied in a zombified tone. "What made you decide to grace the wild Sizwe with your presence this afternoon?"

She glanced out at N'damu, splashing in the water as querghil launched fountains from their blowholes. "Ivy said the beaches by this river were beautiful."

"Isn't it a little dangerous for someone so delicate?" Noba asked. "I might not be able to protect you *and* N'damu."

"Please," Enah said, sliding her specs down from her forehead and rolling onto her back. "Rigel Kong is with me." She pointed at the Oshunese Commander of the VEOs. "I'd imagine the Sizwe should be more worried about *him*." Kong's trench coat flapped over his black VEO armor. He never took it off, no matter the heat. He had more straps, holsters, and pouches than one could count—pulse rifles under his arms, an array of hand blasters around his waist, and a proton cannon on his back. "The man is a living weapon. I wouldn't be surprised if all his weapons had little weapons."

"A man who needs that many blasters is compensating for something." The lordling winked.

"Don't be jealous, Norbo. Your stick is cool too!" Calitro Frigg had a way of sneaking up.

"Thanks," Noba said with a proud grin, tapping his spear in the gravel. He never seemed to detect sarcasm. "It's Noba, actually."

"Looks like your deity is floundering again," Frigg said with a chortle.

"Who in the Barren Void would want to spirit link with a querghil?" Enah asked. N'damu and S'ike swam near the shore, hoping to hop on one of the creatures as they popped out of the water.

"Querghil are one of the strongest animals on Inana, Princess," Ivy Freya said.

"Strongest-smelling maybe," she replied. "On Earth, they had animals called hippos. Basically, small querghil with legs."

"There are animals on Oshun that would make a quick snack out of one of those fat fucking slugs." Rigel Kong lit a spliff as he stared out across the river. "The real alphas lurk in the Konga at night."

"Homo purists are the true alphas." Enahdra sat up, tying up her hair in a bun as she looked out at the action. N'damu flailed wildly in the water as a three-ton querghil came up from under him.

"Grab her spikes!" S'ike cried out from the water. The barb-covered worm flopped in and out of the river with N'damu on its back. The prince gasped for air each time the querghil came up, his cheeks puffing like bubbles on the way down. "The spikes. The spikes!" His hands seemed to slip each time he tried to grab one. N'damu screamed like a small child. "He senses your panic."

Waddling up onto the beach, the prince rolled off the querghil's back, tumbling through a gauntlet of spines before smashing into the mud.

Frigg burst out in laughter. N'damu looked over, sulking in the riverbed as S'ike Novojoh swam over and helped him up.

"Be quiet, dwarf," Noba said. "Enah, aren't your men supposed to be covert?"

"Shut up, Calitro," Enahdra said with a scornful tone. "Rigel, get the VEOs out of sight. You can take post up over the ridge." She pointed to a small hill looking over the valley.

"What about you, Princess?" Rigel signaled to Ivy and Calitro, and they began to march off.

"I'm lying on the beach, hardly noticeable."

"We can't leave you unguarded, Princess Vesta," Ivy said as she turned back. "Lord M'demke would have my head."

"I thought you already gave him your head," Frigg said with a chuckle as he did mock fellatio on his thumb.

Enah rolled her eyes. "Don't worry, Ivy. I am with the *legendary* Noba Sadah." She puckered her lips as she patted the ground next to her. "You'll stay here and protect me, won't you? Brave soldier of Sadah." She batted her long lashes as he plopped down next to her. "Now go, Commander. You'll have a better vantage from the hill anyways. You have your orders."

"Suit yourself," Rigel said as he toted his blasters up the riverbank in a huff.

Across the waterway, another group of querghil was exiting the river. S'ike hopped on the giant mother slug while pointing N'damu to the pups. "Try a little one," he yelled out.

"None are little, in my estimation," the prince replied, looking up at the two-thousand-pound baby querghil. S'ike held out his hand as if focusing some invisible energy. Then, much to Enah's surprise, the beast seemed to calm, and N'damu finally vaulted on.

"Hold tight," S'ike said. He lowered his hand as if relinquishing his hold, and suddenly the bony worm began to flail around the beach.

N'damu cheered, grinning from ear to ear as he straddled the slimy slug. Holding its shoulder spikes, he followed S'ike up and down the riverbed, slithering in and out of the grassy shallows. "Are *you* controlling him?" the prince asked. "Or am I?"

"It's not control, N'damu," the querghil kota replied, bouncing on his mount. "The querghil must want to heed your wishes. N'jikota is a consolidation of wants and desires."

Enah leaned over, her pink lips an inch from Noba's ear. "Sounds pretty sexy."

The lordling crinkled his nose, shuddering. "Nothing coming from S'ike Novojoh is sexy to me." The boy was portly and unrefined to be sure; his wild hair looked perpetually unkempt. The Novojoh was not an olden clan. Their lineage arose on Inana, genetically engineered from the start with this wild planet in mind.

"Oh, come now, he's only thirty-five," Enahdra said. "I think he's adorable." The prince's laughter echoed across the river. "I bet he has a big—"

"Gross!" Noba seemed to shudder.

"Very mature, Noba!" A parade of young baby querghil scurried from the water and circled S'ike Novojoh, snorting playfully. She could smell the bitter odor of their moss-covered hides, even from her side of the river.

"Well, we don't all mature as fast as *you*, Enah," Noba said.

She shot him a poisonous scowl, then rolled away onto her side. "I don't know what you're talking about." But of course she knew *exactly* what he was talking about—in fact, the entire Tri-Worlds knew Enahdra Vesta's dirty secret.

Twelve cycles ago

The ambiance of rainfall filled the throne room as the storm season raged. The courtiers and councilors seemed glower like the weather outside, glazed over, sulking in their seats as Enahdra's father announced the speakers in succession. The princess, however, was enamored with the politics of it all. No issue disinterested her, whether it be border disputes, quarrels regarding taxation or trade, weddings, and name-days, parturition celebrations or funerals, Enah's eyes were always wide open in court.

King N'joku, on the other hand, seemed less engaged, to say the least. His legs draped over the arms of the Seat as he laid back, half asleep. *Disgusting,* Enah thought. *How can he not care about his kingdom?* She watched his gut shrink and expand. His golden toga looked soiled with sweat and stained with blotches of sauce. *How can this oaf shepherd humanity anywhere, other than perhaps the buffet?*

Prince N'damu sat off to the side, playing holo-games. As always, he had his little natural friend by his side. "Ahdia, imagine if Father made a natural orphan a member of *our* guard?" She shuddered. "Ahdia. Can you imagine?" She looked over at her sister. "Ahdia!"

"Wha–what?" Ahdia Vesta jerked awake, shaking out her silky blue hair.

"How can you be sleeping?"

"Uhhh, how can you be awake is a better question, Enah." She crossed her arms and let her head go limp again.

Enah looked up at the Seat again. Queen Anaqua sat on the other side, with Ala and Aku. In front of them, N'joku's chancellors stood in a line. Other than her father, they all looked expressionless—vacant and without focus. *Thank Khanya for Father. At least someone here cares.*

"Sorry I'm late," a voice called out, reverberating through the throne room. The princess looked back over her shoulder as the court collectively gasped. Enah's cheeks went pink as her dimples raised. "Blasted rotations are hard to get used to when you come from a planet that doesn't spin." N'joku Atalay's ward, Theodus Darius, stumbled down the crimson carpet, past the court of callers, and up to his seat beside the king.

"Lord Commodus has no trouble," Enahdra's father said with a cold frown. "Nor do any of the countless Anutians here today."

"It is incredibly disrespectful to interrupt these proceedings, young Darius." The queen scolded him sternly. Enahdra might have been in awe if she could take her attention away from Theodus for a single second.

"I love his hair," Enah whispered. Ahdia made only a soft wheeze, on the verge of snoring. "And his eyes, they're bluer than the oceans of Earth." As soon as he sat down, he scanned the court. Enahdra scooted up, sitting as tall as she could until finally, he noticed her, flashing a kinked grin as they locked stares.

"My love," the king said, his voice booming, loud enough for all of Inana to hear. "Theodus has that Darius blood." He patted him on the shoulder with a hoot. "That Izlagosi passion for life that cannot be bottled ... right, Son?"

"Absolutely." Theodus nodded, clearly disinterested in anything but Enahdra. "Right." It felt like they were alone somehow, concealed in an attraction that seemed to transcend reality's limitations. Enah's forehead beaded with sweat as her heart pounded faster. The feeling was alien to her, an all-new fire deep within. She bit her bottom lip, fighting the urge to run up to him.

Her interest in court disappeared as callers came and went. Theodus wetted his lips with his tongue, winking at her with a smoldering expression. He was sixty-seven cycles—exactly twice her age. *Twenty-six in Earth years,* she'd thought. She knew he was too old for her on either world. And that he was not "Atalay" enough for Father's approval. Still, she didn't care. Enahdra wanted him. She shot a coy smile, brushing her index finger down her neck and across her chest.

After another hour of ogling, Enah nodded toward the hall, ever so slightly. Theodus stood up, interrupting two squabbling nobles as they argued over an inheritance. "If you will excuse me." He bowed low to the king, who was again barely awake. "I need to tinkle." N'joku waved him off. Enah's father scoffed as the lordling skipped around him.

She glanced at her sister as Theodus disappeared through the archway, exiting the throne room. "Ahdia, I'm not feeling well. I'm going back to the suite for a nap." Her head was hanging to the side as she snored away. "Tell Father, okay?" Ahdia mumbled in her sleep. "I'll take that as a yes," Enah said before slipping down the aisle and out of the throne room.

"Is something wrong, little princess?" a guard asked. Enahdra had a trick for times like these.

"I am having a feminine issue," she replied, looking up at the burly man in golden armor.

He immediately looked up, scratching at his neck. "Oh … um." *Naturals are so dumb.* "You mean … um. You're … uh—"

She grimaced and clawed at her abdomen. "Oh my. Cramps…" She didn't have a menstrual cycle, but what natural would question a purist girl her age on such things? "Do you want to check down there yourself? It's a bloodbath."

The golden sentry cringed and nodded her on. Enah hurried down the hall, groaning and pretending to favor her belly. The moment she turned the corner, however, someone grabbed her and pulled her behind the tapestries. She'd thought it was a guard for a moment until she felt a frenzy of kisses moving up her neck.

"Oh, Theodus," she said as she wrapped her arms around his neck and her legs around his waist. He smelled like japhid spice and ganja smoke. His stubble was rough against her skin as he slid his cheek up across her chin and kissed her. The passage of time became impossible to track. Eventually, they came up for air, poking their heads out. The moment the hall was clear, they took off running, hand in hand.

Every time they passed a granite column or a statue large enough to hide behind, he pulled her in for another secret kiss. "My father will kill you if he finds out about this."

"Come now," he whispered, gasping for air between kisses. "You heard the king. I have that old Darius blood." He put his warm tongue back in her mouth.

"The king is *not* my father." Enah brushed her fingers through his blonde coif. "Father takes his daughters' courtship very seriously. We are a prized asset."

"I don't want to be your husband," he said. She could feel his hardness grinding against her dress.

"But my fath—" Theodus pressed his finger across her lips.

"Don't worry, My Princess." He sniffed around her neck with an animalistic moan. "*He's* not your father anymore." The Anutian's words perplexed her. "*I'm* your daddy now, and you're going to listen to me." Enah knew she should be offended—repulsed and upset. Intrigue, however, was her only sensation. "You're mine now. My property. *My* prize asset." Her body was ablaze as his hands moved over her dress, groping her curves ravenously.

Enahdra had never felt such a rush. "Yes, Daddy."

Now

Rain began to patter down as clouds rolled over the Sizwe. Enah sat up and tied back her long hair, peering across the banks. N'damu and S'ike still roared with laughter. The querghil seemed delighted to play in the rain, slipping and sliding through the mud with the boys on their backs.

Noba was less content. "I can't stand any more of this rain." He cozied up to Enahdra as if to keep *her* warm. "Where the hell is Chuku? It's her time to babysit."

"You're going to just leave me out here?" she asked. Enah bumped his shoulder playfully.

209

Seemingly out of nowhere, Noba leaned over, puckering his lips for a kiss. *What the fuck.* She slapped him away. "Noba! No."

"I–I'm sorry." He hopped up and grabbed his spear, pacing down the riverbank before turning back. "I don't understand. Why do you pretend to be so virtuous, Princess?"

"I'm not here for that—"

He laughed, bobbing his shoulders. "Whatever, Enah. I don't care. We're both young and attractive. I thought to myself, 'why not.'"

"You should have your eye on your prince, First Spear of Atalay."

"Khanya knows *you've* never done anything inappropriate." Noba's eyes rolled back to their whites as he threw up his arms. Enah wasn't sure, given his limited grasp of sarcasm, but he seemed to be mocking her. "Maybe I should get my whips and make you call *me* Master." He laughed so hard, he choked.

The princess's face flushed. She popped up and slapped the lordling. "You'd never be worthy of a Princess of Vesta."

"Atalays ass, Enah." Noba scoffed. "I will be the Lord of Sadah. General of an army that carries my name—the greatest standing army of all time. None under Atalay are more worthy."

Enahdra looked out at N'damu. "Maybe I am not willing to settle for less than Atalay." *Not this time,* she thought, shielding her face from rain as she watched the prince.

"Try to make them circle now," S'ike yelled out. The querghil chaotically splashed around the shallows of the riverbed as N'damu held his hand out. His brow curled as he tried to focus his will. Enahdra felt a pull stirring inside as she watched the prince's determination. She'd never been attracted to him, not like her father would have wanted. Yet watching him, out in the elements—when she squinted just right—he looked handsome. *Maybe his muscles will fill out.*

A blast suddenly rang out, echoing across the water. Enahdra looked to the ridge. "What was that?" The querghil began to scatter as blaster fire erupted from the tall grass.

"Bandits!" Noba shouted as he sprinted into the water with his spear twirling. "With energy weapons? How?"

One of the blasts landed in S'ike's gut. With an agonized grunt, he hit the mud. Without the Kota of Querghil to soothe them, the bony slugs flailed and thrashed in panic, throwing N'damu as they broke for the river.

"Agents of the Volturis! N'damu!" Enahdra shouted as she waved to the ridge. Armed bandits began to spring from the bushes as she watched from the opposite banks. Noba was a quarter way across the river. *He'll never make it in time.* "Where is my firepower?" Their green rhybite-leather hoods were stitched to long flowing broadcloth capes—garb typical to tribesmen of the M'lilo forest. *The savages had better not harm N'damu.*

The prince staggered through the mud as the bandits moved in on him. By incompetence or design, their erratic shots seemed to land all around the prince. The mother querghil launched itself out of the water as the enemies converged, taking N'damu in their sights, point-blank. The beast lashed its long pink tongue, coiling it around him before lapping him up into her mouth as the bandits opened fire. His horrendous screams went mute as the animal swallowed him whole, then dashed back into the water.

"N'damu!" Enahdra screeched in horror. "No! No–no–no."

The Womb Of Inana

Twelve cycles ago

"No–no–no," Enah said, scoffing. "Drugs are for naturals. I'm not going to poison myself with that nonsense." She sat in Theodus Darius's bed as he pushed a tray of yellow powder in front of her. The Ward of N'joku had a palace of his own in the north wing of the Tower of Atalay. He had his own guard as well, Izlagosi legionaries loyal to Clan Darius alone. Over the past oct, she'd become adept at sneaking into his chambers. It appeared every servant in the tower had a price.

"Do as Daddy says. Ether will only expand our love—our passion." Using an Eden's Ace card, he scraped the powder into neat lines and handed her a small tube. "Close one nostril and suck it up through *this* with the other." She didn't want to. The room was already spinning from the two bottles of Vhimhilian vintage he'd ordered her to drink. Ganja smoke clouded the posh chamber, and their clothes were strewn about the floor amongst the whips, paddles, leather binds, and chain restraints. Speakers pounded with Anutian dance-pop as he leaned over and kissed her again. His lips were so delicate and thoughtful. "I love you, Princess. No. My *Queen*!" She grinned, blinking like a rapid-fire blaster.

"Okay, Theodus." Enahdra reached for the straw, but he pulled it away at the last moment.

"Ah, ah, ah." His finger waved in her face.

"Okay … My King!" He handed it to her with a satisfied smirk. Without hesitation, she snorted up the lines of ether. The princess fell back on the mattress, suddenly happier than she'd ever been. Theodus kissed her again as the world began to beat like a heart. *He is perfect. We are complete together. Father wants me to be queen—and now I am.*

"Oh, My Queen," he said, bouncing up on the bed, bowing as he laughed hysterically. "You are truly a vision meant to sit atop the Tower of Atalay." She lay back and writhed through the sheets like a querghil in mud, laughing so uncontrollably, she thought she might vomit. "Not that fat degenerate, N'joku." Theodus held up his pinky finger. "Or that little cock, N'damu."

"It should be a real man," Enah said. He bounded back down next to her, and she ran her hands through his blonde hair. "Someone with a golden crown already."

Suddenly, screams rang from outside the door. Izlagosi guards shouted a warning before an eruption of blasts silenced them. "What the fu—" Theodus sprang back up.

The princess continued to chuckle as she sniffed up her nasal runoff. Sounds of battle ensued right outside the door as Theodus stumbled for his sword in a panic. "This ether is so exciting," Enah said, smiling as she slid off the edge of the bed backward, propping herself up on her head as her hair spilled out on the carpet like an indigo ocean. "Did ya know on Earth they got drugs from plants?" She writhed with laughter as the blaster fire shook the chamber. "Yeah, where humans evolved, psychedelics grew from the ground like magic."

"My Queen, you need to hide," Theodus said, kicking the bondage gear under the bed. Suddenly, her stomach churned. "Do as Daddy says, now—" Enahdra began to spew yellowish vomit. It ran down her face like a river as she hung upside-down, mixing with her hair before she fell over.

213

The door burst open. "There she is," a voice shouted. *Rigel?*

A stream of blood spattered her face the moment Enahdra looked up. Commander Kong mauled Theodus as a troop of VEOs surrounded him. Ivy Freya picked her up, cradling her as she moaned. "No," Enah said. "No, don't hurt him."

"Lord Vesta's orders, Princess," Ivy said as she brushed the sick from her hair.

"I–I." Every time Theodus tried to speak, Kong bludgeoned him in the gut. Still, his love for her was so real, and he would not be denied. "I—love—you."

Rigel dealt him a knockout uppercut as Ivy carried her out of the topsy-turvy room and back to the Lord Chancellor's chambers.

Now

Enahdra knew what it felt like to be swallowed by a monster. She looked on in tears, helpless as the querghil's shadow disappeared underwater. The M'lilo forest bandits turned their fire on Noba, screaming in their savage, broken tongue. He dove down to avoid their blasts as Enah hid behind a mass of stones.

"They work for the Volturis!" Enah shouted.

The bandits converged around S'ike Novojoh, picking the wounded boy up by the hair and holding him out. Another came up with a sword cocked, ready to execute the young Novojoh. However, just as he began to swing, a barrage of sniper fire came from upriver. S'ike hit the mud with a thump, the bandit's severed arm landing on top of him. The errant sword swing landed in another bandit's chest, too far embedded for him to pull out.

Noba sprang from the water, twirling his wet spear before hurling it into the heart of the swordsman. The Sadah lordling somersaulted forward, regaining his spear as ten more bandits piled on him. Blasts ricocheted off his armor as Noba severed arms and legs like a gardener sheering weeds.

Ivy and Frigg ran in with their VEOs on their tail—six in total. They blasted the pile as bandits overwhelmed Noba, bludgeoning him with swords, axes, and spears. Frigg unloaded his hand blaster as Ivy ran up to the mound, executing bandits at point-blank range with her pulse rifle. The forest tribe was outclassed by the VEOs' firepower.

Where the fuck is Kong? Enahdra thought as she peeked out over the rocks to assess the action.

Ivy Freya called back her men as she threw a proton detonator. "Eyes up!" A dazzling white light flashed, disintegrating six opponents in an instant. A moment later, an outlaw drove an axe into her armor repeatedly, screaming tribal war calls. He mounted her as she fell, ripping off her helmet and raising his weapon for a kill strike. A deluge of bloody guts was all that hit her, however, as Noba's blade tore through his stomach. The First Spear lifted the bandit off Ivy, his carcass sliding down the spear's shaft like a fresh maraphite, skewered to barbecue. She quickly returned the favor, blasting two more attackers as they flanked Noba.

"Thanks," Freya said as he helped her to her feet and handed her back her helmet.

Noba simply nodded. "Lieutenant."

With the six VEOs behind him, Calitro focused his fire on the tree line as more and more enemies emerged. Despite his expert marksmanship, three more outlaws sprang from the woods, replacing every one they dispatched.

Enah mumbled to herself as she clenched her fists. "Atalay's ass! Where is Rigel? What will the optics be if my VEO commander is off taking a piss while N'damu is assassinated?"

Noba and Ivy fought back-to-back. Freya used her spent rifle as a club as the lordling of Sadah jabbed his spear at anyone who came too close.

"We need to end this. Now!" Noba said. "The prince may yet still live."

Ivy swung the butt of her rifle into a bandit's face. His jaw exploded as blood and teeth rained down. "Frigg. Boys! Cut loose," she cried out. "Leave it all on the field."

The dwarf charged the tree line with the VEOs cheering. "For Vesta! For Atalay!"

Even from across the river, Princess Vesta could sense the shift. Noba continued to cut them down like a butcher cleaving schmigs. Ivy's armor glistened as she fought, its violet plating soaked in crimson. Finally, Frigg and the VEOs unloaded the last of their charges.

"Fucking stick-hurling mongrel shits," Frigg shouted with a callous scowl, throwing his last detonator into the trees. The foliage became a black silhouette as the light pulse burst.

With that, the tribesmen's tone shifted. Their M'lilo-tongued chants clearly changed from ones that meant *charge* to ones that meant *retreat*.

216

Enahdra stepped out from behind the rocks in a huff. Her indigo hair was matted to her face as the rain began to intensify. She scanned the river for a sign—a hope N'damu might be alive. *I have failed, Father,* she thought. *Again.*

Twelve cycles ago

"You have failed me, Enahdra." Her father stood over her with his monolithic headdress eclipsing the chandelier's soft glow. "You have shamed Vesta. I would expect this sort of nonsense from Ahdia."

"What in the Barren Void does that mean, Father?" her twin asked, visibly shocked by the insinuation. "I'd never fuck that yellow-headed—"

"SILENCE!" M'demke Vesta glowered over Enahdra as he pointed to the doors. "Get out, Ahdia." Enah could only weep. Her throat was too sore from crying to speak. Lips chapped and her head pounding with migraine, the princess's palms had bloody scratches from her clamped nails.

"Awww. And miss all this fun? Happily, Father." Ahdia smirked and gave a sarcastic salute as Ivy Freya escorted her out.

"Kong. You as well." Vesta pointed the Oshunese commander to the exit. "I want to be alone with my daughter." Rigel shrugged as he followed Ivy out and shut the door behind with an echoing clang. Resting his arms on his hips and tapping his foot, Lord Vesta's grimace sank even deeper. Her father's brow was a sea of black wrinkles—his ice-cold eyes suspending her animation like a freeze ray.

"I love him, Father."

"Your love is not yours to give him, I'm afraid." He clenched his jagged yellow teeth. "You are a product of Vesta. I thought you had some idea of what that means."

"I know what it means!" *YOU don't understand.*

Scorn filled his disgusted gasp. "You have responsibilities that far exceed yourself. You are not '*a*' Princess of Vesta; you are '*THE*' Princess of Vesta. Ahdia was too wild from the start." He turned away, shaking his head. "The people of N'gaia have already poisoned and defiled you. It was too soon to bring you here."

She choked on her mascara-filled tears, falling before him in desperation. "I will live up to my responsibility." *As soon as I get out of here, I'm going back to him.*

"My son dead, and now this." He dropped his head and sulked, removing his headdress to expose what thin wires of steel-gray he had left. "Perhaps, there is still time to domesticate Ahdia. But I fear it is not in her to understand the secrets of Vesta."

"What, Father?"

"You are not a child of Khanya. This crude planet could never design you. You were created above the light—for a much grander purpose than being a queen."

"Am I not human?" she asked, sniffling and pushing her hair back. "Aren't purists created to love?"

"You are more creator than creation," he said. "Your DNA is the universe, refined to a self-realized ideal."

"Enough of your riddles, Father!"

"I say this now, only to you, Daughter." He kneeled and helped her to her feet. Forcing his version of a smile, he looked into her eyes with unemotional sincerity. "We are the gods of shadow—sculpting shapes in beams of light. Atalay is an empty figure, cast on the wall by our benevolent hands. We are the shepherd's shepherd."

Enah broke down in tears again. *I just want to be a girl.*

Now

The VEOs kneeled in respect at the edge of the river. Enah sulked on her knees next to Noba as he broke down, inconsolable, it seemed. *N'damu, you can't be dead.*

Suddenly, something stirred in the bushes. She turned to see Rigel trudging out of the forest.

"Where *were* you?" Noba shouted. He grabbed his spear and marched at Rigel Kong until the two were nose to nose. Blows were clearly imminent, Enahdra stepped between the alpha men.

"Rigel was guarding *me*, Noba! I was afraid bandits might come from this side." She lowered her head and sighed. "I thought you would get to N'damu in time."

Noba fell to his knees in despair. Rigel cleared his throat. "Just following orders." Enah squinted at him suspiciously. *He is a terrible actor.*

"I can't believe we failed," Ivy said. "May N'damu fly the atranoch in the Eternal Womb." Enah couldn't escape a strange tickle in her stomach—a whisper in her ear telling her he was still alive.

"Can't you purists just cook up another one?" Frigg asked. "Maybe add a few muscles?"

"Have some respect, Calitro," Enahdra said as she patted Noba's shoulder. She noticed S'ike Novojoh sitting up on the beach. "Young Novojoh? Are you hurt?" The fat boy stood up and inspected his belly.

"Looks like a graze." S'ike stretched out his arms, surveying the carnage.

"That's not how it works anyways, Frigg," Ivy said, trembling as tears rolled down. "A purist Atalay is born the same clone at birth, but they become their own person from there. Environment and experiences shape them. You don't simply make another."

Frigg lit up a spliff and shrugged as he puffed.

"Rest in peace, kid," Rigel said, saluting out to the river. A tear ran down Enahdra's cheek. *But, I still feel … something.*

S'ike chortled, a laugh from deep within his belly. "So dramatic. Those bandits are lucky I was out." He held his hand up and closed his eyes. A ripple formed that soon crested to a mini-tidal wave. Out of the cascade, the mother querghil flopped out. With a wet, booming heave, the mammoth beast regurgitated N'damu—puking him up, covered in pink mucus and bubbly white phlegm.

Noba's eyes lit up. "N'damu!" He ran up and carried him back up the shore. "Thank Khanya."

"Querghil are very protective," S'ike pointed out. "They sometimes swallow their babies for weeks to guard against nagas or crongrins." He laughed like it was a common occurrence. "Noba, did you forget your N'jikota training?"

The lordling didn't respond as he hugged and kissed his prince, right on the slimy mouth.

Enahdra clapped her hands. "Well, everything worked out, just as I planned. Querghil expedition was a wild success, wouldn't you say? Though, I think I'll sit out for the rest of the N'jikota training, N'damu. If that's okay."

Everyone stared at her with blank, vacant expressions. The prince only hacked up an oozing ball of gelatinous spew, then gave her a thumbs-up.

CHAPTER SIXTEEN

Myriam III

A Yosai is not a shadow: a warrior must cast no impression on the physical world.

A Yosai is not a silent breeze; a warrior must be an absence of air, rendering wind impossible.

A Yosai is not empty space or a dark void, imperceptible in the cosmos. A warrior must truly be nothing at all.

The mantras repeated ceaselessly in Myriam Yamada's mind as she traveled across the vast continent of Vrinas. She had not been home in a very long time—a duality of honor compelled her to return as much as to stay away.

She couldn't help but crack a smile as her maglev train came within eyeshot of Long Zenya. The Anutian city had walls that had been ancient long before the empire. Its people and traditions were as old as the first states of Anu.

"It started as a refugee haven," an elderly gentleman said, winking through magnified spectacles from two seats over. "The City of the Dragon's Breath, they called it."

Myriam nodded. "A place for lost souls to begin a new path in life." She stared out of the glass hyper tube as the train slowed at the city limits. Her pink hair—her sword—concealed under a black cloak. "The question is, what is it now?"

"I think people come to find focus, these rotations. To get away from society at large." The man chuckled to himself. He clearly had a story of his own. "Soldiers, fighters—mages and prophets." *Which am I?* she wondered.

"Slaves?" Myriam added. "Social outcasts." *All of the above in some form or another.*

He shrugged, twitching his silvery whiskers. "Iron sharpens iron in Long Zenya."

"It is true. Long Zenya was a warrior's utopia," she said. Her face was blank—emotionless. "A place of brutal reform, with a fierce code of integrity—a place to perfect yourself." Myriam missed it very much.

The city was on the Tropic of Dawn and had an eternal sunrise to the west, sitting in a constant river of foggy mist flowing in from the Dragon Sea. Stone walls and ocean surrounded the urban center, and inside was a city lost in time.

As the train came out of the tube, Myriam calmly left her seat and walked to the rear. Unnoticed by the security guards, she slid into the cargo hold at the caboose. The maglev slowed coming into the station, and she slipped out through an access hatch, avoiding all eyes.

The city was a difficult place to infiltrate, even for a master of stealth. Luckily for Myriam Yamada, she was so much more. She moved through Long Zenya like a whisper on the wind.

Chiseled, vine-covered hedges lined the white stone streets, shielding her from detection. Steeped in vapor, they interconnected the city's intricate wooden houses and majestic marble temples. She'd come to visit the most monolithic shrine on Anu: the Temple of O'jod. It was a towering pagoda on the city's eastern edge, white-walled with brown, red, and gold eaves. There sat the high Clan Shingen and the home to the Knights of Yosai.

Long Zenya was policed relentlessly by the Disciples of Yosai, as she knew all too well. Fortunately, she recognized their routines, all their tendencies, and techniques, having trained many herself.

It was the beginning of the light side of Anu's "night" iteration. Most of the population was asleep in their light-proofed abodes, hidden away from the eternal dawn. Night-phase was the best time to avoid attention. She moved only in shadows, working through back alleys and underpasses, phasing through the city like a ghost. Her business in Long Zenya would be bitterly short and would require flawless intangibility.

For access to O'jod, she would need help—and those aiding her could not be aware of it.

She made her way to the northwest end to the armored holding facility known as Kejima Prison. A tomb of stone and steel, the Yosai incarcerated some of the Tri-Worlds' most dangerous criminals here. She'd put her share here when she was Yon Astra, before her exile.

The prison's security was unblemished—zero breaches. However, that rotation, Myriam planned to break in *and* out. She would come and go as she pleased. Bars may as well have been turnstiles as she entered the hold undetected.

Behind the ten-foot concrete walls was an exercise yard where hardened inmates enjoyed what leisure they could. Spying from the rafters, Myriam was seeking one particularly despicable low life in the crowd: Mok J'honda.

"What? Chu think I'm some kinna asshole? Eh, Asshole?" A particularly obnoxious voice in the crowd sounded like just the right kind of scum.

"Mok … I sw–sw … I'm tellin' truth … I swear it," a whinier man replied.

"Listen up, Nibs, you stupid grat shit. None o' these subhuman scumbags believe a single word pouring outch'yo cum guzzler." Mok had a dry, croaking laugh—even *it* had his thick Vedian accent somehow.

"I swear it, guys," Nibs replied. "That sexy songstress—Spring Graysong? I fucked 'er backstage in Zrilas! On my honor."

"Atalay's *ass*. You neva fucked nothin' 'cept ya palm … much less no Spring-mother-fuckin'-Graysong. Now sit yo grat ass down." Mok was clearly the alpha scumbag.

"Y'aint got no honor, neither, Nibs!" Voices from the crowd of prisoners called out. "Lying sack of schmig shit."

"I fucked 'er raw, trust me. Said she ain't never had no bigger—"

"I fucked Quinn Darius last night-phase!" J'honda thrust his pelvis in the air. Soon enough, all the deprived prisoners were shouting their fictitious exploits.

"I 'ad Ala and Aku in a three-way, and dey was begging fer more."

Mok J'honda's guttural chuckle was easy to track. He was a keg of a man with thick arms and bandy legs. Bald with one eye of brown and another of black glass, his skin had a greenish shade. Though he'd claim he was a natural, there was some apparent chlorosapien heritage in him.

Suddenly the horn sounded, signaling the end of exercise time. Each inmate lined up like a trained dushnah and marched back to their cells. Most guards in Kejima were automated androids, and Myriam knew all their program coding and how to exploit it. Finding a stasis panel, she quickly deactivated the air pressure sensors in the ventilation system and disappeared into the ducts. All too familiar with this stronghold's layout, the former Yosai silently crawled to Sector 6, Mok J'honda's subdivision.

226

Myriam had a particular interest in Mok because she knew he had the specific interest of another. The lowlife was the first in a series of dominos she needed to set up in Long Zenya. He could draw out a former pupil—one who could be her key to the Temple of O'jod.

Myriam played out the cinematic in her mind. Her history with Yukimuro Ito, a street thief when Myriam had found her, picking pockets and selling her body. Yuki was an empty vessel, enslaved by the whoremonger, this piece of mamidon shit, Mok-fucking-J'honda. The girl had a case of loving her captor. When the Yosai shut down Mok's Palace in Ogata, Yukimuro had fought tooth and nail for him.

J'honda'd made hostages of his own girls when Myriam and her team of Disciples raided his holdfast that day-phase. Yuki included. The gangster beheaded three girls before he took Yuki and held his spazer to her throat. Myriam let fly three throwing blades. Each struck true, the first down the barrel of his blaster. Then one to his kneecap and one to his eye, which exploded with a bloody pop. Mok fell in a screaming heap and curled up weeping in the fetal position.

Myriam sheathed the Sword of Pegasus and offered her hand to the frightened girl. She was only feigning victimhood, however; Yukimuro Ito came at her like a feral naga. She drove a blade into Myriam's stomach before being besieged by Yosai.

The Yon Astra buried her emotions, allowing herself no grief. *It's not like a Yosai could have children anyway,* she'd thought. While Mok and all his henchmen went to Kejima, Myriam took Yuki as a protégé.

She trained her hard. When the girl tried to escape, Myriam brought her back. When the girl tried to attack her, Myriam put her in her place. In time, Yuki grew into a committed Disciple of Yosai and a dangerous warrior in her own right. After Myriam's banishment, Yukimuro got a new teacher. *Let's not get ahead of ourselves—one domino at a time.*

Like flipping off a holo-movie, she snapped back to reality. J'honda lay on his cot, smoking some Vanilla Daydream he'd smuggled in. He tapped his feet to the ceaseless march of the sentry androids patrolling the corridors, singing in horrid atonality.

Myriam silently scrutinized his cell as the buffoon screeched like a dying ulanoid. She delicately opened a panel in the shaft wall and synched her comp-band to the access grid. Fortunately, the security codes were unchanged, and she effortlessly hacked into the prison's mainframe. *Time for the patrol to take a break.*

"The sweat of your ... um, something something ... heat of your kiss, something, somethin-ternal bliss." For all her training, nothing could have prepared her ears for such an onslaught. Mok sang on nonsensically but suddenly lost his beat as the sentry's metronomic marching ceased. "What in Atalay's asshole?!"

The incarcerated fool looked to the door of his cell. The light on its handle, usually red, now flashed a vivacious green. His grin streaked ear to ear. Mok J'honda grabbed a blade he'd hidden under his cot and bolted out of the door. Slamming the cell behind him, however, he tossed the knife down. "Kida and Kiyoma," he said. "Bless your *fucking* hearts!" He lit up like a young boy on a holiday morning when he saw what she had left for him: a

228

charged proton cannon. He made no hesitation in disintegrating half of Sector 6, then breaching the outer walls in his escape.

With Mok J'honda loose in Long Zenya, she would not have to wait long for the second domino to fall. Following the freshly minted fugitive, Myriam weaved like a serpent through the trees, under wooden decks, and over bushy hedges. J'honda made his way to the city center. Obviously anticipating pursuit, perhaps he hoped to do the unexpected by hiding in the middle of town. But, more likely, he was a complete imbecile wanting to get his drunk on.

He slipped into a small dive in the lower downtown district as Myriam settled in a tree overlooking it. She held her comp-band to her lips. "Send it." An anonymous prerecorded message to the Yosai authorities transmitted, informing them of J'honda's escape from Kejima. She knew who they would send after this specific scumbag.

She had to wait less than five minutes before patrons began pouring out of the establishment, screaming. *Subtle the man is certainly not.*

Her bait had done the trick. Soon after, the prey she hoped to ensnare came sniffing—Yukimuro Ito arrived on her X-Fantom jet bike. Drifting to a halt, she threw down her helmet and ran to the front of the tavern to question the civilians. Myriam was relieved Yuki hadn't detected her presence immediately—her former student had much to learn still.

"He went in and just started shooting up the place," said a tall, thin man.

"He's crazy," added an old Inanean woman with fire-red hair. "Flipped 'is lid 'cause nobody had ether. This is Long Zenya. Ain't none of that shit 'ere, eh!"

"Don't worry. Please, stay out here and don't let anyone come in. Can I count on your cooperation?" Yuki asked. She had a petite frame, five-feet-tall, with short indigo hair tied in a tight bun on top. Her eyes were slanted and sparkled with a purple hue. She dressed scantily for a Yosai, but it was her style: straps of black leather covering only her essential bits.

She's grown up, the feral child gone. She's a Yosai warrior now. Myriam was still proud, even though the girl had turned on her long ago—with the rest of them.

Yukimuro entered the tavern, locking the door behind her as the onlookers began to amass. First, there were a couple of blasts before the pounding of fists to skulls started to emanate. Myriam could hear Mok J'honda gasping for breath, accompanied by periodic thumping. "Uh, uh, uh," Yuki grunted to an intermittent pounding. Crashes and bangs sounded as furniture broke and glasses met with the floor tiles. *Is she killing him in there?*

Myriam made her way through a window in the upper tier to improve her vantage on the conflict. Her eyes grew wide as planet Ra when she looked in.

Atop the bar lay J'honda while Yuki straddled him, writhing in sexual ecstasy. The two fucked violently on the countertop. Chairs toppled to the floor as glasses fell from overhanging racks with successive crashes. His hairy bare ass made a streaking sound, like a cloth wiping mirror foam, as he pushed his manhood up inside her. The grunts she had thought accompanied punches now supplemented squishing sounds of sex.

For a split-second Myriam feared she had miscalculated Yukimuro's motivations. *Is it possible she still wants him after all her growth?* The concern didn't last long. Yuki reached behind her back and slowly drew her sword from its sheath. She pulled Mok up face to face with her as she thrashed on his hardness, locking her feet around him like a belt. Myriam could see from the look on her face that a fire was building in Yukimuro's loins. She slid the sword around Mok's back, unbeknownst to her coital foe. Yuki screamed in climax. In conjunction with her ecstasy, she ran her blade across her former slaver's neck. Blood sprayed in an initial gush that soaked the bar as his head hit the floor with a thud. Then two, three, four more squirts shot from his throat hole onto Yuki's bare chest, each with less intensity as his blood pressure plummeted to nothing.

Myriam was horrified by the spectacle, a sign of the weakness she fought to destroy. *What the hell has she become? Was this in her the whole time?*

Yuki wiped the gore from herself as best she could before redressing and opening the door to the public.

"The disturbance is at an end," she explained to the tavern owner, patting his shoulder and leaving a handprint of blood. Several lower-ranking disciples of Yosai had arrived on the scene, and Yuki ordered them to assist in the clean-up. "Stabilize the situation and restore order to this sector," she commanded. "I must return to O'jod and give Madam Umi my report. The Yon Astra will want to hear this from me."

The Womb Of Inana

Only two more dominos to go.

CHAPTER SEVENTEEN

N'damu V

A low rumble shook the plains of the Sizwe: the hooves of a dushnah herd, ten thousand strong, roaring across the savannah in a chaotic union. An unending flow of half-ton animals at full charge, like a raging river, they sounded like static thunder.

"Bring them this way, Shar'nah," Sal'aah Novojoh commanded his daughter. N'damu marveled at the massive gray hoard that swallowed the land. They'd ridden south all day to find the herd aback trained, domesticated dushnah. These beasts, however, were wild. "Bone-horses," the ancestors had nicknamed them. N'damu remembered Enah telling him once what a horse was, but he'd long forgotten the details. Earth's version of a dushnah, he supposed.

The spindly Novojoh girl stood up on her mount, held her arms aloft, and closed her eyes as if in meditation. Shar'nah was only thirty-two cycles but already was a respected G'higari kota. She was less than ninety pounds drenched, with dark cocoa skin, scuffed from a day's riding. She dressed in a black leather vest with vibrant red tasseling and boyish trousers that bagged around her little stick legs, at least four sizes too large.

N'damu might have thought it odd to learn under someone who was essentially a child, but he knew offending her would only result in a blackened eye or a kick to the groin. She had an excuse for childish behavior.

As if she were emitting some sort of beacon, the entire phalanx shifted its orientation. The roar increased quickly, dropping in pitch as the herd charged in their direction with no indication of stopping.

"Ummm … I know I'm not supposed to talk … but is this a safe place to stand?" He noticed Noba whispering to Sal'aah from the rear. When his friend had last been to Meadowdell, Shar'nah was *much* younger—not yet Kota of Dushnah. The lordling of Sadah was obviously not yet confident in her dushnah mastery. N'damu's trusted guard gripped his spear with a second hand as if it could save him from the tide of animals. After being attacked by bandits and swallowed by a querghil, the prince, too, had his share of nerves.

The sound of blasters cocking came next as VEO Commander Rigel Kong was the next to flinch. "It's illegal to use a blaster on dushnah—huge poaching violation—*unless* you're protecting a *prince*. They better stop, Novojoh," the commander threatened. The man of Oshun dressed in black armor and hung his ranking badge around his neck. A steel-cast Tri-World pyramid, red on

234

black, a symbol of loyalty to Atalay. N'damu was happy to have Kong with him this rotation.

"Put away your weapon," Sal'aah yelled. "Do the dushnah look like the prince's would-be assassins?" Sal'aah flipped his gray dreads as he jumped from his steed and came face to face with Rigel Kong, fearlessly indignant. "Leave the beasts to my daughter."

"N'damu, come," Shar'nah said firmly. The herd rushed down the valley and up the hill like a flood filling the low ground and rising.

"Go, N'damu, trust her," Sal'aah told him. "Trust my Shar'nah. The time for faith in Khanya is now."

N'damu grabbed the reins, directing his dushnah toward the young Novojoh girl. The animal sensed its rider's trepidation and advanced with caution. The thundering was relentless. The future king's teeth began chattering from the vibrations as the dushnah closed in.

"Stand, as *I* do, N'damu," Shar'nah said to him when he came up beside her. "Reach out. Feel their rhythm."

His knees trembled, threatening to drop him, as he struggled to stay the vertigo before he found his balance and stood upon the dushnah.

"Now, connect yourself to their vibrations." The Kota of Dushnah stepped up to her mount's head as the beast reared onto its hind limbs to elevate her vantage.

"I thought I *was* connected to their vibrations already," he yelled back at her, competing with the stampeding herd's roar, shaking more violently by the second.

"Stop them, N'damu," Shar'nah told him. "Reach out with your feelings, sense their energy with your own. Convey your thoughts to them. Feel."

The prince spread his arms and closed his eyes as she did. He tried to think of what she wanted; his consciousness searched with all his available senses. He shut his eyes as tightly as he could, rummaging in the darkness of his mind, but saw no light. He heard no voices. No smell or taste or hand was there to guide him—no push or pull to force him. The prevailing impulse was to cower in fear—the instinctive response to an impending trampling.

"Any man can bond with a single dushnah, My Prince," Shar'nah said, glaring over from under her hat. "It is as simple as making a friend. The power is in the *mass*. One dushnah will carry you; ten thousand will carry an army!" The young Novojoh was now screaming to reach N'damu's ears as well.

He strained his brain again, and as sweat poured from his brow, tears streamed down his cheeks. The world seemed to spin as though he were on some drug—an ether trip gone awry.

The roar drowned out any further words of encouragement. N'damu opened his eyes as the wall of exophile beast closed in. Closer up, he could see their individual color patterns, which introduced variation into the monotone gray of the herd seen from a distance. Some were charcoal-black, others white as milk, and numerous more every shade of gray in between.

He thought he might soon be nothing more than red ooze on their hooves—his heroic DNA stomped into the dirt. N'damu dove from his dushnah but struggled to get up and run. One foot got in the way of the other in his panic as he tripped and fell over himself, yet again landing face-first in the rough. There was nothing else for him to do but cower on the ground and leave his fate to universal design.

He waited for death when suddenly the rumble turned to hush. All went silent save the pounding of his heart as the prince peeked out between his fingers. Shar'nah hopped to the ground with a soft pat. She caressed one dushnah on its rump, kissed another on the tip of its nose, and continued down the line, greeting and tossing treats to them at random. The herd quickly settled, then dispersed to graze.

N'damu felt the powerful slap on the back that Sal'aah had come to give him every time he failed at something. At first, it had been endearing, but after the number of failures he'd suffered, the guru's pats of reassurance felt more like punishment. Somehow, he still laughed about it, but the prince was starting to suspect he was the worst student the Novojoh had ever seen. "So, the link probably isn't dushnah," Sal'aah said after he'd finished his barrage of condolence. "Shall we camp for the night? I'd sooner face the ride back after a good sleep."

"We should ride now," Rigel Kong insisted, but Sal'aah had already dismounted and was pulling his tent from his saddle.

When Lord Novojoh phrased a sentence as a suggestion, it was an entirely rhetorical gesture—he would have his way.

Trees were sparse on the Sizwe, but the troop was lucky to be in an area with a scant supply of veras. Shar'nah gathered kindling for a fire while Noba helped her father with the tents. Kong looked disgusted at his predicament, but he finally dismounted and accepted that he would have to sleep there tonight.

"Let's walk to the river, N'damu," Noba said, placing his hand on the prince's shoulders. "We will fill the water." The two boys gathered everyone's canteens, and after getting direction from Sal'aah, headed west for a stream he promised they would find.

N'damu's head drooped as he walked along in his torn, sullied training robes, dismayed by yet another setback. The mamidons, the throzeids—the querghil and dushnah—failures. "Why is this so difficult?" he asked.

"Did you think N'jikota would be easy?" Noba asked.

"No … no, I didn't," N'damu said. "However, I did not expect this disaster." *I'm sure the great Noba Sadah had no such issues finding his spirit-link.*

"Nor I," Noba told him. "Though I never imagined *myself* here in the first place."

"When you came for your N'jikota training, was it like this?" N'damu kicked a stone casually, then grimaced from the pain.

The long grasses smelled bitter and made his skin itch as they waded deeper into taller overgrowth. Their sandals began to smack from the damp mud as the tynn became a marsh. "The river is this way," Noba said. The boys used their spears for walking sticks as they pressed on through the soft, wet terrain.

"You dodge my question." N'damu stopped in front of him. "Answer me: was it like this when you came?" Noba was forty-six and had come to Meadowdell four cycles prior. Much to N'damu's annoyance, his friend had never been forthcoming about his experience here. He'd always assumed it was because Noba was ashamed of his bond. "Botsora aren't that bad—as long as you hold your breath."

"Shut up." Noba swatted a pair of quil moths that seemed to orbit his head, making love. He never discussed it. Botsora were not exactly beasts of the heroes. He was the First Spear to the prince and preferred people focus on that.

"Come, my friend," he said. "They don't stink *that* bad." The terrestrial animals slithered two heads tall. Botsora were scavengers that fed on anything they came across: grass, shrubs, carcasses—droppings. Their defining feature was the overwhelming odor they excreted to fend off predators. No description could convey the stink of botsora spray.

"They smell pleasant to me."

N'damu could not hold back his chuckle. "Oh, come now. Did you stand for three rotations atop the mamidon perch? Did throzeids have you puking and shitting yourself for yet another three rotations? How many times did you fall into the mud, Noba? I'm guessing zero?"

"Zero," Noba said as the marshy grasses came to the riverbank. "Who cares?" He removed the lid of the first canteen and held it below the cool stream's surface. "And you can laugh about botsora all you like. My spirit-link to this spear is enough."

"Then why do you never discuss your experience with N'jikota?"

"I've been told not to…" Noba said. "Orders."

"From whom?" he asked as he capped off the canteen Noba handed him and passed him another empty.

"I cannot say, actually," Noba answered with a sympathetic tilt of his head. "Orders."

"Orders? I am your *prince,* if you've forgotten." N'damu hoped to exude his Atalayan authority, though he had his doubts whether it worked. "I order you tell me … now!"

"Okay," Noba said. "They thought it might put too much pressure on you, so I was commanded to keep quiet. I always *wanted* to tell you, my friend."

"So, *what* then?"

"If you insist." Noba shrugged with a pompous smirk. "I rode the mamidon. I resisted the throzeids. I stood to the dushnah herd. Shi'nah Novojoh said she'd never seen a better student in all her cycles." He'd clearly been dying to tell. "I flew with Sho'nee on the atranoch. Man, it was hard not to tell you about it. I tamed ulanoids and querghil, and I bonded with the botsora. Their stench smells a little tangy to me."

"Well, congratulations. No need to boast, though." His jealousy was impossible to conceal. It was apparent why they'd hidden it from him. The pressure would increase now, exponentially, knowing Noba was such a G'higari savant. He was happy for his best friend, but his failures now felt all the more wounding.

"Crongrin … cr … cr…" Noba said, a strange stutter overtaking his voice.

"Oh, did you master *them* too?"

"CRONGRIN!"

N'damu looked beside him and saw a rocky formation he'd not before noticed. The spikey gray rock suddenly split open, revealing bright yellow eyes. Ulanoids burst from the tall grass in a panic, and in a chaotic hurricane of water, a mound of teeth lunged at him. The mighty crongrin had been lying in wait, anticipating the perfect moment—like when unsuspecting fools came to fill their canteens.

He could feel the heat of the animal's breath as he froze. Noba lunged toward the beast with a war cry, twirling his spear without hesitation before lodging its shaft in the crongrin's mouth. "Get the fuck out of here!" Noba shouted as he rammed his spear in farther.

N'damu didn't run, though. He swung his spear uselessly into the rocky hide of the savage beast. His blade only buckled in his hand, causing him more pain than the animal.

"JAM ITS MOUTH!" Noba was slipping. Their only hope was to keep its mouth incapacitated. The jaws of a crongrin produced the most forceful bite on Inana. They could snap a man's arms like sticks of tinkercane. N'damu shoved his weapon into its massive mouth, forming an X with Noba's spear. The crongrin charged in a fury, whipping its spiky tail and splashing violently in the water. The boys dug in their feet but could not stay the animal's momentum, their legs sinking into the mud.

Suddenly, with a pop, a hole appeared in the animal's forehead. The crongrin's eyes changed in an instant from a burning rage to widened panic. Its fear was unmistakable before its head exploded, erupting purple blood, brains, and bone. Its neck spewing gore, the slain crongrin's massive body flopped into the river with a swoosh.

N'damu and Noba were blown clear by the wake. They looked back to the shoreline in a daze, coated in dead crongrin, and saw the VEO commander.

"Ion grenade," he said in his deep, cold voice. Rigel Kong was silhouetted against the blood-red skyline with his blaster smoking as Thraxis set to the south. He looked like some holo-cartoon antihero as he leisurely holstered his weapon. "The IL 300 Series, charge launcher. Cool new Vesta tech I've been dying to try out. It's so bad." He waded out to the boys and pulled them to their feet.

"You followed us?" Noba asked as he sifted through the mud for his sandals and spear.

"Of course. I'm here to protect the prince. I saw what happened when I left him alone with you last time. You're welcome, boy. He's safe." Kong's long black hair streamed over his face as he leaned over and patted Noba on the back.

"Thank you," N'damu exclaimed. "I was not keen on being swallowed a second time!" Rigel gave a quick wink.

They gathered the floating canteens and moved upstream, away from the corpse-tainted water, to refill them again. The sky darkened to indigo as they headed back to camp and was deep violet by the time they arrived.

N'damu and Noba sat with Sal'aah and Shar'nah around the fire they'd made and shared the story with their Novojoh companions over wompa root stew. Noba exaggerated the crongrin exploits, making them out braver than they were as N'damu nodded along. All the while, Rigel paced behind smoking spliffs. He seemed to want no part in the retelling.

"That is a heartbreaking tale," Shar'nah said as she slurped at her bowl.

"Heartbreaking?" N'damu replied, confused. "We were crongrin food *for sure*."

"You should have known not to wade in the tall grassy areas where the river meets the marsh," Shar'nah reminded them. She was young and emotional, yet N'damu sensed she was somehow, morally, on the crongrin's side.

Sal'aah was somber as well, silent as he ate, the ambiance unusually lacking his jolly chuckle.

"That's true," Noba admitted. "We don't have marshlands in the Glass Valley. Crongrins are much easier to spot."

"We were careless," N'damu added.

"Yes, but Rigel's shot was amazing," Noba said. "I mean, we were standing our ground okay, but it was dicey."

"We *weren't* standing our ground," N'damu said, unable to help but correct him. "We were about to go under the beast before Commander Kong saved us."

Sal'aah at last had had enough. He tossed his bowl aside and stood imposingly. "Alas, I was not there to save the crongrin from *him*—from all three of your ignorance."

"Sal'aah—I." He didn't know what to say.

"You have failed—again, N'damu." He shook his long silver dreads out. "The point of N'jikota feels lost to you." N'damu stared into the fire, hopelessly confused. "You could be learning a better way, the true G'higari way, N'damu. But you are surrounded by your friends and their weapons, and you discover nothing."

"What was he supposed to do, Sal'aah?" Noba tried to defend him.

"Khanya will know you are not food if you take the time to tell it. I am sorry, N'damu—for my frustration. It is my fault as a teacher. I know the error in all this, yet I cannot go against the will of my king. I cannot go against *your* will, N'damu, and your

N'jikota suffers for it. I allowed this Vesta supervision. Now a beautiful crongrin is dead, and Khanya weeps." In a huff, the Lord of Novojoh stormed off to his tent and was not heard from again all evening—apart from the snoring.

Rigel finally took a seat with them around the fire, tossing his butt into the flames as he squatted. "When I came to your planet, I thought I would eventually get used to you G'higari. But after all these cycles, I still cannot fathom you." The white-skinned man reclined against a rock, pulling some dried nievahnoid jerky from his bag. "Believe me," he said. "Try spending the night in the Konga. On Oshun, you lose your inhibitions about killing pretty quickly when the mongrels come."

"Perhaps your people lack faith," Shar'nah suggested. "It takes devoutness to spirit-link."

"Little girl, Oshun is teeming with so many mages and wizards—'sacred orders of this' and 'lost societies of that'—I've lost count by this point. Alchemists and pyromancers, hell, Calitro Frigg thinks he's from an ancient race of magical subterranean dwarves."

The boys chuckled, but the sarcasm was lost on Shar'nah. The young Kota of Dushnah was obviously a proud young woman with a strong ego. The prince couldn't be sure if she just didn't get Kong's humor or was unwilling to yield him any intellectual ground. "Why would he not be a magical dwarf?" she asked. "He's little enough."

"I dunno," Rigel replied. "Pretty long way around callin' yourself a midget."

Noba gushed laughter, but the Novojoh girl's face remained frozen in a scowl.

"The beasts of Oshun are not the work of Khanya," Shar'nah said. "They are not blessed by the Womb of Inana. Forsaken by Atalay!"

Commander Kong looked at N'damu, dead in the eyes. "Why did you forsake them, boy? Mongrels, sure, but why the cute little schmiglets?"

Noba's laughter swelled to a second wave.

"Maybe a dushnah trampling would awaken your faith," she threatened. "Rot in the Barren Void!"

"I know, I know," Kong replied. "*The Demons of the Jade Moon* was one of my favorite old books. We have Milushi, G'higari, and S'bu. We have Elewynites and the Joph Razin. Al Rana and the Order of Otu—my head goes spinning, honey. All these lists, ya know? I'm sorry if I offended your daddy, but I only saw blood and teeth and mangled flesh when I blasted that crongrin. No light. No spirit energy. That thing was looking to eat, but a bigger predator came along. Lookin' to survive."

N'damu could see the frustration in Shar'nah's rancorous expression, but he did not want to add to the conflict. Commander Kong *had* saved his life: why speak against him? He owed him a debt and actually agreed with what he was saying. When it's kill or be killed, a man's instinct is to survive. He will do as he must. He was happy the crongrin was dead, and to lament it seemed like wishing he were in its belly, digesting with his best friend.

246

Still, he didn't want to upset his young teacher either, so the prince kept his mouth respectfully shut.

N'damu also shot Noba a squint and a half a head turn. It served as an order to stay out of it.

"I'm sorry for *you*, friend," Shar'nah said as she took a drink of water and stood for a prebed stretch. "The Womb of Inana is a powerful love I feel in my heart. I would only wish to share it with you."

"Well, I appreciate that, sweetie," Rigel answered back with a wink. "And don't worry: if 'the Womb of Inana' tries to eat any of you Novojoh, I won't interfere."

CHAPTER EIGHTEEN

Nalia IV

Nalia squinted as the Eden Star peeked out from behind the mountain ranges to the west, burning at the retinas within her fragile human eyes, evolved beneath another star.

She rode at the rear of the caravan on a pearly dushnah she'd named Aiku, after the blossoms much the same shade of white. At her side rode her fellow spear, Noba Sadah, on his steed of gray-speckled charcoal. Heavily outfitted, as usual, the proud heir of Clan Sadah shone in his glorious chromium armor. Noba's father ingrained the precept that a soldier must always present himself appropriately, regardless of comfort. Still, he seemed to hate armor even more than she did. She chuckled to herself and lovingly patted Aiku's smooth bony back as she watched Noba endlessly readjusting in his saddle.

In front of them rode the VEOs, in trilateral formation. Atop an ash-gray mount was Commander Rigel Kong, as always bearing an array of preposterous weaponry. Nalia often walked through the entrails of his pipe-smoke, clenching her nostrils. His eyes always obscured by specs, the shady man from the jungle moon gave her the creeps. On each side and slightly behind trotted his senior lieutenants, Ivy Freya and Calitro Frigg, on dushnahs of midnight black.

The Prince's Guard all rode far in the back, as ordered by Sal'aah Novojoh, who led the caravan on his enormous mamidon, Jasper. The parade leader was noticeably growing more annoyed with the royal escort on excursions such as these. Such interference with N'damu's training could be the cause of his struggles, a fact that did not go unnoticed by the Lord of Novojoh. He'd made the necessity of remaining inconspicuous clear to each member of the guard moving forward.

Nalia could understand and did her best to cooperate, though she couldn't vouch for her compatriots.

A discreet distance ahead of them, S'ike Novojoh slithered on the back of his enormous, pale yellow querghil. His rotund body rested between the plates of the animal's long bony back. The oldest Novojoh son had inherited his father's belly, which rolled and jiggled with the motion of the two-ton beast. Behind S'ike sat his younger siblings Sab'ina and Sab'ano, passengers holding on for dear life to plates of their own as the massive worm quaked up the mountain trail.

Ahead, his sister Shar'nah directed eight more dushnah, two by two, carrying all the supplies for the treacherous journey up

249

the Sindiswa Mountains. N'damu rode next, on a light gray mount. As usual, he seemed to struggle to control the beast and often had to call back to Shar'nah for the aide of her dushnah link. Scurrying to his left, as near as her bone-horse could trot, was Sar'ah Novojoh, with her flowing cinnamon hair waving back and forth. The distant, muffled sound of their flirtatious giggles made Nalia feel like she might throw up in her mouth. Although maybe it was Sar'ah's throzeids influencing her intestinal fortitude.

At the prince's right rode Sho'nee Novojoh, the eldest of the clan's children. In Nalia's opinion, it was her, and not Sar'ah, who was the most beautiful. This was Sho'nee's tour into the mountains. The climb was necessary for finding the rare animal she was spirit-linked with—the "bone-dragons" of the sky, the all-mighty atranochs. Now and then, she could make out Sho'nee's instructions for N'damu, telling him how to stay safe on the cliffs, how they would find the atranochs, and of the leap of faith he would have to take to fly on one.

"It's so frustrating. N'damu gets to ride up there with two of Inana's most beautiful, eligible noble girls. And I'm stuck back here—with *you*," Noba complained, looking over with discontent on his grimy brown face.

Dust faded the gloss of Nalia's gray-plated armor. Her curly orange mop glistened with oil and sweat, beads of which occasionally dripped down her forehead, stinging her eyes as she trotted along the path. Her brown broadcloth half-cape flapped behind as she toted her long spear tightly under her left arm. She smiled back at Noba with a wink and blew him a kiss. "I thought

250

old grandma Shi'nah was more *your* type," Nalia said, referring to the woman of 265 cycles.

"Well, I won't say it hasn't crossed my mind," Noba replied, waving back his burgundy hair. He squinted at her and pouted his lips, joking of sexual arousal. A prototypical son of Sadah, Noba was an amazingly handsome young purist. Nalia would never admit to the many crushes she'd had on him growing up. Back when she used to think about who she would marry one day—before realizing the limitations of being natural. She'd imagined being with a noble lord that would make her adoptive clan proud—dreamed the king might anoint her a true Lady of Sadah.

It was not the way of the clans, but perhaps one day, if she proved herself.

Nalia Chuku rolled her eyes, then set her gaze ahead, trying to forget her jealousy of the Novojoh girls riding with the prince—the boy that made her forget all others. N'damu Atalay, her forbidden love. Oh, how he'd kissed her in that grotto that evening on their last night in N'gaia. She felt a heat between her legs swell as her dushnah rocked up and down.

"Seriously, though, those two are immaculate," Noba went on. "Sho'nee's skin is so flawless, and Sar'ah's ass! It's driving me crazy bouncing up there."

"I get it, Noba," Nalia said. "But I'm afraid you'll have to wait for your tent tonight. Your palm will be just as '*immaculate*,' I'm sure." She chuckled, letting a small snort slip as she looked up again at Sho'nee and Sar'ah. *He is not wrong, though,* she thought.

"Imagine them both together," Noba fantasized aloud with a grin in far-off wonderment.

"Please stop talking now," she begged.

The ride up the foothills was long but uneventful. The troop erected camp in the early evening as the mother star sank to the south. Sal'aah found an eetee tree filled with ripe beige melons that were the juiciest Nalia had ever eaten. Lord Novojoh invited the guards to join around the fire as they supped and shared stories of the mountains. Sho'nee told them all about her first flight, the day she held her grandfather's neck as he leaped from the cliff and onto his atranoch.

"Atrax was his name," the Kota of Atranochs said. "He was so big he could eclipse Thraxis, casting the Sizwe in darkness at will."

Nalia was certainly impressed, but she could tell her captivation paled in comparison to N'damu, who seemed mesmerized by the notion. She'd heard him go on and on a million times—it was no surprise. The Second Spear knew he'd dreamed of little more than flying the atranoch. If the prince had a choice in his spirit-link, this would be it. He wanted it so badly, and it rubbed off on everyone who loved him: Ala and Aku, the king and queen. The entire Tri-World knew how much he yearned to ride the bone-dragon. The Novojoh knew it—Vesta, Sadah, Darius, Winters. But most of all, Nalia. She prayed every day for *this* blessing from Khanya, for this one dream to come true for the person she loved.

Not long after storytime, complete darkness fell in the foothills. The orange of the crackling fire was all that lit anyone's face as the Novojoh treated them to some ancient Milushi hymns. Though Nalia didn't understand the archaic language, the clan sang in such lovely harmonies; she couldn't help but imagine the stories behind the lyricism. Sab'ina and Sab'ano intoned soaring melodies in their angelic sopranos, while the three sisters chanted in the midranges with flawless tenor vibrato. S'ike and his father filled out the bass with their deep baritone voices, but as gorgeous as the songs were, they had an unmistakably somber feeling that nearly brought her to tears.

Nalia dried her eyes on her cloak as she scanned for the other's reactions. N'damu and Noba whispered back and forth like fools—no doubt more Sar'ah adulation. Ivy Freya appeared to be as captivated as Nalia herself was, although *she* seemed to have more of an idea what the words meant, mouthing along to the verses. Rigel Kong was indifferent, at best—perhaps he preferred the music of his world. *Even that idiot Frigg is crying.*

The final hymn came to a close, and soon after, Sal'aah and the twins were off to sleep, snoring away in their tents. Kong played hands of Eden's Ace with S'ike and Noba. It seemed like the three were unable to get through a single game without accusations of cheating. Freya tended the dushnah with Shar'nah, setting them down for the evening, while the dwarf, Frigg, balanced the target on his sniper blaster, still whistling the Novojoh tunes quietly to himself.

N'damu emerged from the bush behind Nalia, where she sat at the fire chewing leftover eetee melon. She'd noticed he was still fastening his trousers after relieving himself in the darkness. She was disheartened when he sat so far from her. An unusual chasm seemed to be growing between them, both literal and metaphorical. Scooting from her seat, she was about to talk to him, but the words came a moment too late.

Sar'ah beat her to the punch, plopping down next to him and placed her foot in his lap. "Do you see a bite on my ankle? I think a himpheah ant got me." After an unnecessarily thorough examination of her entire leg, N'damu shrugged in bewilderment. Sar'ah only giggled and whispered in his ear, pulling him by the arm to the other side of the fire, where they bantered privately.

"How did you come to the Prince's Guard?" Sho'nee Novojoh asked as she sat next to Nalia, admiring her spearhead.

She paused for a moment before answering as the kota brushed her fingers along the fine metalwork of her blade. "My parents died when I was very young. Lady Sadah adopted me," Nalia replied with a polite smile.

The Novojoh beauty offered a handful of dried ocha-nut berries, which she gladly accepted. The sour sweetness was a delight in her mouth. "My grandfather was a good friend of Simit Sadah, and in fact he trained with him for a time in Ulundia," Sho'nee said. "He was your mother's grandfather, I believe."

"Lord Simit taught my mother everything she knows," Nalia said. "She often regards him as the greatest spearman ever to have lived, though I'm sure she realizes she is better than he *ever* was."

"I always dreamed of becoming a master of Sadah'anah—when I was little," Sho'nee said. Nalia was astounded for some reason. It seemed to her odd that the Kota of Atranochs would care about spear-fighting. Hand-to-hand combat felt beneath her dignity. Sho'nee was so elegant in her lilac robe with tasseled pearl-beaded fringes. The ulanoid feathers intertwined in her reddish-brown braids flashed pink and blue highlights. "I used to practice sticks with Father, but when it came time to introduce the blade, well, let's just say I don't have the nerve for blood. Perhaps you could show me some moves? Next rotation?"

"It would be an honor, certainly," Nalia replied. "It must be amazing to fly through the clouds on your atranoch. *I* wouldn't have the nerve for *that*."

"I will take you for a glide if you like," Sho'nee said. "Would that be a fair trade?"

Nalia was taken aback. "*I* could fly with you?"

"Why not? If you can take the leap, of course." She grinned, flashing her sparkling white teeth. "What kota would I be if you couldn't?" Sho'nee Novojoh seemed halfway between joking and serious as she scooted a little closer. "Is it a *simple* thing to be proclaimed 'Master of Sadah'anah' in N'gaia?"

"Simple is not the word I'd choose," she said. "The spear is the oldest weapon known to humans. It is a bond of its own, like N'jikota. Mother is the greatest spear fighter on Inana, yet she trains every rotation to improve." Sho'nee nodded as Nalia extended her hand, and the two ladies shook in agreement. "I would love to fly."

Sho'nee smiled and leaned closer to whisper. She placed a hand on her leg, causing a wave of goose-pimples. "Just remember, you can't be afraid to hold on tight. Flying together is intimate ... a passionate experience between spiritual creatures."

Nalia put her hand on Sho'nee's, staring back with her intrigue aroused. "You make it sound—indecent." She couldn't help her nervous cackle.

"Well, with your father or your siblings, it's one thing—a shared energy within Khanya," Sho'nee said. "But with someone new, someone you find attractive, it can be almost ... sexual." She ran her nose down from Nalia's ear, inhaling her scent deeply as they grazed cheeks. Sho'nee stopped with her lips a hair's breadth from her own—so close, she thought she might get her second kiss before fate interrupted, as it is wont to do.

Sar'ah kneeled next to them, disturbing their huddle. "I saw some kavah bushes in the brush," she whispered. "You guys wanna come trip?"

Sho'nee took her hands and pulled her to her feet. Nalia's laugh went from nervous to excited, even though she had no idea what Sar'ah was asking.

"Have you ever tried it?" Sho'nee asked with mischief in her eyes.

"What is *it*?" the Second Spear asked.

"Kavah flowers," Sar'ah explained. "They grow naturally. Don't worry. They are quite safe. But, when you eat a few, well, to be honest … the experience can be magical. Transformative, even."

"Psychotropics? You intend to do this, N'damu?" Nalia asked, turning to him, shocked that he would entertain the idea. However, he seemed to ignore her. "You are Atalay! You cannot compromise your genetic—"

"Count me in," N'damu said, obviously trying to seem more masculine than he was. He grabbed Sar'ah's hand and pulled her into the dark brush, snickering like an adolescent. "Come on, Nalia, better keep an eye on me. I'm about to break some rules."

She lost herself in another world for a moment until Sho'nee squeezed at her fingers, reminding her of where she was. "Don't worry," Sho'nee said. "I'll keep you both safe."

Nalia scanned the camp, pondering what to do. Everyone had retired to their tents by then, other than Noba. Her fellow spear was passed out during the last game of aces—snoring away in the grass. She interwove her fingers with Sho'nee's and clutched. "Yes, I'll try some." Nalia pinched the air. "A little."

She clumsily scampered through the dark brush behind Sho'nee. Nalia may have been ungainly, but her inelegance seemed like poise next to N'damu's constant stumbling. Both Novojoh girls, of course, glided over the terrain as if they were supernatural apparitions, hardly making a sound.

"I saw them over that field, in the brush by the foot of that cliff," Sar'ah called out as she led them on.

"I can't see anything," Nalia mumbled to Sho'nee. "It's just darkness."

"Do not worry," she replied. "My sister can sense the throzeids. They give her a different form of perception in the wilderness. Her ability to track is marvelous."

Sho'nee was not wrong, and after a short walk through a damp grassy meadow they arrived at a wall of kavah bushes.

"N'damu, are you sure you want to do this?" Nalia asked. "I mean…" She could almost feel his want in the air.

"Yes, I am certain," the prince told her. "Are you here to stop me?" *I'm here because I love you, idiot.*

"I'm here to do my duty," Nalia said. Even if she wanted to back out, she couldn't, as though there were some invisible blade at her back.

The darkness hid their faces, but the tension between them was not difficult to detect. "Maybe that's the problem," the prince replied in a frustrated tone before turning to the other girls. "So, how many do I need to eat?"

"It takes three flowers to feel the effects," Sar'ah explained as her older sister stretched out, picking the ideal buds. After she carefully made her selections, Sho'nee passed the pale white flowers out three by three. Chalky dander covered the blossoms, sticking to Nalia's fingers. *They smell a little like japhid spice,* she thought.

"The journey can be intensely personal," Sar'ah said. "Amazing and spiritual."

"And don't worry," Sho'nee added. "We are here with you. We are together."

The Novojoh girls crunched them up in their palms, rolling the buds to manageable little balls, and popped them in their mouths with no hesitation. They looked to N'damu next.

Nalia could sense his apprehension as her eyes finally began to adjust to the planet Set's lowlight, a solitary white speck in the sky. "It's okay to change your mind. You don't have to do this."

"I'm so glad I can have my loyal spear here with me, making sure to protect me," he snapped back sarcastically. "Protect me from life instead of living any of it with me."

She was beyond confused. "N'damu, I didn't ask to come."

"Does it occur to you, or Enahdra—or even to my parents, that all this unnecessary protection is the *very* thing keeping me from N'jikota?"

"Yes," she replied. "Everyone knows what you—"

"No one knows ANYTHING!" His brow creased as he ground his teeth audibly. "I have to be a savior to everyone in the Tri-Worlds. Here I am, on the adventure of my life—too fragile to be on my own."

"N'damu—you..." His heartache pained her, but she had no words.

"And you want to know the worst part?" He began to tear up. "You're all right. I've done nothing but be smashed, beaten, and swallowed whole since I arrived in Meadowdell."

259

"Don't forget puked your brains out," Sar'ah reminded him, looking at her sister and shaking her head. "They always forget the throzeids."

Sho'nee patted the prince on the back. "You must have patience, N'damu. You've yet to fly." She flipped back her hair happily, waving her arms like wings.

"You all have this destiny planned out for me, and you follow me through my little maze while I seek the reward of a forced fate I never asked for. What if I don't even want to be king?"

"Everything can change after you fly," Sho'nee said. "Trust me. Trust *us*."

"Yes," Sar'ah said, closing her eyes and rocking back and forth on the balls of her feet. "Eat your flowers and fly with us, My Prince. Sometimes the future just pops into focus."

"Isn't it obvious to you yet that I am not a hero? How many times do I need to fall on my face before everyone realizes the truth?"

"My family believes in you, My Prince," Sho'nee said.

"All of the realm loves you, N'damu," Nalia added. "No matter the outcome out here."

He seemed to cringe at that. "They don't know me, Nalia! I may have been incubated and come out named Atalay, but I will never be what the realm expects of me. I can't even learn who 'N'damu' is because I am not allowed the freedom to live. To bond. Not only to the wild beasts but to the people I lov—"

He stopped as she popped the ball of kavah flowers in her mouth and gulped. Maybe he was right—perhaps Nalia had to protect him, even from her. Or from those who put his life in a box. "What are you waiting for?"

He smiled as he stuffed his dose in his mouth and chewed.

The effects began in Nalia's fingers, tingly needles that moved up into her arms—followed by a sinking sensation, like treading water in a slow descent. Effortless, sincere, and happy. She felt swaddled in nakedness, warm and wet, as though she were lying back in an infinitely deep hot bath.

Music began to color the air, an infectious Xolani tribal beat that enslaved her hips to its rhythm. In perfect sync with her heartbeat, she had no idea if the music was real or fantasy, but it was not long before dance took her feet. The Novojoh girls were swaying around her as well, and she could see N'damu following closely behind as the tempo of the kavah flowers captured him as well. He seemed to be twirling in slow motion, followed by his trail of ghostly copies, lapsed in time—fading to glittery sparkles obscurely as he frolicked. His skin glowed white with an angelic hue she found mesmerizing.

Nalia blinked like rapid fire. Each time she opened her eyes, the ground disappeared more, melding with the sky as up and down grew irrelevant. Stars seemed to flicker as white lines began to spread out, connected them, forming constellations she'd never seen before. A mamidon, a crongrin, a ulanoid, an atranoch. One, however, started to glow brighter, emanating energy as it seemed to take form. It was a naga shaped of solid light with a crown levitating above its head like a halo.

"Do your duty, Nalia Chuku," the naga said. Its voice was like an unnerving hiss forming tones from the tip of its snarling tongue. "Yours is not to question why, Nalia Chuku. Yours is only to do as Atalay wills you." Its eyes turned red as it circled her like a predator sizing its prey. "You are the servant, Nalia Chuku. The material of HIS divinity."

Who? she asked herself.

"Atalay!" the naga replied. "You know who."

N'damu, she thought, looking down at her wiggling toes as she floated over a birthing galaxy. *Wait. You can hear my thoughts?*

The naga rattled, circling faster. "No one can hear your thoughts, no. Those are yours, slave of Atalay."

I'm NOT a slave.

"Empires are built of meat and metal." It lashed its tongue in her face as they moved through rainbow-colored clouds of nebulous gas. "The meat..." She became aware, suddenly, that she was naked. "...and the metal." Her spear materialized in her hand. "You have the implements—everything it takes. You are *made* to worship him. It is beyond your control, Nalia Chuku."

I hate kavah.

The naga sprang for the kill, snapping at her neck. Nalia braced for the bite but instead felt a warm moisture at her neck: Sar'ah's lips, as she danced sensually next to her, kissing up to her earlobe. Warm tremors erupted as she gave in to intrigue. She closed her eyes, letting her mind slip away as the Novojoh beauty nibbled at her ear.

Next, she felt a different hand sliding through her orange coif to the back of her head: Sho'nee—guiding her lips to her own. The Second Spear didn't expect to receive her second kiss here tonight. Nevertheless, one thing was instantly certain, it was one she'd never forget. Her tongue was warm and ingratiating and had the tangy flavor of ocha nut Nalia found inebriating. As she fell into her bottomless kiss with Sho'nee, she forgot, if only for a moment, about her jealousy—her anxiety—everything hidden under the surface.

Sar'ah then tipped her chin to take the next turn at her lips, claiming kiss number three. Nalia began to feel the fire between her legs rage as Sar'ah and Sho'nee clawed at her hips. In the moments she came up to breathe, the Novojoh girls kissed each other passionately as well.

I love kavah.

N'damu almost seemed to disappear as the three Inanean girls rocked to the silent melody. Almost.

Sar'ah finally pulled from the three-way embrace and walked up to the prince. She wrapped her arms around his neck and began to caress him aggressively. Their kissing was even more intense *without* the influence of throzeids. There was something unmistakable between them. It should have been a knife in her stomach, yet the kavah made her hot and cold at once—sweaty and wet.

Sho'nee embraced her; still, Nalia couldn't help but watch the man she loved in the corner of her eye. He was watching her as well. *What does he feel … watching me kissing them?*

She noticed him peeling back Sar'ah's blouse, exposing her to the evening glow. She began to unfasten his trousers, and it was the point of no return for Nalia. The sickness of jealousy that the kavah had dammed suddenly rushed back over her like a typhoon.

She quickly pulled away from Sho'nee, tears streaming down. Nalia readjusted her clothes but knew it was impossible to hide her distress or salvage any dignity. "I'm sorry … I'm *so* sorry. I need to go to bed now. I can't handle … I'm sorry." Her stuttering voice was hoarse under her sobbing. She grabbed her spear and retreated up the field, hurrying back to camp through the dark brush.

***

With tears still flowing down her cheeks, Nalia Chuku crawled into her tent and under the covers of her cot. Her stomach was sick, in knots over what had happened. Not only had she humiliated herself, but she'd also abandoned the prince in a vulnerable state, in a hostile wilderness. If something happened to him, the Seat of Atalay would demand her head. Still, part of her thought that execution might be a soothing relief from the anguish in her heart.

As much as she wished she could stop loving, it would have been easier to cease breathing. Their souls were a perfect fit, in her mind. Damn the world they were born in, where such a love would be forbidden. A world where she must sit idly and watch him marry another, some Sar'ah Novojoh or Enahdra Vesta. Maybe an exotic out-world beauty, a Darius or a Winters.

Get it through your thick fuzz. She sobbed into her comforters, the tent spinning from her kavah trip's lingering effect. *He can never love you back. He can never… You need to leave… you are ruining his bonding. It's you, Nalia. You're ruining his … life.*

A rustling came from her tent's opening. A thin figure made a black silhouette against the dark tan fabric of her tent door. She feigned sleep but slowly reached out for her spear as the specter entered. Her fingers fumbled in the darkness beneath her cot, feeling for her weapon. Just as her index brushed the handgrip, the intruder was upon her.

However, instead of pain, she felt the heavenly kiss she had craved most. N'damu's tongue was the most nourishing thing ever to trace her lips. He collapsed onto her cot, which immediately lost its legs, dropping them to the floor with a thud. They kissed so aggressively, neither seemed to notice.

"Sar'ah?" Nalia managed to get enough air to ask. "Sho'nee?"

He only buried his tongue deeper into her mouth. Never had she tasted anything sweeter or as warm, smooth, and satisfying. "I left after you … I don't know," he replied. "I love you, Nalia. I don't want anything if I don't have you."

"But, the Seat of At—"

265

"Let the Tri-Worlds fall into Thraxis. I love you."

"I love you too," she said as she wrapped her arms around him. The two lovers began to tear at each other's clothes. N'damu's braid dropped into Nalia's face as he pulled his tunic over his head. They laughed for a moment before he tore off her blouse and pressed his chest against hers. Next, she felt his thumbs reaching under each side of her bottoms, and he peeled them down slowly past her knees and off each foot one by one, all the while continuing with their tongue ballet.

At first, she felt a shockwave of pain as the head of his manhood pressed against her wet lips below. The feeling soon became delight, however. He began to grind harder, entering deeper with each thrust. Nalia had explored her body before but never felt anything so big inside her. He might lack muscle definition, but the prince was every bit an Atalay below.

N'damu grunted in delight. She could see in his eyes it was as much a dream come true for him as it was for her. The fire soon built to explosion for them both as they gripped each other's soaked naked bodies in every way possible. The two lovers erupted in perfect unison.

He stayed with her until the Eden Star began to glow in the south, and they both knew the fairytale had to end. But what dream has no end?

Another secret to keep, it seemed. Better to have to hide joy than anguish, at least. The new rotation was coming, and Nalia had never felt more ready.

CHAPTER NINETEEN

Sal'aah II

"There's a ground underneath those clouds, definitely," N'damu said, peeking over the edge of the cliff at the sheer drop. It took six rotations to climb Mount Lapis, the highest summit in the Sindiswa mountain range. "The clouds just make it *look* like there's no ground. But I'm not fooled, Sal'aah. There's a ground. One hundred percent. There's a … ground?"

Sal'aah Novojoh came up behind the prince and gave him a pat on the back that nearly sent the scrawny boy off the edge. "Well, if anyone can find the ground, I *know* it's you," he said with a jovial hoot, surprisingly loud considering the rarified air at this altitude. Even when breathing was a trial, he still had to joke. "Maybe, don't stand so close to the drop-off, eh?" Sal'aah's huge flaxen poncho puffed up with the wind like a parachute, making him appear twice as fat as he was. It looked like a beating heart as air moved in and out of the broadcloth. He had his silvery dreads tied back with twine and decorated with beads and ulanoid feathers of blue and white. Sunshield specs covered his eyes like obsidian pearls, and his gray beard was frosted at the tips by the chill. The Lord of Meadowdell had a habit of underdressing at this height.

"Indeed, we must wait for the atranochs," Sho'nee Novojoh said, standing a safe distance behind. Her robes flapped blue and violet in the wind as she scanned the horizon through her shaded specs. "Though I am glad to see you're so eager."

"I am," the prince replied in a shaking voice. "I've waited for this all my life." Sal'aah smiled at N'damu, forcing a look of confidence. *Is this the moment his Atalay spirit shines through?*

It was the first time in so many rotations Sal'aah had allowed himself to ask the question.

After the long climb, the boy was skinny as ever. The journey of N'jikota could be emaciating. Indeed, he was even using his spear as a walking aid. So depleted, yet somehow focused, N'damu seemed unusually tuned in. Sal'aah couldn't help but think something was different about him. *No doubt Sar'ah's been at him in the bushes.*

"I will fly first," Sho'nee explained. "Atranochs fly in flocks called a valor with up to seven or eight strong. However, most often they fly alone or in pairs. My bond will soothe any in the area and make them more welcoming to new riders. This is how Father and our ancestors, the ones not spirit-linked to the bone-dragons, were able to fly all the same." She pointed down the

268

overhanging ridge, from which poured a picturesque waterfall, five hundred meters tall at least, through the air, until it hit the side of the mountain. "The old boys will swoop in for a sip occasionally. It's the perfect place, easy to hop on."

Sal'aah noticed N'damu tiptoe out to the edge once again. "Perfect … easy," he repeated in a height-induced trance. "Got it. I can do it. Just tell me when to jump. Faith, Khanya, Atalay, and all that." Sal'aah could sense his anxiety. *Perhaps I should stop him?* he asked himself.

"Once I'm up there, I'll give the signal to Father," she said. "You will have to jump with *him* the first time."

"What? No … I can—" N'damu tried to interrupt, but she cut him off sharply.

Sho'nee was a gentle soul, but a strict commandant when it came to her teachings. "No arguments," she shouted.

"Just don't squeeze too tight, N'damu," Sal'aah jested. "I'm known to get gassy at these heights."

N'damu looked slightly queasy at the thought, and he turned his gaze to Sho'nee. "Can't I just fly with you, Sho'nee?"

What? Wasn't one daughter enough?

"Yes, but that would be too easy," she replied. "The idea is to see how the animal reacts to you. My N'jikota may keep the atranoch from spirit-linking to you."

"Yep," Sal'aah jumped in. "They already *know* they don't like me." He shrugged with a jolly chuckle. "The gas, maybe?" He shrugged. "Good thing for me mamidons stink already."

269

"Who did my father fly with?"

"He flew with my father, Sav'ato. He was strong enough to control an entire *valor* of atranochs. Someday, it will be the same for Sho'nee."

"Atrax, was it?" N'damu asked.

"Yes, that was his mega-atranoch," Sho'nee said, clearly in awe of its memory. "I've never seen another one his size." Sal'aah also remembered his father's bone-dragon: midnight black with streaking spots of scarlet and eyes that glowed yellow; there was no doubt that when you were in the presence of Atrax, you were in the presence of the dominant species on Inana. *He* was king of this world, as far as he knew.

"Okay, so, I can't help but ask, Sho'nee. What happens if we just fall? Do you catch us? If we miss…"

The Kota of Atranochs flashed him a mischievous smile then out of nowhere turned and sprinted as fast as she could, leaping off the ridge. Sal'aah looked over at N'damu, waiting for his reaction. Watching an atranoch kota dive from a mountain top was something he'd seen many times. The best part, by far, was seeing the newbies' frightened reactions. The prince's expression was priceless as his chocolate face turned to cream. "Sho'nee," he screamed pointlessly, to Sal'aah's delight. He tried to fight the laughter, difficult as it was, and to focus on his own flight ahead.

"Stay ready, N'damu," he told him, pulling his shoulder, directing him to stand behind. "When she swoops and calls out a whistle, we need to go immediately … no hesitation."

"Yes," he replied confidently. "Got it. Destiny. For Atalay!"

With a screech, a ghostly white atranoch tore through the waterfall's path, showering the mountaintop with a cold spray. "Whoooooooo!" Sho'nee cried out, creeping up its back, gripping its massive shoulder bones like a ladder and pulling herself to her feet. Wind poured through her hair, which trailed behind, whipping with her pastel purple cape. She weaved the creature eastward through a puffy white cloud, shredding it into a thousand smaller ones that swirled and twisted, then seemed to evaporate to nothing. Sho'nee looked to be in full control, leading the atranoch into a corkscrew move before climbing straight up toward the atmosphere's edge. At the highest point, she stopped suddenly, dropping like a stone into an upside-down dive, adding more clouds to its nimbus tail as it tore back up through the mountains.

"Daughter, what have I told you about showing off?" Sal'aah said to himself as he watched her grandstanding for the prince's benefit. Though he could hardly blame her: she was born to the sky. The Kota of Atranochs belonged in the air. It was her true home.

"She's amazing," N'damu said, jaw agape.

"Ha! Oh, I bet she'd love to hear that," Sal'aah replied. "It's a little embarrassing—my daughters don't often get to play host to an Atalay. They grew up idolizing you, you know. Can you blame them if they are smitten?"

"They are both beautiful … astounding individuals," he said. "All of your children are, in fact … but I'm afraid I've met my true love already."

Most fathers would be happy to see their daughter become a princess in N'gaia, but not Sal'aah. He would have them stay his little girls forever. "Oh, young love is a treasure," Sal'aah said. "I hope you will fly for *her* today. Fly for true love, N'damu."

Sho'nee made her pass and gave the whistle.

"Whoooooooo," Sal'aah squealed as he ran and leaped from the edge.

The prince, much to his surprise, jumped right beside him. "Oh, shiiiiiiiiii…!" N'damu shrieked before going hoarse with fear. They fell down the waterline, skimming the surface of the dropping river. Another pearly white atranoch flapped up below, lapping massive streams of water with its enormous tongue. It seemed to pause, hovering in the updraft as if waiting for Sal'aah to land on its back with a splashy thud. N'damu immediately followed, grabbing on to Sal'aah's hips for dear life.

He'd always imagined the first atranoch bonders had done it very much this way, jumping on as the beasts slowed to drink. As the atranoch leveled off after a sizable ascent, he took his stance between the bone-dragon's shoulder frame. Smiling cheek to cheek, he loved the view from up here. *This must be how the gods saw Inana—when Inana had gods.*

N'damu seemed too petrified to move at first. Wrapping both arms and legs around one of the atranoch's immense bone spikes, the prince clamped his eyes. "Come, N'damu, you must see this,"

Sal'aah yelled back. He didn't recall ever seeing this particular atranoch before—her creamy white plating indicated her gender. She had scattered circular spots of red along her wings, which spanned fifty heads at least. Her six stunning eyes twinkled like yellow stars inside her boney exterior skull. She sang out a haunting screech, calling over the Sindiswa.

The prince finally opened his eyes and took in the glory of the world he was to rule. Sal'aah pointed down the mountain. "Look, there is Meadowdell. Just a white speck, and the whole trek, our six-rotation climb, looks the length of my finger from up here." The boy finally smiled but still could not speak, let alone venture to stand.

The Sindiswa Mountains seemed to cleave Inana in two from north to south. The M'lilo Forest was a lush green ocean to the east, and distant to the west were the Griner Valley's laurel farmlands.

Suddenly a shadow overtook them as Sho'nee flew down, eclipsing the sun with her atranoch. Sal'aah swerved quickly to regain the warm rays, wishing he'd worn a thicker poncho. "Okay, N'damu," he yelled. "It is time to attempt the rider's position." He reached back to grip a suitable spike and moved out of the way for the prince. The wind whipped his dreads over his specs. "Sho'nee will keep her stable. Reach out, tap into her energy." The boy still seemed too terrified to move. "It's okay, N'damu. Don't fear. Clear your mind of expectation—let go of your conscious self. Feel her wings. Sense her body and her heartbeat."

Shaking frantically, he finally reached up and began to climb the spikes, making his way toward the shoulder plates. The two atranochs soared through a valley clearing where two mountains split as N'damu took each bone in hand and moved to his knees.

"One more step," Sal'aah encouraged him, until finally the boy took his feet.

The moment of truth.

"Reach out, N'damu. You are linked through Khanya, N'damu." Sal'aah saw the boy's eyes light up as his fear washed away. "Express your will, as you would whisper a dream back to yourself."

Suddenly, the animal's colossal wings began to rise and drop with mighty flaps as the bone-dragon ascended.

"What the—" N'damu cried out in joyous confusion. "I just thought about going up."

"Concentrate … don't lose focus," Sal'aah shouted over his shoulder. *This is it. N'jikota.*

Out of nowhere, the beast dove with a jerk into a corkscrew nosedive that rivaled Sho'nee's earlier aerial acrobatics.

"Whooooooooo!" N'damu screamed, echoing Sal'aah's earlier call of elation.

He could see his daughter, never one to be outdone, emulating the maneuver seconds later. The bone-dragon spread its wings and floated down the foothills, skimming across the grasslands of the Sizwe. The shadow swept overhead again as Sho'nee glided down over them, and near twice the speed, blowing over trees and toppling animals in her wake. She began to flap again, guiding her atranoch back up into the mountains, with N'damu giving close chase.

"Let's not go *too* crazy," Sal'aah said, but he wasn't sure the prince heard him. "This is your maiden flight, after all."

Eventually, they retook the lead, swerving through the foothills, attempting to lose Sho'nee. The two winged titans raced over the trees with a swoosh, then skimmed a mountain lake that reflected their contest perfectly on its crisp surface—until Sal'aah reached down to break the tension with his finger.

They were soon up in the mountain clouds again, where they leveled off, soaring silently side by side. Sho'nee beamed with pride. "So, it is the atranoch. I'm so happy for you, My Prince. This is what you wanted!"

"Wow, I never want to go down again," N'damu cried out, almost in tears. "Thank you so much, both of you." He looked back at him.

Sal'aah's heart felt such satisfaction, yet something vexed him. What, he could not explain. *Why does something feel off?*

"I'm proud of you—young Atalay," he said. "The Atranoch King." *I would see the look on N'joku's face when he hears that.*

"I *do* like the sound of it," N'damu said as they veered around Mount Lapis.

Sal'aah's odd feeling worsened to nausea, like mongrels slashing at his insides. *Flight sickness? I never get—*

Out of nowhere, a crack rang out from the range below, and Sho'nee's atranoch let out a horrible scream. *Blaster fire?* Sal'aah thought.

Bang. Another shot. A proton flare burst through its wing, leaving a searing hole surrounded by burning skin. The bone-dragon screeched again. Sal'aah threw off his specs and looked down, perplexed. He could see only clouds. *Bang.* With another scream from her mighty atranoch, his daughter began to spiral out, dropping uncontrollably into the fog.

"SHO'NEEEEEEE!" he screamed in a desperate panic, doing everything he could to make the atranoch dive after her. Her eyes were wide with fear as she disappeared in the mist. *No. Not her. Not my baby.* "Dive damn it! DIVE!" *My nightmare,* he thought.

"I'm … I'm trying," N'damu yelled. "It … won't … LISTEN!"

Sal'aah knew it didn't matter now. They were already too late to catch her. His daughter was gone.

He moved up to take the rider's position from N'damu when another blast boomed from below. A fire ignited in his stomach. Wherever he had been cold before, he now felt nothing. Everything else was fire as Sal'aah looked down to see a hole where half his belly had once been. "N'damu," he said, looking into the prince's horrified black eyes. "N'damu."

With every ounce of strength he had left, Sal'aah tried to make his body move, but he couldn't even will his fingers from their grip. His legs were without sensation, his arms but pins and needles of ice. N'damu managed to pull him to a more secure

276

spike. His mouth could no longer form words as vomit and blood began to fill his throat. Violently, he hacked a spray of gore on the prince's horrified face as he tried desperately to keep them both from falling off the atranoch. "Meadowdell," N'damu cried out. "Please, take us to Meadowdell!"

But Sal'aah knew atranochs didn't speak the tongue of men. His intestines spilled like tynn grass as he gripped his abdomen, attempting to hold it all in. He could smell the stink of his internal organs, mixing with his bowels, of which he'd lost control. "Meadowdell," N'damu continued to beg desperately, over and over. "Meadowdell—Meadowdell!"

The queen was right: the threats were not a deception. That shot was meant for the prince. Luckily, my fat gut got in the way.

He could see the boy bawling, sobbing, uncontrollably frantic, yet powerless. *Don't worry, Son, I am ready to see my father again!* If only he could tell him. Thraxis began to flicker, a yellowish-orange strobe, as reality bent to his heartbeat's throbbing.

"I love you always, Sal'aah Novojoh," his wife had told him as he prepared to leave on N'damu's atranoch expedition. "Our prince, and our children, couldn't be in better hands." Marique was the most beautiful woman he'd ever laid eyes upon. "Still, please be careful, and fly safely. These threats against Atalay—"

"Nonsense, my love," Sal'aah had said dismissively. "The distraction is the biggest specter. Damn these Spears and VEOs to the Barren Void." He heard himself saying it over and over.

"Nonsense … nonsense." The words echoed in his mind. *Nonsense.*

Kaboom. The sickening thud of N'damu falling again from the mamidon perch, atop the ancient Milushi totem. Sal'aah ran across the tall grass to see if he was wounded. But before he could arrive, he saw the prince again falling from the top of the pole, careening to the soil. "N'damu," he cried as he reached him finally, only his body wasn't there. He looked up to witness him falling yet again—this time onto *him* with a thump. The Lord of Novojoh felt the impact in the pit of his stomach.

N'damu. The sky swirled ochre and lemon as the world seemed to shift, then drop. Sal'aah craved a maraphite sandwich on crumble bread and to bask on the Sizwe riversides like a tucsabura in summer. The thought consumed him while hunger ripped his gut.

"G'higari is the religion Inana has taken, my son," his father explained as Sal'aah looked up at him, fascinated. "But you must know, the ancient Novojoh heralded the Milushi faith." *Father. Alive? I've missed you every day, Father.* The Novojoh ancestors were the first to teach N'jikota to the clans of Atalay faithful, even though they had only ever held reverence for Khanya— rejecting the Doctrines.

"I am Milushi?" he asked his father, Lord Sav'ato Novojoh, whose hand he'd held the day he died.

"Yes," he replied. "And so much more, Son. You are not a remnant of Earth, natural nor Homo purist. You are a child of Inana, though you must be careful when you express that part of

278

yourself. Atalay has forbidden the faith. We are proclaimed a purist clan, and all must be pledged G'higari now. Even your friend, Prince N'joku, would not abide it."

Sal'aah felt like he was going to vomit as his heart rose to his throat. His belly churned with pain, and retch spewed from his lips. It tasted like eetee melon.

"Meadowdell," a voice cried out. "Meadowdell ... Meadowdell."

"I trust my daughter will be in good hands with you, Son," Lord Maxim Duran said as he extended an arm to finalize the marriage pact between their olden clans. Sal'aah looked over at the woman he was to marry, the gorgeous Marique Duran, who had endless brown eyes and snow-white hair smelling sweet as ipabites buds.

"I love you always, Sal'aah Novojoh," Marique told him as he prepared to leave on N'damu's atranoch expedition.

N'damu fell again in the distance, from the Milushi totem's perch. After him came Sho'nee, in a broken heap on top of him. Next was Sar'ah, then Shar'nah, S'ike, and the twins, piling in the tall tynn of the Sizwe. His mighty mamidon reared back. Sal'aah could not feel his spirit-link. The glow of N'jikota went dark, and the Kota of Mamidons lost control completely. With all its mass, the beast stomped down repeatedly. Its hooves crushed the prince and all his children, pounding until they disappeared into a bloody hole in the mud. Lightning shot to his gut as Sal'aah dove from his mount's back, only to land in a soothing lake.

279

The fresh cold water seemed to wake him from a trance as he looked up to see N'damu pulling him from the pond outside of the Hall of Novojoh. Looking up a moment, he noticed a white atranoch flying off in the distance, over the walls of Meadowdell. He was home again. *Did I chew kavah or something?*

"Help!" N'damu screamed in a tearful panic. Sal'aah looked at him with a blissful smile on his blood-smeared face. "Lord Novojoh needs help!" His house guard came quickly to his aide. *So tired. I need a nap.* Sal'aah Novojoh closed his eyes again and slipped into a calm and comfortable sleep, filled with dreams too fleeting to recall.

CHAPTER TWENTY

Myriam IV

The Knights of Yosai had recruited Ishikura Umi as an orphan refugee from the small island of Alerius. Her family died adrift on their makeshift raft, and she had washed up on the coast of Minicius, the sole survivor. Myriam and Ishikura were two budding flowers competing for the perfect spot in the sun. They grew up together in servitude and were both given a second chance by Clan Shingen. They lived, slept, ate, and trained side by side. They challenged each other, as was the way, rising quickly to the top of the Disciples of Yosai.

When the former Yon Justia, Bunko Shingen, was killed in a Port City street blitz, it created a power vacuum within the Yosai. Her younger brother, Azuma, who was then Yon Astra, took up the first mantle, but there was no Shingen to claim the second. In this event, it was tradition to turn to the Disciples to hold a tournament for the honor. Many came to fight, but it was indeed a contest of two. Myriam and Ishikura alone sat on the edge of greatness; both, appropriately, trained by Lord Azuma Shingen himself. It was like a scripted melodrama as they came to spar in the final battle for the Sword of Pegasus. Ishi never truly got over her defeat that day.

Thus were fostered the seeds of resentment.

Myriam moved in the shadows, following her former student, Yukimuro Ito, into the giant O'jod temple. Disciples of Yosai filled the pagoda, going about their humble duties. She knew the rhythm of this place, like in the Kejima prison. Though in O'jod, she needed to be ten times as stealthy. Disciples were certainly not androids, and a true Yon would detect her immediately.

The genetic access barriers were updated regularly, which was why she needed Yukimuro. That cretin Mok J'honda drew her attention, and now Myriam shadowed Yuki closely as she entered O'jod's restricted sector. She arrived at an elevator, taking to the silo, clinging to the car's bottom as it rose to the highest floor.

There, at the pagoda's pinnacle, was the sanctum of the Yons of Yosai. It was a wide-open hall, held up by dark, polished wooden pillars, and smelled a mix of spicy incense and manta-oil polish. All variety of hand-to-hand weapons ornamented the white walls: katana swords, throwing daggers, Sadah'anah spears, diskarmors, sais, and whistler stars. Ishikura Umi kicked at a heavy sandbag with ferocious grunts in the center of the padded black floor. Yukimuro Ito presented herself, taking a knee in front of her master. "Yon Umi, I come with my report." She bowed low.

Ishikura seemingly paid her no mind as she continued her assault on the bag. Repetitive thuds resounded as she picked up her pace.

"I have slain the escaped prisoner, Mok J'honda. He presented a danger to the public and required termination."

Ishi jumped with a twisting spin kick, severing the rope that held the bag aloft. Before it could hit the ground, she kicked it dead center on her second round. At that instant, Myriam slipped behind one of the columns like a specter, seemingly undetected. The bag exploded into sand as it hit the wall. Ishi landed and turned to her pupil. "How did it feel? Killing the man who manipulated you so in your youth?"

"I felt nothing, madam. A Yosai is not a heart of sentiment. A warrior is body and mind, filtered and untainted." Yuki recited the words as she rose from one knee.

"Good." Ishikura moved to another bag and began to kick at it with her shin. Dressed in an ash-gray robe, she had elongated eyes of indigo and bronzed southern island skin, common in the realm of Minicius. Ishi's hair was black with indigo streaks and swung long down her back in a curly tress.

Yukimuro turned from her master as Ishi carried on with her workout, stoically robotic in her demeanor. Myriam could spot the discontent on her former student's face. Yuki must have hoped for something more than an indifferent pat on the head.

"You may go now. I have business with the Yon Justia," Ishi commanded.

Myriam slid around the pillar as Yuki walked out of the hall to avoid her peripheral vision. Then, she put her hand on the hilt of her katana; the time had come.

Yon Justia. Head of the Yosai, Azuma Shingen. Myriam's one true love. Myriam's one true enemy. The *final* domino.

Once Yukimuro was gone, Myriam stepped out of the shadows and drew her sword, facing her former peer.

"I was wondering when you would reveal yourself," Ishikura said. "The girl still has much to learn. She's not born for it; not like you and I were at her age." She pulled a katana from the wall and faced her.

"Yes. Yumi's soul is still in flux," she replied. "Perhaps killing J'honda will be cathartic."

"Nevertheless, the child was your pawn this rotation. Isn't that right, *former* Yon Astra?"

"As we were both pawns of Azuma."

"Did you come to present me with my sword?" Ishi asked, referring to the ancient katana Myriam had taken as a parting gift from the Yosai. Not that they had ever offered it; the Sword of Pegasus was the rightful property of the Yon Astra. "That sword is mine now, by right."

Myriam tossed it down. "Take it," she said. "I just want *him*."

Ishi wasted no time. She picked up the katana, staring Myriam down with a sinister grin. Holding the blade aloft, she charged while she had an advantage.

Myriam sprang from the mat, tumbling across the room. Flipping and cartwheeling, she evaded Ishikura's frenzy of slashes by inches. A lock of her pink hair floated to the floor as Myriam ran up the wall. Grabbing a pair of sais, she vaulted backward and kicked off the ceiling, coming down on Ishi. Sparks flew as the women struck weapons, grunting ferociously.

She locked the Sword of Pegasus in the prongs of her sais. *I will never die by this blade,* she thought as she disarmed Ishikura, flinging the sword across the room. Ishi came around with a heel to her gut, knocking the wind from Myriam's lungs. Next, the new Yon Astra launched into a handstand helicopter kick, repeatedly blasting the former Yon Astra in her face.

Myriam caught one kick by the ankle and with a hard thud flipped Ishi to the mat. She stabbed her sais down, pinning both Ishi's wrists to the ground as she barraged her with head-butts. Screaming with each bludgeon, both women's foreheads cracked open.

In desperation, Ishikura caught Myriam with a head-scissor and flipped her over. The sais went flying as she landed on the mat with a hard thud. Rolling away, she quickly retook her feet. Then they both charged. The two women seemed to mirror each other's every move. Myriam's left hook met Ishi's right jab. Ishi's right shin slammed into Myriam's left. Every grapple met the perfect counter, every hold expertly reversed.

"Why come back here?" Ishikura asked, landing an uppercut. "Fool."

"Because I need to see to him one last time." Myriam returned the uppercut.

"You dishonor the Yosai order by returning to Long Zenya." They both jump-kicked, their soles colliding in the air, clapping like thunder. "You will die for this."

"Halt!"

Myriam looked over her shoulder and saw Lord Azuma Shingen himself standing in the archway of the entrance hall. Ishi gritted her teeth in frustration, picking up the Sword of Pegasus again and taking a knee of reverence. "Yon Justia, she has violated her banishment. She dishonors the Yosai by returning here. She dishonors you!"

Ishi held the katana out. Myriam stared down the blade that had been hers while her rival awaited sanction to swing. They froze motionless, silent. Sweat dripped from Ishikura's brow as she glowered with the hungry look of a predator.

Finally, the soft clacking of her former master's patient footsteps broke the silence as he came up behind Myriam. "Turn to me. I would see your face once more. Look upon me again, before the violet in your eyes fades to white. Before your lips dry and crack, and the rose in your cheeks blackens, look upon me, my former pupil." She turned and took a step in his direction, staring Azuma down while Ishi poked the katana into her back, ensuring her presence not be forgotten. "There she is. I remember the pretty little Jentrillian kiko moda. Oh, I could sense the fire within you from the start. 'What a Yosai she will become!' I told everyone when I vowed to train you."

"I was honored by the faith of Clan Shingen," Myriam said. "It is my deepest regret that I proved unworthy of your confidence."

Azuma was of average height for a man with such a transcendent presence. He had a handsome face that was hard to look away from, coppery skin, and oval eyes the color of graphite. The hair on his head was receding but still lush and black. With facial hair perfectly groomed into a mustache and goatee combination, he had wisps of silver mixed in the murk of his whiskers. He wore a golden robe embroidered with a red dragon—the symbol of Clan Shingen over his heart.

Ishi raised her blade to the back of her neck. "Master, let me execute her now."

"Leave me with her."

"Master!" Ishikura fumed, allowing her emotions to betray her. This was personal for her. Too personal for a Yon Astra, who was supposed to feel nothing.

"Leave the sword as well," Azuma snapped his fingers. "We will address this outburst later."

Ishi seethed as she tossed it at her master's feet, then hastily marched from the hall. Azuma picked the Sword of Pegasus up and flipped it 180 degrees. Catching it on his index finger, the sword balanced, perfectly upright. "It's a beautiful blade, to be sure," he said. He lay the katana across his forearm and took a knee in front of Myriam, offering it back to her. "I will take this sword back only from your lifeless corpse."

She accepted the blade and sheathed it at her hip, nodding in acknowledgment of his threat.

"Come, shall we take some air on the terrace? It's been so long." Azuma walked to the curtains and opened them to the balcony screens, translucent white and decorated with golden dragons, nagas, and incerta. He slid them aside, and they stepped out into the Thraxian warmth. "It *would* be a beautiful day to die." He put his hands to the rail and stared out over Long Zenya, steeped in its sea of perpetual morning mists.

"Kill me then," she said. "Do your duty."

"Is that why you've come?" He chuckled condescendingly. "Why you've violated your banishment and embarrassed my Disciples of Yosai?"

"I'm leaving Anu if you refuse," Myriam said. "Let's end this, once and for all. Before it's too late."

"End ... what, exactly?" He held up his nose to her. "I banished my failure alongside you. The lack of closure is meant to haunt you, Myriam Yamada."

"But darkness spreads in me like cancer. I am infected. Evil. This is the last chance for you to stop me." Myriam lost her words as the emotions she had fought to bury now boiled to the surface. Despite her best intentions, a tear streamed down one of her cheeks as she looked up at him. "This will be our last meeting. If you do not kill me now—"

"Myriam, my dear, you sit on the border of darkness and light. Between Barren Void and the Eternal Womb. You are trapped in a purgatory of your own making. You come seeking closure, permission to move on from the light for a place devoid and black."

"Is that so wrong, Azuma? My sin was falling in love with you. My weakness…" Myriam lamented. "I come here now to ask you to free me from my darkness—to kill me. Put a sword through my heart. Something must stay the weapon I am becoming—the evil that flourishes within me. As a Yosai, you must fight it. For the sake of Atalay."

Azuma shook his head in disapproval. "Your disgrace in my eyes now stands complete. I preach 'no emotions,' and you hear 'fall in love.' Your failure is my greatest shame, and now you ask me for the satisfaction of my forgiveness? The mercy of my blade?"

"It is no longer about *us*," she said. "It's about what I'm becoming. I've killed already—"

"And you will kill many more, if that is your destiny," Azuma replied. "That is another shame you must live with. A sentence that will not end until you are ripe and old and withered to nothing. Only *then* will I relieve your pain with my blade." *Liar. I know why you won't kill me. I see it in your eyes.*

Tears began to stream down her face in torrents as Myriam lost grasp of her last shred of humanity, finally engulfed in the blackness. "I am going to kill the Prince of Atalay. Then you will have no choice but to do your duty."

He chuckled, shaking his head. "Your weakness will prove you unfit for the task. The weakness in your heart will burn bright in the Light of Atalay."

"Then I will die on Inana," she replied. "Food for the nagas."

"That is not your destiny," he said. "Leave Anu, fine. There is nowhere in this cosmos from whence you won't return to me." He took her hand in kissed it gently. "Your fate will be fulfilled. I never told you how I truly feel." Azuma leaped onto the ledge of the balcony railing and turned back to her. "I allow only *you* this window to my dormant heart. I do love you, as I hate you for making me love. Your end does not come on some distant world, but by my blade, as I hold you in my arms and weep over your old corpse." His hair waved in the wind as the mists of Long Zenya shrouded him. "When the oceans go dry and the cities are dust—when the Eden Star is black in the sky, we will reunite and do battle. At the end of time, when the universe is cold and empty, our souls will remain, locked in eternal melee." He spread his arms, then flipped backward and off the terrace. "Until then, Myriam Yamada."

She was thankful no one was there to see the tears raining from her violet eyes. Myriam Yamada was a master of stealth.

CHAPTER TWENTY-ONE

N'joku IV

"I am sorry, My King. Atranoch flight is hazardous, as you know. My VEOs lost sight of N'damu, momentarily—but long enough." Lord Chancellor M'demke Vesta explained the situation in the south, looking up to the Seat of Atalay with a grimace wrought with despair. The king was shattered by the news he'd just received. Queen Anaqua sat on the seat a gradient below, sobbing uncontrollably. "When the shots were fired, they had lost all visual. The blasts could have come from any number of mountain populations."

"It's this *Volturis* that armed them, I know it." N'joku's veins began to boil. His fingers throbbed, pained from clenching fists of frustration and strangling nothing. There had more and more whispers of the Volturis's gathering forces. The wild desert and forest tribes, Stone Sea pirates, and savage mountain bandits had reportedly congregated in the south, illegally armed and under an anti-Atalayan flag. "Incompetence, Vesta." *Suspicious that the vaunted Vesta tech "lost sight" of the future king?*

"Princess Vesta had her finest men in place, but Lord Novojoh was *very* resistant to their presence. I only wish he'd been more cooperative."

"Dammit, Sal'aah!" he yelled, pounding the arm of his throne. "Did you forget *again* who is king?" *Foolish Milushi. Deep down, his ego overpowered his love for Atalay.*

"Clan Vesta will pray to Khanya for his recovery and the safety of the prince," M'demke declared. "But beyond that, rest assured: my VEOs will not sleep until we find out who took those shots."

Ala stepped up beside M'demke next. "Father, Aku and I are progressing in our ulanoid training. Some shorter carrier routes are coming back with reports already. Outlaws from Tilo country are flocking to the east with calls for mercenaries." Her golden mail shimmered in the sunbeams that poured through the windows. N'joku could see the urgency in her eyes as her bone-hawk screeched on her shoulder. "I am afraid more stand against Atalay than we knew."

"This solar storm catastrophe exposes their true colors," Aku said, shaking her wild red dreads. His other daughter had a fire in her voice, as always—like him, she was prepared to act. "Naturals are pouring out of West Icici—all the way to the shores of the Summer Sea. The land is inhospitable. Volturis is offering them food, weapons, and credits to fight in his army—"

"We need to be offering them more," Ala snapped, tapping her spear in the stone as the court cheered in support.

"My Princesses, please." M'demke adjusted his collar, then turned to the court. "We are doing all we can to aid the natural communities, I assure you." He puffed out his chest and turned up his nose. "But I refuse to put blasters in the hands of Inaneans. We will see more wanton death than any solar storm could inflict, I assure you."

Anaqua's wailing overtook the court, a horrid shriek that sent the ulanoids into the rafters and froze the slithering nagas. "What about my son? He is not safe out there. I don't want to discuss anything else until N'damu is home in one piece."

"Indeed, My Queen," Vesta agreed, twisting his beard like a weed in the garden. "The future of the Tri-Worlds hinders on N'damu's security.

N'joku Atalay finally stood from the Seat in his shaggy robes of gold satin, then took three steps down toward the court. Urnas and Usoca circled him uneasily, their anxiety a clear reflection of his anger at this affront. He turned from the court and stared past the arches, out into the endless mural of the cosmos. His face burned orange and kingly gold from the glow of the torches. None knew as well as N'joku Atalay the threat lurking out there. "General Sadah!" The Chancellor of Peace stood behind, armored head to toe in silvery implements. "Prepare the Soldiers of Sadah. The golden armies of N'gaia march to Meadowdell as soon as possible."

"Hear, hear!" Naris Commodus cried out in support of Atalay—likely flattering him, as he usually did before bursting his bubble with the outrageous price tags his commands incurred. "Though, as Chancellor of Finance, I'd be remiss in my duties if I failed to remind you that solar storm relief efforts have meant a hefty investment in crown credits and men." The noble Son of Anu's gilded silver vest sparkled, giving his paste-white skin and yellow hair a pale glow befitting the treasures he guarded.

Finance was the furthest thing from N'joku's mind, however. He hooted condescendingly at the court. "I'm sure you can find the credits, Lord Commodus. Certainly, you would not spare expense when it comes to your prince's safety."

Naris bowed low in compliance. His etiquette was impeccable, as always. However, for all his courtliness, N'joku couldn't help noticing a few drips of chaladha nut butter on the backside of his pearly trousers. They looked like shit stains.

"My King," Vesta interjected, waving his dark blue cape as he turned and paced back across the room. "We must not allow this one instance to draw us off guard." He constantly checked his servants and whispered to his assistants between speaking, like the old man was simultaneously conducting a symphony of business dealings. "Before this attack, we weren't even certain the threats against the prince were valid. Enahdra and her VEOs will be more than capable of—"

"M'demke, are you absolutely *certain*?" asked Queen Anaqua as she peeled back her silvery veil and cleared the tears from her lush fern eyes. "The fact is this spirit-quest was too dangerous. It was a mistake to allow N'damu to go. And now *this*, under Vesta Enforcement's watch."

"And under the watch of the Two Spears as well," M'demke added as he adjusted his oversized Vestian headdress like a young stud in a contest of pageantry.

Perhaps he has forgotten who is king here. Maybe the whole of the Tri-Worlds has forgotten me. I will remind them. "I am the Naga King!" N'joku growled imposingly. His baritone shook the throne room as he flipped his wild mane of flaming dreads, like an animal displaying supremacy. "These grats dare take shots at my son? They wound a lord of the olden clans, and you think I should leave retribution to *your* daughter? A princess? While she is a capable woman, you don't *really* expect me to do nothing? No, no, no: Usoca and Urnas will taste the blood of these vile barbarians. Jambi, prepare your soldiers to move, as I say."

"Yes, My King," Lord Sadah answered. "Though I'm afraid it will take some time to mobilize."

"Clan Sadah is simply not prepared for such rash action, My King," M'demke intervened once again. "The forces I have already deployed in Meadowdell are in excess of necessity. These are the acts of guerrilla terrorists—they will not attack castle walls. These are cheap cutthroats who work in stealth, who hide in shadows. They will not simply stand and fight you honorably. They wait for a mistake, a foolish act of passion, and only in your moment of vulnerability do they strike."

"Is this true, Jambi?" N'joku asked. "Are you not able to do your king's will? To protect your prince?" *A Sadah will never back down from a challenge to his ego.*

"Clan Sadah's spear is for Atalay," Jambi announced with a fist to his chest.

However, the confidence N'joku had grown up seeing in the general's eyes looked weathered. At 151 cycles, Jambi was not much older than the king himself.

"As always, we will do what must be done, old friend."

"And what of N'gaia? What of the Tower of Atalay?" Lord Vesta continued, not willing to relent. "Your wife and daughters."

"I am *king!* Why should I have to choose?"

"I second *you*, Father," Princess Ala chimed in, tapping her spear to the ground repeatedly. "Aku and I will be more than capable of defending the Seat in the absence of Clan Sadah." *The fire of Adam Atalay burns within her.*

Not to be outshined by her twin, Aku, of course, added her input as well. "Besides, Lord Vesta, you said it yourself: they will not attack us as an army might. These villains are most likely rogues from the wildlands. Let them experience our strength." His daughters were as dangerous as they were gorgeous; it occurred to him from time to time that the realm might be in better hands with one of them than his son—or even than with *him*, in fact. Ala and Aku were both fierce as wild nagas.

"This is about your brother," M'demke said with a sour scowl. The king was not used to seeing Lord Vesta face such opposition on a matter. It was oddly satisfying. "Lord Novojoh is on the brink of death. Puffing out our chests like Earth apes does little good. N'joku, please: we are old men, and you are not the hero you once were—we are long past our time of valor. Our war is over."

Little does he know the hero inside me, starved for battle. "Lord Vesta, I know you would never question the strength of Atalay or the resolve of my reign."

"I would like to hear from Lady Li'asaga, if we may," the queen suggested as she finally collected herself enough to speak clearly. As the Chancellor of Faith, Elle Li'asaga was the spiritual guide to the king. "What council have you for the court, Elle?" It was her duty to counsel him in all matters religious in nature.

"Long have the G'higari abhorred violence between men," Lady Li'asaga said, standing in her holy robes of lavender, jingling as her many links of white beads, polished crongrin teeth, and rare ichnid pearls shook with her movements. As the G'higari Chieftain in N'gaia, the king had always loved her as a boy would love his mother—a fact his wife was well aware of, as she no doubt was seeking her support. "All Khanyastic faiths preach natural equilibrium within the Womb of Inana. Since the natural-born Inaneans arose to let go the old way, we have preached only the cultivation of harmonious balance with the biosphere. Keep in mind, harmonious balance does not mean peace. When wrought with violence, one must sometimes fight

297

and, if necessary, even kill to survive. Apex predators must exert their dominance as hapless prey fall by the wayside. Cycles pass with or without us. Khanya existed long before man arrived at Thraxis and will thrive long after we are dust. This rotation knows our king, N'joku Atalay, as apex predator—for, of us Homo purists, he is alpha. The stars aligned with the spirit of our people to show the path to the Eden Star, only by the will of Atalay, Shepherd of Men."

"Our forces move at dawn," N'joku proclaimed again. "I will accompany you."

"N'joku!" his wife cried out.

"Father, you cannot be serious," Princess Ala also interposed.

"I am the king, and my son is under threat," he said in a thunderous voice. "Any who would say I am too old, too weak, might challenge me and allow me to show the power I wield."

"You will *not* be leaving this tower under any circumstance," the queen reiterated.

"King N'joku, if I may." The Chancellor of Science, Serivicious Starr, bowed low, finally interjecting after being quiet and contemplative all morning. "While being Atalay is an amazing thing, and your great conviction is commendable, it behooves me to point out that you are a man of *flesh*. One errant blast would have every bit as much effect on you as it did on Lord Novojoh." Dressed in stately magenta tunic and trousers, he was always a man of cold calculation and would never simply tell N'joku what he wanted to hear. "All the faith in Khanya will not resurrect you once you're gone—or prepare the Tri-Worlds for

298

life without your benevolent rule." The man of Oshun bowed his head in reverence, his words hitting the king like a punch and leaving a hollow pit in his stomach.

"The Tri-Worlds would be left in ruin without you, My King," Naris Commodus added. *The sniveling shit.* An Atalay would never fear death over weakness—over failed ambitions or letting his ancestors down.

"You all support a war, yet not when your king would fight it himself?" M'demke Vesta commented once again. "N'joku, surely if we are to send our men into such danger, patrolling the impenetrable Sindiswa, I can understand your desire to stand on the front lines. While I do not support this act of aggression, I am not a believer in half measures. Clan Vesta will back you, if this is your will. Should we die, let it be with honor. In our prodigy, we must trust." Vesta looked to Ala and Aku with an old, bent smile. N'joku felt only confusion at the strange turn in the old man's stance. Perhaps the disease of age was finally taking the Lord Chancellor's faculties.

While he had much love for Vesta, the king's ego would never allow the Tri-Worlds to believe that any clan could rival Atalay. Therefore, it would be N'gaia's forces that brought justice to these criminals. That would be enough to keep his son safe and to remind the Tri-Worlds of the prominence of Atalay.

"I will stay in N'gaia," N'joku announced meekly. He felt a sharp pain in his chest and massaged his breastplate. "My responsibility is to my people, however much it grieves me not to fight with the men my orders send into the fray." The shame burned his heart like acid reflux.

"Fret not, my friends. Our children will represent us well, I swear to you," Lord Vesta assured him once more. "Princess Enahdra will keep the peace." However, the king couldn't help but wonder why his friend was so determined to make the princess the hero of this campaign. "She will lead the joint armies valiantly. With the Soldiers of Sadah and the Gold Knights of N'gaia behind her, order will quickly be reestablished."

"No," N'joku said. "My daughter Ala will lead the campaign." *Even Clan Vesta must learn their place.*

Princess Ala bowed in reverence to her father. "It would be an honor, Father," she said as her agitated ulanoid flapped its wings. "Though I'm not—"

"What has gotten into your mind, you old fool?" Queen Anaqua quickly interrupted. "Our goal is to get our children *out* of the line of fire, not send them running toward it. Ala is young still—Enah as well. You ego-driven mamidon asses! They all need to come home immediately."

"You are right, of course, My Queen." M'demke had a sparkle in his deep blue eye as he smiled at the king like he was holding a *packed dynasty* in Eden's Ace. "Perhaps someone with more experience should take command. Lady Sadah, perhaps? There are none more honorable."

"Yes, I second that," Ala said in a soft, graceful voice that the king recognized: a daughter afraid to undermine her mother.

"I concur," Aku added, not to be forgotten. Though she was only minutes younger than Ala, she was still very much her little sister. She pounded her staff into the cold stone floor. "Shyla Sadah will find the Volturis and chop off his manhood."

"What if it's a woman?" Ala replied, taunting her sister.

"Enough!" N'joku snapped. "Shyla Sadah, Sword of Atalay and commander of my Royal Guard, will you go to Meadowdell and bring back my son?"

Shyla stood and peeled back the white hood of her broadcloth kandora, releasing her vibrant black hair. With a twirl, she whirled her mighty long spear aloft before driving the hilt to the floor with an echoing clank and kneeling before him. "My spear is yours, King N'joku."

***

N'joku found no rest that evening as he sat up in his royal chamber, staring at a crystalline chandelier hanging over his bed. The transparent prisms gathered just enough starlight to cast ghostly rainbows upon his polished quartz walls. The king imagined they were the glimmer of his forefathers' spirits come to watch over him. He constantly shifted in the sheets, avoiding the areas of mattress he'd recently soaked with his pooling body sweat, which had now gone cold. Whether it was anxiety or blood pressure, he wasn't sure, though the stress-eating before bed probably didn't help. *Yeah, that twelfth tinkercane bar was perhaps a mistake.*

He looked over at Anaqua, envious of her rest. She, at least, was in an uncomfortable state of slumber—finally. *N'damu was unharmed; I should be thankful.* The mental debate was exhausting. Should he go to Meadowdell himself and reject his council's logic and advice? *This Volturis and his savages have the wills of fools if they think Atalay can fall. My war is far from over.*

The acid in his stomach began to move up to his chest, causing him to sit up and plop his chubby legs over the bed's edge. *What respect do I command when my own people attack my son? MY SON! The future of Atalay.* Thoughts screamed inside his head, loud enough even to drown out his wife's snoring. *They think I'm beyond utility—a figurehead king—a fat stuffed ornament of worship.*

An ache twisted in his chest. For a moment, he worried it might be a heart attack until the sensation moved to his throat. *Am I just old and used up—protecting my family from a chair, half a world away?* Suddenly, his bladder raged as well. *Is the great Naga King incapable of avenging a fallen comrade? This is what they think in that court.*

Putting his dry, cracked soles to the floor, N'joku nearly stumbled. Pins and needles spread across his feet as he wiggled his toes to life. *The "Shepherd of Humanity" might as well be a rusted lamp—a decayed pot of flowers.*

Usoca and Urnas slept together in a coiled heap upon their lavish cushions. N'joku crept around them carefully. Unlike his wife, who'd long since become accustomed to his late-night trips to the urinal, his nagas were easily stirred. *Don't need those damn beasts rousing the entire realm.*

He knew the guard on duty was Haldir Nolan. Though he trusted the man with his life on a battlefield, he had less faith in his ability to stay vigilant during the graveyard shift. Despite the king's hefty frame, his bare feet made only dainty pats as he snuck by the snoozing guard. *We do need to improve security— this is far too easy*, the king thought as he slipped around the corner of the hall and into an elevator lift. *That is the problem, for myself, for N'damu. It's just not possible to contain an Atalay!*

The elevator capsule came to a halt with a light jerk, and N'joku stepped out into his secret hall. His personal quarters were on a level only he could access; it was a cave of solitude where no one could encroach on his whims. "Lights." The hall lit up instantly with soft yellow torches, illuminating his mural-covered walls. He loved to paint, though so many of his works ended up abandoned, unfinished. Though the arts enamored him, the king's focus was always fleeting. *So much easier to be the hero here—alone,* he thought.

N'joku also loved music, though he'd never had the confidence to play in front of anyone. The king had perfectly maintained stations set up for every musical instrument imaginable. Each boasted the most refined craftsmanship the Tri-Worlds had to offer, from authentic tribal percussion kits from the Jade Moon, symphonic string sections carved in rich Inanean blackwood, and even the latest New Vrinasi synthesizers.

He could not deny that the thought of throwing a spear or thrusting a sword excited him more than any instrument he had here. *If I go to war—if I swing my diskarmor in battle again, would I be doing it for N'damu or myself?*

He liked to imagine sometimes what an ensemble of virtuoso musicians or masterful artists might create in there, yet this place was for *his* eyes and ears alone. His style was sloppy, his music loose and off-key. His poems were lazy, and his dancing always late by a step. All the same, N'joku was a genius at everything he did in this room. The ghosts of his ancestors always cheered and applauded.

Would it be fear or reason that kept him in N'gaia—on his uncomfortable throne?

The king sat at a corner desk on his soft leather chair on wheels and rolled in front of a control board lined with fader pads, nobs, and meters. He cued up a Centralian opera on his media system and began to stuff his smoking pipe with a load of ganja. *Doctrine Three: Atalay does not demand loyalty. All humans have freedom of thought and will.* He gazed hypnotically at his collection of exotic nude sculptures and puffed rings of smoke.

A violent fit of hacking cut short his thoughts—yet he still took another haul of smoke before fully recovering his breath. *Is Atalay only a shadow on the wall—keeping the high clans in line?* He let loose a lung load to more coughing, then buried his forehead in his palms, running his fingers down his face, massaging his wrinkled brown skin and pinching anxiously at his silvery beard. *What happens when the shadow is gone?*

It was then he realized perhaps his call to action was not to fight but to find the courage to stay. His valor was in humility—in sending his warriors to fight for him while he remained chained to the Seat.

Once the high settled his brain, the king did as he always did when stress was too much. He grabbed his ankahbra zhuru from its stand, flipped on the amplification module, and began to pluck its shiny strings, losing himself in sorrowful melodies.

***

N'joku marched to the O'taji Fortress with the rise of Thraxis. His nagas trailed him with regal obedience as he went to show support for the warriors of N'gaia, loyal soldiers who might never see home again. In his famed golden suit of mail, he held his diskarmor proudly over his chest as he strutted the halls. Capped by a shimmering crown, his helm's grill was gilded with crimson jewelry and showed only the glow of his eyes underneath.

The king felt empowered in his armor, though the breastplate was much tighter than it had once been. In fact, his weapon felt heavier as well, like his heart. Nevertheless, it was the least he could do, considering parents might be leaving their children forever orphaned. He had seen so many of his friends die on the dark side of Anu. The scars from that trauma still lingered.

He had claimed the war a victory, but it was really the locals who brokered the truce. The Mahr Meca, leader of the darksiders, moved the Charon armies out of Izlagos and back to their dark islands—and N'joku took his armada back to Inana. It never *really* felt like a triumph. Weapons of mass destruction like the electron atomizer frightened everyone. Anu could have been destroyed were they to unleash such a weapon. So, both sides conceded, accepting a bitter peace. *Another painting, unfinished.*

He opened the polished-gold gate to the *Angkor*, his royal war chariot. After Usoca and Urnas slithered on, he secured it behind him. The hovercraft was pearl white with gold trim, powered by quark flux thrusters, and stabilized by state-of-the-art gyro-tech. It was a vehicle for a king.

It was no easy thing to send men into the dangers of the mountains. The tribes were ruthless and would undoubtedly kill many of his subjects. Soaring over the city, he could see N'gaia bustling as it prepared for mobilization. Lowering his chariot over a crowd of Sadah soldiers, he lifted his helm and shook out his locks again.

"Great warriors of Inana, hear me now! It grieves me to beg this calling of you, this rotation. I love you all, and I take nothing more seriously than your place in our great kingdom. As I would never ask you to live for nothing, I would never ask you to die for nothing. Atalay is my name, and while I would never claim that I am the same as all of you, I can tell you with all certainty that as the cycles pass, I envy you all. They call me hero; they call me king, and yet my reverence is for *all* of you. We of the G'higari love our place in the Womb of Inana, together, and humankind has long hailed Atalay as Shepherd. But the people are the saviors of Atalay, for you are the living creators. The

306

blood in my son's veins holds the oldest and holiest DNA. As we preserve knowledge and technology—as we preserve great works of art and music, so too must we defend the Homo purist genome. For the honor of N'gaia, we will not let our great society come to ruin, vandalized by darkness or time."

The soldiers amassed as his speech went on, and soon the shadow of his chariot floated over a sea of cheering warriors: Sadahs, VEOs—soldiers and fighters from all corners. "I implore you, heroes of N'gaia, great soldiers of Sadah, bring these would-be assassins to justice. Desert warriors of the Fuza, Atalay beseeches you: avenge this attack on my brother in arms, Lord Sal'aah Novojoh. Spearmen of Ulundia, mountaineers of Vaccavane and the Zola, VEOs of Centralia: secure Meadowdell and ensure my son's safety. Noble children of Asa, Oba, and Duran, sons of Anu and Oshun, I beg, please heed my desperate call. A darkness is coming to the Tri-Worlds, and we must first unite if we are to survive together. The Volturis and the vile inhuman fiends who aid him have maimed our brethren. Go forth and serve these villains the justice of Atalay!"

CHAPTER TWENTY-TWO

Enahdra III

Transmission one

Enahdra Vesta had always had more than her peers. More wealth, beauty, and influence—none of it seemed unusual. Even the life of a king did not leave her wanting, on a material level anyway. Power and worship, on the other hand, were enticing.

Father had taught her well. In polite Atalayan society, it was rude to speak of your superiority to those of a lower station. Since there were none higher than Clan Vesta—they'd always quietly been the Clan of Ghosts. *Unborn, undying ... we are the silent souls, the specters in the garden—the truth behind all humankind.* Enah thought about those sayings her father would whisper in confidence as he tucked her into bed.

The planet was crippled after the coronal mass ejection devastated Inana's electro-magnetosphere. A problem for all, purist and natural alike—yet nary a concern for Vesta. She and her select allies had Quantum Net Transmitters, which transferred data instantly and over vast distances through particle entanglement. The princess would have told everyone she had coms but always reminded herself: *it's impolite to speak of your supremacy.*

"N'damu is safe, Father. Don't worry." Enah looked up at Lord Vesta's likeness cast in blue light emanating from her silver ring. "You can assure his deviant father." She stood in the command bridge of her megamagnus, now parked on the lawn of the Hall of Novojoh.

"I certainly will," her father said. "Once I factor in the latency of this information's travel time, of course."

"Why are we keeping the QNTs so secret anyway?" she asked, holding up her finger in awe of the tech. "Or the ultranium eleven engines, for that matter? Surely, Inana could use—"

"Sweet daughter, there is nothing we can do about the satellite grid for now." He wrapped his finger around his beard, squinting as he honed his glare. "Every advantage is opportunity, Enahdra. We cannot simply *give* this tech away because there is a need. Until I decide how to exploit our tools best, they must remain classified."

"I understand, Father."

"Does anyone else have a Q-net device?" he asked.

She shook her head. "Only us, Father. Not even Ahdia has a ring."

"Give me a logistics report," M'demke said. The hologram detailed his crooked teeth flawlessly as he leered. "I like to know where my chess pieces are." Her father loved Earth games as much as she did.

"The majority of the VEOs have been directed to the Sindiswa to find the brigands who shot Lord Sal'aah. The Two Spears and the Novojoh children are still up there as well, camped in the basin of Mount Lapis. The prince is here in Meadowdell at his master's bedside."

Father fiddled his fingers together as he stared off in thought. "Your focus must be on N'damu and N'damu alone. He is vulnerable on his own."

"I know," Enah said, scrunching her nose and looking down at her feet.

"Atalay is the most powerful Vesta tech ever created. Protect it. Bring honor to our clan, Enahdra. Remember what happens when you don't."

Twelve cycles ago

Tears gushed down her cheeks like waterfalls as Enahdra watched Theodus Darius dragged by his hair down the throne room's crimson carpet. The gold-armored guards threw him at the feet of N'joku Atalay. The king's nagas were in a frenzied panic, as though feeding time was near. She wanted to scream out or to rush the floor and offer herself to Usoca and Urnas. Enah glanced at Rigel. *Would he save him if I ordered it? Would he kill everyone here—leaving only Theodus and I to be king and queen?*

"You have dishonored Clan Darius, boy." The fat, ugly king shuffled down the steps. Theodus struggled to his knees while the nagas rattled, sniffing him up and down. The lordling of Darius looked utterly defeated. With blackened eyes and bleeding from the lip, he was limp and spent. "What do you have to say to the court?"

"Does anyone have a spliff?" He chuckled as Usoca snapped an inch from his face. "No?" He looked around the court, flashing his dashing smile. "A glass of Vhimhilian?" The court swelled with laughter. Even the vile king cracked a crooked smirk before Father noticed, and he quickly returned to a mock scowl.

"Death for this dishonor to Clan Vesta," her father said from his Lord Chancellor's podium. "Feed him to the nagas, My King."

"Father, no!" Enahdra cried out finally. The court was aghast.

"Enahdra," he said calmly. "Silence, child."

"No, I will not! This was *my* fault, Father." Lord Vesta nodded at Rigel, and he immediately came up behind her and covered her mouth with his hand.

"You are hereby stripped of your wardship," King N'joku said as the nagas slithered away from Theodus and cuddled beside him. "I denounce you. I shame you and deny you the Light of Atalay. I exile you from Inana, never to return. It is only because you carry the blood of Darius that I let you live out your disgraceful cycles on Anu." The king smiled at Enahdra, though she was unmoved, glaring back at him with ire. "Most importantly, you are never to contact the princess again. Not a word, nor even a glance."

"Fine!" He hacked out a gob of blood and puss. "Where are we on that ganja?" The golden guards of Atalay carried Theodus out unceremoniously.

Enah knew what her father had done, manipulating the moron king like a puppet on strings. The obese fool would never kill on Father's order—his ego would never allow it.

She squinted at her father, creasing her brow with juddering lips as she tried to compose herself. *He wouldn't want a purist lordling killed—he would consider it a wasted commodity.* The Atalayan alliance with Clan Darius was a crucial cog in Vesta's influence on Anu. His death would be … problematic.

Transmission two

Enahdra slid her fingers through the holographic field of her Q-Net ring.

"Does your father know?" Rigel Kong asked as his hologram materialized in front of her.

"He knows what he *needs* to know!" Enah confidently flipped her indigo hair back. "What I want him to know."

"Well, remember, Princess: secrets don't come cheap on Oshun."

"That's because you're a moon of degenerated jungle mutates," Enahdra said, doubling her decibels. "You like credits; I get it. Do you think it's an accident that my fingertips create credits? I just type in a number. It's the magic of Vesta. It's better than mind control."

"Well, if your daddy finds out—"

"My *father*. Never call him 'daddy.'"

Rigel tipped down his shades and sneered. "That blue-bearded son of a mongrel will have me disintegrated." She could count

312

the times she'd seen his eyes on one hand, yet the worry in them was unmistakable.

Enah lurched over, laughing. "I know."

"One less Oshunese *natch*, eh?" Rigel asked. The princess poured herself a glass of vintage and took a sip, its blood-red tint staining her lips.

"No, no. I *need* a low-breed like you; you know that, Rigel. Or should I call you 'Volturis?' I can't employ those disgusting bandits on my own. If I were caught supplying weapons to the wild tribes, image the scandal."

Rigel shrugged. "I just don't get why you would let 'em *use* those weapons. They coulda wasted the prince on the river."

"They almost used them on me!" Enah shook her fists. "I don't want another debacle like the attack at the river. They were just supposed to scare him."

"It would have been the perfect time to kill a Novojoh, at least."

"Death has no part in the plan, fool. Purist blood is a precious product. I'd never waste it." Enahdra paced the command bridge before taking a seat and crossing her legs. "I'd kill the incompetent dupe who blasted Lord Novojoh." She sipped from her glass again.

"That fucking kook had it comin'."

"Again, you are the gun, but I am the trigger. You don't shoot anything I don't say."

"Gun?" he asked. "What the fuck is a gu—"

"Just keep Noba and the Novojoh spinning in circles up in the mountains, searching for N'damu," Enah said, scoffing at his

Earth-lore ignorance. "I need time alone with him. This is the perfect opportunity."

"Get on with it then." Rigel shook his head. Since they'd left Centralia, his frustration seemed to escalate. "All these lies and fake threats. Colt Dunkarr, Volturis—I'm going to lose track."

"Just pushing a few Atalay buttons—no big deal," Enah said with a giggle. "How else could I get invited on N'damu's most *private* religious pilgrimage?"

"Seems like a lot of work just to get that scrawny little shit alone."

"Yes, well, seducing a deity is not easy," Enah said as she rubbed her brow. "As one myself, I know. It takes finesse."

"The Chuku bitch doesn't seem to have a problem with it," Rigel said. "Saw him sneaking in and out of her tent on the way up Lapis."

"WHAT!" Enah threw her glass through Rigel's hologram in a rage. It shattered against the wall as the distorted light came back into form. "That is impossible."

"I have had my eyes on that squirt every second. I saw what I—" She ended the transmission before he could finish. Pacing the room, the princess could feel her heartbeat on overdrive. Enahdra had no idea why she felt so enraged—so animalistically jealous over a boy she'd never had carnal desires for.

She tried to pour another glass but couldn't steady her hands enough to hold the bottle. The princess thought about N'damu, naked with that natural—inside *her*—that baseline slut. *I am losing my mind.*

Screaming, she threw the bottle and toppled an entire table filled with dishes and glass. *Why am I angry about this?* When

314

they'd left N'gaia, she had no real attraction to him beyond the politics of their union. Even in Centralia—seeing him newly resynthesized did nothing to stir arousal. He was a Prince of Atalay and she a Princess of Vesta, something her father never let her forget. She'd always loved him, yet never *lusted,* until now. That moment, a spark lit a flame within her—a fire she'd never been able to ignite.

"It may not be true," she whispered to herself as she steadied her breathing. As if some haze encompassed her thoughts—some hypnotizing black magic seemed to make her look at him differently. "I need to make my move. Now." Enahdra Vesta couldn't afford to invest in the wrong king again.

Twelve cycles ago

"I need to make my move, now," she whispered to herself. The night was dark and ominous. The glorious golden capital that she was so excited to come to now seemed like a prison—a hallucination of the Barren Void. Enah slipped out of her bed, softly tiptoeing past Ahdia as she snored. She had no idea what to do—how a little girl in pajamas could rescue Theodus Darius and escape N'gaia.

A Princess of Vesta was no fighter nor covert operative. *What would Father do?* she thought. The answer to that was clear: he would use his puppet, N'joku, to free him. He did not need weapons to get what he desired. *Theodus's sentence is Father's doing alone. He gets to keep the peace on Anu AND get me away from the man I love.*

Unfortunately, M'demke Vesta was more formidable than the focused totality of Atalay. All she could do was beat him at his own game. Enahdra poked her head out her chamber door and whispered to the two VEOs standing guard over her. "*Psssst!* Guard."

"The hour is late, Princess," the VEO said. He was a young Centralian boy, newly arrived at the capitol. *He looks gullible enough,* she thought.

"I cannot sleep, for fear." Enah bit her lip and trembled. "Will you accompany me as I stroll the halls?"

"I'm afraid the Lord Chancellor has ordered you remain in your chambers," he explained with a squeak in his tone. "Until the exile is deported."

"I want to speak to Commander Kong myself." She felt a tap on her shoulder.

"I've had my eye on you since your foot hit the carpet," Rigel said. Enah's shoulders dropped, and she shook her head. "Go to bed, Princess. There is nothing to fear." He brandished a sword at his hip. "A katana forged in krotrium. Pretty fuckin' beautiful for a weapon you have to swing. You're safe, girl. Trust me."

"Impressive blade," she admitted. "Father pays you handsomely, for an immigrant natural."

Rigel only snickered, grinning at her with shades on, even at night. "Ha! Your daddy knows the score. Unlike you rich, spoiled, tube-babies, I'm the type with absolute loyalty to one thing."

"Credits," she said with a nod.

Rigel Kong slouched. "Credits, weapons, tech—and M'demke Vesta has the most."

"Not necessarily." Enahdra's navy blue eyes sparkled in the starlight. She hurried over to her closet, swung open the door, and began rooting through her bag. She pulled out a small ring and tossed it to Rigel. "That is a QNT ring." She beamed every time she talked about tech. "It's a cutting-edge prototype. I can assure you, it's worth a great deal more than Father is paying you."

Kong held the ring up in his palm with a curled lip. "What the fuck does it do?"

"It interfaces with the Q-Net, which I'm not about to explain to you now." She stood up to him with authority, though her nose barely reached his navel. "Do you want it or not?"

"What use do I have with the Q-Ne—"

Princes Enahdra held up her own ring, revealing a holographic field filled with virtual buttons, screens, switches, and nobs. She flipped an image in the air, spreading out her hands to increase the size. "These are your accounts, correct?"

He clenched his teeth as he loomed over her like a trench-coated mountain. "I wouldn't mess with my creds, sweetheart." Rigel patted the scabbard at his hip to remind her of his sword.

Unintimidated, she waved her finger through the field in a circle, increasing his bankroll as though she were winding an Earth clock. "My father is an old man—you are young, Commander Kong. When he is gone, I will be in command of all that is Vesta. When he is gone, what do you think will happen?" Enah reversed the direction of her fingers, and his account balance dropped. She could feel his palpable rage emanating. "You could be the Commander of the Vesta Enforcement Officers until you die. Endowed with the greatest tech and limitless wealth for a lifetime." The princess brought the number back up and down—up and down. "Or you could be shipped back to that mamidon turd of a moon you came from, without a single cred."

He nodded and put on the ring. Enah smiled as she added zeros to his bottom line.

"It is custom to hold up your weapon when vowing your blade to a princess."

Rigel took a knee as he unsheathed his katana and held it out. "What do you ask of me then, Princess Vesta?"

"I want Theodus Darius," she said.

Rigel nodded. "Simple. But you know he is grat-shit insane, don't you?"

"Watch your tongue, Kong. He will be your king one day." Enah began to riffle through her closet, fingering through clothes hangers. "Gowns—gowns—gowns," she mumbled.

Her new servant chuckled as she looked through her role-play attire. There was no reason to hide anything from Rigel now.

He turned his back. "You're too young for that shit."

"Don't be a prude, Kong. Let' see. No, not schoolgirl. Not Charonese slave. Kandora? No. Yosai warrior, *hoya hasta gi*? Earth girl! I *wish*—but, no. Oh, here we go." She held an Izlagosi Guard uniform over her silk pajamas, flipping back her silky blue hair. "You will smuggle me in with Theodus's guards. I'm going to Anu." She put her fingers over her lips. "Hush now, don't tell Father."

Transmission three

"My Queen, finally, you answer me," Theodus Darius said, his hologram grinning like a desert drifter who'd at last seen water. "I have been lost without you. Please, talk to me. Tell Daddy you still love him." Sadly, this would be their final conversation. As parched as he was for her affection, Enahdra was a mirage in the sand—a dead salt sea that would only doom him.

"I am professing my love to N'damu," Enahdra said, with her back to the hologram. "I want *you* to know. I want it to be the last thing you hear from my lips. That I will be the queen—the *real* queen—without you."

"HA!" Theodus went into a tizzy, flipping over tables, throwing chairs, breaking windows, and thrashing furniture. "Enjoy it while it lasts, my love. 'Til the hitman comes to hit."

Enah jeered. "Tsk, tsk. My golden-haired atlas, it's so unlike you to be fooled by whispers." She walked up to his proxy, formed of light. "The Volturis is a shadow on the wall, cast by my hands." Leaning over, she kissed the hologram. "No threat of regicide has been uttered without my knowledge."

"HA! The Volturis?" He spat at her—a gob of holographic light that passed through her cheek. "You always were a stupid, spoiled little cunt." He unzipped his pants and let them drop to his ankles. His hologram cock pointed straight at her. "I can't wait to have you back."

Enahdra laughed as she reached down, her fingers passing through the intangible organ. "You will never touch me again. Perhaps your sister, Quinn might be avail—"

"Shut the fuck up, you sick little girl." He lit a spliff and stroked himself. "Just keep the Seat warm for your master, whore."

She snarled like a naga, taking the straps off her dress and letting it fall, exposing her naked body to him. "Do you think N'damu will enjoy this?" She puckered her lips, squeezing her breasts together as she kicked the gown aside. "As much as you did, back on Anu?"

His eyes lit up—bright as Thraxis. "Oh, he will," Theodus said, his holographic hands moving over her body like a ghost's. "Let him give you what pleasure he can before my assassins arrive."

Enah tilted her head, perplexed. "What assassin do you have?"

"Assassins—plural," he corrected her. "But this one will be enough. My Yon Astra gone afoul—my Yosai turned away from the light." The hologram suddenly cued footage of a woman, pink-haired and dressed all in black. With a whirling katana, she cut through at least twenty of his Izlagosi Guard like they were newborn schmiglets. "You better enjoy your pathetic little prince while you can. Myriam Yamada is the most dangerous human alive, and she might be on Inana already."

Princess Enahdra seethed as she watched the footage. "You are disgusting." She trembled, horrified to the core. "Is this real?"

"How do you address me? Slut."

"Is this real … Daddy?" She bowed her head and sniffled.

He bent over, propping himself on his knees as he laughed. "Ha! As real as our love, my queen of queens." Theodus's hologram flickered as he kneeled in front of her. "Myriam

Yamada is as real as death is imminent." He blew a puff of holographic smoke into her face as she scowled. "I suffer without you, Princess."

"Call her off, please."

"NOOOOOO! No-no-no-no-no!" His bloodshot eyes seemed to spin in opposite directions as he hooted and hollered.

"I love him." *I love him?* she asked herself. *Really?*

"Look what Atalay has done to you! You are under a spell— the Light of Atalay is a laser beam coring out your brain and enslaving you."

"It's not!" She frantically shook. "It's not?"

"Yamada will cleanse you of his toxin," he said. "Then you will return to me."

Enah began to punch the floor, bloodying and bruising her fists as she screeched obscenities. Hopeless, desperate, she begged him. "Theodus. Master—Daddy—God, please. Don't kill him!"

"Was this how you pleaded with your father to save my life?" He stood with crossed arms, chuckling to himself. "I would RATHER have died than lose you. I need my queen back!"

"Killing N'damu won't get me back, Theodus." Tears trickled down as she pulled her dress back on.

"Then I'll kill M'demke too. And Ahdia. I'll kill N'joku, Anaqua, and those bitch twins. I'll kill every last person on all three worlds if that's what it takes." He stared through her. Enah couldn't remember seeing a man more indomitable. "I will be king, and you will be queen. If we are to rule over three worlds filled with corpses, so be it."

She fell to her knees, weeping as his hologram faded.

CHAPTER TWENTY-THREE

N'damu VI

"You must develop an eye for the smoothest stones, my son, for of all the rocks that line the riverside, most would sink straight to the bottom. So few have those perfect, rare attributes: flat and even enough to dance over the surface." N'damu's father was a poet as well as a great warrior and a Tri-World-class rock-skipper. The prince was less sure about himself after his hundredth attempt plunged into the river with a single plop.

"I'm terrible at this, Father," he said, whining as he tried to do as instructed, kneeling into the stony riverbank but wishing they could return to the tower. "Noba has done fifteen skips before."

"*Ha*! Only fifteen, you say? When I was a boy, my pebbles would disappear over the horizon. Khanya knows how many times they skipped, but trust me, it was well over fifteen," N'joku Atalay boasted. "I would show you again if it wasn't for this phantom's elbow." His father worked out his joints like a stiff axle. He always had one pain or another, a new discomfort in his body that made being old seem awful.

"Well, my record is three," the prince said, wistful as he tossed another failed attempt with an embarrassing *kerplunk*. He felt such shame that rotation, as though he couldn't achieve the most straightforward task.

"It will come, Son. You're barely twenty. You have yet to discover the strength within you." The king glowed with pride as he reached in his knapsack for a couple of grats, which he quickly hurled into the river. In an absurd panic, his adolescent nagas wrestled each other to get to the water first, and in a fury of splashing, they converged on the boney treats. "Look at Urnas and Usoca. They're still young hatchlings. Wait till you see what they can do after a bit of training."

N'damu crawled out onto a spiky gray rock that jutted from the banks, hoping to get a good look off the edge. Lying down on his belly, he reached into the chilly water, feeling around the riverbed for smooth stones. A family of querghil flopped around the opposite bank, taking a cool drink in the Thraxian heat and rolling their spiny tan hides in the mud. Ulanoids sang their sweet songs as they landed on their hulking backs to scour for attached maycon clams. They got a meal, and the querghil got a good cleaning. He could remember how, even at that age, altruistic behavior amazed him.

He recalled the strange feeling that moment, a chill on his neck, though the air was warm and humid. A silence he could remember to this rotation, as though everything around him sensed something he'd completely missed. Suddenly, the ulanoids dispersed in alarm as the querghil plopped onto their bellies and began to bounce up the bank. All Inana seemed to tremble, and N'damu only understood when he looked at the side of the rock he was hanging on and realized it was looking back at him. He sensed himself being lifted in the air as the rock split in two, revealing rows of razor-sharp teeth within. After that, he only remembered his father's scream.

"N'DAMU, crongrin!" His thoughts must have been faster than his words. Before the prince could react or the creature's death grip could take him, he was knocked out of harm's way by Usoca's tail. Next, Urnas went at the crongrin's neck in a frenzy. After landing at least twenty meters away in a bush of olyin yara, N'damu remembered watching the little nagas reduce that full-grown crongrin to an empty husk in a matter of minutes. It was only after a great deal of time passed that he looked down to notice a giant gash in his soft palm.

"I'm okay, Father," he said. "Only a small cut. I think it happened while reaching for skipping stones."

Not only was that the first time he had seen his father unleash the power of his spirit-link, but it was the first time he'd seen his own blood. He'd walked those banks since before he could remember and would walk them for cycles to come, but everything changed after that brush with mortality. N'damu learned the power behind N'jikota and how fragile life could be. Even for an Atalay.

His focus returning to the present, he looked down at his hands to find them covered in blood again, more than he'd ever seen. A bitter iron flavor lingered on his tongue as the warm crimson flowed between his fingers like molten lava. Death permeated his nostrils as sweaty lake water dripped filth from his forehead, burning his eyes.

After he helped carry Sal'aah Novojoh to the healing house, N'damu fell to his knees in shock. Meadowdell's medics went to work on their liege lord in a fraught panic, determined to stabilize him. Sal'aah's chest still showed signs of faint breath, though his eyes were rolled back to their whites, fluttering as his mind seemed to tilt in and out of consciousness. Next, the lord began to whisper something that at first seemed like nonsensical ramblings but N'damu soon realized was a strange language he didn't know.

"*Vharta tan khama du toah tut'tahsa.*"

A lovely language, he thought. He took two steps closer and cupped his ear before the medics pushed him back. N'damu fought to keep Sal'aah's face in his line of sight, hoping against hope his mentor might revive.

"*Soh mana umai tut'mahra fo'afoh.*"

Finally, Marique Novojoh arrived by his bedside, understandably upset and struggling to remain focused. Born a noble in the aeronautic culture of Duran, she understood high-pressure situations, but no one could prepare for seeing the father of your six children with his stomach spilling out.

"*Vharta tan khama du toah tut'tahsa.*"

"You're not going to die, my love," she said, grasping for her husband's hand. "How did this happen? N'damu, please focus. Tell me what happened."

He knew he needed to speak, but the shock kept his lips frozen and his spine trembling uncontrollably.

"*Nei ee soh f'humana zo Atalay.*" N'damu couldn't help noticing the one word he did comprehend. His name, being chanted by his mentor in prayer—in the face of death. Is this what it meant to be Atalay? Whether he liked it or not, a man he loved expected him to be a savior. In his darkness, Sal'aah was crying out to him, but no matter where he searched inside himself, he had no strength to share.

Hands worked tirelessly sewing his teacher's wounded stomach back together while connecting tubes to his veins, transfusing blood, and resuscitating his lungs artificially. As more medics rushed in, the mute prince was eventually pushed out of the room entirely.

"N'damu." The voice calling from down the hall was Princess Enahdra Vesta, who came running up to him beside herself with worry. "Thank you, Khanya. You are unharmed, My Prince." She embraced him, and her familiar scent washed away his anxiety for a moment. Enah had a soothing glow about her—a warmth that alleviated his pain. The princess kissed him on his cheek several times, one or two pecks lingering at his lips.

If he weren't in shock, he might have thought something of it. In any case, the power to speak returned. "Enah ... I ... I." She pressed her forehead to his and held him tightly. "I was flying. I genuinely felt it. Finally, I was flying the atranoch, Enah." He looked up into her tender indigo eyes. "It was completely amazing—and then they just started blasting. Sho'nee. She fell. I don't know wha–what." The prince lost his composure again and began to sob uncontrollably.

He began to see stars. Exhaustion or hunger, he hoped—though they were eerily similar to the visual distortions he'd experienced in the solar storm. Princess Vesta hugged him again, even tighter than before. He could feel her heart beating against his chest and was calmed by her honeyed perfume. "It's not your fault, N'damu."

"But it is," he said, pulling away from her. He looked out the window in contemplation, squinting at the orange sun as it began to sink below the wooden rooftops of Meadowdell. "They were shooting at me. Sal'aah is dying in there, and Sho'nee is dead because of blasts meant for me. Because of *me*. Because *I* was born Atalay."

"It is *because* you are Atalay that if they die, it will be with honor," she replied. "You don't need to apologize for being who you are, N'damu Atalay. Your making was no accident. It was the summation of human will that begat Atalay. I would give my life for you, just like any of your subjects. Don't underestimate the love your people have for you. Some can't imagine life without you."

He'd never felt this vigor from Enah before. The princess was an amazing woman. What a queen she would be for some lucky man. She'd always felt like home, and he needed her now more than ever.

"Come, let's get some fresh air. There's nothing you can do for Sal'aah now." She took his hand and squeezed it tightly. After ordering ten VEOs to aid the Novojoh guards, she led him to the courtyard to take air in the gardens.

"We need to get word to the mountain caravan. The Two Spears will not know why I've not returned," N'damu said as he walked the path uneasily beside her. "They may all be in danger up there."

"They are with my command unit. Believe me, the ones who take on Rigel Kong will be those in danger," Enahdra said as they strolled through the grassy glade, flowers sweetening the air. "Besides, I am one step ahead of you. I sent out riders as soon as you arrived. They will inform the company accordingly."

"Thank you, Enah. But how did you already—"

"Take off your boots, My Prince. The stress is not healthy for you. Feel the cool tynn on your soles with me. Please?"

He did as she beckoned, kicking off his bloody mountain boots, then followed her across the grass and under a glen of meridian falls. The shaggy purple trees seemed like a curtain from the world. Even the Seat's all-seeing eye in the Tower of Atalay couldn't see through their canopy of lush violet vinery. The haven did nothing to ease the stabbing pain in his heart. The beauty of the scene and his gorgeous company were lost on him. *Nalia would love this.*

He looked at Enahdra, who smiled at him so adoringly. *It's so romantic. Could Enah have brought me here for...?* N'damu stopped himself midthought. How *easy* it could be to fall for a girl like her. The princess was a Vesta, noble and powerful, and so beautiful his eyes felt concussed every time he looked at her. Still, his love for the low-bred orphan girl was undeniable in his heart, now, more than ever, in the presence of the perfect specimen of a woman. The sick whirlwind in his heart yearned for Enahdra—perhaps a bandage for the hurt. Nevertheless, his mind wouldn't budge.

"I heard some other worrisome news—rumors, really." Enah fluttered her lashes as she took his hand. "I'm not one to believe gossip," Princess Vesta explained. "However, rumor has it something happened with you and the natural girl." *How could she know? Spies in the grotto?*

"No. It's not tr—"

"N'damu, I understand the inclination, believe me," Enahdra continued. "Just don't forget about those who are counting on you. Your purity is no trivial thing. Mixing your genetics with a natural-born? The Doctrines forbid this. The future of the Tri-Wo—"

"We didn't *do* anything. I mean, we did," N'damu explained. "We snuck away from camp with the Novojoh girls for a while one night. It's shameful to admit, and I hope you won't tell my parents, but I tried some kavah flowers. *We* tried some, Nalia and

329

I, and … well, she sort of had a panic attack." He shook his head, staring at his feet. The lies were bitter on his tongue. "Caused by the drugs, no doubt. She passed out, and I carried her to her tent, hoping to avoid getting caught—and that was *all*."

Enahdra avoided eye contact. Deceiving her was notoriously tricky. Like her sense for tech, the princess had a nose for botsora shit. "You wouldn't lie to me, would you, N'damu?"

"Enah, if I lost my virtue, do you believe I would not tell you?"

She stepped up to him slowly, gazing with her deep regal eyes as she wormed her toes on top of his. "I always thought I would be there—losing mine with you." Enah brushed his cheeks with her glossed lips, yet the notion of her sexual attraction hard to believe. "I thank Khanya you're safe and that the moment hasn't passed me by to tell you ... I love you, Prince N'damu Atalay."

"Enah, I love you too," he replied quickly. He took her hands in his and smiled with sincerity only he could conjure. "In the Light of Atalay."

"No, My Prince." She bobbed her head and giggled. "I love you as a woman loves a man. Not as my prince. Not as Atalay, Shepherd of Men. Not as a sister loves her brother—or a friend loves a friend."

He broke her gaze. Painfully, awkwardly. It would break his heart to break hers, and N'damu Atalay wasn't sure his could survive another breaking. Still, he knew Enah could see his sorrow—his confusion, where she would see delight if he loved her back.

Enahdra stepped off his toes quickly. "I *had* to tell you. If you were to die and I had never said anything … life is fleeting." The tension between them became palpably uncomfortable.

"I am sorry, My Princess. Any man would be fortunate to be with you, but I am not ready for things as weighty as love. I'm afraid that's just not where my heart is at."

She seemed to get oddly indignant. Turning her back to him, she spat. "And where are *your* affections, *boy*? With the baseline stray?"

"In the sky with the atranochs, I'm afraid," he told her. "And on Sho'nee and Sal'aah. On the happiest moment of my life juxtaposed with this tragic attack. My dreams were answered when I flew…"

She turned back, only to roll her eyes at him. "Botsora piss! What about in N'gaia? Before Meadowdell. Surely you considered who might become your queen one rotation."

"I'm sorry, Enah. I just never—"

"I asked about your heart—a mistake with all men," she said scornfully. "I should have asked where your cock is at."

"You would be a worthy Queen Enahdra, but if *that* is what you think of me…" N'damu said before she cut him off.

"You really should check up on Lord Novojoh. I've kept you too long."

"Enah, please, let's talk about this."

331

"I've sent riders north as well to inform N'gaia of our situation," Enahdra said as she slipped back into her boots. "The king will send half the kingdom to defend you now." Not bothering with his boots, he scrambled after her, confused by her extreme reaction. She walked ten paces in front of him as they entered the healing house of Meadowdell—instead of hand in hand, as they'd left.

When they finally arrived at Sal'aah's chamber, Enahdra simply walked by with no interest in his status, continuing down the hall in a spurned huff.

CHAPTER TWENTY-FOUR

Nalia V

The peaks of the Sindiswa mountain range were a pitch-black silhouette on the deep violet starscape. The galaxy's rush made a creamy river, splitting the sky in two and illuminating the wilderness with a low purplish glow. Rasp dragons buzzed thick in the air, nearly drowning out the symphony of nocturnal wildlife as they called out for a mate or a meal. Nalia Chuku relentlessly combed the canyon. Dried branches scratched her skin as curtains of leaves did all they could to impede her search for the prince. Her hair seemed like a flickering flame, bouncing in and out of her light cannon's field of luminance. She'd left her heavy armor behind, opting for the speed and maneuverability of gray fatigues.

How can I even hope to find him, stumbling in this darkness? She swung her long spear to help clear the bush ahead. The sounds of sticks breaking behind her grew closer, accompanied by several sets of hurried boot falls. Lieutenant Ivy Freya emerged from the thick in her violet armor, glimmering in the low light. Her brunette curls were frizzy and disheveled, carrying a collection of sticks and thorns acquired in the brush. Nalia paused for a moment to wait for the troupe of VEOs. "No sign of him, I'm assuming?"

"That bone-dragon could have him halfway to the Quiniso by now," Freya said. "Searching on foot is *beyond* futile."

"Any word from Meadowdell? Princess Vesta?" Nalia asked desperately.

"Yes, her riders arrived hours ago," she said. "None of them have heard from the prince or Lord Novojoh. Listen, Chuku, we need to report back and get reinforcements. Our numbers are not adequate for the threats in these mountains."

"That is precisely why we need to find N'damu, immediately," she demanded, likely failing to disguise the love that drove her concern. She spun her spear, shredding through a thick pewter growth of olyin yara with a high-pitched *shoooop*. "Go back if you must, Lieutenant Freya. Refresh your men so that they might return to the search." Nalia ran into the dark pathway she'd freshly cut, not even waiting for a response.

The orangey light of Set poked through the canopy of black trees, creating a strobe effect above her as she ascended the mountainside forest. Never in her life had she felt such determination. She finally had N'damu: he loved her despite everything that meant, and she was not going to lose him now.

Soon, the mountain became too steep to run up. She clasped her spear to her backstrap and began to grapple the rocks, vaulting herself from the trees that grew horizontally from the cliffside. Breathing was laborious as sweat soaked her face, yet she pressed on. *I know he's alive ... I know it.*

"You must *really* love him," a woman's voice cried out below. Ivy Freya again, this time alone. She had not expected any of them to follow. Obviously, Freya's men lacked the fortitude she possessed.

"He is Atalay."

"Oh, no. A girl doesn't embark on such a fruitless endeavor out of religious duty," Freya said. "This is the act of a desperate lover. Believe me, I know."

Nalia scowled down at her. "Well, you don't *know* me," she said with a grunt, continuing to climb the ever-steepening mountain's face. "I'm adopted. A low-bred, baseline natural. What interest would the prince have in me? I could never—"

"Your butt looks wondrous from my vantage," Ivy said. "That would interest many—men and women alike. The great Atalays may think they are better than us, but they *do* have genitalia, right? Otherwise, how perfect could their genetics really be? So, I figure they're just like the rest."

"N'damu is the Shepherd of Humanity," Nalia replied. "He is above such carnal motives." *Does she know? How could she?*

"Yet if you were honest with yourself, you'd admit he isn't." Ivy laughed below. "Don't forget, I oversaw his resynthesis back in Centralia. I saw Prince Atalay in all his glory."

"Perhaps this is how it works in Centralia. Sex might sell where *you're* from," Nalia said. "In N'gaia, honor drives our purpose, and there are none more honorable than Atalay." She hoped singing N'damu's praise might divert suspicion. Nevertheless, she had to confess, Ivy Freya's words did not land quietly. The prince was willing to throw away his honor and the faith of the Tri-Worlds. He would deny eons of legacy and tradition and forgo his holy purpose just to be with her. "Believe me; my backside isn't that appealing."

"Well, that is admirable," Freya said. "But between you and me, I think you would be an adorable couple."

Nalia's heart melted. The thought took her back twenty cycles, reducing her to the little girl she'd been, with lyverna flies fluttering in her belly.

She'd never forget the rotation she met N'damu Atalay. It played back in her mind as she climbed, like a hologram cinematic.

King N'joku was a mountainous human—an icon on his white throne. "Lady Shyla Sadah, my old friend, and First Sword of Atalay, for your loyal service, I offer this gift on your name day. I know you *had* a child—a beautiful daughter, taken from you by Khanya. The recent skirmishes in Xolani have seen much bloodshed, battles between the armies of Rhyolite and war-mongering barbarians of the Fuza." The king's voice sounded like that of a god to Nalia as golden guards led her into the immense throne room of the Tower of Atalay. "This girl's parents died with honor, fighting for Atalay on the field. I believe her parents' blood, though natural, is fused with the nobility in their hearts—and their daughter now has no home. Her name is Nalia Chuku. I offer you this ward."

She remembered looking at the woman who would become her mother, tears of joy dripping down her brown cheeks. Her soft, warm, motherly face made no secret of her immediate love for Nalia. "It would be my honor to foster the girl," Shyla Sadah said, kneeling. She looked down with forlorn eyes, placing a hand over her stomach. "Thank you, My King—my faith is affirmed. This is a wish come true." Her mother was always a soft-spoken woman of few words. She'd usually let her skill with a spear do her talking.

"I'm happy to hear it," the king said with a comforting smile. "I'm sure you'll make a great warrior of her."

That was when she noticed the skinny boy sitting on the lower throne, playing holo-games with a look of boredom, and with two terrifying baby nagas asleep at his feet. He had an orange bun on the top of his mohawk, the beginnings of a princely braid. She thought he was so handsome—his black eyes were so mysterious, so intriguing. The entire court seemed to fade away for a moment, dwindling from reality as her heart all but exploded in her chest. "Perhaps she might even serve on my son's Prince's Guard if she trains hard enough."

"I can see in her eyes a great intelligence." Shyla kneeled in front of her new ward. "And this beautiful hair—must be the fire

337

within her, burning bright. Would you like to learn to be a warrior?"

Nalia nodded.

"Of course she does," the king had said. "Her parents showed such valor. Such loyalty to Atalay in their sacrifice. I'm sure this girl will be as honorable."

"She's pretty," the prince said unexpectedly. The compliment flattered Nalia to no end. She hadn't noticed he'd even looked up from his game. It was the last thing she'd expected: that the prince might even see her, let alone find her in any way beautiful. The queen and princesses all agreed in turn.

"Her hair looks greasy," a young girl cried out from the court.

"Enahdra! Silence." Lord Vesta seemed like a terrifying wizard with his pointed blue goatee and gangly smile. "Forgive my daughter for her jealousy of your beauty, young Nalia. Natural-born Inaneans have such stunning features indeed." His words were kind, but she couldn't help being nervous of his hideous headdress.

"Pretty, yes, but can she swing a spear?" the king asked. "What do you say, little one? Would you like to learn to be like Lady Sadah? A golden warrior of N'gaia!"

Nalia humbly kneeled before N'joku, reciting the words she'd been ordered to say if ever called upon to talk. Children of her lineage were rarely allowed to speak in the presence of Atalay. "I am given by Khanya to serve in the Light of Atalay." Words that always rang true the moment they left her lips.

A branch suddenly broke beneath her boot with a blast, snapping Nalia's consciousness back to the present. She fell abruptly as the stone supporting her other foot broke away from the mountainside, unable to bear her full weight. Her heart shot to her throat for a second before Ivy Freya caught her forearm, clasping her precariously over the deadly drop that awaited. With a grunt, Freya hoisted Nalia onto the trunk that supported her. "Dammit, girl, this is no time for daydreaming."

"That branch was solid. I think something shot out the—shi—" A flurry of blaster fire ripped along the cliffside, cutting a path of destruction in their direction.

"Guerrillas," Ivy yelled as she pulled her blaster from its hip holster. Nalia looked up to confirm. The flaming contrails had emerged from an outcrop above. Some bandit sniper had them in his sights. "How are these heathens getting blasters?"

Freya returned fire just in time to stay their blasts. She flipped around the branch for cover. Nalia, however, sprang from the tree, boldly vaulting toward the enemy.

"Cover me, Freya," she cried out as she sprang up the branches like a gymnast from the Great Vrinasi Games. The Second Spear bobbed and weaved up the tree. Ivy provided a spray of proton bursts, minimizing the bandit's ability to get any sort of lock. Nalia spun from one branch and flipped through the air, drawing her spear as she landed on the ledge where the guerrillas perched.

Somersaulting forward, she avoided a barrage of clumsy, short-range fire, coming up with her spear embedded in the

339

sniper's gut. She counted eight more bandits behind him, standing at the mouth of a small cave. Another one had a blaster, unusual armaments for mountain outlaws. *Must have slipped through Vesta's fingers.* The rest drew their hand-to-hand implements: two with long swords, three spears, and three whips.

"Damn, boys, yeah lookie 'ere. Da gods must be lovin' us, eh? Another sweet lil treat. Throw 'er in wit' da other one." A whip-wielding bandit licked his lips creepily—obviously their excuse for a leader. Nalia could smell his body odor from ten paces. His skin stained as black as charcoal, the guerrilla's teeth were foul and broken. "Bet she got a real warm and wet one too." His black dreadlocks had patches missing, exposing festering head scabs that covered half his scalp. She sensed nothing but darkness in his pale-yellow eyes. "I get to fuck her fir—"

The thud of his decapitated head hitting the ground replaced his yammering. The dirty guerrilla's body followed as Nalia brought her spear's spin to a stop beside her. The falling corpse hit the severed head, sending it rolling off the cliff's edge. For so long, she'd wondered what it might be like to kill. It gave her no pleasure, but she would slay everyone in the Tri-Worlds if it meant saving N'damu. Herself included.

"Where is he?" she asked. Nalia lunged her weapon without hesitation into the chest of one of the spearmen to an explosive gush of blood. With a *frippp*, a whip restrained her arm. The next spear lunged at her from the opposite side. She tumbled again, jerking at the whip and jolting its holder to his knees, in line with his comrade's swing.

"Adam fuckin' Atalay!" he screamed, looking down at the jagged spearhead buried in his belly. The guerrilla's eyes rolled back as he fell with a thump, and she quickly pulled her spear from the other bandit's chest and returned to fighting stance.

Next, the two swords rushed her. Nalia repelled their clumsy swings with ease, her form of Sadah'anah so reminiscent of her mother's. No wasted movement, the blade, the shaft, the blunt of her hilt struck in tempo as she spun her spear with seamless precision. Like a musical instrument, the whir of the twirl ended in a devastating clank as she disarmed one swordsman, then ripped him from balls to brain on the rebound.

Another whip's lash snapped, this time around her waist, restraining her enough to allow the remaining swordsmen to graze her thigh with an errant swipe. Nalia cried out in pain, falling to her knee as blood poured down her leg.

Clunking footsteps pounded her way next. Another spearman charged. At the last possible moment, she spun out of his way, tripping him with a spin kick and ending his rush with a smash into the rocks. His spear flew into the air as he landed with skull-breaking impact, leaving a bloody smear on the stone. A master of recovering fumbled spears, Nalia caught the twirling shaft expertly. In a liquid motion, she drove it into the final swordsman's neck.

Unexpectedly, a slew of ulanoids converged on her head as the last guerilla spearmen approached in a fighting stance. Two ulanoids—one pink and one blue—landed on either shoulder of the remaining whip-man as he stood behind, unspooling his weapon. *A spirit-linker in the fold.* Feathers created a cloud around her as more and more bone-hawks flew in to swarm her. They pecked violently at her face as she swung her weapon, franticly swatting at them in vain. Their razor-sharp claws scratched as she fell from her feet and began to tumble toward the ledge. Just before she was about to roll off, however, the ulanoids started to disintegrate, one by one, in bursts of flaming plumage.

Nalia looked up, delighted to see Ivy Freya come to join the fight. The VEO's blasts scattered the ulans in a panic. Clearly, the fear of energy weapons was more potent than N'jikota. Without hesitation, Nalia threw her spear once again. It landed like a dart between the eyes of the ulanoid bonder. Finally, she turned to the last bandit as Freya stepped up behind her, reaching over her shoulder and drawing her blaster on him.

He quickly laid down his weapon and kneeled in submission.

"Where did you get the blasters?" Freya asked. *Her Vesta agenda is well engrained.*

"Mercenary gave it t' us," he replied. "Tons o' creds too."

"Name!" Freya demanded as she stepped out from behind Nalia, brandishing her blaster at his forehead.

"Dunno. Jus' called 'imself Volturis." *Volturis?*

"We should keep him alive," Nalia said. "He said they had someone else! The 'other one' your friend mentioned. You're going to take us to them."

"Ya, no problem, eh? But t'aint gonna matter none. She prolly dead by now." The guerrilla repeatedly bowed as he backed away on his knees. *She?* Nalia thought. *Dammit, it must not be him.*

"Dem boys had their way wit' her last night, eh? Real rough like. Glurg found her broken on the mountain anyway, bleedin' out, so they figured: whatever." Nalia picked up her spear and held it to his throat, trying to think of a reason not to remove the man's head. "Wasn't me, ya understand. I was just excited the bitch had ocha-nut berries. You can ask 'er yerself. I didn't lay a hand on 'er." *Ocha-nut berries? Sho'nee?*

The oldest Novojoh girl had been munching them the entire journey. A coincidence perhaps. Still, Nalia turned to the bandit. "Where is she?"

"In 'ere, in da mountain," the bandit said. "Probably a corpse by now."

"Well, if she is, then you will join her soon enough," Freya threatened as Nalia nudged her spear against his neck, drawing a single bead of blood.

The two women followed the defeated bandit into the tunnel, Nalia poking her spear-tip into his back regularly to remind him of her presence.

"Chuku, we need to stop and wrap your leg," Freya suggested. Nalia refused, however, determined to move forward. "You should have waited for me. There is a reason I carry a blaster."

"You should have moved faster." At the back of the cave, she saw an auburn-haired girl curled up naked. "It *is* her," Nalia said

343

with an emotionless expression, unsure if she should rejoice or grieve. "Sho'nee." She shoved him aside and ran to her. The Novojoh girl rolled over, moaning as her broken bones adjusted to movement. Blood coated her face, as well as other less than dignified fluids.

"N'damu ... N'damu," Sho'nee whispered, wheezing as her eyes rolled back, clutching at reality.

"He's fine," Ivy said, lying to appease her. "Relax, you're going to be fine as well. Come on; I'll carry her. We need to get her back, Nalia."

Nalia began shredding her shirt into strips. "We stop her bleeding first."

Freya held her blaster at the guerrilla. "Take off your clothes," she commanded. The man stripped, his little cock hiding, shamefully retracted in his wild pubic bush. Nalia tended the worst of Sho'nee's gashes, using every strip of fabric her shirt had to offer while her own leg still bled profusely. Afterward, Ivy covered her bruised, cut-up body in the dirty bandit's clothes and hoisted her up.

"Vol–Volturis." Sho'nee mumbled nonsensically as Freya carried her out of the cave, led by Nalia and her prisoner. "Kong. Ri ... Rigel."

"Did she say Kong?" the Second Spear asked as she bound the bandit's arms and drove him to his knees by the cliff's edge. Reduced to her bra straps, the mountain air was bitingly cold.

"The girl's been through a trauma. She's delirious," Ivy said, laying her down in the grass.

"N'damu … is he? Is he?" Sho'nee asked, struggling to open her eyes, now bloodshot red.

"We don't know," Nalia said. "We need to know what happened to him, Sho'nee. Where is N'damu?" She cradled her head in her lap, petting the Novojoh girl's matted hair and holding a canteen to her dried, peeling lips.

"We have to move," Freya said. "There could be more guerrillas in this area."

"Oh, there are," the naked prisoner said with a chuckle. His voice seemed to trigger something in Sho'nee as a cold scowl washed over her stained face. "You girls better be far away from 'ere when dey get back, eh?" Nalia could see Novojoh clenching her fists, her teeth grinding. "Gonna be a lot of 'em—and dey ain't like me, ya know." Sho'nee closed her eyes and seemed to disappear into meditation, humming a strange hymn under her breath. The wind gradually picked up, as steadily as the bandit's confidence. The hair on the back of Nalia's neck also perked up. "Dey are deviants fer sure. 'Course, I'd never lay a hand on any o' *you* lovely ladies."

A shadowy black hole traversed the cliffside, like a dark rain cloud eclipsing the light of Set in the night sky. The guerrilla grew darker and darker, unaware of the imminent specter. His face disappeared in shadow as a colossal atranoch dropped into the canopy with an explosion of leaves. The bone-dragon screeched as it flapped wildly, impaling him on its massive wing

345

spike before ascending again. Some of his blood sprayed across Nalia's face as the guerrilla flailed in his final throes of death, then disappeared into the heavens, an ornament for the beast's wing.

Sho'nee went limp—exhausted. "He touched me with something *else*, and I didn't like it."

"Sho'nee, what can you tell us about N'damu?" she asked. "We need to find him."

The Novojoh girl's grimace turned to Ivy Freya. "It was them—*their* men. Volturis is the VEO commander, Rigel Kong. As they raped me in turn, the bandits bragged all night long how he hired them to shoot down the prince. He even gave them the power weapons."

"Impossible. That's not true," Ivy said, clearly taken aback.

"A perfect plan, I guess," Sho'nee continued, still wheezy from her distressed lungs. "Lead him up to the mountains, make it look like outlaws. Cheap and effective. Kong is clever. I'll give him that."

"These are debased mountain savages."

Nalia raised her spear to Ivy Freya's chin. "Put down the blaster."

CHAPTER TWENTY-FIVE

N'damu VII

N'damu slipped into the healing chamber to peek at Sal'aah. The old Lady Shi'nah Novojoh sat in her wheelchair, grievously sobbing at her son's bedside. "Oh, My Prince, thank you for bringing my son home to me."

"Yes, N'damu, you are a hero this rotation," Lady Marique said, reinforcing her mother-in-law's notion that he'd actually been helpful.

"I'm sorry, ladies, but this is my fault," N'damu explained. "I was selfish to come here knowing I was under threat. Putting you all in danger was unforgivable. Wrong of my father as well. He—and I—just didn't believe it. Atalay begs your forgiveness."

"Every Atalay I've ever met has been such a self-important drama queen," the old lady joked dryly. "Sal'aah didn't believe it either." She scoffed. "This is *his* school. His expertise. He's at *least* as dumb as you and your daddy, boy."

"How is he?" N'damu asked, turning his focus to Marique. "Will he live?"

Her response was to peel back the sheet to show him the extent of her husband's wounds. He'd been sewn and cauterized, cleaned and disinfected, yet still the cuts pulsed with scabbing blackness and bubbling yellow pus. The answer to him seemed a resounding no. "Due to the solar storm, our resynth chambers are defunct. Medics are doing their best—but I'm afraid—" She grew too distraught to speak.

"Would it be too risky to move him? Perhaps to Centralia?" The silence seemed to be answer enough. Family and friends and medics alike came and went. N'damu never left his side that night, slipping in and out of uncomfortable sleep beside his nursing bed and checking Sal'aah's vitals every time he jerked awake.

His guru still whispered occasionally in the strange language. He assumed it was the tongue of Milushi. "*Vharta tan khama du toah tut'tahsa.*" N'damu would open his eyes one moment in Sal'aah's dim healing chamber, and when he closed them, he would be somewhere else: a field of tynn, speckled with bourgeoning skylar roses and aiku blossoms. His toes were wet from the grass once more.

Open

348

"*Soh mana umai tut'mahra fo'afoh,*" Lord Novojoh chanted, his mind gone in some fever dream. His body convulsed as the technologically crippled doctors struggled to keep him functionally alive.

Closed

Looking up a mounded foothill where the Sizwe met the Sindiswa, he could see the mamidon perch he'd stood on those many rotations, the great Milushi totem from times long considered ancient. N'damu noticed a man reclined at its base, smoking pipe weed, face obscured in darkness. He ran with all swiftness up the grassy hill.

Open

"*Nei ee soh f'humana zo Atalay.*" Sal'aah jerked in violent spasms, loosening his hairnet and unintentionally releasing his disheveled gray dreads. His breathing had a sickening wheeze to it as the medics pumped air in and out of his collapsed lungs.

Closed

"Life and death in perfect symmetry. The Womb brings disorder into balance," the man beneath the totem chanted in shadow.

"Who are you?" N'damu asked.

He exhaled long, a series of smoke rings before standing with a content stretch and stepping into the light. "We are all the people of Atalay," Sal'aah said, standing before him in perfect health.

"Sal'aah! You were dying," N'damu cried.

Hooting his joyful chuckle, his guru patted him on the shoulder, much more forcefully than N'damu would have liked. He smiled before letting out a loud fart, sending the ulanoids off in a panic of fluorescent feathers. "I guess I *do* need a shower."

"You're bleeding out on a table. What in Khanya is going on, Sal'aah?"

"What's going in is: I have a little scratch, and you're sobbing uselessly by my bedside." Sal'aah plopped down on a tuffet, cross-legged with a *thwamp*. "I'm going to sleep for a while, N'damu. We will have time to commune, but you need to help my children, N'damu, My Prince. My King."

The prince noticed then that he was in his father's golden Atalayan armor and hoisting his krotrium diskarmor.

"My father will send help, Sal'aah," N'damu explained.

"You are N'damu Atalay, dammit," Sal'aah said. "You do not need Jambi's silly armies. I have no faith in *them*—or capitalists like Vesta or Winters or Darius. Puppet puppet-masters.

Darkness is coming, N'damu. Only *you* can save them now. I have seen your power today."

"Flying was amazing, Sal'aah, but many have been atranoch bonders. It does not make me as powerful as you might hope."

A strange voice came from behind him. "I'm sorry to tell you this, N'damu, but you did *not* spirit-link with the atranoch." A man of at least two hundred cycles, hunchbacked and potbellied, stood behind him. His braided dreadlocks of white hung past his knees, over his leathery, dark-brown skin, covered in Milushi ink.

"And you are?" N'damu asked, perplexed by his dream more and more. As aware as he was of it, he still could not seem to force himself awake.

"I am Sav'ato Novojoh. This fat old man is my son."

"Daddy, I've been waiting for you," Sal'aah said. "You look as I remember you." The two embraced like they'd waited an eternity to reunite.

"You look happy, Son!" Sav'ato said with a smile. "Fat, but happy!"

"Sorry, but if I didn't bond with the atranoch, how was I able to control it?" N'damu asked, awkwardly breaking up the reunion.

Sal'aah only shrugged.

"Sho'nee!" Sav'ato blurted out. "Somehow, you were able to channel *her* N'jikota."

"How is that—I mean, um." N'damu struggled to make sense of it, searching for logic inside his dream. "Is that a thing?"

"In the Light of Atalay, N'jikota is mysterious indeed." Sav'ato scratched his chin through his fluffy beard, squinting as he looked the prince up and down. "A puppeteer of the puppet-masters? The old Milushi legends speak of N'jidia, the Kota of Kotas."

"Milushi is—arcane." N'damu slouched over, hopelessly more baffled.

Sav'ato shook a finger in the air. "She controlled the atranoch—for you. Somehow, through her affection for you, the two of you became entwined."

"Her affect—?"

"Daddy, you really shouldn't gossip," Sal'aah interrupted. "N'damu, you must forgive my daughters their little crushes. You are the Prince of Atalay, after all."

"What in Atalay's asshole makes you think it's only a crush?" Sav'ato asked. "The girl *has* a heart. Believe me, N'damu, my son is new to this spiritual dreamscape thing." He sneered at his son, holding out his arms to present the world around them. "But I've seen everything. Sho'nee's heart is pure. A bright light she has given to you, young prince."

"Still, how could he have channeled N'jikota?" Sal'aah asked.

"He could be the N'jidia," Sav'ato said, looking wide-eyed at N'damu.

"No one has ever controlled another human being through a spirit-link."

"Indeed," his father replied. "But all the same, N'damu temporarily tapped into Sho'nee's power of influence. Be it the will of Khanya or some strange science, I am too simple a man to say, I'm afraid. I would think love had something to do with it." *Why does everyone seem to be falling in love with me?*

He figured being an Atalay meant contending with the undying adoration of all. "A lot of good it did her—loving me. Trusting me," N'damu grieved aloud. "The moment I fly, and I feel like my life begins, hers tragically ends. It's just not worth it."

"It would explain why the boy's influence on the atranoch faded when she ... when she..." Sal'aah couldn't finish his thought. Even in N'damu's dream, it was too painful.

"Well, here's some good news for you," Sav'ato said, smiling as he put his arm around his son and faced N'damu. "When you wake up, get yourself together. The children *all* need you, and *Sho'nee* is still alive."

Open

Explosions rang in the distance. The Hall of Novojoh shook as the ambient war cries seemed to get louder and louder. N'damu looked over at Sal'aah as he pinched his arm. *Awake,* he thought. N'damu ran to the window. To his horror, legions of bandits amassed in the field outside the hall. They besieged the

Ghost Ship of Vesta, looting its stockade of weapons—no doubted improving their artillery by a hundredfold.

M'lilo outlaws. Tribes of the Sizwe—and the Red Savanah. Mercenaries from Ghost Creek and Shadow Hill. Guerrillas from the Sindiswa and pirates of the Stone Sea—every criminal on Inana looked united in rebellion.

"What is this madness?" He looked down in desperation at Sal'aah, then back out as the attackers hijacked the Ghost Ship and began advancing it to the front door. The guards of Meadowdell were well trained—dangerous spirit-linkers out in the wilds, but their numbers were just too few within the city and against power weapons.

"N'damu!!!" Enahdra burst through the door with Rigel Kong behind. "We have to run, now." The entire mansion buckled as the megamagnus rammed the face of the hall. *All those artifacts and ancient relics—destroyed.* He stood with his mouth hanging open in shock.

"Now, boy, or there ain't no getting out." Rigel heaved his proton cannon from over his shoulder and charged it.

"I won't leave Sal'aa—"

"He's meat," Rigel said. "Like the crongrin. It's let die or die, Atalay."

"N'damu!" Enah was irate. "Now. We don't have time. You are *all* that matters."

He planted his feet as the building quaked again. "Help me get him out, Enah." The shouting got louder as the invaders flooded in down below. The prince held out his hand, touching her shoulder. "Please."

She shut her eyes, massaging her temples and groaning—like her mind was possessed. N'damu could sense her conflict radiating. The ground quaked like Inana was breaking at the faults. The cries of dying warriors of Meadowdell echoed from the hall. The smell of death mixed with bitter blaster discharge, permeating the air.

"You make her stay, she dies, Atalay!" Kong blasted out the window and latched his grappling hook to the ledge.

N'damu looked at Enah as she agonized. Tears dripped from her cheeks as she stared back. Then he looked at Sal'aah. "Be with your father now, my friend," the prince said as he grabbed Enahdra's hand and pulled her behind Kong. Rigel lifted them both up to the window as invaders began to pound at the door.

"Go!" Rigel opened fire, unloading his proton cannon at the entrance, disintegrating the door and the bandits behind it.

"Are you coming?" the prince asked.

"N'damu, let's go." Enahdra began to climb down the rope. The enemies poured into Sal'aah's chamber, overwhelming Rigel Kong as N'damu slipped out the window. The prince could hear the commander's earsplitting shriek as he cried out from the throes of death.

"Rigel!" Enah screamed as they rappelled down the side of the hall. They landed in the hedges and quickly took cover. "Oh, Rigel."

"He was a hero, Enah—as was Sal'aah. My they find bliss in the Eternal Womb." They crept through the bushes, trying to avoid all eyes, yet it was a long way out of Meadowdell. The invaders executed the citizens systematically. The bandit outlaws filed innocent civilians out of their homes, lining them in the streets for execution. N'damu looked on with horror as the carcasses of his people began to pile up. *Follow the Light of Atalay to the afterlife,* he thought. "Khanya bless them," he whispered as they reached the edge of the garden.

There was a wide field of tynn between them and the grove of meridian falls that would mask their escape. "They'll see us, N'damu," the princess said. "It's impossible. We will never make it."

He knew she was right, but there was no other way. "The Womb of Inana has exacted a heavy enough toll for one rotation. We have to believe." *Don't see us,* he thought, over and over. *Don't notice us. Don't see.*

Enah grinned and took his hand. The two ran across the field as fast as their feet could carry them. *Don't see us, please. Don't notice.*

N'damu's prayers seemed answered. He and Enahdra disappeared into the grove, making their way out of city limits under the shadowy tree cover.

CHAPTER
TWENTY-SIX

Nalia VI

"Give me the blaster, Ivy."

"Chuku, this is ridiculous," she said. "Why would I—?"

"You should have no problem giving me the weapon then, just until I can sort this out," Nalia replied. "Trust me, Ivy. I believe *you* have nothing to do with this. But can you say the same about Kong?" Immediately, Freya removed the proton charge from her blaster with a loud click and tossed it off the cliff—then handed it over.

"Satisfied?" she asked. "Look, I *know* Rigel Kong. He's a moral man—under the grim visage. He may not love Inanean customs, but he's a long way from the Jade Moon. He may cheat at Eden's Ace—his best friend is a smarmy little dwarven pervert, but he is no regicidal conspirator."

"Sho'nee … Ivy … will you help me get to the bottom of this?" Nalia asked as she clicked her spear into its backstrap holder. "And find N'damu?"

"Yes, there must be a good explanation," Ivy said, loosening a length of rope from her bag. "If we hurry, we can make it to camp before Thraxis rises, but it's a long climb down."

"You helped save me, Lady Freya. I will give you the benefit of the doubt," Sho'nee said. "But those bandits had no cause to perform some recital for my benefit." The Kota of Atranochs trembled, looking to her feet. "As they defiled me—those outlaws thought I was as good as dead—no reason for theatrics. Rigel Kong did this. The real question is, did someone *else* give him this order?" Nalia could see the pain on Sho'nee's face, the quivering in her voice. *I can't imagine what she's been through,* she thought. *I would never have such strength and focus were I in her place.*

"Come. Let's get a stretcher together," Nalia said as she looked down from the ledge. "The descent is long. We need to hurry, for N'damu."

"All right, but it would be much faster if we go up," Sho'nee replied.

"But the camp is in the valley." Nalia looked back at Sho'nee in her oversize bandit's garb.

"It will take five rotations to maneuver down the mountain," Ivy said as she collected branches for the stretcher.

"The camp is down, but the atranochs are up," Sho'nee said, looking to the summit. "Besides, I owe you a flight. Don't think I've given up on those spear lessons, Nalia."

***

The climb was treacherous and tediously slow. Carrying Sho'nee in the makeshift stretcher was not easy, even for two strong women like Nalia and Ivy. They were cold from lack of clothing, starving, and bleeding as they climbed. Snowfall began, fluttering at first but soon whipped in the violent winds, forming frost on their exposed skin.

Every few hours, Sho'nee forced them to rest, despite Nalia's disagreement. The Second Spear knew if Rigel Kong was duplicitous, then any number of VEOs could be as well. *That little shit Calitro Frigg, no doubt. All* her friends might be in danger.

Hoisting Sho'nee up the cliffside, Ivy stumbled to one knee. The cold bit at her ears like himpheah ants on the dunes of the Summer Sea. Frostbite tickled the soles of her feet like a playful mother with fingers of knives.

"You need to rest, friends," Sho'nee said. Nalia scoffed as she tried to force Lieutenant Freya forward.

"This nook looks perfect," Ivy replied. "We'll camp here a while."

"Dammit," Nalia shouted. "Do either of you care about N'damu?"

"He *could* be safe," Sho'nee said, sitting up in her A-frame stretcher. "He may well be back in Meadowdell by now, eating Grandmother's maraphite stew." She held up her legs, stretching her knees out and wiggling her blackening toes.

"He could be dead," Ivy said as snow caked in her hair. Sho'nee slowly took her feet, willing her body to heal.

"How much would *you* care?" Nalia scowled as she began working on a fire. "It's Vesta that you serve, when you get down to it."

Ivy harvested some egg-nut-root from under the frost, then sat down across from her. "You are upset; I understand." She gnawed a root as she passed her canteen to Sho'nee. "But let's not be childish. We've both had weapons on each other, so what can words do?"

"You're going to love flying, Nalia," Sho'nee said. "It will restore your faith, whatever N'damu's fate."

"Don't say that." Nalia clenched her fists. "I can't even think abo—"

"You must come to terms with the possibility." The Kota of Atranochs shook her head with a sorrowful stare. "And remember, death is never the end. We will dance around the fire again on the plains of the Eternal Womb."

"Yeah, Chuku," Ivy added. "Sometimes it feels like there is no Nalia without N'damu. Maybe that's your true fear, being nothing without him."

"I don't want to hear this right now!" Nalia launched her spear into a vera's trunk.

Sho'nee smiled. "You told me it had been N'damu's dream to spirit-link with the atranoch. You said you wanted it so badly for him. Let me ask, did you ever want it for *you*?"

"Now who sounds childish?" Ivy interjected. "N'jikota requires Homo purist DNA. Naturals can't—"

"Or so *purists* would have you believe," Sho'nee said. "Plenty of naturals spirit-link."

Ivy gasped. "Blasphemy. The Doctrines of Atalay forbids them even to seek N'jikota."

"Purist society conveniently forbids naturals from doing a lot of things." Sho'nee winked at Nalia. "Sometimes, to live, we break the rules."

Nalia grumbled, crossing her arms and staring down the mountain. "Something is wrong. I feel it. Nagging at me— rattling a can in my mind incessantly."

"You're dedicated," Ivy said. "I'll give you that. I don't think N'damu needs a spirit-link—he has you, Chuku."

"Not if I get him first." Sho'nee winked, then cuddled up to Ivy with her hand out to Nalia. "Come, try to sleep, Nalia."

"You two get some rest," she replied, retrieving her spear and pacing the nook in the mountain. "I'll find no rest until I get back to him." *Are they right? Is my love for N'damu some blissful enchantment?*

***

The snowfall stopped, but Thraxis rarely shined on that face of the mountain, making it all that much colder. Nalia hunted all morning, bagging a fat rhybite. Its sour meat filled their stomachs, and its skins fortified their garments, and soon they were on the move again. Recovered enough to climb on her own, Sho'nee took the lead that rotation. Finally, they came to an enormous thar'vak tree that jutted twenty meters out from the cliff.

"This will do perfectly. We need to climb out." Sho'nee pointed to the giant bushy brown tree covered in scarlet moss. Her determination was admirable. It was amazing how strong she seemed, considering the ordeal she'd just endured.

"Couldn't the bone-dragon just pick us up down in the valley?" Freya asked.

"It could," Sho'nee replied. "But do you want to end up impaled on a wing talon? This is the safe way." She crawled out onto the branch, loosening an avalanche of snow, dirt, and dead bark.

Nalia had been fighting vertigo for two rotations. "Safe— great." With no time to waste, she latched her spear and shimmied out behind Sho'nee. The icy-covered branch shook, dipping uncomfortably as Ivy followed. The icicle-covered thar'vak would have been a mighty tree in its prime, but now it was slumped over, frozen gray branches rooted out by ulanoids. Nalia could see it wouldn't be too long before its roots gave out, and it would topple from the mountainside.

The valley seemed bright at this hour as the combined might of the gas giants, Set and Ra, provided dueling sources of luminance. It was not long before they hung by their arms, looking down at certain death. Sho'nee again closed her eyes, apparently calling out with her mind to her atranoch friends. "Drop when I tell you. You cannot hesitate. She will sense your fear." It was not long before her spirit-link responded, and an enormous silver atranoch came, spotted in reddish-yellow blotches that reminded Nalia of the abstract paintings she'd done in her youth. "It's Arvexia."

"Arvexia. Wow, she's stunning," Nalia said. Four more atranochs followed—all shades of white—exoskeletal frames flapping their leathery wings as they stretched into the drafts.

As the beast soared under, Nalia expected Sho'nee's call. Her teeth clattered as her fingers strained to grip the slick branch. The valley was an unfocused blur below, obscured by clouds and distance.

"Wait!" Sho'nee cried out with terror in her eyes. The atranochs screeched, tones of similar terror as they flapped past.

"I sense something—no." The Kota of Atranochs turned around. "Go back. It's too dangerous with *him*—"

"What?" Nalia asked. "We can't go back. It took too long to get here." Panic swelled up like a lump in her throat.

"Nalia, I think we should listen," Ivy called out, already retreating slowly up the thar'vak trunk.

"Vartek is near," Sho'nee explained. "A rare breed of mega-atranoch—he is the most dangerous animal on Inana, I'm afraid. His will is too much for one kota—his influence will override the entire valor of smaller atranochs."

Something wouldn't allow Nalia to budge. An invisible spear in her back nudged her on. "Is it possible, Sho'nee?" Vartek's low-frequency shriek rang out from miles away.

"We may go unnoticed, but it's very risky."

Nalia saw the atranochs rounding the valley. It seemed like she felt it before she could see it. *They're making a second pass.*

"Chuku, we're wasting time," Ivy said. "If we need to climb down, we need to get going."

"Sometimes, to live, we break the rules." With a kinked grin, Nalia grabbed Sho'nee's hand. "I have faith." She could feel the Novojoh girl squeezing her palm as Arvexia soared under foot—sparkling in the sunshine.

"Khanya, protect us." Sho'nee smirked.

Ivy cleared her throat. "You've got to be kidding."

"Drop!"

***

Nalia would never forget the majesty of flight. Sho'nee led the winged animals safely out of the valley and away from the mega-atranoch. The air was crisp and cold and genuinely smelled like nothing.

Ivy clung to a pearly white spike beside Nalia. The Centralian woman was composed, not afraid—not overly taken with the experience. "Much better than walking," she said with a shrug as her brown curls whipped behind her head.

The Second Spear's obsession with N'damu took away from the grandeur. For every rainbow-speckled waterfall—for every crystalline lake or misty glade they soared over, she thought of him. The business of finding her prince, the feeling inside her that told her he was alive and needed her. *If Sho'nee is alive, he could be too.*

Nalia patted Arvexia. Her hide was hairless, smooth, and soft, like freshly shaved skin. She was a beautiful atranoch, beaming with the Light of Atalay, yet Nalia still craved only the real thing: his touch, his voice—his kiss.

"Do you want to try the rider's position, Nalia?" Sho'nee asked.

"I don't want to slow us," she replied, shouting over the wind resistance as her afro whirled in chaos.

"We have to circle the northern range before we head south for the base camp." Sho'nee took Nalia's hand and led her to the position between the beast's two shoulder spikes. Holding them like handles, she beamed as Sho'nee stepped back. Arvexia seemed to vibrate with satisfaction. "Reach out to her, Nalia. I can feel her through you. She is connected."

"What?" Nalia asked. Ivy scoffed behind her.

"Yes, Nalia," Sho'nee smiled ear to ear. "Do you feel it? A visceral emotion you can't explain. A sound you can see—a smell you can taste. A glow you sense in your heart?"

"I thought it was N'da—" She stopped herself. "Ahem. I do feel it."

"N'jikota!" Sho'nee cheered out. "Arvexia is spirit-linking to you, Nalia."

"How can it be that simple?" Ivy asked.

"Often, the ways of Khanya are that simple—that pure."

"What does it feel like, Chuku?" Her only answer was N'damu. Perhaps she was spirit-linked to him.

"It feels like—love," Nalia replied. "I can't believe this. I never—"

A horrifying screech came out of nowhere. An ominous blackness from below she could sense through Arvexia.

"It's him!" Sho'nee stepped up beside her as the atranoch quaked. Like the wind was knocked from her gut, Nalia couldn't

366

breathe. "Vartek!" The mega-atranoch plowed into Arvexia's soft underbelly once more, jabbing her with his talons.

The valor of atranochs scattered, but Vartek focused on Arvexia, clearly aware of her riders. Breaking into a corkscrew, the enormous black bone-dragon sideswiped them. Nalia's heart flew up into her throat as she rolled down Arvexia's spine. With all her fingers might, she held to her tail spike, looking down wide-eyed at the valley, miles below.

Vartek's wingspan was all-encompassing as he came up from under her feet. Nalia's fingers began to slip. She could feel her bond with the atranoch slipping, and soon Arvexia began to whip her tail as if trying to get rid of a parasite.

"I can't control her!" Sho'nee screamed.

Ivy began to descend the spikes like a ladder, trying to reach her hand out. Another violent shudder rolled through Arvexia, ending with a tail lashing that sent Nalia soaring. A shadow flashed over her for a moment, and the atranoch flew away. Clouds whipped by as she free-fell. The mountains rushed up from below. Spinning out of control, she careened through the atmosphere like a meteor. *I have failed.* The pain of the thought killed her. With all the love in her heart, she reached out to N'damu in her final moments so that he might know it. His face formed perfectly in her mind, and instead of falling, she seemed to float.

Like landing in the blackest of oceans, the mega-atranoch caught her in his wing. Bouncing her like a child on a trampoline, the beast maneuvered her onto his back, droning eerily. Vartek was ten times Arvexia's size, at least. His call was deafening as thunder. The valor descended, circling as the midnight-black monolith began to flap its colossal wings. Nalia's heartbeat began to normalize as she dared to take Vartek's rider position.

***

Nalia Chuku soared masterfully through the air aback the charcoal black mega-atranoch. Vartek's eyes blazed orange and seemed to match her wild hair, flickering like a flame in the wind. She scanned the Sindiswa for a sign of N'damu. The megalithic bone-dragon seemed to glow below her. His glossy black spikes were twice as tall as she stood, lined like two stone-spire fences down its back. Her arms could feel the air under its wings like they were one and the same, flapping in the hot updraft. Thraxis cast the animal's jagged silhouette on the mountainsides.

Their spirit-link was unmistakable. She could Vartek's essence—could know the winged serpentine's very being. His mind churned with a language of magnetic pulses, evolved long ago on prehistoric Inana. They cannot abide the words of our kind. What use could they be to a god of the sky? The world was silent and lacked to touch of skin she understood, but solar radiation lit up the vista like a vibrant painting—avant-garde yet somehow a map the bone-dragon could understand and navigate by. The magnetic field flowed through his body as well, somehow nourishing him, stirring the beast's core and generating

368

an energy akin to food. *That explains why they never come down,* Nalia thought.

She thought *dive*, and he dove. Nalia flew into free-fall until she thought: *catch me,* and he softly hovered under her, allowing her to land with a gentle pat. His smooth black skin formed to her bare feet, soft and warm—she often lost track of where she ended and the atranoch began. *So, this is the feeling of N'jikota.*

CHAPTER TWENTY-SEVEN

Enahdra IV

Neither Enahdra nor N'damu was fleet of foot. Growing up in extravagance does not involve much running for your life. She didn't have to pretend to trip and stumble—or to feign exhaustion as they stammered east across the Sizwe. Her game of deception was past the point of no return. With hands washed in blood, the Princess of Vesta was too far from the shadow's comfortable obscurity. She knew she was flying dangerously close to Thraxis. *Father would be aghast.*

"If we head into the mountains, we can find the VEOs," she told him as they pressed on. "Noba as well."

"And Nalia," he said, looking back and gasping for breath.

"Of course." She looked past him, straight through like a ghost of pure light. His desperation felt strangely exhilarating—the sense they were in this together—that he needed her. Enah's black silk dress was tattered and torn by the brush. A more suitable outfit *did* occur to her, but she wanted the misery to be wholly authentic. She had killed for this chance to be alone with him—caused so much death when she ordered the siege of Meadowdell. "Can't you reach out to the atranoch?"

N'damu closed his eyes and tried again. It had been his hundredth attempt and became his hundredth failure. Enah took his hand as they began to tread through a soggy marsh. "I feel nothing. I don't understand it. It was so powerful before."

She tightened her grip. "Really? Nothing at all?"

"Only your hand, Enah. And believe me, I'm happy to be holding it, now more than ever." His words seemed to rinse over her, soaking her in satisfaction like a warm bath. Like an addict away from their drug too long, she only knew then how much she'd suffered before. As the rush washed over her, the princess knew it had been worth it. The collusion—the lies in court, the blackmailing of Colt Dunkarr, bribing of Rigel Kong, and raising an army of heathen militants. Now add the sacking of Meadowdell. N'damu couldn't know any of it, or he would never choose her for his queen.

They walked for hours across the savannah. For all N'damu's training, no animal would bear them. Dushnah scattered, and mamidons ignored him completely, but the more he tried, the harder it became for Enah to look away. As sore as her feet were, she was happy not to share him, even with an atranoch. If they were to wrap their legs around anything, it would be each other.

"You need to rest, Enah."

"I can't, N'damu. Think about all those people. About Sal'aah and Rigel—dead."

"They will find their light, Princess." He put his hand on her shoulder. His dimples flexed in as he smiled with lips calling for her to kiss them. Enah could forgive him for sleeping with that beast of a natural, as long as he did what was right. She deserved adoration—to be Queen Enahdra Atalay. In this scenario she had created, N'damu was sure to fall in love with her. When her VEOs took back Meadowdell and brought justice to Sal'aah's assassins, how could he deny her?

"The rebels will not have my sympathy or Clan Vesta's mercy."

"Do not forget, Enah; those 'rebels' are *my* people." N'damu wrapped his arms around her as she pretended to sob in his chest. "I will look each one of them in the eye and ask why they betrayed Atalay." His heart was so innately good, it made her envious.

Perhaps I overestimated his outrage, she thought, nodding in agreement. "The Volturis was real all along."

"It's all turned out to be true, Enah." The prince grimaced, clenching eyes, teeth, and fists at once. "Everything Colt Dunkarr warned my father of." A rattly droning rose low in the air as they plodded out of the marchland onto an open field of tynn.

"But we may have more immediate danger." Her heart sank when she realized her blunder. Again, she'd underestimated the Sizwe. "I'd recognize that rattling anywhere. Not a rotation went by in court where I didn't hear—"

"Nagas," the prince said. "These tynnlands are vast. We will never outrun them."

Enah pressed a finger to her lip. "*Shhhhhh.*" Despite the danger, their heightened awareness seemed to bond them even more.

All they could do was stay low and creep through the long beige blades of tynn. Unlike Earth-grass, which Enah preferred, tynn had a pasty resin that stained your skin white and stank like sour jupiter juice. The prince held out his hands and scooted on his knees ahead of her. She could see he was not afraid—giving himself over to his faith in Khanya. *Earth-lore is filled with men like him,* she thought, crawling closely behind. *Horus, Odysseus, Krishna, Buddha, and Jesus Christ.* Atalay was a true conduit of faith, whether Vesta created them or not.

Enahdra wasn't sure how much conviction *she* had, however, as a rustling in the grass caused her to recoil. She'd always considered such mythic characters to be social tools. Like brushes and paint to a painter, she wanted to be a wielder of such implements. Atalay needed no power outside of the idea that he had it. The belief that he was otherworldly and benevolent was a formidable societal weapon. But useless, unfortunately, against a rabid pack of nagas.

Perhaps the princess had been as impetuous as N'damu in the Glass Valley—running out on lessons that needed learning—taking on the world too soon.

A naga shot past their line of sight, almost a shadow, but its form was unmistakable. Prong-covered worms, snarling and savage, she'd always hated Usoca and Urnas with a hot passion. *At least we will die together.*

The rattling intensified as snarling and hissing seemed to surround. One of the serpentine predators whipped its tail, tripping out Enah's ankles. She rolled hard into the shrubs with a harsh thud. The prince dove over her, shielding her as the naga coiled like a spring. Another naga side-swiped it before it could strike, and the two creatures began to wrestle in a furious whirl. In this momentary distraction, N'damu pulled Enah up, and they shuffled away.

She tripped and stumbled behind. "I think my ankle is broken."

N'damu stopped and turned to her, taking both of her hands as the rest of the pack converged. "Only faith can save us now, Enah." He looked to the sky. "Only the mercy of Khanya can avail us." She felt her sanity drift as the prince seemed to emit a pulsing glow. The ten-foot nagas burst from the shrubbery, circling them in a frenzy.

The princess dove into the bush as N'damu stood his ground. With her ear to the turf, she heard it—felt it: a rumbling steadily rising. Then, she sensed a pull to N'damu as he raised his hands in a "V" to the heavens. The nagas snarled in his face, lashing their slimy violet tongues and snapping their prongs.

The prince smiled in the face of death. The rumble soon became a roar as Enah retook her feet and stood behind him. Startled, the nagas began to circle faster as a herd of dushnah came storming down from the foothills. A spire of light seemed to emanate from N'damu. *A trick?* Enah thought, rubbing her eyes. *Another solar storm burning my retina with neutrinos?*

Enahdra began to throw stones at the nagas. She didn't know if this was the Eden Star, Khanya, N'jikota, or Atalay's own luminance, but something compelled her to protect N'damu. One of them snapped at her from behind, lodging itself to her lower back with a chomp. She screamed out in agony as the animal gnawed on her hip. Suddenly, the naga exploded behind her with a thunderous crunch, and a towering mamidon cast a shadow over her.

"Sab'ano! You're not supposed to kill the nagas."

"Oops. Sorry, Sab'ina." The young Novojoh twins sat upon the lumbering animal, smiling and waving. "Hey, Princess! Need a lift?" *Novojoh?* She looked up, plain-faced and dripping in naga gore. As happy as Enahdra was for rescue, the pain overwhelmed her. Not from the gashes the naga had left in her back, but the hindrance to her plan.

The herd of dushnah overwhelmed the rest of the naga pack, scattering the slithering predators. S'ike Novojoh slithered over on the back of his fat blob of a querghil, fending off the final naga with its massive belly as it moved in on N'damu. *Barren Void. Are they ALL here?*

Enahdra felt a hand on her back, and a soothing cold and relaxing warmth came on at once over her wound. "Let my throzeids heal you, Princess Vesta."

"I'm fine," Enahdra cried, pushing Sar'ah Novojoh off her.

"Wild naga bites are incredibly poisonous," Sar'ah said. "Their saliva is a micro-biome of viral species. Luckily for you, I can treat you without your permission or courtesy."

"Impressive, Sar'ah," Enah said, nodding. "Thanks." Shar'nah hopped off a dushnah and ran up to hug N'damu. As the prince scooped her in his arms, Enahdra could feel her pulse pounding in her forehead.

Just then, Noba jumped out from over her shoulder. "Surprise!" He kissed her on the cheek. "You ruined another dress, Princess."

Enahdra punched him hard in the nose. "Get the fuck away from me!" Noba scowled at her as blood rushed from his nostrils. "You'll never touch me again without my consent, you smarmy—"

"What's gotten into you, Enah?" Sadah went into a half-stance as though she might attack again. "Oops. I guess you *wanted* to be naga feed."

"Don't take credit, you fool. I didn't smell botsora spray."

Noba squinted as he pinched his nose to stop the bleeding and held his head back. "Who told you—"

"Everyone knows your spirit-link is botsora, idiot," she said. "No one has *that* much gas, Noba."

He shrugged as N'damu ran up and hugged him. "You answered my call!"

"I saw a strange light," Noba said, pointing up. "A beacon in the sky. I thought, perhaps a distress call."

The prince had a confused expression. "I saw no light," he said, scratching his mohawk. Shar'nah allowed the herd to scatter as S'ike hopped off his querghil, waving happily as the bone-slug bounced away.

The twins slid down their mamidon's leg. "We were *all* drawn here," Sab'ina said. "Strange."

Enah cringed as Sar'ah took the next turn hugging N'damu—she even dared to kiss him.

"I just knew you needed us, N'damu," Shar'nah said.

"Odd indeed," S'ike added. "I could have sworn I saw a spire of light also."

"Hey, N'damu," Sab'ano said. "I found my spirit-link!"

"*We* found, *WE*!" Sab'ina waved her finger at her brother. "We both bonded to mamidons."

"Barren Void, Sab'ina! I wanted to say it!" The little boy pouted as his sister giggled. "You're always copying me."

"Watch your language, young man!" Sab'ina said as her twin brother grumbled. Then she whispered to the prince, loud enough for all to hear. "I linked *first*, N'damu."

"No!" Sab'ano hopped in the air, spinning completely around. "*I* linked first. What can I say? N'jikota is powerful with me, like Father!"

"He will be proud of you both," Sar'ah said, finally taking her claws off N'damu.

"Where is he, My Prince?" S'ike asked, plopping down on a tuft and drinking his canteen. "We have been searching for you all since Mount Lapis."

"What happened during your flight with the atranochs?" Shar'nah asked with her arms crossed tight. "Where were you?" The young Kota of Dushnah tapped her foot impatiently.

"Where's Sho'nee?" Sab'ina and Sab'ano asked in tandem.

"Children, please," Sar'ah said, taking command as the oldest present. "Let the prince speak." She looked at him, bobbing her head and giggling. "So, did you link to the atranoch, N'damu?"

"I thought so," he replied. "But I was wrong. It was something—else."

"What?" Noba massaged the bridge of his broken nose. Enah felt invisible, as though N'damu had all the answers they desired.

How little they knew. "Can you please do better than 'something else'?"

"It was not N'jikota," N'damu said, scratching his mohawk. "Yet the atranoch answered my commands. I flew on its back, and it knew my thoughts."

"It sounds like you bonded, N'damu." Sar'ah hugged him again as Enah scowled.

"He didn't," Enahdra said. "As soon as Sho'nee died, his control faded."

Sab'ina screamed in horror as S'ike fainted, hitting the turf with a thud.

"No–no," Shar'nah said, shaking frantically as she held Sab'ano in her arms.

"Sho–Sho'nee?" Sar'ah squealed with throbbing eyes raining tears.

The princess enjoyed their dismay, dying to tell them their father was dead too. Enah couldn't explain this newfound hate for them—this new sense that the Novojoh were more competitors than allies. "Is Sho'nee, really … dead?" Shar'nah asked, turning to N'damu.

"I don't know," he replied, staring at Enahdra with displeasure. "We were attacked during our flight. She fell from her atranoch."

"Oh, Sho'nee." Sar'ah tumbled to her knees, sobbing. "Not my sister."

"Tell them the rest, N'damu. The truth." Enah walked next to the prince and put her arm around his hip, smirking over at Sar'ah. "They deserve at least that." *Is this what it's like for Father? When he uses N'joku to destroy his enemies.*

"What truth?" Noba asked, kneeling to comfort Sar'ah. "Let's get on with this. I am the First Spear, don't forget. I need all the information here, N'damu."

"I'm sorry to have to tell you this horrible news, my friends." The prince's eyes welled as tears tinkled down his cheeks. "Sal'aah—your father was—" He cleared his throat, collecting himself before continuing.

"Lord Novojoh was gravely wounded, I'm afraid." Enahdra couldn't control the impulse to help. All her father's tutelage seemed to be fading. "N'damu heroically got him back to Meadowdell. However, the rebel army of the Volturis invaded while your father convalesced. N'damu and I narrowly escaped. Sal'aah, sadly, did not."

The shrieks echoed across the Sizwe. N'damu shook his head, staring her down with anger she'd never seen on his face. Like an atom-breaker engine of rage, a shock wave of heat and energy seemed to radiate from the prince. Enah fell to his feet. "Enahdra! Your tact is unacceptable—"

"I was bearing *you* the burden—"

"No!" His scream drowned out the weeping Novojoh children as they huddled together, lamenting their loss. "Something has *possessed* you, Enah." Love and hate seemed to overwhelm her at once. She tugged her filthy tangled hair as blue eyeshadow ran down her cheeks.

"I love you, N'damu," she said.

"Wa–what?" Noba chimed in with his jaw hanging open. "Since when?"

Enah ignored the idiot lordling. "Don't worry. You don't have to reject me again. It doesn't change the fact that I've done everything for you." She pointed at the pile of grieving Novojoh siblings. "Vesta is here to do the dirty work, as always." The princess scooted over on her knees and put her lips to N'damu's sandals. He quickly pulled away. "I can't even kiss your feet, My Prince? Tell me your will for me then. I can feel it, but I can't understand."

"You feel it?" Noba asked. "Enah, are you crazy? These kids just lost their sister and their father."

"It is *I* who does not understand, Enah." N'damu took a knee beside her. "Help me understand, and I will help you." His hypnotic black eyes entranced her. *It's him,* she thought. *He is the ether in my veins. The kavah flower that led me away from my right mind.*

Princess Vesta pressed her palms to the side of her head and screamed as a burning sensation consumed her. Sanity was a shadow, it seemed, disappearing in the light. She began to yank out strands of hair, panting like an animal as she slowly crawled away from him. However, as hard as she tried, she couldn't seem to escape his influence. "Let me go!" she begged. But Enah was chained to N'damu's will. "Let me go!" She rolled on the ground, shouting. "Let me GOOOO!"

"What the fuck is wrong with her?" Noba scoffed. Enahdra could hear the Novojoh weeping in the distance. *My brain lights with reward at the notion of their pain. Why?*

"She's been through so much, Noba. As have we all." N'damu tried to help her up, but all she wanted was freedom from the agony inside.

"I have to go," she said, stumbling to her feet like she was drunk. "N'damu—I. Stay away from me."

"Enah."

She recoiled when he offered his hand.

"N'damu, perhaps the Novojoh would benefit from your attention." Noba grabbed the prince's other hand and tugged. "If there is a time for the Light of Atalay, it's now. Where will she go anyway?"

Enahdra began to walk off. The air felt thick like syrup, and the ground seemed to adhere to her soles. "Don't leave me, Enah," N'damu said. "I need you." She turned around in an instant and ran back to him. Like a magnet to metal, she clung to his body, wrapping her arms around the prince and kissing him deeply. *Yes, yes. No—stop. Go on, do it. Don't, please. He doesn't love me. He is Atalay, I am Vesta.*

Her lips seemed to force his mouth open. Whether or not he was placating her was unclear, but his tongue began to massage hers back. Enahdra's stomach churned at the awkwardness. Between her legs, there was only numbness, pins and needles, while her mind lit up like a thousand orgasms.

"Enahdra!" Noba sounded repulsed. "N'damu! Please." The lordling was jealous, though she wasn't sure of whose lips. Enahdra pulled down her tattered dress, exposing her breasts and shaking them against N'damu's chest. With Noba dry heaving and the Novojoh children in tears, she looked up at N'damu's miserable expression.

"It's the natural, then? Isn't it?" The prince looked away as she pulled up her dress. Enah sneered. "What kind of Atalay *are* you?" He shook his head and stepped away.

"Not a worthy one," he said.

"You fucked her."

"What?" Noba shrieked. "Who?"

"The orphan," Enah said with a chuckle. "The baseline natural."

"Nalia?" He looked at the prince, wide-eyed with a gaping jaw. N'damu's demeanor betrayed him—his eyes said it all. "How could you—I don't underst—" The First Spear shook his head in disbelief. "What if people find out about this? What if she got pr—" The words seemed to stick on his tongue, and Noba stormed away in a huff.

"He wants you too," she whispered with an off-key melody. "Everyone loves N'damu. Everyone loves N'damu."

"I've never seen this in you before." He didn't smile or frown. If the feeling were light, she would be blinded—if it were gravity, she'd be crushed.

Enah rubbed her upper arms as she hugged herself. "Everyone loves N'damu," she sang quietly. "Everyone loves N'damu." She tried to reset, to find a happier place inside, one with darker shadows to hide. *Resist,* she thought, hoping to stave off the madness. *You are Vesta.* "Everyone loves N'damu." The princess lay in the grass, rolling back in fourth to a tempo. "Everyone loves N'damu."

"Is she all right?" Sar'ah Novojoh asked, still sniffling from grief. Enah continued to roll in the soil, humming her ominous tune with eyes turned back to their whites. *Is it her? The throzeid witch—controlling me with her microscopic slaves? Driving me insane?*

"Everyone loves N'damu." *She wants him. It's Sar'ah.* "Everyone loves N'damu."

"No," he said, kneeling over her. "She's far from all right, I'm afraid." *The Novojoh are after the Seat. She could control us all with her throzeids. Too dangerous.*

"Everyone loves N'damu."

"I can help her to sleep," Sar'ah said. "The princess is overwhelmed."

"Everyone loves—" Enah snapped out of her trance and sprang at Sar'ah like a naga. The princess punched the Kota of Throzeids over and over, tackling her to the ground. She gripped her throat and squeezed while she pounded her nose bloody.

"Enah! Stop this madness now," the prince cried out.

She immediately released her chokehold. "I need to protect you, My Prince!" Noba pulled Enahdra off the Novojoh girl, kicking and screaming. "Noba! Kill her now. She manipulates our minds!"

"I can't do that," Sar'ah said, crawling away.

"Liar!" Enah stepped behind Noba. "Drive your spear through her head before she takes control of you too." The rest of the Novojoh children made a line in front of their sister.

"Leave her alone," Sab'ina and Sab'ano shouted in unison.

The prince gasped, shaking his head. "Enough, Enahdra!"

"The Novojoh are after the Seat!" She ran to the prince and clawed at his vest. "You know me, N'damu. My brain is besieged. We need to kill them all! Noba, protect Atalay."

"Sar'ah, make her sleep." The prince embraced her, patting her hair and shushing as everything went black.

***

383

Enahdra Vesta's eyes blinked open in the dark of night. Campfire embers flicked at her toes as Noba snored beside her, propped up by his spear. The oaf was clearly supposed to be on watch as N'damu and the Novojoh slept. Enahdra felt clear again—free of the phantom mind-control. *I have to get away while they sleep,* she thought. *I need to contact Rigel.*

As the lordling of Sadah snoozed, Enah crept off into the dark savannah. She knew the VEOs were encamped in the foothills—strategically away from Meadowdell's siege. The princess fumbled through the dangerous wilderness, crossing the tynnlands until finally reaching tree cover. The home star began to leak its morning light, yet it was still dark enough to hide her. Enah pulled up her dress, unclipped her QNT ring from her navel, and placed it on her finger.

Commander Rigel Kong suddenly appeared in light-form in front of her.

"You look like shit," he said.

Enah rubbed her temple and clenched her eyes shut. "Get a fix on this transmission and send the VEOs immediately. I won't last long out here."

"Frigg is not far," the commander said. "Freya and Chuku have not returned from searching for Atalay. Should I come—"

"No. We need the Volturis to fortify Meadowdell. The Novojoh are coming soon. Summon the throngs."

"I've called half of Inana here already," Rigel replied. "Naturals outnumber purists on this rock twenty to one. It ain't too surprising they don't enjoy licking your boots." She smiled ear to ear as the hologram showed the armada he'd amassed outside Meadowdell. A legion of fighters blended into the horizon. "Rebels from Nolwazi and Xolani Valley. Every disgruntled outlaw in Tilo. Every bounty hunter of the Blood Plains and nomad of the Fuza has come to fight with the Volturis—great freedom fighter that I am."

"You play the role well, Rigel," she said.

"I've found the access tunnels to the ancient Milushi dungeons under Meadowdell, as you commanded."

"Excellent," Enah rubbed her palms together. "So, they *are* more than rumors."

"They're derelict—dank and crawling with grats," Rigel said.

"Dark." She smirked at the flickering hologram then looked up at the rising sun. "A place even the Light of Atalay won't shine."

"It's a fucking torture crypt."

"The forces of N'gaia will arrive soon. I want the Novojoh exterminated before then. They're grief-stricken. They know we have their mother and the old crone. Those kids will be stupid and arrogant enough to attack, especially with Noba beside them. It won't be long now."

"Good," Rigel said, cocking his ion-grenade launcher. "I'm ready to collect some heads."

"Just don't reveal yourself—to anyone. Not yet." The commander of her VEOs slipped a black helmet over his head, decorated with a single red jewel on the brow. In his sleek armor, charcoal black with crimson trim, the Volturis was her obsidian knight. He had an enormous proton cannon latched to his back and pulse rifles over each shoulder. "I don't care who you kill; just don't hurt the prince. Get him away from the Novojoh before they corrupt his mind as well. Make sure he is safe. I need him."

"Yes, Princess." Under the Volturis helm, his voice was distorted, modulated with a menacing low-pitch. "I will secure the commodity and soak the streets of Meadowdell in Novojoh blood." The hologram flickered out.

CHAPTER TWENTY-EIGHT

N'damu VIII

"She's gone." Noba shook the prince's shoulder, stirring him from sleep. *Nalia?*

"Wha-what? Who…" He'd been communing with Sal'aah Novojoh in his sleep again. N'damu had so much to learn, far too much to absorb from fast-fading dreams. "Nalia?"

"Enah—she snuck away in the dark." His heart sank. For a moment, he thought Enahdra Vesta's breakdown might have been a dream as well—a nightmare.

"Barren Void!" N'damu sprang to his feet and scanned the sprawling plains of the Sizwe. "She thinks herself invincible." They'd been fortunate enough to be saved from the naga pack; indeed, she would not sneak out on her own were she in her right mind.

"Fool-hearted Vesta. For all her allure, she's completely insane." Noba Sadah squirmed into his armor in a hurry. "She'll never survive alone out there."

He looked to Sar'ah Novojoh, sitting with the twins at the fire. "Sho'nee said your throzeids give you an extrasensory perception." Her auburn eyes flickered with the flames' reflection, glazed over as she snapped out of her grievous trance and nodded. "Can you locate Enahdra?"

Sar'ah tied back her hair and closed her eyes. "If Princess Vesta is close, I will feel her micro-biome." Streams of dried tears veined down her dirty cheeks as she hummed softly. "It may take some time."

N'damu meditated as well, reaching out to Enahdra with what dull senses he had. *Nothing.* Sal'aah had told him, again and again in his dream, about the power of N'jidia, a foretold ability to channel the N'jikota of those around him. The concept was difficult to embrace, however. The propensity for divination was not in the Atalay design. The Doctrines warned against human prophecies, and with good reason, they were always wrong.

He could feel something: a warmth, an invisible radiance in all his friends. The throzeids, perhaps, yet he could not sense Enahdra.

"I can't feel her," Sar'ah said.

"What about Sho'nee?" the prince asked. "Nalia?"

Sar'ah slouched, shaking her head.

The morning sun crept up from the mountains to the south as violet skies gave way to yellows and oranges. Thunderclouds loomed over the Sindiswa to the west—the storm season's wrath moving down from the mountains. The ominous sight made more ill-omened by the fact that the two women N'damu loved most were out there. Vulnerable and exposed because of him.

Shar'nah Novojoh came out of the brush with a cold scowl. The young girl had two rhybites, one in each fist. "Eat." She tossed the skinny bone-cats to her brother, who sat by the fire, lost in melancholy. "Gather your strength." S'ike and Sar'ah were older than Shar'nah, yet she was the alpha, it was clear. "We are taking *back* our home. I won't let another rotation pass with those infidels in the Hall of Novojoh."

"If Father is dead, then I only care about revenge," Sab'ano said, pounding his tiny fist in the dirt. Sab'ina hugged him and began to sob again.

"You can't avenge him from the grave, my friends," N'damu replied. "Better that you honor his sacrifice. He would value your lives above all else."

"Father would not be content to leave our home in the hands of outlaws." S'ike skewered the rhybites and put them over the fire to a greasy sizzle. N'damu's stomach rumbled as the savory odor hit his nostrils.

"I agree," Sar'ah added. They all nodded at once. Even Noba tapped his spear in support. "This cannot stand—but they have Mother and Grandmother."

"Unless *they* are dead as well," Shar'nah said as she raised her fingers to the sky. The ground began to shake as she summoned the dushnah herds.

"We must be cautious, Shar'nah." S'ike gobbled a bite of meat, burped, then passed some to the twins.

"The Volturis will have commandeered the magnus fleet by now," N'damu said. "We need to find Enahdra and reunite with the VEOs." Noba tapped his spear again as the prince continued. "The Vesta Enforcers will be necessary. Commander Kong's arsenal alone will be worth a thousand rebel bandits. In two or three rotations, we will strik—"

"Not good enough!" Shar'nah snapped. "I will not allow this insult to my family. This is an affront to all G'higari." She threw her black hat into the dirt and flipped back her long, wild red hair. "These rebels spit on Khanya, and you, N'damu Atalay. We do *NOT* need Vesta!"

"Don't underestimate N'jikota, N'damu," S'ike said as he handed him a leg of rhybite.

"They have proton cannons," Noba said. "I must agree with the prince. We will find Enahdra. Sho'nee and Nalia could be out there as well. The VEOs are proven warriors with superior tech."

"Technology is only a human construct," Sar'ah said with a chuckle. "We draw our power from Khanya—from the Light of Atalay." Herds of animals formed around the camp, dushnah, querghil, and mamidons alike.

N'damu could feel them through the Novojoh children, as he had felt the atranochs with Sho'nee. Were the ancient Milushi right? Could he be the N'jidia: *the* Kota of Kotas? At first, he rolled his eyes. *Humans love their 'chosen one' tropes,* he thought. The prince wasn't sure if it was true, but he *could* somehow sense all their spirit-links. A warm sensation, a light drawn from the entanglement of souls. As if he'd been training in his dreams, he knew, unlike before, he could harness it.

"We are outnumbered," N'damu said, unsure if he should risk attacking now. "I think it would be unwise to rush to offense."

"Our advantage only lessens the longer we wait," Sar'ah said with a grave face. "Don't forget, throzeids outnumber them a million to one." The prince realized; *she* was the secret weapon. The army of throzeids Sar'ah commanded gave them the invisible advantage. The idea set him at ease as his own internal microbial society became perceptible.

"I am the Prince's First Spear," Noba said, stepping between him and the Novojoh. "I'm sorry, I cannot allow N'damu to enter a battle."

"You can, and you will," the prince replied.

"You don't even have your spear!" Noba stomped his foot down.

"I have strength you do not understand, my friend."

"And *you* do? You can't ask me too—"

"I am Atalay," N'damu replied. "Asking you, only for faith." *Please, Noba.*

The Son of Sadah nodded, tapping the butt of his staff in the dirt.

"There are thousands of dushnah on the Sizwe," Shar'nah said as she leaped on a bone-horse's back. "I will take Meadowdell back myself if need be." Emboldened by N'jikota, the prince gave in. *Let's do it,* he thought. *For Sal'aah.*

"For Sal'aah!" Noba climbed on a mount, a dushnah of ash gray with white stripes. "I am with you," he said, hoisting his spear in the air. "*We* are with you!" He reached down and pulled N'damu up behind him.

Sab'ina and Sab'ano scaled a bull mamidon as it knelt for them. "For Father!" Sab'ina cried out as her twin whistled back to the pack of lumbering beasts.

Despite the animal forces, numbers worried him. N'damu saw the Volturis's army with his own eyes and knew what it would take to overcome the magnus fleet, especially the Ghost Ship.

S'ike climbed onto a querghil followed by Sar'ah, who straddled the writhing bone-slug behind her little brother. The clouds grew darker as rain began to pour down. Beasts steadily joined their numbers as they rode east, forming a throng—an army of Khanya. Five thousand dushnah at least rolled down the foothills behind them like a comet's tail. At least a hundred querghil and half as many mamidons flanked the riders as well. *If only Sho'nee were here,* N'damu thought. *A few atranochs wouldn't hurt.*

The mountains grew smaller behind them as they crossed the tynnlands headed to Meadowdell. A pungent aroma filled the air as botsora began scurrying from the brush, snorting in the rain as stomping hooves steered around them. The prince had never felt so happy to sniff their sweet stink. Noba grinned back at him with water dripping down his face. "Do you smell flowers?"

N'damu patted his best friend's shoulder. "Yes … yes, I do!" No spirit-link could be stronger than the one he had with Noba, save for one. *Nalia.* He wished so badly for her to be at his side yet was so thankful to have her a hundred miles away from this fight.

Suddenly, warning horns sounded. Meadowdell was only a distant speck as the enemy line came upon the horizon. The hair on the prince's neck stood up as he stared out at the legions. Tens of thousands of Inaneans rising against Atalay—tens of thousands of people he'd failed. People his father and grandfather failed, now formed a cheering rabble. Their taunts grew increasingly louder as they approached, eventually overtaking the thundering herd in volume. Engulfing the horizon, they screamed in a hundred languages, all with a unified tone that needed no interpretation—"death to Atalay."

Noba looked back with eyes wide as Set. How could so many people rise against him? His life in N'gaia had clearly been coddled. So much hate concealed from him. *How many truths of the world have been hidden from me?*

"There are too many," his First Spear cried out. The shadows of the magnus fleet made silhouettes behind the host of rebels. Zolani mountain-men comprised the front line, hulking goliaths with ten-foot pikes. Beside them were archers from the Griner Valley mixed with knights from Oba and Asa, all in gilded Tri-World armor—warriors defected from N'damu's own kingdom.

"They are far too few for me!" Sar'ah stood on her charging querghil, hair streaming rainwater behind. The animal bounced, launching her into the air. With an acrobatic backflip, she landed on a black dushnah and surfed on its back to the front line beside N'damu and Noba.

The Zolani surged, roaring like monsters. Sar'ah scowled as the pigment in her eyes faded to milky-white. She held out her hand like it was spraying some invisible enchantment, and suddenly the entire line of mountain warriors keeled over, puking their guts out. Knights ripped off their chrome helms, spewing vomit like garden hoses—the smell of retch mixed with the botsora spray to create a stomach-wrenching green smog in the air.

Shar'nah took advantage as she steered the deafening herd of dushnah into the haplessly sick enemies. Spears and arrows

393

bounced off their wet bone-plated hides like lyverna flies against a castle wall as they mauled the rebels. She targeted the archers first, stifling the most expert bowmen on Inana. Lighting flashed, periodically lighting the sky. The bone-horses thrashed and trampled, skewering armored knights left and right without relent.

In retaliation, the magnus fleet began to advance. Only the Ghost Ship remained back—certainly, that was where the Volturis was hiding. The tanks started to launch ion grenades into the sea of dushnah, each exploding to rushes of bone and gore. N'damu could feel a pinch in his spine for each one that died, and he knew it was worse for Shar'nah.

"Protect yourselves!" N'damu cried out.

"This attack was foolish," Noba yelled as he drove his spear into a vomiting Zolani rebel. "What was I thinking?" The warriors from the south were known to be brutal and remorseless. Their skin was black and their eyes ghostly white. The rusted Zolani armor was crude but thick and heavy. One threw his weapon only for Noba to catch midair. "How did you make me allow this?" Twirling the pike, he flung it back through its thrower's neck.

"I didn't!" N'damu said as he clung to his guard's hips. *Did I?*

Noba looked at Sar'ah, then out at the troop of sick Zolani warriors, then back at Sar'ah like he was putting puzzle pieces together. "Maybe Enah was right," he said. "*Something* is corrupting my mind." He knocked on the side of his chrome helm with a clang, shaking his head. "I have to get *you* to safety!"

A cloud of dust followed the herd as they passed back and forth, bloodying the mud with trampled rebels. The prince wasn't sure what was happening—*who* was in control. Was this murder self-defense or valor in battle? Was this blood on *his* hands? Shar'nah's? The dushnah? "This was *my* command, Noba!" he said. "Mine alone."

Another pike came flying from the left, behind Noba's head. As fast as N'damu could think, a white dushnah reared back on its hind legs, blocking the blade with its neck. The animal's six yellow eyes went dark as it fell with a wet gurgle in the dirt. The prince glared at the Zolani warrior as his satisfied chuckle was broken by another bone-horse impaling him through the heart with his horns.

"Did *you* do that?" Noba asked. N'damu nodded as he summoned a mount to his side and hopped on. Dushnah rushed to surround him, circling, pummeling any enemy who dared come too close.

"I don't know if we can trust the Novojoh," Noba said, looking back again at Sar'ah with a suspicious squint. "Something has compromised me. My reasoning is—"

"Trust that *my* mind is sound," N'damu replied. "If you want to protect me, win this battle, noble soldier of Sadah." Noba shouted a war cry as he charged off at the enemy. It was unlike his friend to comply so readily to anyone's command.

The next line of enemies came down the field. N'damu felt a single dry swallow moving down his throat like a worm. Hundreds of M'lilo bandits, in spiky war armor, wielding broadswords, maces, and bows. They began to chop down the herd, chanting ominous, archaic Milushi hymns as they fought.

395

"Noba!" Sar'ah called out. "N'damu—get behind me." As they fell back, she activated another wave of throzeids. The bandits who didn't vomit fell flat on the ground—asleep. Others began to rip off each other's armor and fornicate on the battlefield, feverishly overcome by lust. "S'ike, send in the querghil!"

S'ike Novojoh held back with the twins behind the dushnah herds, waiting to cue his querghil. The flopping spike-covered slugs bounced their hulking bodies across the ailing horde of M'lilo fighters. Blades were useless against the beast's thick hairy hides as they rolled over, squashing the bandits: sleeping, puking, and fucking alike—crushing them under their tonnage. S'ike seemed to glow with delight as he rode through the field, thrashing armor with his querghil's massive tail barbs.

N'damu grinned as his confidence grew. *I'll not let them fight alone, not when I have so much power.* He leaped from his dushnah and sprinted toward the fighting.

"What in the Barren Void are you doing?" Noba shouted.

"Upgrading!" The prince climbed up the blubbery rolls of a particularly immense querghil, like he'd trained in a forgotten dream. N'damu grabbed its shoulder spikes and expertly straddled its squirming neck. The massive bone-slug began to shred through M'lilo bandits, ripping them in half with their mandibles, shredding their armor shells and swallowing the meat inside.

A legion of guerrillas attacked next, mountain brutes from the Sindiswa. Snarling and spitting, they shouted profanities as they charged in with spears twirling, swords swinging, and whips lashing. The wild men of the mountains knew how to work together against the animals. Whip wielders wrangled the head horns of dushnah and querghil alike while their swordsmen cut out their throats or bellies. Animal intestines added to the medley of foulness as their numbers started to wane.

A whip lashed across N'damu's face. With a blood trail following his head, the prince flew from his querghil into the mud. The beast swallowed the guerrilla whole as N'damu stumbled away. Four enemies converged on him, circling with spear tips while archers barraged the slug, landing arrows in each of its eyes. It flopped wildly in the mud as N'damu scooted back. "Why are you doing this? Where did Atalay fail you?"

One of the guerrillas spat in his face and kicked him onto his back. As the enemies formed a wall between him and the herd, N'damu could feel his connection to the animals fading instantly. *Are the Novojoh too dispersed?* Perhaps, he needed to be near them to channel their N'jikota. For the moment, he was on his own.

"Atalay ain't nothing ta us!" Another gob of spit hit his eye. The barbarians seemed like callous cutthroats, not the sort of people he'd ever imagined lived in his kingdom.

"Keep yer tower, boy! Fuck you and your chair. The return to Milushi is at hand."

He hated them for a moment before reminding himself he didn't understand their plight. "You are Milushi?" N'damu asked.

"G'higari scum!" A woman of M'lilo threw a chunk of mud into the side of the prince's head. "No longer will we hide in the forests … or remain isolated in the mountains."

397

"Are you *all* Milushi?" He shouted in the downpour a second time so all his aggressors might hear over the chaotic conflict.

"We are," a rebel knight from Oba said. This soldier knew very well who he was. With a crooked smirk, he maneuvered his sword under N'damu's princely braid. "We have no reverence for you." The orange lock of hair he'd had from birth fell into the mud with a slice. A lifelong part of him sinking in the sludge seemed the perfect metaphor. "Naturals will no longer lick the boots of test-tube kings."

"What reverence do you have for the N'jidia? The Kota of Kotas!" N'damu shouted with a voice as booming as his fathers.

"How *dare* you speak of—"

"How does the clone devil himself know of the Milushi legends?" the Oban knight asked.

"Atalay and the N'jidia are one," he proclaimed. All he could do was pray to Khanya they would feel his light—that they would believe his desperate claim. "Which of you would dare assassinate me?"

The crack of proton cannons resounded in the distance. The cloud cover was dull-flaxen ash, occasionally lit white by the lightning. An obsidian-skinned older man balked as they stepped back, one by one, wide-eyed and jaws agape. "Get out of their heads, you shit." He slapped one of his comrades. "He lies! Atalayan witchcraft."

"Then *you* strike him down." The Oban stepped back, raising his sword and pointing at N'damu. Rain streamed down his grimy brown face. The air reeked of slaughter, animal and human alike. "I'll not risk killing the N'jidia—nor do I want to be the one to slay the Prince of Atalay."

The old one scoffed as the rest backed off, lowering their weapons. "Fine! *I* will kill him." He cocked his spear, scowling ice-daggers. Suddenly with a loud *shoop*, a blade cut his head in half like a melon. His tongue flopped out as the top of his skull slipped off above his spinning eyes and hit the stony ground with a plop. Noba vaulted over the old man's falling body, quickly covering N'damu. He pushed the prince down, twirling his Sadah spear like a circular saw above them for protection. His weapon and armor were not like the bandits' crude implements. Noba's krotrium blade ripped through their steel shields like tree bark while their jabs all ricocheted harmlessly off his shiny coat.

"These men have yielded, Noba!" The rain pounded hard over the roar of the combat. N'damu knew Noba heard him; still, he did not stand down. His Sadah'anah technique was flawless. He had never seen his best friend's skills truly unleashed. It was glorious—impressive but frightening. A pirate futilely gouged his sword into Noba's chest plate, making a juddering clang. The lordling retaliated, ripping out his guts, spilling violet intestines in the marsh. Next, a mountain tribe woman lashed her whip around his wrist. With a jerk, he yanked her toward him, skewing her on his spear tip.

"I'll do what I must," Noba said.

The stink of botsora intensified as another wave of adversaries hit. Tribesmen of the Red Savanna, more pirates of the Stone Sea—armies of bandits from Tilo and the Blood Plains assembled as a phalanx. His First Spear continued to cut down the Milushi who'd refused to kill him. *How many must die?* he asked himself.

"Noba!" *They deserve Atalay's mercy, at least.* There were circumstances for all these people. If he was the Shepherd of Humanity, then *they* were his flock—perhaps the ones that needed his light most. "These people have yielded!" The company of Milushi raised their hands to concede.

Noba flipped off his helmet and looked back. "I am made to fight your wars, N'damu. For ugly deeds deemed less divine." The conflict ripped the prince in half. He realized then how little he'd understood war. He'd been so naïve—so selfish to lead his friends away from N'gaia and to persist despite death threats, solar storms, and assassination attempts.

"We must *be* the better way, my friend." N'damu stared into his embattled eyes. Noba looked back like he was fighting off a trance. He seemed stuck in some limbo, stunned and incapable of fight or flight. A squirt of blood suddenly erupted from his mouth. Noba Sadah's deep brown eyes turned bright crimson as a spear tip came exploding from the center of his forehead, tearing his face in two from the mouth.

N'damu shrieked with dread as he collapsed. One of the Milushi who'd surrendered a moment ago drove the entire shaft through Noba's head. Skewered at the skull, he flipped N'damu's friend's dead body through the air and into the turf with a humiliating crash. The prince's childhood friend—the only brother he'd ever know, lay dead, destroyed in the mud.

What have I done?

Surfing the dushnah herd, Sar'ah and Shar'nah broke through the line of bandits. The prince crawled toward Noba's body. "No, no. This—this just can't." Shock raced through him as reality began throbbing—spinning like gears with too much grease. The rain masked his tears as he scowled at the bandits. N'damu could feel his control returning as the girls drew closer. He held out his hands, sending the throzeids in their bloodstream into a frenzy. Noba's killer was the first to grip his stomach. His face turned green, and suddenly he buckled, shitting himself as he heaved over. He started to dig his fingers into his throat, ripping his neck open as he choked on bile. Clearly, another skill learned in his dream-training, the prince focused the throzeids, thickening the murderer's veins. Blood vessels started to burst all over his body as the Milushi bandit dropped from a heart attack, writhing in the wet grass.

N'damu picked up Noba's spear without emotion as Dushnah bucked the remaining Milushi, keeled over in misery. The bone-horses pulverized them as the prince walked up to Noba's killer with a plain face. He cocked the spear back, breaking down in tears. "Why do you choose this? WHY!" *How can I live on now— without ... my brother?*

Despite all his rage, he held down the spear and turned his back to the dying Milushi. The next wave of rebels hit the herd hard as N'damu collapsed beside Noba's body again, weeping uncontrollably. The Novojoh charged passed him, shaking the ground as the mamidons finally rolled in, leveling the battlefield in their wake.

"Get up, N'damu!" Sab'ina cried out as she skipped across the dushnah's backs.

"You're a sitting ulanoid down there!" Sab'ano added.

The magnus fleet was advancing, a wall drawing closer. The megalithic mamidons reared back and came crashing down repeatedly, stomping the rebels two at a time. The Novojoh twins rode the biggest one, hooting and hollering down from the omnipotent animal's back.

He looked down at Noba, tenderly petting his blood-matted hair one last time, knowing he had to fight now. N'damu had led the Novojoh children into this, and he had to get them out.

S'ike and his querghil engaged a troop of pirates, overwhelming them with their girth as his sisters took on the savannah tribes. N'damu raised his friend's spear and charged into the battle. Dushnah circled him like electrons orbiting an atom, creating a barrier of charging bone spikes. Two querghil cleared the path, plowing their obese bodies through the struggle according to the prince's mental command.

He saw a familiar mamidon ahead, Rosalie, the animal he had tried to ride during his first lesson with Sal'aah. She'd refused him that rotation yet this time kneeled for him straight away. *How is that possible?* he thought. More dreamscape training in the dark recesses of his consciousness. Toting Noba's spear, he scaled her back and took the rider's position with confidence.

Only the mamidons stood a chance against the magnus fleet. Proton cannons erupted from the enormous land tanks, disintegrating dushnah by the dozen, leaving piles of smoking ash. The white spray charred the tynnlands, generating an increasing wild fire. Glowing embers floated through the air like reverse snow, singeing his chest as he charged with Rosalie.

Clouds of smoke hazed the field. He could only see the white flashes of the proton fire, yet he could still sense the Novojoh's throzeids. "Magnus shields are too strong," Sar'ah called out. "I can't feel the throzeids inside." N'damu reached out with his mind, and through Sar'ah, he could sense it too. The magnuses

402

were all dark spots on the battlefield that even N'jikota couldn't penetrate.

Converging on the first land tank, N'damu felt his shield of dushnah thinning as the pulse-rifles began to fire from the cupolas.

"Whooooooo," Sab'ano hollered as the twins drove ten mamidons into the hull. Sab'ina pumped her fists, cheering behind him as the vehicle began to rock back and forth. The blaster fire grew dangerously close to the children. Smoke pumped from its exhaust as it tipped farther, teetering for a moment before finally collapsing onto its side. The air filled with chemical stink as fumes began to waft across the field. Rain doused the fire as desperate pirates poured out of the floundered magnus, burning alive.

Intrigued by the scent of cooked flesh, the querghil all went wild, gobbling up the scorched men like little charred morsels. S'ike rode his slug around the burning magnus, snuffing out the sweltering tynn as his beasts feasted like insatiable gluttons.

The prince squinted and shielded his eyes from the rain, focusing on the fiery wreck. *Ultranium Eleven engines.* N'damu remembered the instability of the element that ran the commandeered Vesta vessels. "S'ike! Get back, NOW!!!" White flashed behind the Novojoh boy as he looked back in confusion. A distorted crack hit the prince's ears as he watched the Kota of Querghil disintegrate in front of him. A bloody pop that disappeared instantly. The next shock wave sent him flying from Rosalie as a dark mushrooming cloud spewed over the exploding magnus.

Sar'ah's head popped up from the mire. "S'ike, no." She dropped her face in the sludge, weeping for another fallen loved one. "Not you, beautiful brother." Shar'nah was stone-cold. She plowed her dushnah over the shocked and burning enemies without hesitation. The querghil, however, went into an infuriated state, now out of control without S'ike. N'damu felt no connection to them with their kota gone. He climbed back on his mamidon as she stumbled back to her feet.

The twins charged the next magnus, unaware of their fallen brother. The prince directed Rosalie after them, wishing she were fast as a naga. "We can't destroy the magnuses!" The rambunctious pair proved why children, of course, had no place in battle.

With a "woohoo," they slammed into the next magnus, still carelessly unaware of their extreme explosiveness. Rosalie plodded as fast as she could, but it was too slow.

"Stop! Sab'ina ... Sab'ano!" He tried to call back the mamidons, but it was too late. The twin Novojoh already had masterful control over them. They tumbled the second magnus with a sickening metallic crunch, as other mamidons began to buck the remaining tanks. Flames began to emerge from the hull as more incinerated bandits poured out. The twins started to stomp rebels as a pack of hysterical querghil roared down the field. The slugs began to bum and slash mamidons at their legs. Spooked, Sab'ina and Sab'ano's mamidon-mount reared back, and a fat bone-slug barreled into its hips.

"Why are they out of control?" Sab'ano cried out. "Damn, querghil!"

404

"S'ike," Sab'ina said as her tears joined the rain shower. She closed her eyes. "I can't feel him."

Sab'ano began to wail, balling his fists and punching the air. "He's dead too?" Cued by the children's rage, the herd of mamidons began toppling magnuses in force across the battlefield.

The prince fended off the out-of-control querghil with Noba's spear, trying to wrangle them away from the Novojoh kids. "Stop them," N'damu cried out as Rosalie skewered a querghil with her tusks. He hopped off the mamidon and grabbed Sab'ano under one arm. "Make the herd stand down." Scooping Sab'ina under his other arm, he stammered back toward Rosalie. "The magnuses are like weapons of mass de—"

The second land tank exploded. He dove behind the mamidon as the shockwave pummeled into her hide, crushing her ribcage inward. Next, Rosalie skin burst into flames as she absorbed the heatwave, trumpeting out in agony. It felt like a knife in the chest.

Sar'ah and Shar'nah still held the dwindling line. *Why don't they retreat?*

The Novojoh sisters fought valiantly. The throzeids crippled every rebel the Volturis could throw at them as dushnah arrived in droves to replace the fallen. N'damu patted out the flames on Maribeth's broken corpse and with a swing of Noba's spear sliced open her belly. "Hide inside, now!"

"Ewwwww." Sab'ina recoiled in disgust.

"No way," Sab'ano said with a scowl.

I don't have time for this, he thought. *Just do it. Get inside, NOW!*

Without another complaint, the children's eyes went blank. They climbed into the gory stomach of the dead mamidon, resigned to wait out the battle in hiding.

The wind whipped the rain into N'damu's face. Shielding his brow, he gazed out across the smoke-obscured field over the raging battle toward the walls of Meadowdell, which loomed in the distance. The portcullis was rising, and with it the prince's stomach sank. Thousands more rebels began to file out of the city, followed by the colossal Vestian monstrosity, the Ghost Ship.

The magnus fleet rumbled over the battlefield, crushing the herd like himpheah ants. Dushnah were useless against the land tanks. The querghil were lost, and N'damu's control over the mamidons was tenuous at best. *It's over,* he thought. He held up his arms, hoping to direct the animals back to the foothills. *Retreat.*

Shar'nah called out as she rode up. "No, N'damu, we cannot retreat!" He looked back at the Ghost Ship. *He's in there. I know it—the Volturis.*

"We have no choice, Shar'nah." He screamed over the ruckus, pointing out to the battle. "Would you see every last dushnah slaughtered?" Another flash of white erupted from one of the magnus's proton cannons, rendering a pack of mamidons to ash.

"These zealots are killing my family," she shouted back. Shar'nah's eyes were red with hate, her innocent young voice soaked with ire. "I'll follow them to the grave before I retre—"

An arrow pierced her chest with a horrible crunch. The Kota of Dushnah grimaced as she gripped the shaft and ripped it out of her sternum. Blood erupted from her chest in little bursts as she clenched her fists, screaming in a fury. "I will see you all in the Barren Void!" She charged her bone-horses into the army of rebels, killing as many as possible as she disappeared in a sea of swords and spears.

N'damu ran back desperately as his sense of the dushnah faded. The herd flipped modes like a switch, from predator to prey, scattering chaotically in a bid to escape.

Sar'ah stumbled up from behind, clothes shredded and bleeding. "Dead ... all of them." Tears poured down. "I can't feel my family, N'damu." The army of rebels circled with pikes drawn as the magnuses slaughtered the last of the mamidon.

"Take the prince," a defector from Asa shouted, a general based on his armor. "The Volturis wants him alive, for now."

Sar'ah grabbed his hand, bawling as she looked back in terror. The mountain savages glared at her with wide eyes, licking their lips at the young beauty. "They'll torture us." She leaned over and kissed him, then looked up. "I can feel their lust—their hate for G'higari—for Atalay." Her face was covered in grime yet beamed with dignity. "We can't let them take us alive, N'damu."

"No, Sar'ah, do not." Tears streamed from both of their eyes, and they squeezed each other's hands. "Don't do it." He sensed what she wanted.

"One last lesson on throzeids..." Her fingers trembled as she gripped him. The enemies circled and closed in. "They can provide mercy when all else fails."

Stop, he thought.

She pressed her lips to his ear. "Don't make me." He knew what they could do to her—what perverse things they'd do to them both if they take them alive. "My family is dead, N'damu.

I'm ready to move on as well. This is the end, but we can join our ancestors on *our* terms." The Ghost Ship rumbled up from behind the horde of rebels, eerily quiet as its shadow slowly swallowed them. "Join me in the Eternal Womb."

"I won't give in," N'damu said, squeezing her hand tightly. "We can still—" The megamagnus crawled to a halt, lowering its steel skirt to the ground, smoking exhaust as its engine whir vanished.

One of the rebels grabbed Sar'ah by the hair and pulled her away. "Volturis only wants him," the dirty, pale-skinned Zolani said with a commanding tone. "We do what we like with the Novojoh—fucking traitors to Milushi!"

"Please, N'damu." The Kota of Throzeids pulled away, making the rebel gag on a gush of vomit as she ran back to his arms.

"How could I condone killing ourselves?"

"Then let me go!" Sar'ah's pleas burned his chest like acid. In battle, with the blood of war on his hands, he realized the weakness of Atalay. He couldn't touch the Volturis on his shoulder and offer him blessings, nor would Noba's spear avail him now. "Let me die, let me join my family with dignity." The desperate look on her face was heartbreaking, yet still he couldn't even think it.

The Ghost Ship's access ramp lowered as a crowd of rebels poured over them. Milushi zealots hoisted Sar'ah in the air, one on each arm and foot as she kicked and screamed. They shredded her clothes with ravenous intent as she swung helplessly.

"Please, N'damu!" She wailed as a Milushi priestess began painting sacrificial runes on her body. He was confused—

helpless. He knew then he should have gone with her. *The Eternal Womb would be a better fate,* he thought. *Don't let them have you, Sar'ah.*

At that moment, her body went limp in the rebel's arms, her eyes rolling back to their whites. The young Novojoh beauty's ruby hair sprawled in the mud as they flung down her lifeless heap. "Say hello to Sal'aah," he said as he hung his head and sobbed. With a face void of expression, the prince realized he could no longer sense the throzeids. The feeling was disorienting.

"What a waste." A distorted voice came from behind with a foreboding, low-registered resonance that hissed with feedback between breaths. "A girl like that has great value in your culture of rapists and religious fanatics." N'damu looked at the megamagnus as a knight in obsidian armor stepped down the ramp with soft clanks. *Volturis.* "Impressive, getting her to beg you to kill herself. Pretty kinky. How *DO* you do it?" His long crimson cape dragged behind as he stepped onto the muddy battlefield, looming over Sar'ah's body.

Two huge Zolani men held the prince up by his arms, forcing him in front of the imposing black knight. His massive dark helm split into two horns at the crest and reminded him of the Lord Chancellor's headdress in its magisterial presence. However, its red jewel-encrusted eye was unmistakably like the eye on the Seat of Atalay itself. The Volturis carried two proton cannons, like an X on his back, both humming, blinking yellow lights indicating a full charge. He had blades across his chest, and hand blasters lined the sides of his arms and legs, magnetically adhered to his armor's glistening black surface. *He has as many blasters as Rigel Kong.*

The Volturis chuckled through his robotic vocalizer. "You thinkin' of going for one of these?" He pulled a blaster from his hip and cocked it. "Good rationale, boy. That spear ain't gonna cut it." He held it out his for him. "Take one." N'damu looked down at Sar'ah, sniffing the dripping, bloody snot back up his nostril.

The rebels pushed the prince closer to their master.

"May she walk the great savannah of the Eternal Womb with her family," N'damu said, blessing her with his light. "Sar'ah is beyond evils reach now." He looked at the Volturis through his dark visor with regal sincerity in his eyes. "May these people find Khanya's forgiveness as well, for today's atrocities. Atalay has failed you, but the Novojoh were innocent."

"The Novojoh are all dead now!" The horde of rebels cheered the black knight's sentiment. "For nothing—neither your animal friends nor your magical light meant shit in the end." The red jewel in his forehead was mesmerizing and altogether sinister.

"You're right, Atalay failed them, but they did *not* die for nothing."

"Oh, they did." The Volturis chuckled softly to himself as he brought the barrel of his blaster to N'damu's temple. N'damu thought for a moment he recognized the laugh. "They died for you." He pushed it like he was driving a dull spike, grinding it against his skull. "And you are 'nothing' if I've ever seen it. A useless runt—propped up like a prize of creation."

N'damu did not wince. "Then why not kill me and be done with it," he said, slowly shutting his eyelids.

"Because the Homo purist culture needs to learn from this." The villain's voice crackled as he reached out and wrapped his

410

fingers around N'damu's scrawny neck. "They need to know *they* are the beta mongrels." He felt helpless again. All delusions of N'jikota or N'jidia and their empowerment faded, and he was on the mamidon perch again. The world was too much again. The Volturis squeezed his cold grip and lifted the prince off the ground. "The naturals despise you," he said, pointing out to the sea of rebels, slaughtering what remained of the herds. "Any love they've shown was a mirage. Your fat lazy king is hated on all three worlds—believe me. I've been to 'em." N'damu did not struggle, his legs dangling as the giant knight held him up to the hull of the Ghost Ship. His head banged hard against the steel, yet he did not cry out. "Let everyone see how strong you are. Let them see!" The entire army of rebels seemed to have amassed around the megamagnus.

Yes, let them all see, N'damu thought.

The Volturis pulled a long dagger from his chest. Moving his grip to one of the prince's arms, he slid him up the tank. With a jarring crunch, he drove the blade through his wrist. Scarlet squirted as he embedded it in the hull of the magnus like a spike. Then he let N'damu drop, hanging pinned as blood gushed down his arm and soaked his body. The rebels cheered madly, pelting him with clots of mud, yet the Prince of Atalay stayed silent.

"We will tour Inana, boy," the Volturis said, grabbing his other arm and extending it across the blood-splattered hull. "It's time you meet your people. Duran, Asa, Oba—Centralia—and eventually, your triumphant return to N'gaia!" He drilled another dagger into the second wrist, leaving N'damu hanging on the magnus like a fresh kill drying in the sun. Crimson flowed down the magnus, pooling in the mud as the Volturis stepped back to

411

admire his work, laughing softly. However, the cheering of the rebels seemed to be dying out as the prince stayed his emotions.

N'damu could hear them chattering as he hung sprawled out. "Why does he not scream in agony?" The torturous display didn't seem to satisfy them as the Volturis intended. "What man would not react to—" He looked up, scanning the crowd of people who'd risen against him, trying to make eye contact with as many as possible.

"Were we wrong about Atalay?" the Asan general asked. *They need this,* he thought. *They need to know I am not a god but will endure—for them.*

The black knight's laughter turned to a growl, and he ripped what remained of the prince's shirt and threw it aside. "Impressive. Are you challenging me, runt?"

"I told you, you can kill me." The horde went silent. "I've been trampled and poisoned. I have leaped from a mountain and been swallowed alive. I watched my best friend die. What sweet relief comes in stopping my heart, Commander?" The Volturis paused for a moment before lowering his head and removing the dual-horned black helmet.

"Was it the mongrel reference?" Rigel Kong asked. "Or the Oshunese accent?" He tossed the helm, pulled a cigar from his belt, and lit it up. "Perhaps my affinity for proton cannons. I really can't help it. What gave me away?"

The detachment of your laugh, he thought. "Why, Rigel?" Realizing he'd get no answer, the knight in black drew another needlepoint dagger and pressed it to the prince's breastbone.

"I prefer 'Volturis,'" he said as he slid the knife up under his neck. "Just sounds cooler, right?" He began to twist the blade, piercing his soft sternum before ripping the knife slowly across his chest. N'damu made neither sound or expression as the black knight carved over his left nipple and stopped at his ribs. "Princess Enahdra came up with that one." *Enah knows about this?* The thought hurt more than the cuts; still, he gave no indication. Kong began to slice across his abdomen in a horizontal line, stopping at the other rib. "Brilliant girl—very dangerous. Hell of a lot more dangerous than me." Next, he cut up N'damu's right breast, stopping at the point of incision to form a bloody, mangled triangle across his chest. "Never really got over the Darius thing. It probably wasn't a good idea to spurn her, boy. Look what it caused. I would have just popped you, but not her. She's crazy." He pointed back out to the battle-devastated fields of the Sizwe filled with burning deceased, Noba and the Novojoh among them. Finally, Rigel carved three circles down his chest plate, each larger than the last as he moved to the bottom of the pyramid. The rabble quieted as the blade ripped and shredded through his skin. The work of art was, at last, done: the symbol of the Tri-World Alliance engraved on his chest.

N'damu continued to look at the people, but his vision was fading. Unsure of the silence was real, or if he'd gone deaf, not a single ulanoid's caw carried on the static air. His mouth was tasteless—neither wet nor dry. The prince felt the pain. He knew what it was, but the hurt was more soothing in the knowledge he did this for them. *Atalay will endure, a shepherd to show the way.*

The world got even darker as he struggled to hold his head up. N'damu strained to focus as an ominous black cloud seemed to grow and expand overhead. Spreading out over the Sizwe, it cast the rebel army in its gloom as it took over the skyline. When he was a young boy in seminary, he'd watch the storm clouds from the window and imagine they were a valor of atranochs, soaring in to rescue him from his torture.

CHAPTER TWENTY-NINE

Nalia VII

N'damu ... I can feel him down there.

Vartek's scaly skin formed around Nalia's feet, filling the space between her toes, helping her adhere to his back. The megalithic atranoch soared over the combat-devastated tynnlands west of Meadowdell, its shadow slicing the landscape like a scythe. It was clear the beast's presence alone caused the rebel forces to scatter in panic. Sho'nee flew in the distance ahead of a valor of bone-dragons, divebombing hordes of treasonous outlaws with Ivy Freya unleashing sprays of proton fire.

The warzone had a red hue from above, undoubtedly the blood spilled by the thousands of fallen. *Did the Novojoh do all this?* Nalia asked herself as she scanned for signs of N'damu. Vartek tilted suddenly, dodging cannon fire from the few remaining magnuses. She braced herself with his shoulder talons as the atranoch went perpendicular to the horizon, dropped its spike-covered wing, and dragged it across the fiery countryside. She vibrated violently as he plowed through the rebel army like fields of tinkercane stalks, scores of anti-Atalayan deviants shrieking as they tried, in vain, to avoid impalement.

Next, the aerial goliath leveled off, shaking the gore off his wings with a few flaps before drilling his tail through an enemy magnus. The land tank exploded behind her violently—Nalia could feel the heat of the flames as though the atranoch's tail were her own. *Ultranium Eleven*, she reminded herself as her gut wrenched with worry. *We could kill N'damu ourselves if we're not careful!*

Another blast mushroomed in the distance with a lurid clap. Sho'nee decimated the magnus fleet as the rebels set their proton cannons to the skies, lighting up the clouds with vibrant orange and yellow bursts. Nalia could feel an atranoch falling in a tailspin with shredded, burning wings. With its last breath, she could sense Sho'nee compelling it—leading the dying animal to suicide-bomb another magnus. The atranoch slammed into the tank, letting loose an immense shockwave that leveled the surrounding land and everything on it. The pain of its death was grievous to bear and a clear reminder that atranochs could be killed. "We can't let them die," she cried out to herself.

Nalia. A whisper came in the back of her mind—N'damu's voice. She knew then, for certain, he was alive. Another explosion resounded below, its heatwave scolding Vartek's bone underplates. His wings caught the updraft, jolting the midnight-black atranoch upward. *Nalia ... please.* Suddenly, the mighty Ghost Ship megamagnus caught her eye, and she could sense her prince.

Proton blasts erupted around her as Vartek dove again, dragging his belly over a legion of the Volturis's army. The beast knew, through Nalia, to avoid the magnus fleet as it wormed across the battlefield, bounding onto the enemies, crushing them in masses. In fact, the entire valor seemed to understand their threat through their telepathic connections—coordinating their strikes to focus on the standing armies.

Ivy Freya dove from Sho'nee's atranoch, opting to join the skirmish with her blasters. Spending the rest of her proton cannon as she dropped, the purple-armored warrior landed like a dust devil, spinning as she unloaded her blasters in a sea of rebels. She seemed to be making a line to the Ghost Ship as well. Perhaps she expected to find the Volturis; the question is—if he really was Rigel Kong—would Ivy kill him or join him?

Nalia held on tight as Vartek went into a corkscrew maneuver, pummeling the hapless enemies with its powerful wings. Much of the army seemed to be assembled around the Ghost Ship. *Something is going on up there,* she thought as she ran back across the atranoch's back and dove from his tail. *I can't save N'damu on a bone-dragon.* Flipping in the air, she pulled her spear and landed in the mud with a squish. The remaining magnus fleet formed around the megamag and created a barrier of proton cannons no atranoch dared cross. Vartek flew back, joining Sho'nee and her valor of atranochs in returning to the safety of the mountains.

Nalia charged after Ivy, following her blazing trail of destruction toward the Ghost Ship. If she were to save him, it would have to be with her spear. Twirling the staff like a turbine, she leaped in the air, lobbing off a M'lilo bandit's head with a hard swing. Landing on one knee, she drove her blade into a pirate woman's torso and ripped it up through her breastplate with a revolting crunch. As more rebels converged, the Second Spear assumed her fighting stance, jabbing in a series of rapid thrusts. A knife sliced the length of her back, shredding what little remained of her broadcloth scrubs. She never missed her armor so much as a throwing star lodged in her shoulder next. Spinning on her spear, she scissor-kicked wildly before vaulting herself into the air. Skipping over their shoulders, she landed and dashed toward the megamagnus.

Two swordsmen from Redsnow came at her next—though slightly inattentive in their attack. One swung his crimson sword, slicing a lock of her hair as Nalia ducked in a split. Somersaulting under his legs, she drove her heels into the burly man's testicles, leaving him collapsed and crying like an infant. Hopping up into her stance, she jabbed at the second swordsman. He deflected her clumsily, staring toward the Ghost Ship as though it was drawing more of his notice than the fight at hand.

"Did you see what he endured?" he said, waving his sword disingenuously. "He feels no pain!"

Nalia squinted, tilting her head as she relented. "Who are you talking about?"

The man threw down his sword. "The Volturis misled us," he said. "He told us Atalay was only human."

"N'damu? Prince N'damu? Where is he?"

He pointed to the megamagnus, parked on the hill. The outlaw rabble ahead of her seemed increasingly distracted as well. Rebels were dropping their weapons in droves and trying to get a view—congregating like schmiglets, struggling for a nipple.

Nalia pushed her way through the crowd, more motivated than any of them to get a glimpse. Forcing her way past the awestruck forest bandits, mountain tribes, and Tri-World defectors; she could never have prepared herself for what she saw next.

The Prince of Atalay hung bleeding—spread out on the Ghost Ship's hull with the Tri-World crest carved in his chest. The man she loved with all her being dangled, tortured to his limit. Nalia's heart pounded in her head as rage consumed her. She would summon Vartek to destroy them all if not for the look N'damu gave her after battling to raise his head. In the silent sea of rebels, their eyes locked. He seemed to glow brighter with every blink after she rubbed her eyes and refocused. The prince looked happy in the misery, as content as he was on the terrace of the Tower of Atalay, excited to begin his journey.

He was leading them like a good shepherd. N'damu was showing them all—he was glad to bear this in atonement for his people's suffering. "Enough," she mumbled to herself. Tears formed around her sand-brown eyes, yet she could not move closer. Her thighs strained to take a step, but control of her muscles was lost. The prince winked as blood flowed like waterfalls down his arms and chest. "He can't last—can he?"

"IS IT TRUE?" A barrage of blaster fire erupted between Nalia and N'damu. Ivy tackled a mountainous black armored knight. "You're the fucking Volturis?" she screamed, putting the blaster to the side of his helmet and unloading. Unfazed, the knight kicked her in the gut, driving her into the mud with a jarring thump. Nalia squeezed the hilt of her spear, trying again, in vain, to advance. *Why can't I—what is going on?* She looked at N'damu again. *You? How are you stopping me?*

"I was gonna tell you, baby. Was just waiting 'til the time was right." The Volturis pulled off his helm and let out an arrogant laugh as recognizable as his face. Nalia cringed. *Commander Kong. So, it is true.* He kicked her blaster aside and kneeled to help her up. "Believe me, my love. I did this for us."

Ivy jackknife kicked him in the face, backflipping to a safer distance. "My father told me not to marry an Oshunese." *MARRIED?* Nalia's jaw hung open. "You betrayed me. You betrayed Vesta!" She went for another blaster stashed at her hip.

However, Rigel's quick draw was unmatched as he fired a blast into her chest, demolishing her armor. "I would never betray the princess. You know that." He kicked off his wife's headgear and held his blaster to her temple. "My love for credits is unwavering—and she has the most."

Nalia stared back at N'damu. *Let me help her,* she thought. *Please, N'damu. I know you want to protect me, but I need to fight.* Suddenly her spear grip tightened again, and her legs sprang into action. The Second Spear darted past the entranced rebels, pole-vaulting into a flying kick. Her heel slammed into Rigel Kong's skull with a crack. The villain in obsidian armor flew off Lieutenant Freya, smashing his shades as he collided with dank, blood-soaked turf. Kong went quickly for his cannon, but Nalia flung her spear, destroying its capacitor as it slipped from his muddy hands. She picked up her weapon as he began to fling daggers, pulling them from his chest in succession. She sent each one ricocheting as she cartwheeled toward him, her final flip landing with her spear tip in his thigh.

Rigel laughed as he twisted his leg, taking her off her feet by her own shaft's grip. *Stupid, Nalia.* He palmed a wad of her hair and slammed her face down, grating it across the dirt. "Why do you serve these freaks?" He picked her up. They both grunted, wincing in pain, and frothing with anger. "Naturals are real … what a human should be. Not these clone copies!" Nalia raked his face with her fingers, clawing into his soft, squishy eye sockets—with a moist plop, each eyeball exploded out, hanging from veins and nerves against his face.

Next, she walked up and drove her knee into his nose, unleashing a spray of blood as he fell on his back. With her blade to his throat, she stood over him, kicking aside his array of weapons one by one.

"What will you be without all these?" she asked as she looked down at his destroyed face. She poked her spear into his skin, drawing the tiniest bead of red. "What are you without this fine armor Vesta has given you?" Nalia ripped off his shiny black coat of arms and tossed it aside.

"Infinitely more than you, cunt." Rigel spat blood at her, and she pushed her blade into his chest, harder. The factions of the Volturis's army began to draw back, one by one. Rigel groaned, panic in his voice for the first time as he heard them walk off. "Get back here! This fight isn't over yet!" The Stone Sea pirates, outlaws of Tilo and Rhyolite, tribesmen of the Sindiswa, M'lilo, and the Fuza all fell back, abandoning their blinded general to his fate.

"Hummmm, what shall I carve into *your* chest, Kong?"

"I doubt you're much of an artist," he said with a wet cough. "Stupid child, living out your little love story." She looked over at N'damu once more. "She needed him alive. It's the only reason he's breathing." The last of the rebel army disappeared down the valley as Nalia dragged her blade across his chest, over his heart.

"You're right; I'm a shit artist," she said, crinkling her brow as she scowled down at him. "But I am a decent killer now, thanks to you."

"You were always a killer," he said. "Atalay is a murderous line of psychopathic genocidal frauds. You are a slave, girl. Your clone-kings ain't real."

"Maybe." She pointed to N'damu. "But *he* is real."

"Awww, adorable," Rigel said with a smarmy croak as scarlet bubbled from his nostril. "I knew it was a love story all along." Nalia lifted her spear, about to bring it down on his heart, when she felt a blaster barrel at the back of her fiery afro. Its energy-charged whir made ominous music with the beat of her heart as she awaited probable death.

"It's a love story," Ivy Freya said. "But not hers, unfortunately."

"Ivy—"

"Toss the spear, Chuku." Nalia froze. She noticed a strange shift in the air as a sound began to carry up the hill—an ambient vibration, building, high-pitched like thousands of horrible screams. "The VEOs are here. It's over." Ivy pushed the barrel into her skull harder. *Not again,* Nalia thought. Too hard to ignore the sound, they both looked down across the field. Hundreds of armed Vesta soldiers rounded up the retreating rebels, executing them methodically. A company of VEOs in dark navy-blue armor rode toward them on hovering chariots. *Wow, more and more suspicious Vesta tech, immune to the global power outage.*

"He is responsible for all this, Ivy." She looked back at her but did not relent her spear. "All this death—how can you abide—"

"I'm sure you can relate to loving someone you're not supposed to!" Tears rolled down Ivy's soft, pale cheeks. Nalia looked to N'damu again, hanging impaled on the magnus, this time for guidance. Like a ghost, come to double her strength, she felt his phantom hands joining hers on the spear's hilt—one finger at a time, covering hers and tightening their grip. "I will kill you, Chuku. Stand down!"

Together, they plunged the blade down into Rigel Kong's chest, deep into the villain's vile heart. He gargled up a geyser of bubbly gore, trying hopelessly to get out one last word. "I—I—Iv—" Nalia knew at that moment Ivy was wrong—no love stories were playing out here, only tragedies. Rigel's limbs fell limp in the mud, his fingers trembling as he wheezed.

Nalia turned and pressed her chest into Ivy's blaster. "Kill me if you will, otherwise help your prince down."

Ivy grimaced like she was trying to lift a million pounds. Her eyes strained as her forehead pulsated with throbbing vessels. "I ca–ca–can't pull the tr–tr–trigger." Her teeth grinded, squeaking painfully back and forth. "Something is stopping me." N'damu nodded at her, and Nalia took the blaster from Ivy's frozen fingers.

"What is going on here, Ivy?" Princess Enahdra hovered in on her shining azure chariot with fifty VEOs in tow, all in shiny black and blue armor.

"She killed Commander Kong!" Ivy's hands shook in the air as she struggled to regain control of her functions.

Enahdra hopped off her chariot. Her face turned white when she looked up at N'damu, bleeding out on the magnus. Then she turned her stare to Rigel Kong's stabbed carcass. "Killed the Volturis, you mean." The princess reached out and took her hand. "Thank you, Nalia, for doing your duty, an act that would have caused either Lady Freya or I a great deal of heartache. You know the love we bore for our friend Rigel. You cannot fathom our feeling of betrayal."

"I couldn't have done it without Ivy," Nalia said as she ran to cut down N'damu, but the princess squeezed her hand.

"Nalia, please wait." Enahdra wore an urgent expression that made the stakes clear. She pulled her close, whispering in her ear. "I need you to trust me; this has to be done." She twisted a metallic teal-colored tech band on her wrist and pointed it at the prince. A force blast kicked her arm back, pulsing through the air and landing with a *whomp* in N'damu's forehead. VEOs converged around Nalia, taking her spear and restraining her as she kicked and screamed. His head lay limp as blood still gushed down the magnus. "It was only on stun, girl. I'd never hurt N'damu. I love him more than you will ever understand."

Tears poured down her cheeks like rain. "You have a funny way of showing it," Nalia said, looking at the unconscious prince. "Get him down!" The princess nodded at her men and they quickly and carefully helped N'damu off the magnus.

Ivy drew her blaster and took Nalia in her sights again. "My Princess, she killed the commander of our order—the man I love."

"Ivy, stand down," the princess said, stepping between Nalia and her loyal soldier's blaster. "Nalia, he is dangerous." Enahdra raised her eyebrow. "I'm guessing you've felt it too. Noticed his control over you. Your irresistible desire for him. To serve him … to do his will." Nalia knew, of course. She never wanted to admit it, but looking back, it was clear: she'd never had a choice in loving him. "Have you noticed people acting strange? I don't know if it's N'jikota, Khanya, or some other strange magic—I don't think he even realizes it, but he's controlling our minds." If he was, she didn't care. Who ever chooses the people they love? Their feelings made them slaves to each other until the end of time. A give and take of benefit and sacrifice; if N'damu controlled her mind, she trusted him to give her free will.

Enahdra nodded at the guards once she calmed down. Nalia grunted as they let her go, massaging her bruised arm. "You are a hero here then," she said, giving the princess a poisonous scowl.

"No, Nalia!" Enahdra cracked a crooked smile and giggled. "*You* are the hero of this battle, I'm happy to declare. Tipping the fight with your atranochs, defeating the Volturis and saving the prince—the Tri-World is indebted to you. Shyla Sadah will arrive with the king's forces within the oct. In the meantime, let me help N'damu. My people have technology that can get to the root of this mind-control phenomenon. I will keep him safe."

"You will keep him prisoner," Nalia said, shaking her head as the VEO medics took the prince down with care. Still, she was powerless and had no choice but to let him go—to have faith. *Enahdra healed him once,* she thought.

"We will bring peace back the Sizwe region," Enahdra replied. "And secure the south for Atalay."

"And genocide to the rebels?" Nalia looked down the field as the tribes were being lined up for the disintegration squads.

425

Enahdra had no response or clearly any intent to stop it. "N'damu gave them faith again. They deserve another chance."

"Maybe Rigel did too!" Ivy shouted at her with hate-filled scorn.

"In any event, we'll return Meadowdell to the surviving Novojoh," Princess Vesta proclaimed. Nalia gave a faint smile at the sight of Sho'nee walking their way, holding hands with her twin siblings on either side.

"And bury the dead ones," Nalia said with a sniffle. All three looked emotionally spent—clothing tattered and covered in death.

"Yes—and Noba as well. The Son of Sadah deserves a grand memorial for his sacrifice."

Noba ... dead? He was more than her brother in arms. The news of her fellow spear's death broke what foundation she had left, and Nalia collapsed under the weight of the battle's toll. *How could Noba be so careless?* The moment the thought formed in her mind; she knew he couldn't. N'damu gave Noba's will a nudge as well—to his death. *The Novojoh—Lord Sal'aah, the king and queen—Noba. Me. So many could have been unknowingly under his spell. Perhaps he really is a danger.*

She watched as they carried the prince on a stretcher up the chrome ramp and into the dark recesses of the Ghost Ship. "Rest, Nalia, and be thankful," Princess Vesta said as she followed him up the ramp. "We've won. N'damu is safe and getting the help he needs, thanks to you."

"I want to stay with him," Nalia said.

"We *all* need to rest and mourn," Enahdra replied with a grin. "Please respect our purist ways." Sho'nee came up and hugged

426

Nalia, resting her head on her shoulder. "Celebrate your victory, Nalia Chuku. You were a worthy Spear of Atalay today. Your mother will be so proud when she arrives!" Enahdra stepped back into the darkness of the Ghost Ship, and the hatch shut with a loud clang behind her.

She watched as her prince rode away in the megamag, rolling across the land toward Meadowdell. Nalia picked up her spear and shielded her eyes from Thraxis as it dipped below the mountains.

Sho'nee handed her a canteen, and she happily took a deep swig. "My mother and grandmother are still alive. Apparently, the rebels had some mercy in them."

"More mercy than Vesta has in return, I'm afraid." She offered a bag of ocha-nut berries next. Both women reached in and chewed quietly for a moment—staring at the dark-orange sunset together. Sho'nee's strength was awe-inspiring. She'd just lost half of her family, yet still, here she was, comforting *her*. Clan Novojoh would still be a mighty force indeed with her as their lady. "What will you do now, Lady Sho'nee?"

She pointed her spear tip to the mountains and winked. "The Tower of Atalay is blind to the people's hatred—I will make them see. Inana needs to know what happened here. The suffering and loss will not be for nothing." The Kota of Atranochs gleamed with hope. "Legends will tell of the sacrifices our brothers and sisters made. The lessons of my father will resonate for generations. Inana will know of Noba Sadah—and the torture Prince N'damu Atalay endured without complaint."

Nalia took in a deep breath and let it out slowly, her dimples caving slightly as she squinted at Thraxis. "Shall we get on with it then?" She extended her hand to Sho'nee, and they began to walk toward Meadowdell in the dimming violet twilight.

"And you? First Spear of Atalay—rider of the mega-atranoch—what will you do now?"

It was not a difficult question to answer. Nalia Chuku and N'damu Atalay were intertwined and belonged together, without exception or condition. She would continue to defend him, even if he slept a thousand cycles. Her resolve was unquestionable. "I will patrol the heavens and wait for him to be reborn again."

EPILOG

Martellus

Long had Clan Duran stood behind Atalay, from the northern spaceport city that carried their clan's name. As ancient as the *Pegasus Space Ark*, their ancestors had come together from the heavens to settle this system. Duran was the hub of Inanean space flight, where the Ship Masters resided. North of the Quiniso Savanna, where the great Fuza desert meets the polar mountains of Gonothi, lay their city.

The entire metropolis was one giant aerospace terminal for the Tri-Worlds. The deep auburn clouds over the city broke apart regularly as gargantuan cargo freighters parted them, descending the lower atmosphere with their off-world passengers and consignments—Griffindactyls from Oshun, Anu, or somewhere in deeper space. Smoke-billowing Atranoctryx cruisers screamed their banshee cries through the air, only ever drowned out by the boom of the outgoing atom-breaker engines. Duran was a loud place to live, but still, Martellus Duran proudly called it home.

Each step squeaked as he climbed a steel stairway, running his fingers dreamily along the rails. When he came to the podium at the top, he stopped and gazed out onto the rust-colored airfield at his latest batch of aerospace masters. The Duranauts were Atalay's elite space force. With the warm wind whipping his dark gray hair and bushy mustache, he slipped on a pair of black-tinted specs to shield his eyes from the sun. Today was their first jaunt to space after a cycle without power. Having finally restarted the planet's electrical grid and brought atom-breaker engines back online, they were ready for the orbital hardware repair phase. This would be their maiden voyage, aimed at reestablishing Inana's communications network. Duran's finest pilots, engineers, and scientists would spend three rotations in orbit performing satellite restoration before docking with the space station M'demos One—the Vesta Alpha Station.

"Oy, my Duranauts!" Martellus waved his arm to signal for their attention. The men and women in sleek reflective suits immediately turned and saluted reverently. "We are the Masters of Aeronautics! It's a proud rotation, an unforgettable realization that we can overcome the worst of what Thraxis can throw at us. I remember standing where you are, fifty cycles ago, when I was an active pilot. I'd be looking up at my father, Lord Maxim Duran, giving this same speech, thinking, 'Shut up and let me fly, old man!' Well, that time has come. You are all fine purists of the Tri-Worlds, a symbol of human unity: Anutians, Oshunese, Inaneans, all Duranauts alike, working together. Truly, in space,

430

we *must* work together to achieve the vision of the Tri-World Alliance. We are the lifeblood that connects our worlds."

The Lord of Duran wore a tan-colored flight suit of mylar-fused nylon, with a dark-brown utility belt for his holo-comp, clearance keys, and radiation burn creams. Around his neck hung a long white scarf with the symbol of his clan embroidered at each end: the Earth Ark silhouette in black over a field of Thraxian orange. He was a man of ninety-eight cycles who had served his time in space and in the air, flying X-Pod raids during the Charonese War.

"The universe is meant to be traversed," he explained. "Space itself is only an empty vacuum. Indeed, it is the *matter* that is of consequence. It is quite simple: asteroids are your enemies, as shields are your allies. Space has no moral interests, my Duranauts. Coronal mass ejections are your enemies—thrusters and ion boosters, spectral energy analytics, all allies. The people are the wild card up there. The unpredictability you can never quite calculate. Because when it comes to humans, the lines of friend and enemy can dissolve; loyalty can be fluid, a shifting spectrum dependent on external pressures. Allegiances can change, flip, and intersect. This is why we train as we do, because the bonds we make together on the ground might be the very thing that gets us home one day, instead of dead adrift."

His geriatric father, the Lord of Duran, was now crippled, blind, and turned only to his son for guidance. Maxim Duran had lost all his power to reason, yet no influence of command. Martellus's older sister Marique was newly widowed. The Lady of Novojoh was needed in Meadowdell, now more than ever.

Indeed, given his sibling's absence and his father's extreme age, the controlling interest of the Inanean Fleet and Space Agency rested with Martellus.

"My clan has *long* sent heroes of your character into space," he continued, gleaming down at his disciples. "A tradition I'm very proud of. I have every faith in the training you've received. I am confident you will find only allies in each other on the missions to come. Now go forth and remember, young Duranauts: 'We are the captains of the void. We are the connectors of three worlds.'"

A crawler slowly moved their Alterian Three craft into liftoff position. It was the finest vessel in the system, designed by the most advanced engineers on Inana. Although Duran was an essential cog in keeping the Tri-World in space, they could never do it alone. Vesta Technologies emboldened the agency tenfold. Martellus and his clan might have provided the expertise, but the Lord Chancellor was the one providing the tech to get off-world affordably. Duran had the specialists, the pilots, the runways, and the ships, but to get in and out of interplanetary space on a regular basis, you needed atom-breaker engines. Atalay kept them heavily policed under Vesta's jurisdiction. The atom-breakers were the most dangerous weapons on Inana and in the hands of a militant could be deadly.

Martellus gave a farewell salute as the Duranauts filed up the service ramp one by one. He took note of all their faces as each disappeared up the stairs into the cruiser. Nikiu Freya was first— by far his best student; it was *her* in which he had the most faith among the group. A ward of Clan Vesta, she had grown up in

432

Centralia, being groomed from childhood to someday lead the Vesta Enforcement Officers in space. This was a monumental day for Nikiu.

Next was Trung Hon Lu. An island boy with a love of flight, he had come all the way to Duran from the remote island of Alerius in Anu's Sunrise Sea. Trung was already an ace charioteer, but it was time for him to fly bigger ulanoids. None were bigger than the interplanetary cruisers that launched here. Twin sisters from Asa came after, Jintagi and Jeuinga D'aganu. From another purist clan known for aeronautics, they had a famed line of great aviators. Last up the ramp were two newer recruits from the Jade Moon, two of Konga Dreau's finest: Edrick Summerlong and Regimund Evergaze, both bright, eager young lads in whom Martellus had high hopes.

"He just wants to get rid of me, I think," a voice said behind him. "I dunno, Martellus, sometimes I think Father is going senile!" He turned to see Ahdia Vesta, the commander of today's mission. "Alpha Station? His precious Enahdra would never get a botsora shit assignment like this. M'demos One is an orbiting sandbox for children."

"Ahdia, please," he replied, patting her shoulder. "Reestablishing communication to Anu and Oshun is critical for the Tri-World Alliance—leading this mission is an incredibly honorable calling. You serve Atalay well. And *Vesta*, your father has always been proud of *both* of his daughters."

"Please," she retorted. "The man has no interest in a daughter who doesn't want to be called princess. Or any woman he can't control, for that matter. That is why he never married one—and

433

why he *loves* Enahdra more. Vestas are made in pairs, and she's the successful trial."

"You're *both* extraordinary daughters, I'm sure."

"Like you're not a real Vesta unless you're trying to fuck an Atalay somehow. Now they want *me* off-planet?"

"You always do your duty well, despite the injustice," he said. The girl had a strong personality, but luckily Martellus had a way with her types. Dodge. Barrel roll. Like evasive maneuvers back on Anu. He cared little for the internal bickering of high clans.

"Not as well as either of them. The Tri-World pimp and his prize whore. They'll fuck anyone, metaphorically or literally, as long as *they* can be on top."

Treasonous words. "I wouldn't presume to gauge the Lord Chancellor's interest in the opposite sex," he said as he watched the fuel tankers pulling away from the Alterian. "Nor your sister's, for that matter."

"Neither would I, but some scandals are *not* hidden well enough," she replied with a look of hurt frustration. "Trust me: knock before entering a Centralian lavatory. It could be the difference between freedom and exile."

"Noted accordingly." He narrowed his eyes as he appraised her. He could already smell the chemical aroma of the engines priming and knew time was short. "Ahdia, should we scrub this mission? Or are you able to focus yourself?" *I know she is a strong mind, but I cannot endanger my Duranauts.*

"Do you know what *really* goes on up there?" she asked. Lady Vesta had an unblemished, cocoa-skinned complexion—a perfect copy of her sister but in no way a princess. Ahdia Vesta always hid half her face behind bug-eyed black specs and wore a bulky flight suit that hid all indication of feminine features. Her hair was long, black as night except for a hint of deep blue— beautiful but generally veiled by a pilot's skullcap.

"I get the same reports as you, I'm sure," Martellus said with a shrug.

"How sure?" she asked. "Because something doesn't add up. He sends Enahdra to play nursemaid to the prince and simultaneously sends me off the fucking planet? Something is off with him." As alike as the girls looked, their level of refinement set them worlds apart. Where Enah was the epitome of decorum, Ahdia was the embodiment of gruffness.

"Ha! Ahdia, for you M'demke Vesta is 'Father,'" he said, "telling you to eat all your egg root greens and go to bed." The Lord of Duran lifted his shades and grinned sincerely. "But I fought under the man. N'joku gets all the credit, but believe me, the Charonese War would have looked very different without your father reining in the Naga King."

"Yeah, well, maybe he thinks it's time to take credit for everything he's done," Ahdia suggested. "I'm just asking you to have an open mind, Martellus. Something's off, and I'll be powerless once I leave this launchpad. Just talk to him—see if his behavior seems peculiar to you. Duran is powerful and influential."

"Ahdia, you must focus now on the mission ahead of you," he told her. "Don't concern yourself. I will speak with your father. And I won't alert him of your suspicions. Remember, your mind must be concentrated on keeping my Duranauts and yourself safe. Fly well, young Vesta."

He was disturbed by her words but did all he could not to show it on his face. Accusing the Lord Chancellor of duplicity was seditious in itself. And if what she was suggesting were true—if Vesta had somehow turned on Atalay—the entire Tri-World Alliance would fall into chaos. *Where would Duran stand?* As faithful as he was to Atalay, a severance with M'demke Vesta would bring ruin to his people. Perhaps the Lord Chancellor should hear of his daughter's whispers—or, more likely, he was already aware of them, and this was the very reason he was sending her to Alpha Station.

Ahdia Vesta did as she was instructed and boarded the cruiser, all prepped for launch. The last fingernail of light from the docking bay disappeared as its hatch sealed. The atom-breaker's growl rapidly exploded to a deafening roar; Duranaut scientists had not yet solved the challenge of quieting nuclear fusion. The crawler slowly cleared away as Martellus returned to the pad. Then he mounted his speeder and took off down the landing strip. Out of an eruption of light, he skidded across the runway as the Alterian Three broke the barriers of Inana's thick yellow atmosphere. He could feel the humid warmth on his back. With an ungodly crack, the ship disappeared into a glow behind the fire and smoke as the atom-breakers seemed to light clouds aflame. It was nothing the Lord of Duran hadn't seen a thousand times.

He was a man who believed deeply in the unity of worlds. For all the love he had for Inana, the planet of his birth, Martellus could see how much they stood to lose without the other two worlds. The beauty, the culture—the technology and the wealth. *Ahhhh man: the food!* He pulled his speeder through the compound gate and up to Norm'an Command, the agency's mission control hub, and the house of Clan Duran. It was named for Norm'an Duran, the founding father of the Duranauts. The castle fortress was a garrisoned station of black iron and concrete, overly defensed, always having been a potentially sensitive military target in times of war.

M'demke Vesta had spent his tour of duty here during the Charonese War, controlling everyone like pieces in some board game. *If he would ever betray Atalay, why not then? Instead of making N'joku a hero time and time again.* The king was a hot-headed egotist and would not have stopped. It was only after the advent of the electron atomizer bomb that M'demke finally convinced his friend to broker peace with the Mahr Meca of Charon and come home. Even Vesta could not conjure such a weapon. If it were to somehow end up in the hands of the *grays*— it would have been unthinkable.

Norm'an Command was a hulking concrete citadel covered in antenna and transmission dishes. The walls were covered in access panels, pipes, and vents, speckled with blinking and flashing lights of every color, with purposes beyond count. The halls always bustled with Duranauts at the task of managing space traffic by the quanta-cycle. Mission control personnel, monitoring systems for propulsion, quantum dynamics, bio detection, orbital operations, and all other sub systematic

437

disciplines. Martellus demanded the utmost efficiency under his command, and those beneath him were usually eager to please.

One of his ranking defense officers approached from the opposite end of the hall. The warrior in sandy-brown armor wore an urgent expression. "Lord Duran, you have an emissary from Princess Vesta waiting to see you in the war room. Lady Ivy Freya."

"That's unexpected," Martellus said with a chuckle. "Two Vestas in one rotation—how uncanny." He immediately made his way up the stairs to his main conference area. *This cannot be a coincidence.* He climbed each step, past the white braziers and blackened stonewalls. *First, Ahdia approaches me with borderline treasonous claims, and now her sister seeks my attention.* A pit of nerves began to pain his gut as he entered the chamber and saw Enahdra's loyal purple knight.

"Lady Freya, I heard tales of your bravery in the Battle of Meadowdell," he said as he took his seat at the command hub. Martellus grinned, scratching at his scruff and waving for her to sit. "Duran thanks you for your service to Atalay. Our hospitality is yours."

"Thank you, Lord Duran. The VEOs fought with honor. We were—fortunate." Ivy bowed gracefully, then pulled a small silver ring from her satchel. "The Princess of Vesta sends her regards. She would be here herself were she not overseeing the prince's resynthesis personally."

"Clan Vesta is always welcome in this city." He looked up with a dreamy gaze, thinking for a moment about his Duranauts on their mission. "Soon enough, comms will be back online—and we can holo-link at least. Such trouble sending *you* this far north. Tell me, Lieutenant Freya—"

"Commander Freya now." She looked at her feet, shaking her head with a trembling lip.

"Ahhhh, yes, I heard Commander Kong fell in battle. My condolences. He will be remembered as an honorable leader." Martellus's tone was somber. "But what business requires Enahdra to send such a high-ranking and trusted ambassador?"

She leaned over, placing a silver ring on the table in front of him. "Only to give you this."

He leaned back in his chair and crossed his legs, taking a good look at the object. "And what exactly is—this? Not a wedding proposal, I hope. I've seen too many summers."

"This is a Q-Net Ring—a highly classified piece of tech. The global communications problem is not one Vesta shares." Ivy stood and bowed again, respectfully, before turning to the exit. "The princess trusts you, Lord Duran. May Khanya bless you, friend." Martellus watched the Centralian beauty walk out of his war room with confidence in her step.

Suddenly, in a flash of white and blue light, the holographic presence of Enahdra Vesta appeared over his table. Her sequined dress shimmered under her shoulder-padded cloak—the hologram made her look twice her actual size. Her eyes were sharp and her words to the point. "Lord Duran, my father sends his greetings."

"Thank you, My Princess." He tried to hide his confusion, deciding not to question the secret tech making this transmission possible. "Duran is grateful for your father's amity."

"Vesta is equally appreciative of our alliance." The hologram jittered for a moment as she peeled back her hood. *Wow, they are true doppelgängers, those Vesta girls.* "I speak at the Lord Chancellor's behest. He has urgent matters that require his attention." *She is all grown up. Such Atalayan etiquette.* "He asks first if my sister has been seen off on her—mission."

"Yes," he replied. "She will dock with M'demos One in three rotations."

"That's good." Enahdra Vesta's holographic avatar brushed her long, delicate fingers through her silky blue hair, causing more agitations in the light form. "She was not pleased with the delegation. I was concerned she might have perhaps behaved ... childishly." He had to admit, it did seem odd of M'demke to force his daughter into any service she protested—and he'd never had an inkling of doubt in Ahdia's character before. *I don't know what in the Barren Void to make of any of this.*

Martellus decided to play it close to the vest. "Well, she realizes the importance of what we do here. She has my crew of Duranauts up there. Believe me, if she were off her game, I would not have allowed her to fly."

"Yes, Ahdia is integral to Atalay moving forward," she said, taking one step closer, her hologram enlarging with a flicker. "As are *you,* Martellus."

Immediately he dropped to one knee in salute, bowing his head across his forearm. "Duran flies for Atalay."

"I trust in *that*, my friend. My father loves you like a companion in arms." She cracked a crooked smile across her glossy black lips. "Your clan's loyalty was never in question, to be sure."

"What would Vesta ask of me?"

"I need first to know that the words spoken between us now evaporate in the ether when this transmission ends," she said sternly. "I would pass on sensitive information to you— information that would instigate panic in the Tri-Worlds if it became public knowledge."

"I swear silence, My Princess," Martellus promised. "You can always trust in my complete confidentiality." It was no lie. He prided himself on his trustworthiness.

"The Volturis is vanquished, but my intel has discovered an even greater threat on the horizon." Martellus dropped his face in his hands, then ran his fingers through his thinning gray bangs.

"Tell me what I must do."

"Dark forces on Anu plot against Atalay, my friend. But, together, I believe you and I alone can quell this threat. How much trust do you have in your Duranauts?"

"My faith is unwavering," he replied.

"No one else can know this. If King N'joku were to hear what I'm about to tell you, we'd risk another Tri-World War."

"I assure you: no one listens here but us." *More treachery from Clan Vesta?*

"Clan Darius has designs on the Seat of Atalay." Martellus couldn't help but notice the soreness on her face as she spoke. "Theodus wants to rule the Tri-Worlds—intact or in ashes."

"M'demke would certainly not take that lightly," he said. "Your father's hatred for Darius is well documented. Your history with him—"

"My history with him is *why* I know this is serious," Enahdra lamented. "Theodus has employed an extremely dangerous assassin, a former Yosai called Myriam Yamada. She is on her way to Inana, tasked to kill the prince."

He picked at his silvery mustache as he paced around her hologram. "How can you know this? We've not had communications from Anu in over a cycle."

Enahdra tapped her holographic foot with fists on her hips. "We're communicating right now, Lord Duran. As you well know, Vesta is charged with technology and its responsible use."

"You think it's responsible?" Martellus's brow wrinkled as he massaged the sides of his head. "To leave all of Inana in the dark—in silence? While my Duranauts work around rotation and risk their lives to restore our planet?"

"Nothing new for my clan, Martellus!" Her tone sharpened, causing another flash in the hologram. "Imagine if my ancestors gave yours access to atom-breaker engines before they were tested properly—prepared to *help* lives, not take them."

She has a point, he thought, looking to the floor. *Who am I to question the ways of the high Clan Vesta?* "I learned long ago not to apologize for possessing tech others do not." She scoffed and rolled her eyes.

"Apologies, My Princess," he said, kneeling. "Forgive an old fool his dementia-induced paranoia." The Lord of Duran belly laughed with an overexuberance that made it clear he was joking.

"Atalay is counting on your sharpness now."

Martellus stood again, looking up with a plain face. "Duran flies for Atalay!" He puffed out his chest, patting his sternum to signal his loyalty. "Duran controls the air traffic on Inana. No vessel gets close to low-Inana orbit without our clearance. Every passenger—every parcel of cargo will be accounted for. Theodus Darius's assassin will never step foot on this pla—" A sharp pain suddenly struck his back, followed by a sick feeling in his gut. The searing pain moved to his abdomen next. He looked down to see red pooling on his shirt as a point pressed out from his stomach, forming a pyramid of blood-soaked cloth.

"Bad job, Marty," a strange voice said from behind. *Minician accent,* he thought. *Who?*

Everything went cold as he looked up at Enahdra's hologram. "Lord Duran," she cried out as a sword pierced through the shirt, ripping open his stomach before retracting. "Someone, help him! Help your lord!" He knew the princess's cries would be far too faint to be heard. Martellus collapsed forward, helped along with an indignant kick to the backside.

"You ridiculous Homo purists are all the same." A pink-haired woman stepped around him with his blood dripping from her katana. "Helpless without the people you've enslaved to save you." Enahdra Vesta crossed her arms in a huff as the hologram flashed in and out. "Overindulgent gluttons, drunk on your own legend—like so many humans before you."

"You've come to kill N'damu!" Enahdra spat at the assassin. The holographic gob of spit disappeared inches from her face. "I know who you work for, Myriam Yamada. You think *you're* not a slave?"

"I've accepted that long ago," Myriam replied. "Only my masters have changed." She reached across the table, taking the Q-Net ring in her palm. "So, I've come to kill the master of masters."

"You'll never find him," Enahdra said. "He's mine. Atalay belongs to me!" Martellus groaned as he looked up, confused, trying to hold on to his senses. *What is she talking about?* "You dare challenge the might of Clan Vesta? My father is Lord Chancellor. I am Princess Enah—" The assassin, all in black, locked her fingers over the ring, and the hologram blinked out of existence.

Martellus rolled over, grimacing and groaning in misery. Myriam Yamada turned to him once more, holding her katana aloft before driving it into his sternum. Piercing his chest plate with a jolt, the blade penetrated his heart. Torrents of blood squirted from his chest, spraying on his face as his heartbeat slowed. She kneeled over him with an indifferent expression as she wiped her sword clean on his scarf, obscuring his family crest in crimson. The Lord of Duran reached for her hand, connecting his stare to her violet eyes. "The light—of—Atalay—is—love. For-give-ness." She stood back up and slid her glistening blade into its sheathe. "The Womb of Inana—is waiting—" He closed his eyes, too drained to speak.

"One in a long line of stories for times like these, old man." She walked to the doorway without looking back. "Worshipers of death crave no afterlife." Martellus Duran rested his head, imagining a crystal-clear night's sky. *A sad thought.* His breathing slowed as an endless panorama of space encompassed him, sprinkled with shimmering stars that slowly faded to black with his last breath.

The End

of Book One of

Ages Of Atalay

BOOK TWO COMING SOON

THE TWO SIDES OF LIGHT

MATTHEW NORTH

GLOSSARY

Ahdia Vesta – Born 30,278 - 52 Thraxian Cycles (19 Earth years) Second twin daughter of Vesta, Ahdia is a stubborn-willed adventurer. Rejecting her Homo purist designations, she devotes her life to the space agency in Duran.

Aku Atalay – Born 30,273 - 57 Thraxian Cycles (22 Earth years) Like her sister, Ala, Aku is bonded to the ulanoid, though she uses the bone-hawks more as feathery decorates than as weapons. Head of the Asan Guild, she is a progressive-thinking politician who embraces being a Princess of Atalay with all her heart.

Ala Atalay – Born 30,273 - 57 Thraxian Cycles (22 Earth years) One of the binary Princesses of Atalay and head of the Oban Guild, Ala is a willful politician as well as a mighty warrior. Her spirit-link to the ulanoid makes her an especially formidable combatant.

Anaqua Atalay – Born 30, 195 - 135 Thraxian Cycles (51 Earth years) Queen consort of King N'joku Atalay, Anaqua came to N'gaia from the Stone Sea, eldest daughter of Clan Tattrila, master oceanauts.

Anu – (Ah-new) The third world out from Thraxis and second settled by humanity, the tidally locked planet has a climate similar to Earth. Colonized by King N'assar Atalay in the 240th Thraxian cycle, the continental light side quickly became a thriving technocratic society, the great Empire of Izlagos. The dark side of Anu is primarily aquatic, with scattered islands now populated by a social fringe culture of gray-skinned, warmongering people called, Charons.

Atalay – (At-uh-lay) The most heralded line of Homo purists, Atalay was created to lead humanity. Aboard the Pegasus, they were captains and eventually became kings. With selfless altruism engineered in every strand of DNA, every Atalay is noble, trustworthy, generous, and fair, never putting self over duty.

Atranoch – The great bone-dragons of Inana, these megalithic winged beasts soar the skies unchallenged. Limbless other than their massive wings, these spikey arial monsters can reach lengths of 800 meters.

Azuma Shingen – 30,232 – 98 Thraxian Cycles (38 Earth years) Yon Justia of the Yosai, most would consider Lord Azuma the most dangerous fighter alive. Leader of the Knights of Yosai, he is one of few men in the Tri-World empowered to cast ultimate judgment.

Botsora – Limbless exophiles covered in bone plating, they expel a rancid defensive odor to repel predators.

Calitro Frigg – 30,237 - 93 Thraxian Cycles (36 Earth years) A mutate hailing from the dwarf tribes of Oshun, Frigg is a sniper and master of blasters. He serves as Rigel Kong's right-hand man in the VEOs.

Carrico – (care-e-ko) Vastly wealthy Anutian technocratic clan specializing in AI software and advanced quantum networks.

Centralia – The largest city on Inana and the center of commerce, this splendorous technocratic society is home to Clan Vesta.

Charon – An island-chain nation on the darkside of Anu. Oft considered radical and warmongering, little is known about the Charonese people, who have adapted over the ages to life without daylight.

Commodus – Established during the Imperial Age of Anu, their clan serves the Tri-Worlds as Masters of Economics.

Crongrin – Stealthy river-dwelling carnivores, these massive half-ton beasts stalk the banks mimicking rocks with their bone-covered hides and snapping up prey with their powerful jaws.

Darius (Der-eye-us) The Masters of Robotics established during the first Thraxian epoch, Clan Darius is charged with overseeing the safe use of automata as well as preventing the dangerous overreach inherent in artificial intelligence. During the imperial age, Clan Darius ruled the light side of Anu as emperors of Izlagos.

Don Hoya – Born 30,231 - 99 Thraxian Cycles (38 Earth years) The second son of Clan Hoya, Masters of Combat, he is often considered the most dangerous hand-to-hand fighter to ever live. He serves in Atalay's Royal Guard with his fists pledged to N'joku.

Duran – The Masters of Aeronautics of the Pegasian age, Clan Duran maintained the great vessel in space. From the famed city that bears their name, they head the most advanced spaceport of all time, the Duranauts.

Dushnah – The first Inanean animals successfully domesticated by humans, they were dubbed bone-horses by early settlers for their similarity to the Earth animals. The spike-covered quadrupeds thunder across the savannahs in herds of a thousand, feeding on the wild fields of tynn grass.

Earth Ark 12 – Dubbed the Pegasus for its originally intended destination, the constellation Pegasus, this civilization-sustaining vessel was humanity's twelfth iteration of star-spanning ships to leave the mother system in search of a new habitable home.

Elle Li'asaga – Born 30,160 - 170 Thraxian Cycles (65 Earth years) From the proud and pious realm of Oba, she is the matriarch of House Li'asaga and the high priestess of G'higari. She's served most of her long life as a member of the Royal Court of Atalay as the chancellor of faith.

Enahdra Vesta – Born 30,278 - 52 Thraxian Cycles (19 Earth years) Princess of Centralia and eldest twin daughter of Vesta, Enahdra is a charismatic technocrat socialite and a formidable political tactician.

Eshe – (Eh-shh) High clan charged with all systems of communication. In the Pegasian age, Clan Eshe were prodigious navigators. Now they maintain all connective networks on scales spanning from galactic to quantum.

G'higari – (Jee-gar-ee) The most common religion in the Tri-World, G'higari is an amalgamation of the defunct Milushi faith and the old way of Atalay. It embraces the Khanyastic ideas of the Womb of Inana, the Eternal Womb, and the Barren Void in accordance with the Doctrines of Atalay and acceptance of the Pegasian and Earthen origin stories.

Grat – Squirmy, limbless vermin mainly living underground; they burrow networks of tunnels with their tiny two-pound bodies.

Haldir Nolan – Born 30,245 - 85 Thraxian Cycles (33 Earth years) The first son of Clan Nolan, he grew up as a desert survivalist and warrior of the Fuza. He now serves as a Gold Knight in Atalay's Royal Guard and N'joku's personal sentry.

High Clans – Established aboard the Pegasus in the year 104,500 AD in an age of civil war. To stabilize the population, the ancient evolutionaries engineered seven lines of specialized DNA, each with critical roles in balancing their spacefaring society, including: communications, cosmology, biology, engineering, military, technology, and governance. As the centuries passed and humans arrived at Thraxis, the seven expanded into many niche clans mastering geoengineering, agriculture, and even spirituality.

Himpheah Ants – Tiny exoskeletal mites that amass in colonies numbering in the millions.

Homo purist – Once called clones, Homo purists are genetically modified humans incubated in gestation chambers by the evolutionaries. They were a necessary step in Homo sapiens' evolution, critical for surviving the bombardment of radiation to which life in space subjected them.

Hoya – Desert-ranging clan of the Fuza, none are more adaptable at survival in Inana's most arid conditions. Their ancestors developed the deadliest hand-to-hand fighting style known, the art of Hoya Hasta.

Inana – (In-ann-uh) Second planet from Thraxis and the first of its system settled by humankind, Inana is a medium-sized rocky world with a size comparable to Earth. It boasts a diverse array of life-rich biomes sustained by a sub-crust ocean that seeps frugally to the surface forming a network of interconnecting seas and rivers. Its lifeforms are primarily exoskeletal. The planet is rich in dynamic megafauna across air, land, and water, as well as countless cultures of microfauna. Early settlers began to experience a strange symbiosis with Inana's wildlife, often forming an enigmatic life bond with one particular species in a phenomenon called N'jikota.

Ishikura Umi – Born 30,257 - 73 Thraxian Cycles (28 Earth years) The current Yon Astra, second in command of the Yosai, Ishikura is one of the most skilled combatants in the Tri-Worlds. A master of the sais, she grew up in servitude in Port City before rising in the order alongside Myriam Yamada.

Ivy Freya – 30,253 - 77 Thraxian Cycles (29 Earth years) From a Vestian vassal clan known for the finest armor in the Tri-Worlds, Ivy grew up in the Princesses of Vesta's guard and now serves as a lieutenant of the Vesta Enforcement Officers.

Izlagos – Also known as the Pearl City, it has long been the capital of Anu and home to Clan Darius. Considered by many as humanity's ultimate utopia, inhabitants have enjoyed an unprecedented era of peace across Anu's idyllic northern continent which shares the city's name.

Jambi Sadah – Born 30,184 - 146 Thraxian Cycles (56 Earth years) Lord of Clan Sadah and Chancellor of Peace on King N'joku's council, Jambi is a master tactician. As general of the Soldiers of Sadah, the Silver Knight trains and commands the finest standing military on Inana.

Kat'har Rio – Born 30,215 - 115 Thraxian Cycles (44 Earth years) Dwarf from the jungle moon of Oshun, Rio is now a significant player in the sordid underworld on Anu, ruling from his domed fortress, the Hangar.

Kavah – A bush growing in large walls throughout the savannahs of Inana. Their flowery white buds are famous for their hallucinogenic properties.

Khanya – A concept of a visceral one-ness of all life on Inana, creating three interlinking realities. The first is the objective world, known as the Womb of Inana, which interconnects two distinct after worlds: the Eternal Womb, for those whose lives reflected valor and virtue, and the Barren Void, designated for those who lived with evil and malice in their heart.

Kota – The most masterful rank of spirit-linkers, Kota's are revered guides to N'jikota, devoted to helping G'higari pilgrims find their bond.

Li'asaga – Atalay's Masters of Spirituality, this ancient clan is now the central leader of the G'higari faith.

Lyankoh – (Lie-ank-oh) The Masters of Biology, the evolutionaries of Clan Lyankoh not only preserved the sanctity of the Homo purist DNA through the depths of space but continued to evolve new specialized lines as humans adapted to the environments in colonizing the Thraxian worlds.

Mamidon – Massive elephantine herbivores covered in bony spike-covered plating. Spanning up to three tons, these lumbering quadrupeds migrate through the Inanean savannahs in herds as large as fifty individuals.

Maraphite – Aquatic animals that populate Inana's seas and rivers in various sub-species. A staple food for early colonizers, they continue to drive a robust angling industry.

Martellus Duran – Born 30,226 - 104 Thraxian Cycles (40 Earth years) Lord of Duran and Captain of the Duranauts, Atalay's most elite space force.

M'demke Vesta – Born 30,161 - 169 Thraxian Cycles (65 Earth years) The Lord Chancellor of King N'joku, M'demke has always been like an older brother to the king. As lord and patriarch to the High Clan Vesta, he is the Tri-World's principal technocrat with ultimate rule over technology regulations. Ruling beside Atalay, he also commands the VEOs as well as his elite company, Vesta Tech.

Meadowdell – The home of Clan Novojoh and the holiest city to the G'higari, thousands of pilgrims come here each cycle to learn the ways of N'jikota.

Meridian Falls – Medium-sized trees with curtains of bushy foliage ranging from violet to dark forest green.

Milushi – A religion arising in 5,000-5,600 TC during the Dark Age when the phenomenon of N'jikota first appeared. The ancient spirit-linkers disavowed any alien origin story, believing themselves to be one with Khanya and a creation of the Womb of Inana.

Myriam Yamada – Born 30,255 - 75 Thraxian Cycles (29 Earth years) Natural born on the Anutian continent of Minicius, she overcame a sordid upbringing to earn a place amongst the revered Knights of Yosai. One of the most dangerous humans to ever live, she was exiled from the Yosai in disgrace and now wanders as a lost-soul bounty hunter.

Nalia Chuku – Born 30,288 TC - 42 Thraxian Cycles (16 Earth years) Natural born Inanean adopted as a ward of Clan Sadah for her parents' courageous sacrifice serving Atalay. She has trained all her life to become a formidable warrior in the art of Sadah'anah spear fighting and now serves the Royal Guard as the prince's Second Spear.

Naga – Elongated serpentine carnivores, they are generally considered Inana's top predators. With snapping talons around their necks that help them attach their tooth-covered faces to their prey, nagas' robust exoskeletal bodies are sleek and aerodynamic as well as impenetrable.

Naris Commodus – Born 30,174 - 156 Thraxian Cycles (60 Earth years) Izlagos born, he is the first son of Clan Commodus. As a Master of Economics, he serves on the Royal Court of King N'joku as the chancellor of finance.

N'damu Atalay – Born 30,288 - 42 Thraxian Cycles (16 Earth years) Genetically engineered prince and the next in an endless line of deified monarchs set to rule humanity. He is a devoted G'higari and beloved figure, eager to find his spirit-link.

New Terra – The fourth planet in the Thraxian system, this mega-sized terrestrial world is covered in a white haze, hiding it from observation for the most part. Early attempts to settle the wild planet were deemed impossible due to its monolithic wildlife.

N'gaia – Also known as the Golden City, or Aras's Landing, it is the capital of the Tri-Worlds and the home of Atalay.

N'jidia – A hero who bonds with all wildlife, prophesized by the ancient Milushi. Also called the Kota of Kotas.

N'jikota – Also known as a spirit-link, it is an unbreakable nonphysical bond between a human and a particular species of Inanean wildlife.

N'joku Atalay – Born 30,187 - 143 Thraxian Cycles (55 Earth years) King of the Tri-Worlds, hero of the Charonese War, the Naga King, N'joku is the Shepherd of Men, the great Atalay made to lead humanity. Bonded to the savage naga, the great warrior sits on the Seat in the tower of Atalay at the center of the golden city of N'gaia, ruling beside his queen and counsels.

Noba Sadah – Born 30,283 - 47 Thraxian Cycles (18 Earth years) The eldest son of Jambi and the next in line to command the Soldiers of Sadah, he is a master tactician and unparalleled spearman serving as First Spear of the prince's guard.

Nolan – N'gaian Masters of Arms, this vassal clan of Sadah has always served faithfully in the Royal Guard as chief protectors of Atalay and leaders of the Golden Knights.

Novojoh – (No-vo-joe) Clan established in the first Thraxian epoch, Masters of Fauna, tasked with studying the diverse

Inanean wildlife. With the rise of Milushi culture, they became the great kotas and Masters of N'jikota.

Olyin Yara – A common wild bush constantly dispelling buttery yellow clouds of dander.

Port City – Southernmost Anutian city under TWA rule, it sits on the line separating the darkside and the light. Known for lawlessness, wars with the Charonese have been staged here for eons.

Querghil – Bone-slugs of the savannah, these two-ton amphibious omnivores live in families of eight to ten members. They slither their rotund bodies around the riverbanks, slurping up anything they find.

Ra – The fifth and most distant planet from Thraxis, this gas giant swirls with a collage of blood-red storms. An ever-present eye named for the ancient Earthen god, the behemoth is a staple symbol of many ancient religions. Orbited by a system of desert moons, the most notable of which is the dune-world, Katonda, colonized for a short time before being abandoned for lack of resources.

Rhybite – Small quadruped omnivores adapted to every Inanean biome. From the ranges of the Sindiswa to the Fuza desert, these three-pound spike-covered exophiles eke out a niche and are vital prey to larger animals.

Rhyona – (Re-own-uh) Established in the first Epoch as Masters of Dushnah, devoted to domesticating the great bone-horse herds.

Rigel Kong – 30,245 - 85 Thraxian Cycles (33 Earth years) The Commander of the Vesta Enforcement Officers and a master of guerilla warfare, Rigel is as much an expert in ordnances as he is obsessed by them. He came from Oshun at the behest of M'demke Vesta to serve as the princess's personal guard.

Sab'ano Novojoh – Born 30,010 - 20 Thraxian Cycles (8 Earth years) Youngest son of Novojoh, the rambunctious twin has yet to find his spirit link.

Sab'ina Novojoh – Born 30,010 - 20 Thraxian Cycles (8 Earth years) Youngest daughter of Novojoh, the meek young twin has yet to find her spirit link.

Sadah – (Sah-dah) The Masters of Warfare, Clan Sadah is designed to keep the peace. Tactically rational Homo purists with peek physical prowess and a stomach for distasteful realities, they are made to maintain social amity through force if necessary.

Sal'aah Novojoh – Born 30,200 - 130 Thraxian Cycles (50 Earth years) Lord of Meadowdell and patriarch of Clan Novojoh, Sal'aah devotes his life to leading young G'higari pupils in discovering their spirit links. A Kota of Mamidons, he rides aback the massive animals with the ease of walking on his own legs.

Sar'ah Novojoh – Born 30,288 - 42 Thraxian Cycles (16 Earth years) The Kota of Throzeids and the second eldest daughter of Novojoh, Sar'ah commands microbial armies with a simple thought.

Serivicious Starr – Born 30,179 - 151 Thraxian Cycles (58 Earth years) – Hailing from Oshun, he is the first son of Clan Starr. As a Master of Cosmology, he serves on the Royal Court of King N'joku as the chancellor of science.

Set – Closest orbiting world of Thraxis, the buttery-yellow gas giant forms a strong binary system with the home star, narrowly failing to become a star itself. Its system is abundant in distinct, life-rich moons, including the jungle world, Oshun, settled by humans in 13,500 TC by King N'erik Atalay and Emperor Galerius Darius jointly. Set is believed to emit a mysterious radiation field with interconnected transmutational properties on Oshun's lifeforms, dubbed: the Darwin Field for its hyper-evolutionary effects.

Shingen – Anutian clan residing in the mystical city of Long Zenya, they are Masters of Law under Atalay. Clan Shingen is most known for its ancient order of justice, the Knights of Yosai.

Shar'nah Novojoh – Born 30,294 TC - 36 Thraxian Cycles (13 Earth years) Third daughter of Clan Novojoh, she is the youngest Kota of Dushnah ever, masterfully controlling her legion of bone horses.

Sho'nee Novojoh – Born 30,282 - 48 Thraxian Cycles (18 Earth years) Eldest daughter of Novojoh, Sho'nee is Kota of Atranochs. One of the greatest bone dragon riders to ever live, she can bend an entire valor of the colossal winged beasts to her will.

Shyla Sadah – Born 30,221 - 109 Thraxian Cycles (42 Earth years) A master of Sadah'anah, she is revered as the greatest spear fighter ever. One of N'joku's Six Swords, Shyla is one of Atalay's most trusted defenders.

S'ike Novojoh – Born 30,294 - 36 Thraxian Cycles (14 Earth years) Eldest son of Clan Novojoh, he is the quiet but powerful Kota of Querghil.

Skylar Rose – The most beautiful flowers on Inana, they bloom in white and blood-red.

Starr – The most brilliant cosmologist ever engineered; Clan Starr was made to comprehend the vastest concepts of reality. They are the keepers of humanity's infinitely expanding universal understanding.

Thar'vak Trees – The mighty mega-trees of Inana, they are now few and far between but were once believed to cover the planet.

Theodus Darius – Born 30,248 - 82 Thraxian Cycles (31 Earth years) Eldest son of Clan Darius, Theodus is a vastly wealthy and influential businessman groomed to be the next Steward of Anu under Atalay. He also commands the Izlagosi Guard and the robot special-ops unit known as the Hounds.

Thraxis – K-type orange dwarf star oft referred to as the Eden Star or the Second Sun, it is an idyllic system of worlds with a surfeit of habitable zones. It was discovered in the year 210,900 AD by Clan Starr during the reign of Queen Aleigha Atalay. She commanded the first Pegasian course change after two hundred thousand years of space travel, the prospects of Thraxis too enticing to pass up.

Throzeids – Airborne microorganisms invading the bloodstreams of most terrestrial life on Inana. Mainly inert in nature, they were hardly considered consequential until spirit-linkers began to harness their biochemical altering capabilities to great power.

Tri-World – The combined realms of Atalay spanning three worlds: Inana, Anu, and Oshun. Often referred to as the TWA (Tri-World Alliance,) its emblem is three descending circles encased in a pyramid.

Ulanoids – Feathered winged exophiles often called bone-hawks. The colorful creatures weigh up to twenty pounds and gather in flocks of five hundred.

Tucsabura – A spike-covered quadruped usually found in the forests and riverbanks of Inana. Though generally docile, they can roll up into a spiny ball and spin wildly when threatened.

Vera Trees – The most common leafy tree on Inana, its pitch, known as vera, is a typical lotion and soap and has numerous healing applications.

Vesta –The second of the seven high clans, Clan Vesta are the keepers of all human technology. Engineered to engineer, these overseers of human advancements control the dangerous horizons of experimentation, delegating resources, and seeing that progress comes at a pace not detrimental to human existence.

Yon – A high-ranking mantle among the Knights of Yosai, they are the elite leaders of the order.

Yosai – An ancient Vrinasi order started by Clan Shingen during the Reign of Madness, they are the Tri-World's most skilled operatives, committed to upholding justice among social elites as well as ordinary citizens.

Yukimura Ito – Born 30,283 - 47 Thraxian Cycles (18 Earth years) Former slave from Old Vedia, Yuki is now a rising disciple in the Knights of Yosai.

Zharr – The chief spaceport city on Anu and the home of the lawless facility known as the Hangar.

ABOUT THE AUTHOR

Matthew North was born in 1980 in Yakima Washington but spent most of his life in Canada. An avid fan of the arts, he grew up drawing, writing, making movies and music. Obsessed by great storytelling and fantastic worlds, he was never far from a comic shop or a bookstore. His first passion was always the X-Men, connecting with the diverse array of characters as well as messages of peaceful coexistence for all humans. He also developed deep appreciation for intricate lore's of J.R.R. Tolkien, Frank Herbert, and George R.R. Martin. After spending fifteen years in Montreal, Quebec, starting a family, playing in bands, and working in audio, Matthew now resides in Eastern Canada writing his debut science-fiction fantasy series, Ages of Atalay.

www.ingramcontent.com/pod-product-compliance
Lightning Source LLC
Chambersburg PA
CBHW021212260626
47172CB00002B/391